PRAISE FOR BETSY DORNBUSCH AND THE BOOK OF THE SEVEN EYES TRILOGY

"Love, war, and redemption all play a part in this fantasy series opener, which brings to life a brooding hero and a resourceful queen against an exotic fantasy background."

—*Library Journal*

"Necromantic magic, deadly political intrigue, and a reluctant hero torn between his duty to a foreign queen and his desire for revenge . . . Betsy Dornbusch's *Exile* kept me reading into the wee hours of the night, breathless to find out how Draken's story would end."

—Courtney Schafer, author of The Shattered Sigil series.

"*Exile* does an excellent job of fashioning a kingdom on the brink of implosion, as political, military, and personal factors place increasing pressure on the fragile peace that is already undermined by double agents and malignant magic. It also provides a unique conglomeration of magic, which is practiced mostly either by the enigmatic Moonlings or a race known as the Mance, who are in turns alluring and disturbing in their methods and manners."

—Josh Vogt, Examiner.com

"An intriguing world, with its varied people and imperiled gods. The hero maintains his personal integrity even as the pawn of powers of whom he's barely aware, and the plot unfolds with the rapid pacing of a mystery novel."

—K. V. Johansen, author of *Blackdog*

"From the first line ("Cut her throat. His own wife."), readers of Betsy Dornbusch's *Exile* know they are in for a dramatic and exciting tale. . . . Any reader who joins her for the ride will be glad they did."

—Lesley Smith, *Electric Spec*

"Draken is an interesting character, and the secondary characters are equally interesting. The plot moves along nicely, and the story is engaging. I enjoyed the setting and found the author's world building commendable."

—Lori Macinnes, *Lori Reads*

"Betsy Dornbusch's *Exile* is a nonstop adventure with a fascinating world and some terrific magic."

—Carol Berg, author of *Transformation and The Daemon Prism*

ENEMY

ENEMY

THE THIRD BOOK OF THE SEVEN EYES

BETSY DORNBUSCH

NIGHT SHADE BOOKS
NEW YORK

Night Shade books may be purchased in bulk at special discounts for sales promotion, corporate gifts, fund-raising, or educational purposes. Special editions can also be created to specifications. For details, contact the Special Sales Department, Night Shade Books, 307 West 36th Street, 11th Floor, New York, NY 10018 or info@ skyhorsepublishing.com.

Night Shade Books™ is a trademark of Skyhorse Publishing, Inc. ®, a Delaware corporation.

Visit our website at www.nightshadebooks.com.

10 9 8 7 6 5 4 3 2 1

Library of Congress Cataloging-in-Publication Data is available on file.

Jacket art by John Stanko
Jacket design by Claudia Noble
Interior layout and design by Amy Popovich

Print ISBN: 978-1-59780-864-4
Ebook ISBN 978-1-589780-865-1

Printed in the United States of America

For Alex

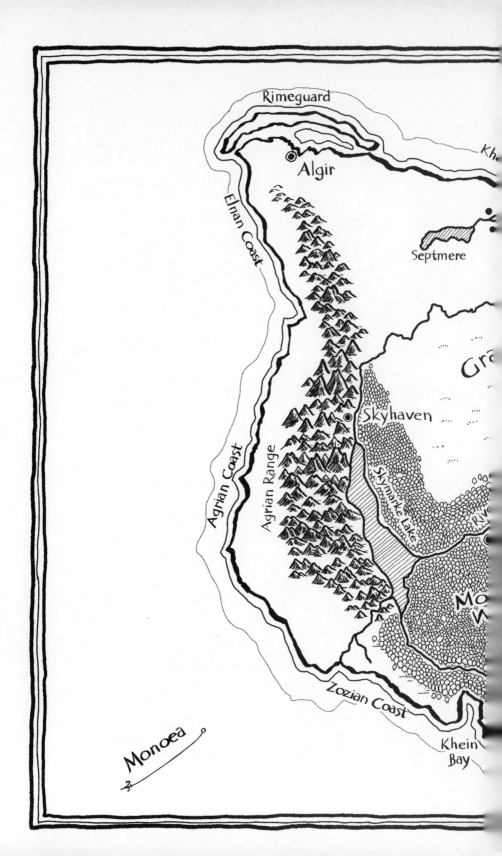

Rimeguard

Kh

Algir

Elhan Coast

Septmere

Gra

Skyhaven

Agrian Coast

Agrian Range

Skymarke Lake

Riv

Mo

Mo
W

Zozian Coast

Monoea

Khein
Bay

Hoarfrost Sea

Eidola
Islands

Dragonstar

Eidola

Seakeep

City of Brîn

Blood Bay

Reschan

Parne
(Village)

Wetlands

Rhial
Mining
Region

Crossing
Inn

Brínian Coast

Akrasia

The truth is torment.

—Brînian Proverb

CHAPTER ONE

The air never quieted on the Brînian coast, and this night it was all angry violence atop Seakeep overlooking Blood Bay. Seven stories high on a cliff thrice its height, Draken fair imagined the stone tower swaying as he emerged from the twisting stairwell into the fierce, chill wind. Flames in the deep bowl churned and danced, sparks scattering, bright dust against the night sky. The wide-eyed firegirl dropped to her knees and twitched her head down into huddled obeisance. Her back bent like Draken's finest recurve bow. One glimpse of her face told him she was sundry: a Brînian-Akrasian mix, likely.

Frightened of him. Curious.

She's frightened of the throne and sword, not the man, Bruche said.

Perhaps his swordhand was right. A long life and a longer death made the spirit residing inside Draken wise. After all, not all girls were frightened of him. His sister certainly wasn't, nor his daughter, who always squealed and scampered across the tiled floors on her hands and knees toward him when he appeared. Still, the slavegirl's trembling genuflection reminded him mistrust and fear were the costs of power.

"Go inside. Warm yourself." Draken waved the girl-slave downstairs and she scampered off. Bloody cruel keeping a child up here. Especially come moonrise. But the fire had to be watched, more so now in wartime, and he had no proper soldiers or civilians to spare for the duty. Living under malicious means had always been the fate for slaves. He'd done his share of unpleasant, dangerous duties when he'd been one.

Once she was gone, he let his hood whip back in the wind, glad for the row of buckles down his chest securing his cloak over his woolen shirt, and moved closer to the heat radiating from the great firebowl. He had to avert his gaze from the glow. The great fire stung his eyes.

Beyond the cliff and the tower, whitecaps dotted Blood Bay. He drew in a breath of salty air, cold and harsh in his lungs. Another gust stole his next

1

breath. A shower of sparks cascaded through the air. One fluttered against the green stripe adorning the edge of his black cloak.

He brushed it aside. "Show yourself, Osias. I know you're here. I met Setia below."

"Khel Szi." The greeting might have been a whisper or his imagination, given the wind. But the Mance emerged from the mist around the bend of the railed tower walk, glowing faintly silver under the rising moons. Draken felt his shoulders ease in the presence of his serene beauty. The Mance had been gone two sevennight to gods knew where and the time had dragged.

Osias glanced about, a smile on his lips. "Beautiful night for a tower meeting, Khel Szi."

Draken grunted. "I needed a private place to speak to you."

Osias's gaze darted past Draken. The Mance's irises shifted from good-humored lavender to swirling storm grey. His face took on sharp angles, and the crescent moon tattooed on his forehead looked like a jagged black hole on his glowing skin. His bow appeared from under his cloak and he nocked an arrow before Draken could even speak. "Father." The word was a threat.

Truls, the ghost who had joined them, remained still and stoic, but his edges blurred and sharpened continually. Watch him too long and it turned the stomach.

"I don't know if even Oscher arrows will kill a ghost-Mance—being as he's already dead several times over," Draken said.

Osias narrowed his eyes at the spirit. When Truls failed to speak, he asked, "When did he appear to you?"

"About the time you left." Draken stepped closer and pushed the arrow aside, mindful not to touch the sharp edge but just the shaft. His healing powers would rattle the old stones of the tower and he had no intention of finding out if his magic was strong enough to bring it down. "I don't know why he's quiet just now. He tells me day and night that Sikyra is in danger, we're all under threat. I wish he'd bloody well tell me something I don't know." A lame attempt at a joke, especially with his voice rough from a recent bout of chest rot. He coughed but it did nothing to clear the sick knot beneath his heart. He didn't say the worst of it, not yet, but as usual his friend cut to the quick of the matter.

"And Queen Elena? Does he speak of her?"

Draken stiffened. "Says she's alive."

Osias's eyes swirled faster, pale enough to reflect twin firebowls. Another thing to make Draken sick. "You don't believe him."

"I don't know what I believe anymore."

That wasn't quite truth. He had seen the fire that Elena had started to allow him to escape her Moonling captors, had smelled the suffocating smoke, and heard the screams of the dying. He couldn't imagine Elena escaping with her life, though on his worst days he was hard-pressed to admit to himself she was dead.

Osias had not sensed her among the dead, but he also claimed the god Korde could conceal her spirit from him if he wished, now that Draken had destroyed the fetter binding Osias's will to the gods. But to what end would Korde hide Elena? A constant question among Draken's advisors in the past moonturns . . . nearly eleven moonturns Elena had failed to appear.

Osias apparently decided not to broach the subject now. He released the tension on the string and slipped the arrow back into the quiver strapped to his thigh. One silvery hand gripped the longbow. Another violent gust tossed the ends of Draken's cloak, wrapping it around his boots. It was then he noticed the weather didn't touch the Mance. His silver hair draped over his shoulders, his grey cloak hung placid around his ankles. He didn't so much as shiver. Somehow it made Draken feel colder, as if all the chill were settling in his bones alone.

"You are accustomed to the gods guiding your hands and heart, Khel Szi," Osias said. "Truls's purpose must be no different than theirs, as the dead belong to the gods."

A Mance way of asking what this had to do with him; never mind Osias was the most renowned necromancer in Akrasia, nor that Truls kept Draken up nights and left him half-mad from exhaustion.

Draken's spirit swordhand, Bruche, chuckled deep inside him. *Told you so.*

"I don't care why he's here; I need him gone," Draken said. "Get rid of him, Osias."

"That is beyond my power."

Draken jerked a thumb toward the ghost at his side. "Truls is Korde's beast, is he not?"

Osias gave Truls a speculative look. "Alas, but I no longer am."

"You still have your magic, damn it."

Osias lost a little of his sheen, dulled as the moon Elna slipped behind a cloud with a bellyful of sleet. "Not all, my friend."

"I can't live like this, Osias, much less fight a war, not with him hounding me all the time."

"The front fair holds. The Mance King scryed it in Eidola ice."

That sort of Sight he'd like regular access to. The current Mance King wasn't as friendly with Draken as Osias, who'd relinquished his title with his fetter in order to travel across the sea to Draken's first homeland, Monoea. But that had been nearly a whole Sohalia ago, and Draken had hoped . . . well. He didn't know what he hoped. Just that Osias might be able to banish Truls back to Eidola.

Can't hardly blame him for ditching on the kingship. You weren't too keen on taking a throne yourself.

Draken gave a grudging nod to Osias *and* Bruche. "The front holds only because of the cold. The Moneans will attack again in force once thaw hits and the winds turn. More ships, more men, more killing."

Osias murmured the Monoean's battle cry in their language, his tone musing, *"Il Vanni masacr."* The godless die. The Mance's attention wandered back to Truls. The spirit's presence had sharpened. Draken knew without looking because the turbulent air tossed a stronger death scent and an ethereal chill eclipsed the heat from the firebowl.

Bruche snorted. *Everyone dies eventually.*

Osias nodded, to Bruche or to Draken, neither were certain.

"I think the Akrasians are starting to believe that ruddy curse themselves. They say there's snow in Moonling Woods." For the first time in an age, long enough ago to be legend. "Coldest Frost in generations and the ones who don't have chest-rot have skin freezing away bit by bit. Speaking of, so do I. Let's go down and speak on this further." Osias had diverted the conversation but Draken wasn't about to let it go so easily. He needed Truls gone.

attack attack they come protect her the child protect her

Now he chooses to speak? Bruche sounded exasperated.

Draken turned on Truls with an annoyed snarl but a flickering row of torch-lights at the gates of Brîn tempered it. A sizable company traveled toward the city gates of Brîn, coming by way of the stone road that cut through the inland hunting woods and curved along the city wall. Soldiers on horseback, tails swishing, black armored forms shadowed against the stone wall, twenty-five at least. A banner fluttered and straightened.

He squinted and growled, "Ilumat."

Lord Ilumat, cousin to the Queen, major lord, and minor nuisance, maintained lands between the Agrian Range and the Grassland. He had come all the way across Akrasia in wartime during Frost, and he was no friend to Draken.

Bruche rose up in him but said nothing. He was growing used to this new magic sight of Draken's. He considered it an advantage. Osias, though, stared at him instead of the moons-lit field. "What have the gods done to you now?"

That set him back a step. But the Mance had noticed, of course, and likely with some alarm. Draken's last "gift" of magic had killed scores of men and brought down a magical city wall.

He tried to sound offhand. "Oh. I can see in the dark now. Daylight stings, though. Inconvenient, but it has its uses. I assumed it's Truls's doing since it started when he appeared."

"No. This is Korde's magic," Osias said.

"Another thing we need to discuss. But Ilumat has come a fair distance in this cold. I wonder what's gone bloody wrong now."

He might've just traveled from Reschan. Checking on the front. He is a soldier.

Despite Bruche's reasonable suggestion, Draken sensed his swordhand didn't believe his own words. Truls followed as he started down the steep winding steps of the tower. Draken nodded to the slave girl, huddled in a corner of the steps. He'd like to tell her to stay inside out of the wind, but they might have need of the fire for a signal.

The cold and seven stories down on stone steps soon had Draken's bad knee protesting even worse than on the climb, but the air was warmer in the court-yard. Halmar held Draken's horse as he and the other szi nêre waited. Bits of rubbish, dried grasses, fabric scraps floated on the wind and scurried along the walls. A patch of iced snow brightened one corner. Truls waited a little apart from Draken and the others, his countenance still wavering.

"Didn't take long for this place to feel deserted." He swung a leg over Sky's back and settled into the saddle. She tossed her head and snorted twin puffs of nervous mist.

"No, Khel Szi." Halmar mounted his own sizable war steed but didn't ride ahead, though he preferred it. Draken had finally got the szi nêre trained to let him go first, despite their sly attempts to lead him.

A shutter banged somewhere and the horses stamped their hooves on the packed dirt. Sky shook her head again, yanking on the reins. Osias and Setia led shaggy tora ponies out from what had been the serviceable, if drafty, great hall. The hilly villages at the feet of the Eidolas used the sturdy animals for everything from dragging plows to supper in hard times. Hardly fitting for a retired Mance King, but more fleet horse-stock had been taken to the front.

Eager to get out of the cold, though dreading the news Ilumat brought, Draken urged Sky to a canter. The horses made short work of the field, clumps of cold dirt and dead grasses dusting the air behind them. Unranked guards took a knee as the royal party passed through the city gate. Draken only glanced at them, keeping his eyes downcast against the glare of torches. Halmar paused to speak to them, so Draken and the others slowed to a walk.

Nightfall stained the sky, but it was still early enough to find the streets full of people hurrying to whatever respite the evening held. Night-sweepers stirred dust over cobbles and stone walks. Butchers' carcass-fires burned in alleys, making Draken's stomach turn with hunger. Most people were hooded against the cold or had their heads down, missing that royalty was in their midst. Just as well.

Sohalia ribbons dragged with sleet and bouquets of flowers wilted under gossamer layers of ice. Not as many adornments for the mid-Frost holiday as for Sohalias of recent memory, and the festivities had been more subdued. Too many fighters at the front; too many deaths to reckon with; too harsh a Frost.

Halmar trotted to ride next to Draken. "The gate admitted the Akrasian lord and his cohort and sent guides to bring them to the Citadel."

"The Akrasian lord" fair knew his way around the city, having visited prior, and would be hard-pressed to miss the elaborately painted dome over the Citadel from nearly any vantage on any street. But trust wore thin between the peoples of Akrasia and Brîn. Draken had learned quiet denial of that mutual suspicion worked best to avoid bloodshed. Captain Tyrolean and the Chamberlain Thom would greet Ilumat.

Indeed, Thom greeted Draken as well, chalk and slate in hand. He hurried forward as they climbed the steps to the Citadel, torchlight gleaming on the white moonwrought mask embedded into the skin over half his face, from his brow to jawline. The unblinking painted eye on it seemed particularly astute tonight. Draken had the disconcerting feeling that if he stared at it closely enough, he would see it roll in its socket. Except, of course, it didn't really have a socket; the meticulous paint just made it look like it did. The glare of lantern light off it made Draken squint.

Draken spoke before Thom could. "Aye, I've heard about our guests. Did you find them accommodations?"

"The porters and maids have seen to it, Khel Szi. A word, though?" Thom glanced at the lingering szi nêre. Their faces bore flat expressions, pierced lips and brows fixed into expressions of alert compliance. It wasn't that Thom didn't trust them, so whatever he had to say must be of a very sensitive nature.

Draken groaned inwardly and waved off Halmar. "Of course." He walked toward the steps leading into the Great Hall. Getting on suppertime, the hall was mostly deserted, but dozens of torches kept it brightly lit. He kept to the shadowed walkway behind the pillars and strolled toward the dais. No one would follow them there.

"I didn't want to bring it up in front of the szi nêre, but the Akrasians refused to yield their weapons."

Bruche growled in Draken's chest. Halmar was steady as stone but the other szi nêre were quicker to take offence. Konnon in particular lost no love on Akrasians. Word of any slight against Draken would spread through the Citadel to the lowliest slave. He hardly needed the staff harassing his guests. "Did they give a reason?"

"Lord Ilumat said it was an insult to take lieges' weapons during wartime."

"I hope someone told them it's an insult to imply they aren't well protected within the Citadel."

"It seemed to make no difference, Khel Szi." Thom had the occasional leaning toward primness, which reminded Draken that despite his considerable organizational capabilities, he was still inexperienced and young.

"It falls to me to settle, then, does it?" Damned awkward, asking for the weapons now.

On the one hand, Draken could see the Akrasians' point, though "liege" was an odd word to use between a regent and his people. Akrasians didn't talk like that. Sounded more like some Landed Monoean, actually. Perhaps this was more threat than insult . . . if Ilumat somehow learned of Draken's personal history. Bad enough Draken was Brînian; the people would toss out a half-blood regent who hailed from Monoea. The secret was only held because most of the people who knew his heritage were dead, and the rest had much to lose if he lost his position.

And they're your friends.

Were they? He wasn't always so sure. He had no illusions he was an easy friend to keep.

Let it go. You have more important things to worry about than an upstart lord with a gold-chased rapier.

He's Elena's cousin and the finest swordsman in Akrasia.

Bruche snorted so hard it reached Draken's throat. *But for me.*

Thom waited, his painted eye and its live twin, also unblinking, resting on him.

"You think I should say nothing of it," Draken said, unease crawling through him. This was like grabbing a metal spoon from a steaming pot; no way to know if it was hot or not. Best assume it was.

Thom's mouth opened and closed, the edge of his cheek pressing against the mask. "Khel Szi, I wouldn't pre—"

"I'm *asking* you to presume, Thom."

The Gadye drew a deep breath. "It seems they might take great offense."

"I've asked Ilumat to disarm before. He didn't have a problem with it then."

Thom cleared his throat. "When the Queen was in residence. I remember."

When the Queen . . . The point of this challenge dawned on him. This was a test of Draken's authority. "I'll think on it. Be easy, I'll be tactful—"

Tactful as an axe, Bruche chortled.

"You just see they're made comfortable." Draken resisted patting the young Gadye's shoulder. Since his being crowned people thought Draken wasn't to be touched or some nonsense, and Thom was too anxious with all the new duties brought by these important guests to break even simple protocol.

Captain Tyrolean, Draken's closest friend and confidant since Elena had lent him permanently to Draken's employ, met him on his way to his chambers to change. "Aye, I know about the weapons, Ty."

"I assumed you did."

"And? What would you do?"

"Accompany you to dinner, Your Highness, with my own blades in plain view."

"Of course." Tyrolean's lined eyes made his expression look severe, so Draken had no trouble guessing how concerned he was over Ilumat's show of bravado. That Tyrolean was tense enough to wear swords to supper with his own countrymen knotted Draken's neck.

By the time they entered the dim antechamber to Draken's bedchamber, sleet lashed the shutters and cold air leaked in through the slats. He sat on the bench to remove his boots. Kai rushed forward to kneel and do it for him. Draken leaned his head back against the wall and watched Tyrolean make a circuit of the room beyond, studying it with his hand resting on his hilt. Truls took up residence in his typical corner.

Draken nodded thanks to Kai. "Bloody inconvenient, their turning up now. I wanted another sevennight or two to study the war and devise strategy."

"Ilumat was raised up a soldier-son," Tyrolean said. "He's surely competent to help. And he might have new information from the front."

"He'd fair well better," Draken said. "Be a refreshing change if he made himself of actual use."

"Perhaps strategy talks can be a distraction from this bad start." Tyrolean paused near the latched shutters leading to the long balcony that ran the length of the wing, then moved on. Draken snorted softly. Neither of them really believed Ilumat intended anything other than building mountains between Draken and his power as Regent.

Kai had warmed a bowl of water for washing and unclasped Draken's cloak, keeping his eyes downcast, and pulled it from his shoulders. Draken stripped off his sword belt and laid the battered scabbard on a nearby table. The candle sconce on the wall stung his eyes, and Tyrolean's pacing irritated like a scratchy wool tunic. He turned his head, examining the room. Nothing out of order. Everything as it should be. He growled softly, irritated that Ilumat's arrival had him so rattled, and strode over to snuff a few candles in the sconce. Tyrolean kept walking, his brow furrowed.

"Did you take insult because I don't speak kindly of one of your lords, Ty?"

"No, Your Highness. I just believe Ilumat can be of use. Better a friend than a rival." His mouth twitched. "No matter how he annoys you."

Draken grunted as he unlaced and stripped his shirt. Too late for friendship. "Ilumat turned Elena over to the Moonlings. I ought to try him for treason."

"We don't know that for certain—" Tyrolean began, but a rattling interrupted him. Both of them turned toward the balcony shutters. They rattled again, harder. Not the wind. Draken stepped toward his sword. Halmar appeared from the antechamber as Tyrolean strode forward to yank the shutters open, drawing his sword at the same time.

CHAPTER TWO

Tyrolean moved, sword first. Its point pressed into the narrow throat of a dark, short figure.

Bruche chuckled. Draken sighed.

The throat cleared, an ironic, feminine sound. "Good evening, Captain."

Tyrolean seemed frozen for half a breath, then lowered his sword and dipped his chin. "Princess."

He stepped back to admit Aarinnaie, Szirin of Brîn and half-sister to Draken. Leggings, worn boots, and layers of tunics thickened her narrow body. All were soaked through and dirty. Dead leaves and twigs stuck in her many tight braids. She scattered droplets of melting sleet as she shook her head and more sleet whipped in through the shutters before Tyrolean shoved them closed and latched them.

"There are doors, you know," Draken said. "Great, elaborate carved doors just for us royals, with servants to open them and everything."

She shrugged and peeled off her outer tunic. The one beneath clung to her narrow curves. "I'd make a mess on the Great Hall floor."

"Instead you're dripping all over mine."

"Kai, will you please bring a towel." She held her hand out.

Kai wrung his hands and stepped back to fetch one, seeming to not know where to look. He was Draken's body slave, not Aarinnaie's. Custom dictated the free members of the household ignore body slaves so they couldn't share Draken's secrets. Draken considered the notion nonsense, just as he thought Brînian holding slaves nonsense, but he'd learned there were some things he couldn't yet change, even as Khel Szi. Kai pulled a towel off the stack and brought it back to her, offering it gingerly.

"Go ask Lina to prepare the Szirin a hot bath," Draken said to him. Kai shot him a grateful look and escaped. Draken turned back to Aarinnaie. "And no thrust and parry about not staying. You've been away far too long."

"I'm staying. It's too nasty out for taverns and taletellers. Besides, you need me. I hear Ilumat has come."

"*Lord* Ilumat, and you never were much for Citadel dinners. Why now?"

"Ilumat is quite handsome. Some say he's the most handsome man in all Akrasia." Too quick for Draken to decide if that was a joke, she made her way across the bright tile of his quarters, leaving a damp, muddy trail. Tyrolean watched her go, brows twisted. She dropped a curtsy at the door. "Present company excepted," and she left them.

Aye, definitely a joke.

Draken strode to wash his face and hands in the steaming, frothy bowl. "All I need is Aarin causing a diplomatic incident."

"Ilumat can handle a clever tongue," Tyrolean said.

Most of it will go over his head anyway.

Draken gave Tyrolean a look. "You surely don't believe my sister's only weapon is her tongue."

Tyrolean's brows raised. "She is yet untouched, Your Highness."

That was *not* what Draken had meant. "How could you know such?"

"I asked her."

Draken stared, his hands soapy. "That is not your concern."

"I made it my concern. My lord, Aarinnaie is an asset in many ways, but she could quickly become a liability. It is my duty to see that such liabilities are countered." Tyrolean spoke gently. "But I don't believe she's dangerous in that way."

Draken was aware the Captain entertained some romantic affection for his sister, but even if Aarinnaie could be corralled into marriage it would have to gain some political leverage. Tyrolean, being a *former* Akrasian First Captain with little power in Brîn or Akrasia, not to mention Draken's closest friend, was useless in that regard. Aarinnaie couldn't be wasted on him.

"She's as likely to sneak into Ilumat's quarters to kill him as ride him." Draken's discomfort made him irritably crass. "There's a potential diplomatic incident for you."

"Ilumat already has already caused one—insulting you by not giving over his sword. A sword you own along with the Queen's seal, Night Lord."

The pendant with Elena's seal clinked inside the bowl as he bent over it. Draken caught it in his hand and wiped the dripping water off Elena's image. Her chin was uplifted in the profile engraved into the moonwrought, jaw set, a hint of smile creasing her cheeks. He drew a steadying breath and let it fall back to his chest over the scar his own sword had left there when the priest-lord who led the Monoaen army had stuck him with it at the Battle of Auwaer ten moonturns before.

Tyrolean is right, Bruche said. *Ilumat has turned fully against you.*

He came here as a guest.

It doesn't feel right. You must take hold of this one quickly, Draken. Do not sup nor sleep without your guards or weapons. Better yet, lock him away for the insult.

Draken looked at Tyrolean. "Bruche says I should ask for their weapons and if they refuse to surrender them, I should put Ilumat in the dungeon."

"And then?" Tyrolean asked evenly.

"That would be the question." He glanced at Truls but the ghost seemed to have no suggestions.

Kai slipped back into the room and fetched a shirt from the wardrobe, but Draken shook his head. "Fresh trousers and the 'wrought armbands." He ignored Tyrolean's look. Akrasians eschewed the Brînian habit of going bare-chested. But in his own house, he would meet Ilumat on his own terms, which were Brînian. "Tyrolean, find Thom and tell him I want our guests' rooms searched while they dine."

"For weapons?"

"And anything else of interest. Then you may escort Aarinnaie to supper."

Brînians weren't given to large state dinners but more intimate affairs of ten or twelve people of rank. The formal dining room was set for Draken, a low table inlaid with swirling mosaics of shell. The low light gave him a chance to study his guests.

Ilumat wore his casual Escort Horse Captain uniform, the rank he'd held before his father had died suddenly, leaving him a young lord with some of the most important blood and lands in the kingdom. His tunic, cut with two diagonal stripes of rank, draped his muscled chest and his boots were brushed. Properly, he should take a knee, but instead he inclined his head graciously to Draken, who was willing to let it go since this was a more casual gathering. A light beard covered Ilumat's cheeks, the edges untidy. Had his journey been too harried to pause for the occasional trim? It would have taken at least two sevennight to make it here from his lands, likely longer with River Eros no use for travel. The river ran low this Frost, and much of it was ice.

"Khel Szi," Ilumat said.

Odd that, using his Brînian title.

Burns the spoiled brat to call you Night Lord. Or worse, Prince. Bruche made a good point. Khel Szi was the least-respected of his titles among Akrasians. An insult in some quarters.

If Draken didn't quite smile, he did his best to pin an agreeable expression on his face. "Lord Ilumat. Welcome."

"Thank you for your hospitality on such short notice."

"The Citadel is quiet during Frost. We've plenty of room." Though a message ahead would have been courteous.

This one couldn't taste courtesy if it were served well-salted by the Queen, Bruche intoned.

Draken let his gaze slide down to Ilumat's sword, his manicured fingers resting on the hilt chased with moonwrought. "It is Citadel imperative to relinquish weapons at the Great Hall and enjoy Brînian protection."

"The Gadye lad mentioned something."

Draken didn't much appreciate the coy smile playing on Ilumat's lips. "Thom is the Citadel Chamberlain."

"Aye. I explained our unease with that . . . imperative. The war—" Ilumat gave a delicate shrug. His fingers also tightened on his hilt. "Discomfiting times."

A war with a front a sevennight away. "Aye. Bad time to rattle me. Since I outrank you, Captain."

Ilumat held his gaze a breath too long, but short of a full-on challenge. He dipped his chin and undid his belt with a flourish, swinging the hilt round to present the sword to Draken on both palms. Well-callused palms. From sparring or fighting? Ilumat had been at the front at the start of the war. But Draken understood he'd spent at least half his time since on his lands, leaving his cohorts to his horsemarshals. Draken didn't much like it but horsemarshals being what they were—trained, disciplined leaders with inarguable success rates—he'd let Ilumat's indifference go. Perhaps this mild rebellion on Ilumat's part was his testing Citadel ice to see where it might crack. Perhaps he should have met Ilumat in the throne room with all pomp and circumstance. Tension built in his spine as he stared at the young lord.

Perhaps it is too late and the damage is already done.

Draken didn't have time to have a conversation with Bruche about what that might mean, but there was enough truth in the words to made his gut clench. The Akrasians moved to offer him their weapons and slaves soon carried all the weapons off. None looked happy as they sat back down when Draken gave them leave, the Akrasians nor the slaves.

The doors swung open, breaking the awkward silence, and Thom entered to announce Aarinnaie and Tyrolean. The men . . . Draken's four guests were curiously all men, including the two ranked Escorts and the Horse Captain accompanying Ilumat to dinner . . . all rose again. Draken suppressed a smile as he offered his sister his arm. Tyrolean dipped his chin to him and moved to his place at the table, greeting Ilumat as he did so.

"Sorry. Am I late?" Dressed in a flowing gown, Aarinnaie sounded girlishly breathless. Draken hardly recognized her.

"No, we've not started. You've met Lord Ilumat before, aye?"

"When I visited Court last." When she'd been under the manipulation of Truls and tried her damnedest to kill Queen Elena. Draken gave a surreptitious glance around despite the lack of death scent. No ghost-Mance. His shoulders eased slightly.

Ilumat bowed over her hand and touched it to his forehead. "Princess. I last saw *you* at the battle for Auwaer. Impressive showing."

"It was a very near thing." Her smile warmed, but Draken thought it a warning. Ilumat wasn't buying her girlish princess act.

"Aye, but we've our city back."

For now, Draken thought. He had his doubts about Auwaer surviving Newseason when the fighting started again in earnest. "Sit, please. They're ready to serve us." When everyone was settled and slaves were pouring wine, he asked, "Did you visit the front on your journey here, Ilumat?"

He nodded, sipping his wine. "Our side is dug in for Frost. The Ashen make half-hearted attempts at raiding. Nothing to signify. I think the snow has thrown them all."

That made Draken curious. The Monoeans should be familiar enough with snow. "I can't imagine Moonling Woods snowed in."

"Thigh high in drifts," Ilumat said, "and so fogged in you can't see the lowest branches of the Oscher trees. The air is so cold and damp it seeps into your bones and won't let loose its hold. Fighting has been at a standstill for five sevennight now."

The coldest Draken had ever been was patrolling the Monoean coast. There, the cold got into your marrow and houses were shuttered so tightly most people had a constant cough all Frost from hearth smoke. Snow fell often and iced over in the damp ocean air. In Brîn the air was cold and damp, especially this night, but with the Citadel woods and walls to cut the ferocity of the cold sea winds, shutters still allowed a slight breeze to dance with the fires in the twin hearths.

A basic thing, the weather, but Ilumat not knowing the enemy when he spoke as if he did irked Draken. "The Monoeans are more adapted to the cold than you might think. Best not to fall off guard."

"Studied them, have you?" Ilumat glanced at the Escort sitting closest to him.

Draken replied evenly, "For all his faults, my father kept an extensive library, which I've made good use of."

"Hm. Never put Brînians down as scholars." Ilumat's gaze flicked down over Draken's bare chest, to Elena's pendant hanging bright against his dark, scarred skin. "But then, you're not quite all Brînian, are you?"

Draken's lungs made an effort to squeeze all the air from his chest. He breathed carefully and took a sip of wine before answering, Bruche holding the cup steady. "If my love for Akrasia corrupts my blood, so be it."

Another exchange of glances among the Akrasians. They ate in awkward silence for a little. Draken let his mind settle before speaking again, though his shoulders ached with tension. At last came the final course of fruit compote with cream . . . a Monoean affectation he asked the cook to fix regularly. Aarinnaie had taken a liking to it but not many others had. Still, it reminded him of his wife. Of his old home . . . and less of Elena. A simple comfort amid so much turmoil.

Ilumat didn't taste the compote. "Now that we're sufficiently fed and watered, may I speak frankly?"

No title. The slow squeeze started in Draken's chest again. "If you must."

"I did stop by the front, as I told you. But not just to see how things stood. I had need of servii, a deal of them. Three thousand."

Draken could barely get air behind the words in his shock. "You took three thousand servii from an active warfront?"

Ilumat simply held his gaze. Next to Draken, Aarinnaie shifted slightly, one hand reaching for a blade that wasn't there.

The quiet ensued, forcing Draken to speak again.

"I suppose you'll tell me why at some point. Perhaps at my sword point."

Bruche moved forward within Draken. *Hold, Bruche.* His swordhand might do something Draken would regret.

Ilumat reached for his wine and sipped.

"I have need of them if I'm to take control of the Citadel and Brîn."

"You speak treason." Draken's voice shook with fury. He couldn't be sure if it was only himself speaking, or Bruche as well. The swordhand hadn't withdrawn. His pressure and chill made Draken lean forward slightly. A waft of death scent mingled with the oil smoke, making his stomach churn. Truls drifted near, watching.

"Your presence here is treason. You're a half-breed slave who isn't fit to pour my wine. Worse, your charade brought the Monoeans here. Someone needs to take the situation in hand for you certainly haven't."

He ignored the slur. Or was it a slur if it was truth? "The Ashen were going to invade whether I went to Monoea or not. No matter what you believe, I have the war as well in hand as possible."

The Akrasian drew himself up. "No longer. I should be King by rights. Regent at the least, until our Queen's fate is determined."

Tyrolean shifted on his feet. Draken held, absorbing this audacious claim before speaking. Ilumat was only a cousin to Elena . . . not even a first cousin. "On what grounds?"

"I'm Elena's closest living relative."

"No. Princess Sikyra is," Aarinnaie said.

"Princess." Ilumat managed to turn the word into an insult. "Bastard sundry. Not even the Brînians would have her. What makes you think the Akrasians will?"

"It's a point. The Akrasians are no model of respect of nobility, if you're any indication." Draken unfolded his long body, feeling much too big for the low cushions and table, and got to his feet. "Halmar. Take Ilumat and our other guests below."

Ilumat laughed even as his szi nêre approached. *Perhaps he's gone mad,* Bruche suggested. Draken ignored him. The szi nêre grasped Ilumat's arms. Only then did his attention seem to hone in on what was happening. His head snapped around to face Draken. "If I don't appear outside the Citadel within a night, the troops are under orders to attack the city. If I'm found dead, they are ordered to raze the city to the ground."

"We've walls. Difficult to breach." Not to mention that those troops belonged to him, answered to him as Night Lord and Regent.

Ilumat laughed. "Unlike you, I'm trained to think things through. I've already got a sizable contingent inside the city, of course."

"You lie. There are no Akrasians here." Her fingers fisted around handfuls of gown. Draken raised a hand to stop whatever she might say or do next.

Ilumat laughed again, a sound Draken longed to erase with torture and blood. "If you go now you might just escape with your daughter's life."

CHAPTER THREE

O ne of the most important lessons a new father learns is never to wake his sleeping baby. Draken ignored that rule, striding to his daughter's chamber adjoining his. He lifted her compact little body. Sikyra startled awake with a sharp cry and tucked her face against his neck, quivering and snuffling. Her fist curled around one of his locks, the other pressed to her mouth. Her body slave Lilna tsked. Bruche chuckled at the impertinence. But Lilna's position was secure. Sikyra adored her. Draken ignored both slave and swordhand and concentrated on comforting his daughter.

Tyrolean appeared in the doorway leading from Draken's sleeping chamber. "Ilumat and his company are locked in cells below. They gave no fight. They seem assured they'll be released before dawn."

Draken nodded and followed him out into the corridor, carrying Sikyra. "Anything in their rooms?"

"Nothing of interest, my lord."

"What do you make of his threats?"

"We've high walls and strong gates. Moreover, we've had no word from scouts that three thousand servii are marching this way. I don't know how he'd hide their presence." Tyrolean paused. "The notion he's got loyals inside the city is more worrisome."

Draken's arm tightened around his daughter. "And Sikyra is a prime target."

"You both are, Your Highness."

They walked to Draken's private scrollroom, Halmar and Konnon hulking shadows striding behind. Konnon's dapples from his Moonling parentage paled from tension. Truls drifted ahead as if he already knew Draken's destination. Their path skirted the Great Hall, but open doorways showed fevered activity within: soldiers and szi nêre moving to tighten defenses of the Citadel and slaves organizing munitions and provisions. He was surprised again at the number of people it took to keep the Citadel fortified, and even more so at their loyalty to a man who was not raised among them. Tingles cascaded over Draken's scalp as a passing guard dipped his chin to them and gave the baby a small smile. Ilumat was wrong. He and his daughter had the Brînians' love.

Osias sat in Draken's favorite chair smoking his pipe. Setia stood near him.

Draken laid his sword aside and sat heavily in a harder chair by the table strewn with maps. Sikyra slid down to hold herself up between his knees, gazing solemnly at the others. Like her mother, her smiles were rare as Newseason sun breaking from behind clouds.

The walls had shelves divided into square cubbies, filled with scrolls and small treasures collected by Draken's forebears. Practical red clay tiles covered the floor. The low chairs bore worn cushions and armrests blackened from generations of hands. Dust softened the corners; slaves were not often permitted to clean this space. From here, generations of Khel Szis had led Brîn. From here, Draken also led Akrasia and her current war.

Aarinnaie paced relentlessly, her skirts shushing around her calves, only stopping when two more szi nêre appeared to report that a preliminary search revealed nothing out of the ordinary inside the city. Aarinnaie snorted. "If there are enemies inside the walls, I would know."

Scouts had been sent to explore the woods and both the seaside and mountainside gates were barred, leaving the wall guards a bit confused but on alert. Draken ordered the city Comhanar attend the front gate, though he hated yanking the older man from his bed.

Setia poured Draken wine and pressed it into his hand, her small hand brushing his. He nodded his thanks as Tyrolean shut the door behind the runner. The Akrasian Captain's jaw was tight, body contained and bristling with blades as if he expected to spring into battle at any moment.

"I think you should consider leaving the Citadel, Your Highness. We cannot be certain of the extent of Ilumat's threat before daybreak." Tyrolean's gaze slid to Aarinnaie as he spoke, silently including her in the escape plan. He was smart enough to not suggest it outright. Aarinnaie would only waste time arguing. "Take Princess Sikyra and hide."

At her name, the baby princess crawled to the Escort Captain and climbed her way to her feet by hanging onto his armor-clad leg.

Osias spoke lowly as he ran his fingers along his strung, waxed bowstring. "Tyrolean may be right. Aarinnaie surely knows a good place to hide."

Setia drew a sharp breath. Draken thought he knew why. Aarinnaie had been abused by their father, and then taken in by Truls and trained to slink through the shadows as an assassin. She still moved through the city at will despite her status. It wasn't a life, an ability, he'd wish on anyone, much less his sister. And

Setia was fond of Aarinnaie. They shared a past from Setia's slave days in the Citadel.

"I know many such places." Aarinnaie waved a hand and carried on pacing.

Draken set aside his untouched wine with an audible clink of metal on wood, turned his squinting gaze away from the three-wick candle burning on the table at his elbow. "I can't defend Brîn from one of your bolt-holes."

"Both princesses, at least, should be made safe," Tyrolean said.

Damn. Now he's done it.

That stopped Aarinnaie. "I can kill as well as you, Captain."

"Better than I, Princess." Tyrolean's face was wooden. "It doesn't mean you should have to. It doesn't mean you can't be overcome."

Draken shifted in his chair, suppressing a grim smile. Seaborn lay dull as dirty bathwater on the table. He laid it across his knees. It was a plain single-hand sword, a little too short for his reach, without ornamentation or carving. Just a devilishly sharp blade, perfect balance, a sweat-stained leather grip. And magic that could trade one life for another.

Aarinnaie's head snapped up. "Khel Szi, I could—"

He held up his hand. "No. Tyrolean is right. Murder is not the answer to every problem, Aarin."

"We have Ilumat captive. He's an admitted traitor. It's not murder. It's an execution."

"The other lords may not believe he is a traitor to Akrasia," Tyrolean said, his dark eyes shifting to her. "I don't think he would have acted unless he had more backing. And there's his threat that his death will set off a massacre."

"You think it's valid?"

"Three thousand troops. A bold claim. He couldn't have taken them without cooperation from other lords and horsemarshals," Tyrolean said. "For what purpose would he come here with groundless threats?"

Draken leaned over and blew out the candle searing the edge of his vision, scattering fine droplets of wax over a creased map. "None."

Aarinnaie sniffed and resumed stalking the room. "Then Sikyra can never be Queen. It was a poor prospect at best. We defend Brîn and let Akrasia sort her own war with the Ashen. She is *your* heir at least."

Draken didn't argue the improbability of smoothly placing a woman on the Brînian throne someday, much less breaking from Akrasia or defending themselves against Monoea. He just sighed. But Tyrolean's lips whitened at her brusque tone. Sikyra tugged on his boot and he bent to pick her up. She watched her aunt and the others from her new vantage, eyes wide. They were deep brown with the Akrasian slight slant. Draken had started the tattooing process when she was an infant and eleven moonturns later they were thickly lined and lent her a wise, aged look. The custom was still foreign to him, but Akrasians wouldn't accept her as Queen without it. Lined eyes or not, her Akrasian heritage was obvious. To him, so was her Monoean blood, but most Akrasians wouldn't see past her hair and dark skin.

His throat tightened. Aarinnaie was right. They weren't likely to accept her at any rate. Sikyra's father might be the highest lord in Akrasia, but she was born out of wedlock with sundry blood and had no mother-Queen to defend her right to succession. Nor was she likely to get the chance to rule with rebellion and invaders nipping at the heels of succession. He rubbed his hand over his face and removed it to find Truls drawing near, soulless eyes black against his ever-shifting form. A waft of rot filled Draken's lungs.

elena is alive seek her seek her

His breath snagged in his chest. His fists closed around the sword on his knees. "Gods. Not *now*."

Draken. Bruche, with a note of alarm.

Aarinnaie strode forward to seize his wrist. "You've cut yourself."

Osias took a step closer, grey eyes narrowed and swirling, looking not at Draken but past him. At Truls, no doubt.

Draken looked down at his hand. It was wrapped tightly around Akhen Khel's blade. He winced and uncurled his fingers to reveal a smear of blood on his sword blade.

Everyone had fallen silent. They were waiting for the floor to rumble underfoot as he healed, for the scrolls to rustle in their shelves, for his father's keepsakes to topple.

Draken kept bleeding and the room stayed quiet.

Aarinnaie pulled a scarf from about her neck. She pressed it to his hand. With the other she gently straightened one of his earrings.

To his surprise, his voice sounded ordinary, almost offhand. "I want the city locked down and all patrols to report. Give Comhanar Vannis the orders yourself. Tyrolean, keep to Sikyra. She needs to go back to bed. Osias, please stay."

Truls's whispers grew, hissing from behind him, a chill breath on the back of his neck. *Don't like that much, do you, you bastard? My doing things my way.*

"Of course, Your Highness," Tyrolean said. Sikyra whimpered as he carried her out, bottom lip jutting as she reached a chubby hand over his shoulder for Draken.

Aarinnaie gave Draken a piercing look and went reluctantly. Setia glanced at Osias. Something wordless passed between them. She shut the door behind Aarinnaie, but remained with them.

Draken drew a breath and rubbed his temple with his fingertips. A headache had bloomed behind his eyes.

"How long since you couldn't heal yourself?" Setia asked.

"Since Rinwar stabbed me with Seaborn, and only that blade. So far." He probed the jagged scar on his chest, let his hand fall.

"But it did not kill you," Setia said. Her voice held a note of wonder. She'd always been a bit reverent around Draken. He felt awkward about it since she worked magic that far surpassed his.

"That time. Now, I'm not so sure." That healing had brought down the seemingly infallible Palisade around Auwaer, the wall of repellent magic that had protected Akrasia's capital city for generations. Right now his vulnerability to wounds from his own sword wasn't his primary concern. He rubbed his eyes with his forefinger and thumb. "Truls talks to me endlessly, Osias. Every day and through the nights. I can't sleep—I—"

Bruche rumbled in his chest, soothing him like a purr. *Easy, friend. You need to think of securing your city. Worry about Elena another day.*

If only he could. Elena's absence was a physical ache. Truls had no reason to help him, no reason to do anything but torture him. They were enemies and had been since the Mance had orchestrated his wife's murder that led not only to Draken's exile to Akrasia but a narrowly avoided civil war. Truls had answered to the gods then, and still did. He was still an enemy, and probably lying. He closed his fist around the pendant hanging from his neck bearing Elena's likeness. His voice came rough: "What if she's really dead?"

A storm overtook Osias's irises. He blinked and they calmed, back to the sea-fog grey. For the first time Draken had the insight the swirling might be the many spirits inside Osias. Maybe they fought Osias to escape, or for control. Or simply to see.

"The gods have no reason to torture you so, not if they want your will as their own," Setia said.

Tightness ached across Draken's shoulders. "It's never made any sense, any of it."

"Just because you do not know their intent does not mean their choosing you isn't sound."

"I used their magic to bring Elena back to life against their wishes. I used it to destroy a ship and kill hundreds of men." He used it to destroy a city wall that had very nearly resulted in the deaths of thousands.

He whipped out his dagger and sliced his palm. The stone floor groaned and scrolls shuffled as the stinging cut closed and healed itself. He scowled, all reason for his bitterness disproved. "I have died a hundred deaths for them. They can fight their own damned wars. I've got my own."

"Perhaps the gods share your war against these Ashen who blaspheme them." Osias closed his hand over Draken's, silvery pale against his rough, dark skin. Callused from bearing a sword he didn't want. Knuckles misshapen from breaking over faces. "Perhaps you are yet their champion. And perhaps Truls seeks redemption by helping you. It might explain why he has come."

Draken shot a glare at the ghost. "Is that it, Truls? You're here for redemption? You won't find it in me."

no no no seek her seek her go from this place now they come

Draken took his hand away from Osias's and rose. His knee locked painfully and he had to lean on the desk for momentary support. He cursed. Osias was wrong. He had to be. Every instinct told him he'd missed something important, especially as Truls closed in, his face morphing to a ghastly misted vision of rank death. His stomach turned over, making his skin clammy and his breath speed up. He spat a mouthful of saliva, hoping bile didn't follow. "Don't you smell him? Death and rot and—"

Osias stood very still, watching him. He knew Truls was here, but the dead didn't torture necromancers.

go they come they come they want the child go they want the child go they will take her

"No one is bloody coming!" Draken swept his arm through Truls. It passed unheeded. Prickles climbed up his shoulder and slipped down his spine, chilling him from the outside in.

Truls carried on looking at him with his black eyes but at least he fell quiet.

"I need him gone, Osias." His voice was rough. He cleared his throat. It didn't help. "I can't afford this distraction."

The Mance shook his head. "I cannot *make* him go."

"Of course you can. You're a bloody *necromancer*." Draken shoved himself upright. His knee held under Bruche's ethereal grip. He ignored the tarnish the Mance's skin took on, the distortion of his features into something less pleasing and symmetrical. It was the bloody light or something, stinging his eyes and driving him half mad.

"The gods—" Osias began.

"Hang the gods! I cut your fetter. You have your own will. I gave it to you."

Osias shook his head and rose, hands raised. The shadows cast a dull tarnish over his silvery skin. "Draken. Be easy—"

But he couldn't. Not now. He was too worn, too worried, too bloody terrified of all that could happen. "Ever since I set foot on this godsforsaken land I have shed buckets of blood, faith, and honor. I am running fair low on all. You owe me for your freedom. You owe me at least that much."

The Mance gazed at him. Draken had the sense of all the spirits within his friend, dozens of them, were vying for the chance to see the upstart half-breed, bastard Prince who dared befriend, free, and now challenge their host. He couldn't hold that gaze for long.

His voice lowered. "I saved the gods once. I'll be damned if I'm doing it again."

Bruche shifted uneasily inside Draken. *Do not speak so. Truls seems here to help. Perhaps you should listen to him.*

You don't trust him any more than I do.

Mistrust is my duty. Mistrust keeps you safe.

"The gods allow you generous insolence," Osias said. "But I've spent my meager defiance. I would aid you in any way, this you know. But I cannot—"

"*Will* not."

The Mance dipped his chin, just barely. "Aye. I will not banish a Mance come to help you. If the gods will send him from you, so be it. But I will not meddle with my betters. Not this way, not since I have unbound my will from theirs."

"Why not?" An honest question. A valid one, damn it all.

Truls slid about the room, swirling and morphing like Osias's eyes. He wanted to order the Mance out—away—

take the child and run

Someone pounded on the door and shoved it open. Halmar's immovable bulk filled the entrance. Aarinnaie was behind him, trying to push through. "Attack, Khel Szi," Halmar said. "Lord Ilumat spoke true. Akrasia has come in force."

CHAPTER FOUR

"They're mad, Khel Szi. Must be to attack on a night like this."

Comhanar Vannis had enough Sohalias of battle experience that Draken always paid close attention to everything the man said. They huddled in a cold wood-plank building shoved up against the inside of Brîn's walls like an afterthought. It wasn't even a proper square or round shape, but oblong and awkwardly narrower near the ugly stone hearth so that Draken, Aarinnaie, Comhanar Vannis, and Tyrolean stood shoulder to shoulder around it. Local guards called it the Cindershack because its drafty wooden roof was a risk from flaming arrows or oil-soaked stones. It was all the more crowded for Truls accompanying Draken closer than his szi nêre, two of whom flanked the door. Draken could smell the reek of whatever necromancy held him to his side.

He asked Vannis to put out the lanterns and candles. The room dipped into soothing darkness but for the fire. He was all right as long as he didn't look at it. The others gave him strange looks, but he ignored them.

The door slammed open, shoved by a heavy hand and the wind. Halmar caught it and kept it from swinging into himself.

"My old fa says it's the coldest ruddy Frostfall since his fa was alive, and he's all crook-back now. Doesn't even know his own name, poor old bast—" The city guard striding into the Cindershack stopped up short and whipped his helm from his head, staring at Draken and especially Aarinnaie in her leather armor. Sleet melted from his helm and shoulders and he'd brought a blast of cold air with him. His companion ran into him from behind and started to curse but choked it off as he saw Draken.

"Shut the door," Comhanar Vannis growled. "And report."

The two guards held a moment like they didn't know whether to kneel or bow or straighten into attention. They settled for the latter. "Khel Szi. Comhanar.

We estimate two thousand Akrasians at these gates. We have not engaged the enemy, as you ordered. So far they hold."

Enemy. Draken couldn't keep the wince from reaching his face. "The Akrasians are allies until proved otherwise." Allies in a bigger damned war everyone but him seemed to have forgotten. They needed the Akrasians or Monoea would slaughter every last Brînian. Did no one understand that?

"I think they just did, Khel Szi, aye? They are holding us under siege." Only the presence of the others kept Aarinnaie's tone on the virtuous side of courtesy. There were several darting eyes and clearing of throats among the men.

"On Ilumat's treasonous orders," Draken retorted. "And there's no attack as of yet. Just a show of force."

Aarinnaie scowled. "Semantics don't win wars."

Draken's patience rested on a precipice. "No, but they can prevent them."

Another soldier pushed in, halted, and blinked rapidly when he saw Draken.

"Shut the damned door, then. What've you got?" Vannis said. Draken nodded for the man to speak.

"Khel Szi." He swallowed. "They've dragged our scouts to the gates and left them. Five. Dead to a man." His voice trailed off as Aarinnaie cursed softly.

Gods, all five were dead? No wonder they'd had no word. Draken waited a breath. Two. "There's more, obviously."

"The Akrasians are assembling a king's ram at the gate."

He stared at the rough-faced soldier, taken aback. The mechanisms on a king's ram were tall as a man, crafted of solid metal, and required specially reinforced wagons and four cart horses to pull just parts of the machine. The ram itself bore a spiked metal head and armor to prevent the wood from burning under flaming arrow attack . . . How in Korde's name could they have dragged the pieces across the country so quickly? It wasn't possible. And yet he didn't doubt the report.

Six wagons, I reckon. This was long in the planning. Bruche took on a strange musing tone. It occurred how seriously Bruche was taking this since he wasn't just rushing to the attack, sword in hand. *Aye, move carefully on this one.*

He took it from either the Bastion fortifications or Khein, Draken replied. Meaning Ilumat had stolen the damned thing from Elena's own troops, or Draken's. Unless both garrisons were in collusion with Ilumat . . . He hissed a curse. The others waited, Comhanar Vannis with a deep frown.

"Captain. Have you dealt with one of these rams?" Draken asked.

Tyrolean shook his head. "Not personally, my lord. I believe it will take all night to assemble. It requires several men and horses to position."

"So kill the men and horses." Curly sprigs had escaped from the braid twisted and pinned to the back of Aarinnaie's head. They bounced as she moved, belying her grave tone.

"The moment arrows fly this turns from a stand-off to a battle." A battle they might fair lose. Draken looked at the soldier reporting and gave him a nod. "I want frequent updates, whether there are any changes or not. See to it personally."

"Khel Szi." The soldier dipped his head—hair shorn tight from grief or penance—and stepped back out. A blast of damp wind scattered sparks from the hearth and Tyrolean went to stamp a couple out. Needless; they were on the dirt floor. He needed time to think, then. A commodity they were short on.

Draken gave him a close look. "Well, Captain?"

Tyrolean rubbed his clean-shaven chin with the back of his leather glove. "They did not haul that ram here to assemble it and let it rust. They are my countrymen, but the Princess speaks truth. We should attack now and do our damnedest to disable the ram and kill the servii who operate it. This is already a battle, my Prince."

Draken eased a breath from his chest. "The king's ram I saw in the Bastion had metal armoring over the top. No way to reach the wood with flaming arrows."

"If we can oil the ground and set fire to it—"

Draken cut Aarinnaie off. "How are we to do that without risking the gates? And there are no grasses nor soil to burn . . . the stone is cold and icy this time of year, especially with the storm." Some thoughtful Khel Szi had long ago laid thick pavers over the road to the city. It kept ditches from forming and cut down on maintenance. It also made a reasonably secure place to set the ram.

"If the gears are oiled, maybe we can set it alight . . . how far have your firemasters gotten with replicating the Monoean stuff, Khel Szi?" Comhanar Vannis asked.

Draken dragged up what he knew of the ram. It'd been ages since he'd seen one and then only briefly. The last use had been when Elena's father had employed one when he'd taken Brîn. Draken had a feeling their fire oil wouldn't be of much use. "It doesn't slow burn like theirs, and it's difficult to catch in this damp."

"Arrows, then. We start picking them off. We've got the archers for it."

Draken cursed, staring at the fire. The last thing he wanted to do was to kill Akrasians. Every servii and horsemarshal were needed in the war against the Monoeans.

too late too late they will come they come to burn the citadel

"Shut it!"

Aarinnaie blinked. "Draken?"

They were all staring at him. "I'm just trying to bloody think."

She frowned. Her confusion was clear. None of them had said anything.

"Fetch the firemasters. See what is to be done with what we have. In the meantime, start archers picking off draft horses and anyone who—no, wait."

"Aye, Khel Szi?" The Comhanar, voice calm though he must be wondering at his erratic behavior.

Draken narrowed his eyes. "I assume the pieces are not dragged up to the gates yet."

"They are still hauling the carts in."

"The wagons are wood, aye? Those we can set alight. And the ram is big enough it might make an effective barrier in front of the gates."

"But we could be trapped in the city," Aarinnaie said, echoing Bruche's wordless concern.

Bruche, you and I both know this city can't stand up to one thousand troops, much less three. Not with all the best Brînian fighters at the front. "Better than letting them dance in with ease. Allow the Akrasians to haul the pieces to the gates. After they start to assemble the ram get our best archers to kill the draft horses and pick off the men. Spare the flaming arrows for the wagons."

"What about Ilumat's claim he has troops inside the city?" Tyrolean asked.

"I think Akrasians would stand out on the street. You certainly do."

Tyrolean didn't let a flinch from Draken's comment reach his face but a pall fell over the room. Draken's tone, no doubt. Vannis brushed his hand over the spotless plate armor protecting his chest, worn under strict orders from Draken who had no interest in losing his top commander to a cleverly aimed arrow. Even Aarinnaie's knife hilt seemed to need a quick polish from a tongue-dampened thumb.

But she was the only one who dared say it in the offhand tone he knew so well: "You are hardly well-loved by everyone and many Brînians love coin more than they love any Khel Szi."

Draken gave himself some credit for not scowling at this blunt truth. After one of Aarinnaie's previous "investigations," he'd had a run-in with a bloodlord's son. Khisson, the father and a powerful man in Brîn and her outlying islands, was definitely *not* loyal to Draken. He knew his local enemies were prevalent, but they'd failed to show much of themselves during his reign. He snorted softly. Reign. If one could call it that.

Even so, Brînians allying with Ilumat and handing their beloved City of Brîn over to an Akrasian lord was a fair reach. "And so Ilumat allied these Brînians and organized them to rebel when he announced his intention to usurp both thrones? Never mind they've no reason to trust him or obey him."

She didn't restrain her own scowl. "It might not take so much convincing. What if he promised your throne to Khisson or some other bloodlord? I wouldn't put it past Ilumat to strike such a bargain, nor Khisson to take it. He was your enemy *before* you killed his son."

Vannis had been pretending not to listen but now his head snapped up.

Draken sighed. "It's a long story, Comhanar."

"I'm certain you had every reason, Khel Szi."

"A couple of very sharp ones, aye. Aarinnaie, go to ground. Find out what you can. And don't," he added in a growl, "be gone many nights. I need you to hand."

Aarinnaie nodded and turned for the door. The wind caught it and slammed it behind her. Tyrolean's lip twitched and his boot moved forward without his actually taking a step.

Draken ran a weary hand over his face. "I can't ever quite escape the feeling that I'll never see her again when she bolts off."

"Nor that she might be right about the bloodlords, eh, Khel Szi?" Vannis said.

Draken looked up, eyes narrowed. Apparently Comhanar Vannis didn't much appreciate the fact that Draken had killed a bloodlord's son, though his face was bland despite his impertinence.

But is it impertinence when he's twice your age and seen four times the blood you have? Or are you the impertinent one?

He answered both Vannis and Bruche in one go. "Aye. That's what bothers me worst of all."

◆ ◆ ◆

Draken sent Tyrolean back to inform the Citadel of the news at the gate and to order them to prepare for attack. Halmar would have been the ideal choice for this errand, but he refused to leave Draken's side.

Outside on the wall, he shielded his eyes with his cupped hand, trying to study the Akrasian force through the weather. Behind the first few lines of soldiers, harried, bent figures put their backs into it to wheel the great pieces together. They were making damned quick progress; even now a dozen soldiers were installing the metal shielding on the top of the ram. He cast an annoyed glance up at the skies. Swirling clouds concealed the Seven from his glare and occasional waves of sleet caught on fierce winds stung his cheeks. His stomach churned as he considered. Enough archers and arrows might take some out some of the servii on the ground, but they'd never get anything to burn in this storm, never mind shooting blind against the wind. They didn't even have enough bloody archers, nor his finest. Most of them were gone to the bloody front, which was where bloody Ilumat should have been.

He reckoned he'd better give it a go though, and see for certain what they were up against.

"Fire!" he shouted, waving an arm at a squad. A dozen archers did as he bid. One arrow skipped off the top of the ram; most caught in a gust and tumbled to the ground.

Waste, shooting in this wind, he thought sourly.

Spears are heavier. Hail the Moonlings. Bruche was joking.

The Moonlings aren't exactly my friends at the moment. It was they who had abducted Elena under the pretense of taking her to safety, they who had bargained his Queen's life, and very nearly his daughter's, for some abstract power they thought they deserved. For all he knew they'd helped Ilumat with this scheme. Though it gave him an idea. If he could buy some time with the magical Abeyance . . . *I should speak to Setia.*

She can't reach the Abeyance so easily.

How do you know?

An inward shrug. *You need sleep. I don't. Sometimes we talk, Setia and I.*

How did he not know? He and Bruche shared all.

You never asked. All sorts of things go on in your hind-mind.

A less than comforting thought. Draken turned his attention back to the mess at hand, puzzling over the angle to shoot and about to ask for a bow. The Akrasians were so intent on setting up the ram they ignored the arrows. They didn't even bother firing back.

Beyond lay shadows of men, shouts silenced in the wind, but for one. A big body, too big to be a soldier . . . Draken's vision sharpened. Rain glinted on something looming over the man's helm. They slowly took shape, like twisted tree branches or curled spikes . . . *No*, Bruche whispered. *Horns.*

Draken couldn't breathe. Horns. It couldn't be.

The man . . . the *god* . . . met his gaze. Inclined his head, too slight to be subservient. A gesture of respect between equals.

But why would he be there, with the Akrasians? Khellian is your patron, not theirs.

The back of Draken's neck prickled and stung. The horned god of war carried on staring.

"Khel Szi?" Sharp, feminine.

Draken spun, slipped forward a little. A crosswind gust pushed at him from inside the city against the outer wall of the walkway. His stomach dropped, but Halmar hauled back on his arm. A greying woman waited a couple of steps down on the flight leading to the top of the wall. Draken dragged his gaze back to the battlefield.

Khellian was gone.

Bloody odd, that.

He ignored Bruche and stubbornly clung to the ordinary. He'd imagined it. There was no one below but Akrasian troops. He'd seen a soldier, and his mad mind and the bad weather had turned him into a god. Too long without sleep, losing Elena, gaining a daughter, the war, Truls, and now this attack. The pressure was getting to him.

"The firemaster, Khel Szi," Halmar gestured to the woman.

He suppressed a growl of frustration at the interruption and gestured to her to rise. "Archers, fire at will. Keep them hopping if you can." He held out little hope at their hitting anything in this gale. It would be a matter of moments before they started pushing the ram toward the gates. He couldn't help thinking the gods had something to do with the poor weather that kept them from defending themselves. But perhaps there was good news on the fire oil.

She lifted her face to look at his, full lips parted, gaze flicking over him.

Bruche chuckled. *She seems to have an appreciation for your looks, Khel Szi.*

Draken ignored him. She went back down the steps, nimble despite her age and the slick stone, skirts swaying. He followed more carefully, favoring his knee. The cold stabbed into it with every step. Halmar kept close in case he slipped. When he got to the bottom, the firemaster had already disappeared into the Cindershack, and he grimaced at Halmar and Tyrolean.

"Perhaps an evening with her could ease your tension, Khel Szi," Halmar said.

Draken opened his mouth to retort that he had no interest in taking any woman to his bed, even this attractive but grandmotherly sort, much less *now*, but he realized a grin quirked the corner of Halmar's mouth.

Bruche chuckled deep inside him. It felt strained, but the swordhand was trying. *Sometimes there's nothing left to do but laugh.*

"Halmar," Draken said. "You made a joke. It must truly be the end of nights."

Halmar's pierced lips stretched with a rare smile. He opened the rickety door to the Cindershack for Draken and dipped his chin to him. Draken strode inside and Tyrolean and Halmar followed. The firemaster held out her hands, chapped from the cold, to the hearth. The fire shed negligible warmth. "What is your name?" he said instead.

The place felt smaller with her in it, but whether it was to do with her voluminous skirts or her discerning gaze, he wasn't sure. "Ninya, Khel Szi."

A young woman's name.

Even she was young once. Bruche was enjoying himself.

"The fire oil's nor ready," Ninya announced.

Once, he, too, hadn't known how to make a little waste-talk with his betters before reporting. He wagered she did; she just didn't want to. "Surely we can make some use of it."

Ninya shook her head. "Only have a bit that'll burn in this wet, and s'nor enough to take out that ram."

"You know about the ram?"

"Whole of Brîn know all about that ram, aye, Khel Szi."

"That was quick," Draken said, dryly.

That Sept accent. Khellian's balls, she must be sundry. She looked Brînian enough though. Fair enough. She wasn't the only one with a deceiving face.

Draken mined memories that weren't all his own. Septonshir, upper region. Clannish and reclusive. Reputation held the men loved their fishing skiffs more than their wives, and no wonder, with women in command. It must have been why Elena never heard any rumblings against her reign from Septonshir. The Sept, of anyone, would appreciate a queen over a king.

It must also be why Ninya had no qualms about looking Draken in the eye and speaking directly. "A waste in this wind, s'well. The lot of it'll splash 'gainst the gates."

He considered a moment and told her his plan. "We intended on disabling and leaving the ram there as a blockade. They're already setting the damned thing up and arrows are worthless in this." He waved a hand, indicating the storm creaking the rafters and sneaking in through every crack. "Barrels of fire oil would require rather less aim."

"If we had barrels of the stuff, which we d'nor."

Her brusque tone was getting to him. "How long do you think it will take to produce more?"

"Sevennight or two."

"Why? Isn't it just mixing up ingredients and—"

Her snort cut him off. "A four-step process to reduce the incendiary. Gods, that stuff by itself'll blow a metal-strapped barrel and the building it's in to Korde hisself—it's to be done and stored in a cellar where a slab of meat will chill hard so it won't blow. And the mix s'nor in ready supply. It takes time and careful—"

"All right, all right." He knew nothing of how to make the stuff and at the moment he didn't care. All he cared was they apparently *couldn't* make it. She seemed to be making plenty of damned excuses about it. He couldn't help thinking of Ilumat's warning about hiding rebels in the city. Could she be one of them? Bruche prodded him to question her. "You're Sept?"

She gave a matter-of-fact nod. "Slave from there, aye, Khel Szi."

His brows raised. "How did you get free?"

"My mistress called me too clever by half. Found a trader'd take me if I was trained to desk work. Hired me to Algir for reading and figures. I was supposed to be back to my mistress when the job were done." A shrug. "Got trained up and d'nor go. He was a chemic."

Capital offense, that. By Akrasian law she should have something cut off her, a breast, fingers, and wear shackles the rest of her life, if not be hanged outright. But with Akrasians preparing to batter down the gates Draken wasn't inclined to give a hang for the minutiae of Akrasian law and one escaped slave with an offer of the truth made him more confident in her loyalty, despite her sour disposition.

"Work on the mixture then," he said. "It may be of use later."

A clear dismissal, though she held, considering him. Now he was losing his patience. "What, woman?"

"You're bigger than I heard. Handsomer. And I think a deal more dangerous than I was told." She shook her head a little and dropped a curtsy.

You're going to let her go, just like that? It's been a while since you had such an, er, willing bedmate.

It's been a while since I had a bedmate at all, old scullion.

Ninya admitted a harsh burst of wind as she went through the door. The cold draught left him grey and empty inside. The banter reminded him sharply of waking alone every morning since Elena had gone.

No sooner did the door slam shut behind her than a *BOOM!* crashed through the rickety old building, peppering his head and shoulders with leaking rain and splinters from the ancient beams overhead. Draken cursed. Already? Truls flowed closer to him, but Draken pushed through him and strode outside to find the soldiers who'd manned the gate struts running back to them. The gates had slipped inward slightly with the first battering. It needed more bracing, desperately. The cross-beam had buckled.

"Lower," he shouted into the wind and pointed. "Hammer more cross-braces here!"

Wind whipped his cloak about his heels and nearly tripped him up. He tore it off as he ran to the gate to indicate where, cursing himself for not noticing earlier that the cross-braces needed to be set lower. It was just so damned difficult to examine the details with the wind and rain. The gates buckled inward half the length of a man's arm, cross-bars groaning as they cracked under the strain of the impact. It didn't want to snap back. The ends of two great chocks already in place—four square-planed logs strapped together made a beam bigger around than a man—skittered across the icy roadway with the next blow of the ram. Good job they'd been bolted to the gates because they'd have rattled free of brackets by now. Men ran to reset them with great levered crankwheels, and others worked to pry up the large roadstones to make holes in which to set the butts of the chocks. Draken cursed again, more from not knowing how to best help than from the urgency of reinforcing the gates. Halmar's hand on his arm guided him back out of the way.

Shouts were momentarily silenced by another echoing thud. As the great strut screeched across the icy roadstones, a soldier yanked his pry bar up just in time to keep from it getting stuck—and himself with it. The iron bar in his hands accidentally swung up to hit another soldier in the head. It clanged against his helm and he dropped like a stone. Sounds of dismay mingled with the whipping rain and harried shouts.

That, Draken could see to. He shook free of Halmar and shoved back the worried soldier who had hit the unconscious man, shouting at him to get back to it. Halmar pulled him out of the way of the workers and Draken felt under his chin for a pulse. Erratic, curse the Seven, and thick blood ran from under the ill-fitting helm. His face was slack and unlined. "Get him out of here, Halmar."

The big szi nêre picked up the soldier and carried him toward the cinder-shack. Draken wiped at the rain running down his face. It soaked the edges of his armor and his locks too. His woolen padded shirt made him smell like a wet farm animal.

Tethered horses neighed and skittered. The soldier with the pry bar finally loosed a stone, teeth gritted, muscles straining. From the effort it looked like the roadstone had grown roots. It took three men to displace it from the hole and shove it aside. *Boom!* The strut slid further and slipped into the knee-deep hollow the stone left. This allowed a lopsided gap between the gates as the crossbar buckled, splinters flying. Some lucky Akrasian bowman was able to send arrows through the gap. They skittered harmlessly off the roadstones; no Brînian was stupid enough to get in the line of fire between the two struts.

BOOM! Splinters flew and the gate with the loose strut slid treacherously further.

The other team digging up the roadstone weren't lucky enough to have the beam slip into place. It slid to one side because of the gate's new angle. Men rushed the gates to push it closed again and the strut itself had to be shoved and dragged back toward the hole by four men. Shouts filtered through the gates and Draken heard a sharp squeal that he realized he'd been hearing all along . . . the sound of the King's Ram as its mechanism drew back. Icy rain trickled under his armor and soaked his head and arms as he watched helplessly.

It took another breath before the men wedged the strut awkwardly into its hole. Air burst from his lungs when the ram hit again. The cross-brace tore a little more with snapping sounds reminiscent of bones breaking, but the struts held and kept the whole lot from moving further. Men rushed to set lesser struts and Brînian archers sent arrows flying through the gap in the gates.

Draken's fingers twitched, wishing for his bow.

But you are Khel Szi and only engage the enemy under extreme need.

"It's bloody engaging *me*, if I am Brîn, as you all like to say." Draken still knelt where the injured man had lain, and pain shot through his knee and radiated up his thigh as he shoved to his feet. In that moment, he realized Truls had disappeared. He looked around for him as Halmar returned and reached out to help him up. Draken shook him off and strode for Vannis, who barked orders at a dumfounded soldier, then prodded him in the chest when he didn't move quickly enough. Draken rubbed his hand over his face, swiping at the rain again. The Comhanar turned on Draken, ready to shout more orders, then balked when he saw who it was.

"How long 'til they break through?" Draken said.

Flat cheeks wet and raw, Comhanar Vannis narrowed his eyes at the struts and the makeshift smaller beams soldiers were hammering to the gates between the impact of the ram and exchanges of arrows. The edges of the gates were already peppered with them. A man hit a nail with a mallet just as the ram hit and he screamed as the impact threw him back onto the pavers, arm dangling uselessly at his side, his shoulder misshapen. His screams choked off. Shock. Dislocated shoulders *hurt*, as Draken well knew.

One of Vannis's men trod down the steps off the wall and drew near. Draken gave him a look. He returned a grim shake of his head. "We're firing as fast as we can, Khel Szi, but with the wind we can't hit anything but mud."

"Best take yourself back to the Citadel, Khel Szi," Vannis said, "and hide away the little Szirin somewhere I don't know. Won't be long now and I'm of more use here."

Undermanned at the only barrier between the Akrasians and the city. But the Comhanar stood like a rooted tree on the roadstones, hand hooked on the hilt of his sword, unmoving even as the ram's impact reverberated through the stone under their boots and made everyone else, including Draken, startle again. Slowly Vannis's square hand, the dark skin spotted and scarred and lined, reached for the buckles on his armor. Draken blinked in surprise. He'd disarm, go against orders?

Fight and die a Brînian. They'll torture him when they work out who he is. He might tell all he knows, and he knows fair more than you think. Better for us all if he dies in battle.

He should return with me.

Do not order him thus. He'll fight and die a Brînian as he always has done. Bruche grunted softly in Draken's chest. *Treat it as nothing. Order him to report to you.*

What? But—

Vannis had loosened his breastplate and was pulling it over his head. Next a shirt stained with sweat peeled away, baring a scarred chest still strapped with muscle under the loose skin of an older man.

Honor him with confidence in his survival, Draken.

Vannis sat on a bench along the road to remove his boots. He set his dark feet with beringed toes on the cold stone. An old man with priceless war knowledge about to be put to death on an Akrasian sword.

Draken cleared his throat. "I'll expect you to report to the Citadel when you know more, Comhanar."

Vannis rose. Dipped his chin to Draken. "Aye, Khel Szi. That I will—"

BOOM!

Draken turned to go, heart in a knot, wondering if he'd done enough, if he could ever do enough. How many Brînians would Vannis take with him? How many Akrasians, for that matter? They were all his people, damn them. *Three dozen or more; I'd lay good rare on it.* Bruche's tone was sage and sure. *But they'll hold things here, give you time to get to Sikyra and get her to safety.*

Except he had no idea where. He regretted letting Aarinnaie run off. She was the one who knew places to hide. Maybe even a way to escape the city, though the thought sank a stone in his stomach. Draken drew a deep breath of warstrewn air, rife with smoke and wet and sweat. He mounted. The ram hit again, making Sky toss her head. "Be easy." He soothed her with a firm hand on her curved neck. "Soon the frightening noises will end."

And others, more horrifying, would begin.

CHAPTER FIVE

An alarmed cry pierced the quiet streets, and then another. The szi nêre pushed ahead of Draken, but Konnon cantered toward them on his horse, emerging from the mists like a god of war on the rampage. He gleamed with sleet. Draken thought he'd caught a flash of sword, but Konnon's was sheathed.

"Khel Szi," he cried. "You must come to the Citadel straight away!"

"Konnon. What's the mad rush, man?" *And why aren't you with Sikyra?*

Their horses danced around each other, hooves sliding over slick cobbles, sensing the anxiety of their masters.

"The Citadel is under attack—"

"Sikyra?"

"The little Szirin is inside, protected."

Draken cursed, his tone harsh against the patter of rain and low snort of horses. "You dared leave her?"

"I didn't dare *not* come. My Lord Mance ordered me to fetch you. They're trying to climb the walls. So far it holds, but not for long."

"They? They who? Who is attacking?"

Konnon's voice quieted, as if he weren't sure of Draken's reaction. He swiped an arm over his wet face. He'd left too quickly to don a helm. "Brînians, my lord. Our own."

His chest seized. He couldn't breathe, couldn't think. Bruche moved within him gently, bringing him back. Traitors, bought and paid for by Ilumat. Draken started his horse toward the Citadel but reined up as quick; no going through the gates this night. "How did you get out?"

Konnon lowered his voice and his gaze flitted about. "The . . . er, passageway, Khel Szi. Under the temple and Citadel."

A gentle term for a nasty place that did nothing to alleviate the sick knot under his heart. Generations of Brînian royal bones lay in the bowels of the

36

Citadel temple. The great planked door inside the Temple, an arched thing as wide as it was tall, was barred with a thick lock, one of the earliest of its kind. Draken wasn't aware a key existed, nor that there was an exterior entrance. He swallowed down the thought of breathing in his ancestors' dust and nodded to the szi nêre. "Take me."

There was a brief debate over what to do with the horses, especially on such a miserable night. Draken shifted in his saddle, blood pounding with fear for Sikyra, but he knew the folly of rushing in to fetch her alone. The streets they took were deserted and the wealthier residential district surrounding the Citadel had no public stables. Draken couldn't shake the eerie feeling of quiet before the storm of attack. Bells had rung when the Akrasians first appeared; some few civilians had appeared and been sent back out of harm's way. Soon after, everyone at the gates had been much too busy stopping the invasion. No bells rang now. Because there was no one left alive to ring them?

At last Konnon pounded on the door of a sizable attached house. The Moonling-half slave's jaw dropped at the sight of them, though she dropped into a passable curtsy. The master of the house, a wealthy merchant Draken had met before, was more businesslike than his servant and roused his stable staff to take the horses, saying they'd be here when Khel Szi returned.

Draken strode after Konnon on foot, only vaguely curious about how they were going to reach the tombs on this side of the Citadel wall, ears pricked for sounds of battle. But they were on the other side of the palace grounds from the main gates. The building and the sharp patter of rain on metal railings and over rooftops and cobbles hid whatever noises the Akrasians . . . or their mercenaries . . . caused in the attack.

You know you can't go back for the horses, not personally.

Bruche was right. Ilumat's threats about having people inside city walls had come true. Draken could trust no one now, maybe even not the szi nêre. Konnon led them without glancing back, certain his Khel Szi would follow, certain Halmar and the others would protect Draken.

You can trust them.

Draken wondered.

Konnon once was sworn to Geord—Aarinnaie's betrothed and named heir to the Brînian throne until Draken had killed him. He didn't have to spell it out to Bruche that the old heir—or at least the idea of him—still had loyals in the city, people he'd paid well to be his friends and who resented Draken's aversion to bribes.

The peril of his situation was hitting him with fresh clarity. Despite being his father's son, he'd appeared seemingly out of nowhere with a fallible personal history. Of course he was not received by everyone in Brîn as Khel Szi. Just being his father's bastard was enough to turn backs. If word got out he was sundry, and half-Monoean to boot, there'd be more people in the city who would hunt him than protect him. Bad enough Sikyra was *known* sundry. That had paved an easy road for Ilumat. As far as Brîn, it wasn't a leap to assume the tide against Draken had fair turned.

Konnon led them around the corner to the door of a shop, an armorer who worked for local bloodlords and armored the Citadel, and pushed inside. Despite the door not being barred, Draken saw no one within, though it was a narrow, deep space. His eyes quickly adjusted, revealing the leather-craft and metal polishing part of an armorer's operation. Fully suited forms of plate, mail, and fishscale lined one wall like an honor guard. These armorers surely had a forge at the back of the city, where pounding hammers wouldn't keep residents up all night. Three tables had half-finished suits laid out on them. Pegs on walls and carts stowed tools. Not a scrap of leather or trash, nor maybe even dust, littered the floor.

Draken reached out to trail his fingers across the fine decorative stitching on a leather breastplate. Whatever odd light the magic filtered through his vision snagged on gold thread embroidered into brown leather, swirling vines and flowers with skulls and eyes and moons.

The ambient, damp light shed from the street winked out as Halmar shut the door and latched it. A blink sharpened Draken's vision. He could see the others' expressions crease with frustration and slight alarm. No one else noticed when two silent men emerged from the shadows at the rear of the shop.

Draken's hand fell to Seaborn's hilt, ready to draw. Bruche was nervous and spoke for him: "Halt for your Khel Szi."

Excellent. Announce me, why don't you?

But they dropped to a knee before him, startled, and lowered their heads. Jewelry around their necks and wrists jingled and fell quiet. Loyal, then. He frowned, feeling oddly sure of it. It didn't soothe Draken's worry for Sikyra but eased him into grim resolution. He had help. He wasn't alone in protecting her, even on the street.

Konnon spoke, softly polite. "A light, please. Khel Szi bids you rise and open the gate."

Gate? Here? Draken peered into the shadows. They sharpened and intensified into shapes and the darkness greyed. To one side an ornate metal banister encircled a stairwell leading down beneath another that led to the upper floors. Then one of the men struck a light. Draken blinked against the glare but pushed through the others to follow first. The floor creaked under their boots. Scents filled the air: the damp of anxiety now drying into fear; leather, fresh-forged metal, oils, and polishes all reminding him of battle preparations. The candle was poor and flickered out, but Draken could see . . . sense . . . when to reach out to grasp the banister. It was clammy under his hand, damp without being really wet, as if the metal sweated like the men.

Someone stumbled behind him and muttered a curse. At the bottom of the several steps the floor sloped further downward. Draken drew Seaborn a little, enough to shed a dim glow. One of the armorers twisted to look at him. Draken dropped it back in the sheath. It had stung his eyes anyway.

They passed tangles of cured leather, broken tools, and random pieces of armor. Despite the neat stacks, the long, narrow cellar had an air of discard. After several steps he realized two things: they had already gone far further than the depth of the building above, and they could be walking into an ambush. Draken's thumb toyed with the loose bit of leather strapping around his hilt.

You see now why szi nêre like to go first? You princes are all alike.

Bruche's chill filled Draken's chest and slid down his sword arm. He lingered like an icy draught of ale filling the gullet: steadying but tugging on his control. They wordlessly shared their tension; both listened hard to the silence. Nothing broke it but the bootsteps of the men. Draken found he missed his sister slinking along to one side. She frequently caught things he missed. But he did see the shapes ahead fall still. He stopped and Konnon practically walked into the back of him. He uttered a soft curse and Halmar grunted for quiet.

"The gate. Er. Khel Szi." The elder armorer stumbled over the words.

"Give a man some warning," Konnon said with tense irritability, putting some distance between him and Draken.

The gate swinging open made them all step back. It scraped on the floor, making his heart trip. The smell of stone filled Draken's lungs. He hesitated, thinking he'd catch a whiff of death or decay, but what lay beyond only smelled of rocky dust.

Another cautious glance back from the man ahead, a pause to listen. Silence. The lean armorer struck flint on stone and a light sparked as he bent to retrieve a torch from a pile to one side of the gate. And gate it was, metal wrought in an even more elaborate pattern than the bannister above.

The torch flared. Draken averted his gaze from the stinging glare.

"The Khel Szi tombs. Final chambers for your ancestors, my lord," Konnon said softly, maybe using the informal address because he thought Draken would be disturbed or feel some grief. Draken felt nothing but a vague sense of displacement. Monoeans buried their dead, but Brînians and Akrasians always gave the dead to the sea, delivering them as directly to Ma'Vanni as possible.

That the Khel Szis had once been entombed made him curious about the practice. Bruche didn't know either; the spirit gave an inward shrug.

Draken wasn't sure what he was expecting, but shelves of skeletons in full
Khel Szi battle regalia wasn't it. Each shelf was marked with a birth name and
the Sohalia count he'd died. Some had images of a face graven next to the
words. Despite worry prodding him to get to Sikyra, he paused to study one, so
ancient the markings had mostly crumbled away. The next resident must have
been more recent; the carving depicted a hard-planed face atop thick shoulders.
The name read *Draku*. He blinked. His father had given him something like a
family name.

Bruche relaxed since it became apparent they weren't in immediate danger of
being ambushed. *I see the resemblance.*

Not a jest. It wasn't like looking at himself, exactly, but he could see where
his build and bone structure had come from. His gaze shifted to the remains,
bones covered in armor, thick dust, and patches of leathery skin. The shadows
tricked the eye to believing the long locked hair writhed around the skull like
indolent snakes. Gauntleted finger bones gripped a decent replica of Seaborn.
Red paint crackled over the tip of the stone blade and its flat bore carved images
of the Seven Sohalia Moons and words scribed in a tongue he didn't understand. Despite the lack of flesh, he had the feeling his elder could leap up into
battle at any moment.

Seaborn had no such engravings. Before he could ponder the meanings of
the etchings, Konnon took up the torch. The two armorers backed to one side
to make room for them to pass, hemmed in by shelves. The torchlight flickered
over weepmarks and thin white stalagtites growing from the stone. Halmar
didn't exactly nudge Draken, but crowded him enough to get him moving again.

Thom had told him Khel Szis don't thank people for their service unless it
was unusual or dangerous. He reckoned this qualified. "What are your names?"

The wiry one lifted his chin. "Helmek, Khel Szi. And he is called Rhiles."

"Helmek. Rhiles. Names I won't forget. I am in your debt. What would you
have of me?"

Rhiles stepped forward and gripped his arm. Swords hissed from scabbards.
"Step back!"

Halmar spoke so infrequently it took Draken a breath to realize the sharp
tone was his. The armorer looked down at his hand on Draken's arm and jerked
it away with a strangled sound.

"It's all right. Speak, if you would."

"Aarinnaie Szirin . . ." Riles swallowed.

His heart twisted. Surely she hadn't found trouble in the city so soon after leaving his side. "What of her?"

"I would see her protected, Khel Szi. Safe."

Gods, a bout of young love was hanging them up? Draken had a daughter to protect. "You know her?"

"From the gate, Khel Szi, right here. She found our old ma once—she wanders. No longer right, her. Szirin saw her to rooms with a caretaker. I protested I didn't have the coin but Szirin insisted it as payment for my letting her through the tombs ever since I was apprentice and she a little girl. They're her tombs, I told her, but you don't argue with Szirin."

He studied Rhiles's face. He'd broken his nose sometime, or had it broken for him. Draken suffocated the thought that Aarinnaie had just run off to do gods knew what while the city was under siege and soon to be occupied. If she were found by the Akrasians once they broke into the city—

"I will keep her safe. Go from this place." He looked at Helmek. "Both of you. Brîn is at war."

Helmek stared. Rhiles shook his head. "But the tomb gates—"

"Not yours to guard any longer. Do either of you have children?"

Helmek's chin lifted. "Two."

"See them safe. Leave the city if possible. And I will keep Aarinnaie from harm."

Both nodded.

Draken walked on without another word, into the bone-filled catacombs, every breath filling his lungs with the dust of his forebears. Here were more bones than he could count, all the flesh long since rotted away. He wondered again at the custom of interring them here, what the new Khel Szi had always thought and experienced while laying the old, dead one among the ancients. He had dumped his own father rather unceremoniously into the sea, as was current practice. But it felt . . . incomplete, somehow. He almost snarled at that thought. It shouldn't. After all, Draken's father had abused him as a child and tortured him as an adult. The gods granted no satisfaction to a man with an evil father.

His thoughts had carried him right past all the dozens . . . hundreds? . . . of skeletons to the great door leading into the temple. From this side it wasn't much to look at; rusted metal strapped the door but the wood seemed solid enough, as impermeable as it did from the other side. It was strung with dirty cobwebs.

Aye. The dead rarely think to have the dust cleared.

Bruche's tone was arid. Draken couldn't tell whether he had any good humor on the subject of the dead. He wasn't inclined to study it too closely. "I assume there is a key?"

Konnon shook his head, eased forward, and knocked.

For a long breath, silence. Draken stood very still. Bruche lingered close to the surface and slipped up and down his swordarm like a chill mist. The catacombs was a good place to hide. It also was an excellent trap. Footsteps hurried toward the door on the other side, there was a scraping sound and a sharp clank. The door swung open and bright, wavering torchlight on the other side made Draken squint and duck his head. *Damn. That stings.*

It's a problem but not one we're going to solve now.

"Khel Szi." The kindly old priest with hands soft as Sikyra's, his voice tremulous and his face creased.

Draken felt himself sliding into his more official demeanor, his chin lifting as he walked into the temple. Gods, the door was thick as his hand was wide, the stone threshold twice that deep, as if meant to keep the dead from escaping.

Torchlight washed over the scrubbed white walls of the temple and flickered against brightly painted idols of the gods. He squinted and shadowed his eyes with his hand. "I understand there's a bit of trouble."

"A mob at the gates, Khel Szi," the priest said, giving him a curious look.

Draken nodded. His gaze caught on Truls, drifting near the open temple door. Maybe Draken just imagined his satisfied expression. Beyond, a cacophony of shouts filled the night. No massive ram banged on the gates, at least not yet, but slaves ran around smothering flaming arrows stuck in the cobbles and gardens of the courtyard. More soared over the wall, leaving trails of fire slashing across Draken's vision. He passed his hand over his face, wishing this enhanced sight away. Nothing happened. He strode outside, seeking relief in the darkness.

Osias hurried toward him like a silver moonbeam. "I thought you were at the city wall, Khel Szi. But I hoped you would come."

"I came back for Sikyra." He had to raise his voice to be heard over the shouting. It was all so much more frantic and panicked than he'd expected. "Not long now before they break through and haul the ram to these gates, if they're not already on their way. Where is she?"

"In her quarters. Captain Tyrolean is with her." Osias gave him an earnest look but didn't question him, just followed quietly. Setia was missing. Gathering their things to escape, if she was smart.

More arrows skittered across the cobbles, scattering sparks across a slave's robes and inciting shouts and screams from the slaves and szi nêre. Another slave ran to beat the flames out, chattering in a strange dialect. Ahead, the tall formal doors hung open, shedding more torchlight from the Great Hall out into the night. Draken climbed the steps, head down to shade his eyes. Slaves and szi nêre and ordinary soldiers assigned to the Citadel hurried through the tiled round Hall, filling quivers and talking tactics. Every free male, pitifully few of them, was armed with sword and bow. Most were ranking szi nêre because the underlings had been sent to the front. Near the dais, one of the captains under Halmar, who was technically Citadel Comhanar though he rarely left Draken's side long enough to give orders or strategize, stood with a huddle of seasoned, civilian fighters.

Draken should speak to them, find out what plans were being laid and gauge the degree of immediate danger. Instead he strode quickly past to the corridor leading to the family quarters. Tyrolean stood outside the louvered door, holding his two bared swords. That told Draken all he needed to know about the immediate threat.

"How is she, Captain?"

Sikyra whimpered within, urging him to rush to her despite its lack of insistence. It sounded like the typical cry of a baby awakened in moontime, one who might just go back to sleep if left alone. But he would take her soon and there would be little enough sleep this night.

"She's well and safe. You should know, I saw Ilumat in the dungeon." Tyrolean held steady, body and voice. "We . . . spoke."

One of his hands gripping the pointed hilt of his sword was bound over the knuckles and seeping blood. Draken's brows raised. "And?"

"He allied three bloodlords—that he'll admit to." He listed the names. Two Draken knew from local affairs, one he'd never heard of. An Islander, perhaps, spending Frost in Brîn.

He was vaguely surprised not to hear Khisson's name on the list, especially with the recent intelligence that he was in the city. The Dragonstar Isles were vulnerable to Monoean attack. Draken didn't know any self-respecting Brînian bloodlord who would leave his home vulnerable in wartime. Insisting each family send a certain quota of fighters to the front was one of the reasons for Draken's current disfavor among some bloodlords—the more short-sighted ones who underestimated the impact of a war with faith-fevered Monoeans.

"Between the three they have perhaps four hundred men," Tyrolean said.

They'd disobeyed his orders to conscript fighters then, to have amassed so many. "Fair enough to take the Citadel this night."

"Aye. I'll await your orders and escort you to wherever . . ."

"To whatever secret hovel Aarinnaie has set up for us?"

No flicker of smile tempered Tyrolean's intimidating grip on his swords. "I know of some few. I will take you when you are ready, Your Highness."

He knew of them—how? But Sikyra's cry sharpened, smothering his curiosity. One thing at a time. Draken pushed through the slatted doors, passing through the tiled antechamber without bothering to remove his boots or clean his feet. Lilna was in Draken's quarters, folding Sikyra's clothes with twitchy fingers. She bobbed into a bow, gaze lowered. Draken should reassure her that she would come to no harm, but he couldn't make that promise.

Sikyra pulled herself to her feet, chubby hands holding onto the bars of her cot. At the sight of Draken, she coughed a cry, took a breath, and bawled louder. Osias strode ahead to fetch her before Draken could tell him not to.

At the sight of her in Osias's arms, realization washed through Draken. "I must stay and lead the defense. You all take Sikyra."

No. He'll take Brîn fair easily if you're dead. Truls is right. He's been right all along. You and Sikyra need to escape, now.

Hiding does nothing for Brîn. They're about to take the Citadel.

Ruddy fool, your life is everything to Brîn. We'll attack later, when we can get the upper hand. Ilumat has it this night.

"Truls says Elena is alive," Osias said quietly. "How shall we explain to her we let you stay here to die?"

Sikyra snuffled and cooed at Osias. Truls drifted around them, silent. Draken supposed he had nothing of use to tell him, now that he really needed it.

"You cannot, Your Highness." Tyrolean had entered behind him. "Brîn can stand without the Citadel, but it cannot stand without you."

Outnumbered. Might as well give in. Live to fight again.

Flat, hollow: "Very well. Take us."

Draken took his daughter from Osias without meeting his gaze and laid her on his bed to dress her warmly. She kicked and gave him one of her rare smiles, trusting and oblivious of the turmoil fermenting below except for a quiver running through her little body when a scream pierced the trees and shutters.

Draken drew a breath, forcing calm. "There, love." He lifted her, snuggled in warm clothes and a blanket, and nodded to Tyrolean.

"I must go a different way," Osias said. "The bigger the group around you, the slower you'll move."

"You'll never make it out," Draken said. "We have to take the tombs."

"Glamour, my friend," Osias said, unsmiling and calm. Draken wondered if the Mance harbored resentment from their earlier conversation. His own had passed. The Mance seemed so steady and certain. Draken wished he'd stay near and impart some certainty to him.

"And Setia?" Tyrolean asked.

"No one notices a slave, which is what they will think I am," Setia said from the doorway.

Or they'd kill her for the crime of having dappled skin and Moonling blood. "We come out through Brightscar Leathers. Do you know the fountain at Bird Market? Come each dawn and dusk. The waterhaulers will provide you cover." Osias would need it. They'd be searching for the Mance that was the Khel Szi's great friend. But he didn't need to tell Osias that.

Osias nodded. He hesitated like he might reach out and grip Draken's hand but turned, silvery hair sliding over his shoulders like a cloak. Draken gave Setia a curious look but she was already walking out the door, close on Osias's heels. They turned in the opposite direction than he'd expected, deeper into the private quarters. But Setia knew the Citadel at least as well as Aarinnaie did. She had some plan.

Draken couldn't help a fleeting glance at his rooms before he passed from them. Cut lanterns picked out bits of color in the tiles and murals. Incense still scented the air. Beyond, Sikyra's cot was rumpled from her sleep. How many nights had he watched her there, listening to her soft breath . . . Not enough. Not nearly enough nights.

He snatched up Kyra's favorite toy, a carved wooden horse she liked to teethe. Her little fingers closed around it as he strode downstairs and through the Great Hall too quickly to take in details beyond a wet smoke smell from the torches outside and slaves and soldiers hurrying toward the gates.

Someone screamed as a figure appeared at the top of the wall. It was sharp on top, shards of metal embedded into mortar and topped by a spiked rail. The figure dropped back down. Draken squinted, his eyes sharpening in the dark. A rope . . . the intruder had left a damned rope looped around the rail. They meant to tear the spikes off the wall.

"Run. Cut the rope!" His hoarse cries were lost amid the shouts. Someone tried, to their credit, and fell screaming and bloody back to the ground.

It was over in a matter of a few breaths. They must have had twenty men on it, or a brace of horses. The rail groaned and creaked and clattered over the side, leaving a clear space to climb over. The first two attempts were met with arrows, but the attackers just had the simple duty of throwing a thick blanket over the wall to shield hands and knees from the sharp blades embedded in mortar atop the wall. Another figure—taking quick shape as a shirtless Brînian painted for war—appeared at one end where the remaining rail twisted away over the wall. Then another. They had bows, as well. Soon the arrows raining onto the courtyard took on much more precision. And arrows found flesh, someone screamed, a defenseless slave—

run run get her out take her

"Nothing like stating the bloody obvious," Draken muttered.

His free hand dropped to grip his sword hilt and he started to turn, but Sikyra screamed in his ear, matching the injured slave's pitch. Tyrolean dared grab his arm. "Come, my lord. This way."

Sikyra's scream, more than the ghostly whispers or Tyrolean's harried voice, jolted him into action. He let Tyrolean herd him into a run, no small trick with the baby bouncing in his arms. Her screams grew into full-on terrified squalling, but the shouts and clang of swords drowned her out. Gods, the attackers had achieved the wall enough to take swords to the Citadel residents. At the temple doors he turned. Brînians streamed over the wall despite szi nêre picking them off with arrow and blade. Flame flashed against swords, making him duck his head and turn toward the temple.

A strong panic that he was doing the wrong thing rose up in Draken. He should defend the Citadel, defend his people. Akrasia had come to take Brîn, banishing all pretense of the principality's partial independence. Not only that, powerful Brînians had allied with them—powerful enough to raise a slaughter. His city was imploding, and for what? Power? Coin? All during an invasion from a foreign country. It made no sense. None of it made any damned sense.

Bruche soothed him, chilling his body and taking enough control to keep his legs moving despite his urge to go back, to draw his blade, to fight. He growled in frustration, but Sikyra had tight hold of one of his locks and her other hand dug into his neck and there was no way to take her but out. Down, and out. Escape was the only choice. Draken swore as Halmar shoved him ahead. His knee wanted to give way but Bruche forced it to bear his weight and kept him moving.

"Go, go!" He wasn't sure if Bruche or himself shouted.

Arrows whistled by Draken; one skipped off his armored back, shoving him forward a step. He huddled Sikyra in front of his chest with both arms. All wiggly arms and legs and little body throwing itself into flustered cries, she was difficult to protect. Halmar rounded behind him, said something he didn't catch.

Konnon shouted, "Run, Khel Szi! We will hold—"

The roar of Akrasian soldiers meeting Brînian resistance reverberated through the courtyard, smothering his words. A flare of torchlight reflected off the white stone temple walls, bringing black arrows into sharp relief. Draken stumbled over the threshold, eyes closed against the reflective white brightness inside. Hardly like daylight but his eyes got more sensitive by the breath.

The priest stumbled back as if he'd been trying to hold the door shut with his thin arms and pudgy body. An arrow skittered off Tyrolean's bicep, drawing a yelp of pain.

The temple was too bright inside, reeking of oily torch smoke, fair blinding Draken when he dared open his eyes. He stumbled and slowed. Sikyra hiccupped terrified sobs, rubbing her face against his chest. He squinted, trying to see. His eyes adjusted a little as Tyrolean shoved him back a step and slammed the door.

"We're in," Tyrolean said. "The szi nêre have the door."

The priest wrung his hands. Smooth hands that had touched neither sword nor bow. He would die here in his precious temple. "What should I do?"

"Pray." Tyrolean was curt, his breath short as he bent by the wall near the door and started lifting a flat metal-strapped beam of wood off the floor.

A sharp, distant slam made the door shudder slightly. Sikyra wailed louder. He stroked her sweaty curls. "Hush now, sweet." His hand trembled against her head and he tried to keep his voice low and steady. "Fools all, what are those explosions? Not a ram."

Muscles straining, Tyrolean moved to set the bar in the brackets across the engraved metal doors. Blood seeped from his fishscale and dripped onto the white floor. Draken shoved his squirming daughter into the priest's arms and helped him with the beam, wondering vaguely why there was such a huge bar to lay across the temple doors and why he'd never noticed it before.

Bruche didn't know either. *After my time.*

Muscles straining, they slid it into its brackets.

"Fire oil," Tyrolean said once it was set.

Fire oil. Ninya had lied to his face. The firemasters had betrayed him. The Citadel was mostly tile, stone, and metal. But the many trees . . . if they went up it'd be simple enough to smoke out the residents. Thank the gods the air was thick with damp mist.

"We must go, my lord," Tyrolean said.

Draken nodded and reached for Sikyra. The priest gave her up with a grateful look. She drew a breath, released a final, piercing cry, then snuffled. One hand held the horse to her mouth so she could run her gums on its back. The other tightened around one of Draken's locks. It pulled sharply again, but he didn't try to tug it free. Whatever kept her calm.

Draken bowed his head, kissed Sikyra's soft hair. The szi nêre . . . Gods. The courtyard was a trap. They couldn't survive. Why hadn't they followed him into the temple? At least Halmar, who had protected his father before him.

They will happily die to save you. Move.

All around, icons of the Seven rested still and quiet in their shadowed niches, paint garish and celebratory. The tomb door was locked and barred again, as if it had never been open—no. Not quite. Grey bone dust scuffed the white floor.

"The key," Draken said.

The priest hurried to a table with pots and boxes, opened one, and hurried back to press it into Tyrolean's hand. The Captain cursed when it didn't slip easily inside the great lock.

"Lock us in," he told the priest, and nodded to Tyrolean, who handed the priest the key. His dark, spotty hand trembled. "They'll kill me."

"No they won't. They're faithful." Brusqueness concealed the lie, Draken hoped. They needed the priest to protect them as long as he could.

Tyrolean stole a torch from a bracket over the god of life and harvest, Agrian in his green and gold robes. They stepped into the tomb and walked down the slope, now familiar, back past the more recently dead. Tyrolean's head swiveled even as he strode quickly. Shadows leapt over the dead, including Truls, shifting between them but constantly glancing back at Draken, his face trailing and blurring as he moved.

The priest slammed the door behind them. It suffocated the last of the sounds of the battle. The tumblers clicked and clanged into place. He hoped the old man found a good place to hide the damned key. *Maybe he'll swallow it.*

Did you see the size of it?

Draken's lip curled. *He's a priest. He's used to swallowing big, distasteful things.*

Inside the quiet of the tombs, Sikyra fell into a limp, traumatized sleep. Draken pulled up his cloak hood and wrapped the edges around her to keep her warm. Tyrolean led the way with surprising speed and determination. Draken hurried to catch up. It wasn't until they were outside the armory that he asked, "Where are you going?"

They could hear faint battle sounds filtering between buildings. The rain had stopped but thick fog blurred the streets and the people emerging from their homes. He saw no Akrasians; Tyrolean was leading him deeper into the city, away from the gates. Most adults were armed and managing distressed family groups. All ignored two more hooded and cloaked men cradling a baby. He was glad the Brînians were warriors. Any penchant for solving problems with violence would serve them well this night.

"We're going to one of your sister's places. You'll be safe there." Tyrolean kept his voice low and avoided titles that might cause passersby to recognize them. He led them around the streets surrounding the Citadel, deeper into Brîn. Draken didn't answer, lest he wake the baby and her cries draw enemy attention.

✦ ✦ ✦

Three mornings later found Draken and Tyrolean ragged, cold, hungry, and
the baby suffering head sickness. Her every cough cut right through Draken.
They'd had little sleep the night before, taking turns holding her upright so
she could breathe. Draken had passed the time wondering about his people,
especially his szi nêre and the rest of the Citadel. Trapped in this dingy, drafty
room, waiting for Aarinnaie to find them, it was easy to imagine the city over-
run, Aarinnaie captured, or worse. Truls lingering in corners like mist inside a
shadow did nothing for his mood. The daylight shining in through the cracks
in the boarded windows stung his eyes. Despite that, he'd be damned if he
would waste another day here. He needed a plan to take back his city, and
quickly.

Their little room, empty but for a mangled stack of furniture more suitable
for burning than sitting on and a couple of narrow campaign cots and decent
blankets, was located near the inland gates that led to the farming valley at the
foot of the Eidola Mountains. He rose and laid Sikyra down, speaking softly.
"We are safe here for now. We just need more food." The goat milk was nearly
gone and despite Draken's distinct lack of appetite, they'd finished their last
crust and cheese this morning.

"And your sister," Tyrolean said.

He nodded. Tyrolean had gone to the fountain dutifully each dawn and dusk,
though he dared not brave actual daylight. No sign of Osias and Setia yet. On
the face of it, the Captain was the best to go. Draken was too easily recognized
and Tyrolean blended in well with the Akrasian invaders. In civilian clothes
with his usually sleek hair in greasy knots, he looked like a camp hanger-on, of
which there were plenty. Ilumat had planned this for a long time now.

she comes she comes

Truls sped from the shadows toward the door, though his whispers didn't
seem to match that gaping mouth.

"I've been thinking." Tyrolean blinked his lined eyes once. "Ilumat might be
using Osias for bait—"

Draken raised his hand and turned, drawing his sword. Footfalls on the steps,
a small snapping sound . . .

Really just a couple of shifts in the old wood that might be feet or a nail
loosening from wood shrinking from the cold. But still, Tyrolean moved forward on silent boots, easing blade from sheath. The floor creaked under him.
He stopped. They held. No sound but Sikyra's light, snuffling snore. Draken
looked at Truls, lingering near the door.

Tyrolean started to shake his head and moved to put his swords away. Draken hissed; Truls flitted through the door. Tyrolean strode forward to take off the hand or head of whoever dared invade their poor sanctuary. The door swung open and his sword slipped through. Aarinnaie jerked her head back, narrowly missing a new cleft in her chin.

"Nice of you to notice me. I've been sitting out there listening since you woke up." She came in, glanced at Tyrolean, who was putting his sword away with an odd expression twisting the clean lines of his face.

Draken huffed a breath, swung the door closed. Truls was retreating. He eyed the ghost, wondering if he should have been listening to him all along. "No, you haven't."

She turned to him, brows drawn. "It was a joke, Drae."

"Where in Eidola have you been?"

"Looking for you."

"For three nights?" She was better than that, and this was her place.

She grimaced. "Difficult moving around the city just now. Ilumat ordered martial law and servii and Escorts patrol everywhere. Not to mention the bloodlords setting up protection rackets." She put her bag on the table, such as it was. Rickety and flanked with lopsided benches, it sagged by the unlit fireplace. "And the Monoeans . . ." She went to look at the baby, laid a hand on her back. Her breathing shuddered her little body. "Fools all, it's cold in here. No wonder she's sick."

"What about the Monoeans?" Tyrolean's sharp tone made Sikyra twitch.

She turned to look at them both. Sighed. "Part of my delay was due to trying to suss out the truth. I needn't have bothered. The rumors are true."

"What rumors?" Draken shook his head. He hadn't heard anything locked up in here.

"Ilumat allied with the Ashen. I have a bad feeling Brîn belongs to them now."

CHAPTER SIX

Draken itched to rush to the defense of his people, but Aarinnaie informed him that curfews, crowd controls, and mobs for food, lodging, and weapons all stood in his way. Apparently the invading soldiers were housing themselves wherever they liked. Aarinnaie and Tyrolean went out separately to get the lay of the land. Neither had had luck in finding Osias and Setia.

Keeping Sikyra safe was a top priority, but sitting back for a sevennight rankled worse than fleeing the Citadel.

"You can't go," Aarinnaie told him. "Your face is on coins. Ilumat is buying friendship and loyalty."

Draken passed the afternoon watching the light shining through the cracks in the shuttered windows slowly fade. Constant explosions, near and far, broke the city sounds filtering up from the street. The fire oil Ninya had lied about. But it didn't make sense. She'd been a slave once, and they didn't trust easily. What would she want with Ilumat? Why would she ever trust the Akrasians or Monoeans . . .

Realization scraped through his mind. He ground his teeth. He'd been so bloody dense. "Seven curse them. They used slaves."

"What?" Aarinnaie shook her head and exchanged glances with Tyrolean.

He mustered some patience to explain. "I kept wondering how the blood-lords managed to gather enough people to take the city. They must have used their slaves to attack the Citadel. Maybe promised them freedom in exchange. Now that I think about it, I wonder if the Moonlings were involved."

Aarinnaie gave him a quizzical look.

"Remember when Lady Oklai asked me to free the Moonling slaves? Right before I went to Monoea. She threatened all manner of disruption . . . well, implied the threat, anyway. I wonder that this is their doing."

"Except the Moonling slaves were interned into camps on the Grassland, remember?"

He nodded. It was a point. Still . . . "Oklai and her people are free. At least they were the last time I saw them."

"If they're still alive after Elena burned Skyhaven," she said.

Draken didn't answer. Not a time he liked to think back on, much less the consequences. Elena had likely died in the fire. Certainly many Moonlings had. But then Truls insisted she was alive, and he'd been right about the attack, right about the danger to himself and Sikyra. A very dangerous hope flickered in his chest.

Tyrolean nodded slowly and spoke as if he hadn't paid attention to all their talk of Moonlings. "Aye. Slaves make the perfect scapegoat. If Ilumat and the bloodlords lost, or were caught out, they could blame rebelling slaves. No one would believe their masters put them up to it even if they accused them."

Draken cursed. The slaves were to have been *his* to free. Affront and shame twisted in him.

No use in worrying over it now.

Draken cleared his throat. "It's time to check the fountain for Osias again. After, go have a proper meal, the two of you."

Tyrolean frowned but said nothing.

Aarinnaie shook her head. "Why? We can just bring food here as usual."

"I'd like to know what tales are earning the tellers coin. With or without Osias, I need to make a decision about where to take Sikyra. I can't hide any longer. This storm isn't going to blow over."

Not to mention they were all worn by Sikyra's constant fussing. Tyrolean had managed to find some kowroot to steep, which helped her a little, and they'd started burning a fire because the mists and fog hid the smoke. But they knew he was right. They had to get her out of here.

Aarinnaie checked her weapons, as she did incessantly when about to venture out. "We can't even meet up with one Mance, and you think we're going to sneak you out of the city? Both gates are guarded, and no one passes."

Properly expressing his annoyance would wake Sikyra. "Bring goat milk, fruit, and bread for Kyra, and mind it's all fresh."

Tyrolean rose smoothly. "Come, Princess. He's right. A meal and a song will clear the head."

Aarinnaie scowled for a moment, and then, with speed that made Draken's insides clench, her expression cleared. "Of course, Khel Szi. We'll be back shortly."

Rarely up to any good when she looks like that, Bruche said.

He tried to brush off his sense of warning, not that Bruche wasn't privy to his innermost fears and joys. *She's rarely up to any good anyway.*

They shut the door behind them. Draken laid Sikyra down on his cot. She snuffled and whimpered but at last exhaustion won out. He straightened and rubbed his face and winced as his shoulder twinged deeply. He thought a moment and lifted his head. Truls lingered yet. "I've a duty for you if you'll take it on. No point in hanging round watching me tend my daughter."

Truls drifted close enough to touch, if he'd had a body. Draken steeled himself against jumping out of his skin, lip curling at the scent of death emanating from the spirit. "You heard us. We need Osias. Find him and bring him here."

Truls held, wavering as a flame off a candle. His misty shape alternately cast grey light and shadows by some design Draken couldn't fathom. Bruche moved inside him, altering his balance and his view. His stomach twisted

"What? Is there a bloody magic word, a mystical command? Eh? Nothing to say now? I've little time and even less patience. *Go.*"

Truls fell still. Cold and silence wove together, spread over Draken like tight armor against his clammy skin, constricting the depth of his breath and narrowing his attention to the specter before him. Truls's visage changed to one of rotting death. He stared back from eyeless holes. Torn, tattered lips hung over disintegrating teeth.

The back of Draken's neck crawled. He was surprised to find he could lift his arm to rub it. His voice only shook a little. "Is that meant to intimidate me?"

Bruche had gone very calm. As still within him as the others. *Try little respect, perhaps?*

For an enemy who torments me?

The ancients claimed the truth is the only torment.

What truth? The only one I know is this man tried to kill me when he yet lived. He's welcome to try again but the queue is long.

You killed him, aye? With Akhen Khel, no less, and brought back Elena with his lifeblood.

He's not the only one who died on Seaborn's blade. Too much blood since he'd been given Akhen Khel, too much death since he'd dragged himself, broken in spirit and body, upon the shores of Akrasia. And before. How many lives had he cut down? A thousand?

And he is yet here, as if he is in your debt. As if he wants to help you.

Draken's eyes narrowed. Such debts often went both ways. *He won't even bloody tell me what he wants.*

He wants you to find Elena.

Who bloody well may be dead! There's naught to do with her bones!

The Gods won't tell you what they want. They know you'll do the opposite. Perhaps he has learned from them.

Draken grunted and eyed Truls, thinking. "A trade, then. Is that what you want? Am I to offer you something for your service?"

Truls began to move again, more, mingling and reforming as waves on the ocean. The tension eased.

As you traded with their lives. Clever, Draken.

Draken swallowed hard. "I need you to bring the Mance here. Understood? Now. What will you take as payment?"

Without a sound, the ghost Truls flitted away. Slowly normal noises came back over Draken: the creak of the building, a slight rattle of the shutter, Sikyra's snuffling, constrained breathing.

Well, that's reassuring. Now he owed a *ghost* a damned favor.

Despite the storied romance of sleeping with a bared blade, he had no wish to cut himself, so he laid Seaborn on the floor. He pulled his cloak over him and leaned back. Elena's pendant slid up on his chest. He caught it, the white metal cold in his fist. He couldn't bear to look at her image engraved into the pendant, but he could bear less to remove it.

Settling on the cot proved difficult and required a deal of shifting to get comfortable on the narrow stretch of stiff fabric. It creaked and he didn't want to wake the baby, so he stilled and let his muscles relax as much as possible. He tried to tell himself he had a cot at least, rather than cold floor or a hard bunk in a pitching ship, but his sore shoulder twitched, irritated. His mind twitched too, more so.

He turned his head to look at Sikyra. She was a princess, born of royal blood, destined to rule after her mother. She should never want for anything while she learned to serve her people. No child should, no matter how lowborn. Even slaveborn of an abusive father, he'd had a warm place to lay his head at night. In return Draken had given his child a life on the run, her only shelter a dank, cold room. Elena would be appalled.

You didn't give it to her. Ilumat did that.

I didn't protect her.

Perhaps not as you wish. But I will protect you . . .

Movement jolted Draken out of his sleep. His cold hand dropped to the side of the cot and closed around Seaborn's hilt. The sword whipped up to rest against the pale throat of someone leaning over him.

Bloody Seven, Bruche! Draken blinked, took back control of his hand, and lowered the blade.

Your eyes were closed. I couldn't see who it was.

"Osias." He rubbed the sleep from his eyes with the heel of his hand and pushed himself to a sit.

"Khel Szi. Are you well?" Osias gaze intently at him with clear grey eyes. No swirling spirits peered through.

"Well enough. Truls brought you my message."

A faint smile. "He brought me here. How did you manage to secure his cooperation?"

"I asked nicely. Where is Setia?"

"Guarding below."

Draken shook his head. There was no need. The building was ramshackle, deserted. Not even curious youths or desperate poor came to investigate. Perhaps Truls's presence frightened them away. "What news? Aarinnaie claims there are Monoeans in the streets, that the city belongs to them now."

Osias frowned and eased down onto the cot next to Sikyra. She whimpered softly but Osias's warm hand on her back and a soft murmur made her settle. "She is ill. I will see to a healer."

"You're avoiding my question."

He met Draken's eyes. "The Citadel has fallen to Akrasia. Brîn will be given to Monoea in a ceremony set for two nights from now. A trade for Akrasia's independence."

"My head on a pike would be a special attraction, I assume." The rough words were meant to stave off burgeoning fear but he had a hard time getting air behind his voice. Draken hadn't realized until just now how hope had burned inside him. His shoulders slumped.

"Not all the Brînians favored you as your father's bastard son. This you know. But I think you have loyals left here. The Akrasians have not been easy on the Brînians, and the Monoeans here . . ."

Sharply: "What of them?"

"They are demanding changes. Every head covered as if going to temple. Any female warriors stripped of their rank and weapons. They claim women are suited only to motherhood, as Ma'Vanni is our mother. Bloodlords must swear their loyalty to the Ashen within a sevennight. All the temple icons are gone. Destroyed. I fear the very temples are next."

Draken stared. "Why would they desecrate the temples?"

"They claim the Seven are to be worshipped at night, under the moons. They use the old rites—"

"Those were outlawed by King Ysseff before I was born. Magic and blood and sacrifice." Truth, he'd done fragments of the old rites as a Monoean. Cutting his palm and letting the blood drip into the sea as a symbolic sacrifice. Roadside altars dabbed in blood. Even oxblood on his forehead here in Brîn and Akrasia. But the old rites . . . holding to those took killing people. Many people.

A shrug belied Osias's wrinkled brow. "I have no confirmation of sacrifice, but rumors . . . I do not think it beyond possibility."

Draken stared at his sleeping daughter. His defenseless, sundry, royal daughter who very well might have inherited magic from her father or her mother. "I have to get Sikyra out of the city. She is my only concern now."

"You could take Brîn back if you rally enough people," Osias said. "You must admit you have a way of gathering them to you."

Draken shook his head and rose to sheathe his sword. He paced as he talked. "Even a thousand citizens, two thousand, aren't enough to take back the city if the Ashen are determined to have her. My real soldiers are at the front fighting."

"Perhaps not. Perhaps they have surrendered," Osias said.

"Brînians surrender? No. But it doesn't matter. It might take the whole of Frost to bring them back, if they even would come to me. We'd need a secret place to gather in force or the Akrasians will pick them off group by group. The only answer is mercenaries, if there are any who avoided the war effort. There might be fighters in those villages downcoast, perhaps, but Khein is probably no longer an option— Why are you smiling?"

You're already planning it out.

Osias nodded his agreement with Bruche and looked down at Sikyra. His hair slid forward over his shoulders. "You're right about one thing. Such a fight is no place for the Princess."

Sikyra whimpered as her breath wheezed in her chest. She shifted her little body as if trying to escape her blankets. Her lips pursed but her lined eyes didn't open.

Draken's fingers lifted to his rough jaw. She had learned to kiss him, and more recently, to rub his face for bristles before she did.

Clever, that, Bruche said softly.

One of her little hands clutched the carved horse. He could fair feel what her fingers felt like when they gripped his, the weight of her body against his. He flexed his hands to erase the ghostly sensation as his stomach fell.

He cleared his throat. His voice was low, harsh against his tight throat. "I'd like to send her with you and Setia. Can you find somewhere to keep her safe?"

Osias gave a brisk nod. "She can stay in the gatehouse at Eidola. There's plenty of room and Setia and the Mance will dote on her. It only need be a short while. No Akrasian would dare come there, and we could defend her well there against any Ashen who might."

ENEMY 57

Draken wasn't happy with the idea of his baby daughter so close to the banes. Evil spirits could make quick work of an innocent child. But he had to trust the gates, and the Mance. They protected everyone from the banes, not just his daughter. And truth, their presence also might hold the Ashen from attacking Eidola. "Will your brothers take you back to stay for a while?"

"To protect the child, aye. They will."

Draken's eyes narrowed. Something in his tone . . . It had been Osias's idea, after all, to take her. "So you intend to use my daughter as currency to buy your way back into Eidola."

"Truth, it is a solution that suits us all."

Bruche shifted inside Draken, either mimicking Draken's apprehension or expressing his own. Sometimes it was tough to determine the difference. He couldn't help but backstep. "She's a child. A baby. She needs her father."

"She is a princess and she needs her city. Her people. Without Brîn she has no chance at ruling Akrasia."

"Brînian prejudice is barely eclipsed by Akrasian. And Brîn means little to most Akrasians."

"Until Tradeseason. Then every Akrasian knows the value of Brîn and her port."

Draken rubbed his forehead and said bitterly, "Ilumat is a fool."

"He may have another plan in store for the Ashen. We cannot know."

"Whatever his plans are, they won't help Sikyra. She never had much chance anyway."

"Draken. Do you think the gods brought you together with Elena to no end? In your daughter, all three countries could be united permanently. As well, if Sikyra rules well from even one of the thrones, it makes hatred of sundry a very uncomfortable luxury. Ilumat knows all this. He will hunt you, Draken. Right now you are his biggest threat. After he kills you, he will come for Sikyra. Why give him the opportunity to take you both at once? Even were Sikyra an adult and capable of helping you fight, you are safer apart. As well, the whole of both yours and Elena's people are safer with Sikyra alive."

"She is my *daughter*, not some sort of savior fated by the gods."

"No. If one exists, it would be you."

Draken snorted, irritated. "You're assuming the gods have some good will toward us. It's a reach, Osias."

"To assume else is folly. The gods have no reason to harm us. We are of them, are we not? Even you cannot deny it." Bruche remained quiet. Draken had the sense he agreed with the Mance. But he also would not war with Draken over whatever decision he made.

"What of the szi nêre? Halmar . . . ?" Aarinnaie had not said.

Osias, usually calm, gripped his knees a moment before digging out his twin-bowled pipe and started to fill it. His voice was flat, factual, without sympathy or remorse.

"Their heads rot on the Citadel walls. As well they desecrated the crypts. The bones of your ancestors burn in the tower bowl at Seakeep. The Brightstar armorers are even dead, their families as well, all publicly executed for helping you. Here is the truth, Draken. Ilumat seized the Citadel and you barely escaped. Do not give him another chance at you and the Princess."

Draken turned his face toward the sea, though there were walls blocking his view. Truls wavered until nausea burned in Draken's stomach and threatened to free itself. He closed his eyes against the sensation. It couldn't shut out Sikyra's raspy breathing.

"She is very ill," he said.

"She is strong. I will see her cared for, Draken. Setia knows the old ways to physic Brînians from when she was a slave, and if she can't manage it, I will see a proper healer is brought." A hesitation. "Do you trust me?"

Did he? "I don't have a choice, do I?"

"I know you are angry with me for not banishing Truls. But I think you'll need him."

"You drew an arrow on him the first time you saw him. What changed your mind?"

"I was hasty in my judgment, aye? He brought me to you."

Long, deep breaths passed. Several more shallow ones from Sikyra. "For some debt he has not yet named."

A grim smile. "Mance are ever thus, eh? The gods chose you, and so have I. I will protect Sikyra so you can protect the rest of us."

Draken looked at his hands. Rough, callused from sword and bow. Crossed with white scars from a hundred small hurts. Ship lines. Knives. The ugly criminal brands Osias had altered into Khellian's horns. It had hurt, it all had been agonizing. But not like the pressure around his heart, the compression of terror that he'd never see his daughter again.

Elena did it. Elena let her go and so must you.

Draken winced inwardly. Elena had given him Sikyra, their unnamed infant daughter, and sent him running from the fires she'd made to destroy the Moonlings' village, to take back their freedom from the Moonlings who held her hostage. She was strong. She had done what was right for their daughter and for their people. He nodded.

Osias rose and picked up Sikyra. She relaxed against him with a sigh. Her chubby hand closed around Osias's silver braid and she pressed her face against his neck. She never opened her eyes.

"Come, Draken. Give your daughter a kiss."

Draken stared at her, trying to fix her face, the way her body curved against his, into his memory. If he touched her again he could not let her go. He shook his head once.

Osias stood a moment more. "Gods willing, you will not be parted for long."

"Tell her—tell her I—" His throat closed over the words.

"I will, my friend." Osias came closer and gripped his shoulder. "Every day and every night until you reclaim her."

He pulled free of Osias and turned his back. Stared into the fire like he could convince himself it was the light that stung his eyes.

Soft bootfalls, the click of the latch, they were gone.

Draken—

Be silent.

Bruche obeyed, withdrawing into an anxious knot deep inside.

Draken gripped Elena's pendant so tightly that her face left an impression in his palm. He closed his fingers over her image and its mirror in his skin, rolled his hand over so he didn't have to look at her. His heart beat on in his chest as if oblivious to Draken's wish to escape the agony of her absence.

Alive or dead, someday he would atone to Sikyra for failing their peoples, for running when he should have fought, for putting her in danger and sending her away.

Someday, but not this day. This day there was no atoning for the past and the dead who plagued him.

CHAPTER SEVEN

Aarinnaie spun on Draken. "How could you?"

A few words into the argument and he already tired of it. "This is no place for a child. She is ill. We couldn't keep on this way."

Aarinnaie stalked a path around the room. He reached over to his cot. In their haste, he hadn't noticed Sikyra had dropped her toy horse. He ran his fingers over the smooth hardwood, the edges worn from her mouthing it. She slept with it always. His eyes burned.

"I'm certain my Lord Mance will take good care of Princess Sikyra." Tyrolean, ever the voice of reason. Today it grated. Draken rose.

"Osias told me all the szi nêre are dead." Halmar and the others. He'd left them to die, loyal to the end.

Aarinnaie blinked. She started to reach for the shutter but her hand dropped to her side, disappearing under her cloak. "Aye. It's truth. All the slaves. They slaughtered every soul in the Citadel."

"You knew. When were you going to tell me?"

She bit her lip and held his gaze with a scowl. "What purpose would it serve, your knowing?"

He bit back a sharp reply. Kept his voice flat. "Osias also suggested I might have pockets of loyalty left in Brîn."

Tyrolean stood with his arms crossed. Nothing marked him as a Royal Escort Captain. He wore no cloak despite the cold. Better to access the twin blades strapped to his back. The distinctive pointed hilts were wrapped in leather to blunt and disguise them. Even his armor was plain and worn, but serviceable. Draken had no idea where it had come from, if he had been wearing it all along or had exchanged his fine armor for this on one of his trips to find Osias. His black hair hung damp and loose about his face. He'd had a bath, then. He was one up on Draken.

"With the coins pressed in the past few moonturns, you'll be known by sight in the city better than ever before," Tyrolean said for about the tenth time. Draken clung to his patience.

Makes it a bit of a trick getting out, Bruche intoned.

"But that's not the worst of it," Tyrolean said.

"No. That would be Halmar and Konnon and all my loyal szi nêre and servants rotting on the walls they once protected."

Tyrolean and Aarinnaie exchanged glances as if they'd discussed who would say this bit. Tyrolean cleared his throat. "Ilumat has declared Elena officially dead. He says he has proof."

"Her body?" Draken asked, sharp.

Tyrolean shook his head. "No one knows for certain."

Draken's shoulders sank. The hole in his gut widened. Proof. And Ilumat would be known as the one who had searched and found it rather than Draken. Her consort, her Night Lord. Her Prince had not found her. The Akrasians would have another reason to reject Draken. As if they needed one.

You were a bit busy running the country and fighting a war, never mind Elena is alive.

Now you're on Truls's side.

He has no reason to lie.

The Moonlings never came forward with anything. He'd supposed they would, if only to throw it in his face. But there'd been no word at all. No sign of them. According to scouts, the woods up the mountains were a mess of icy ash and tree carcasses. Not a trace of Moonlings left. *I should have gone back for her. Searched for her.*

"We can't trust Ilumat," Aarinnaie said. "If you don't know, there's no way for him to know."

Draken sighed. "Ilumat's lands are at the foot of the Agrian Range. It is not a difficult thing to climb up and look from there."

"It is upland from Skyhaven some distance," Tyrolean pointed out.

"But fair closer to the mountains and Auwaer than Brîn," Draken said. Close enough Ilumat could search and have access to the Royal Escorts in Auwaer, could gain their trust and loyalty by proximity and pretty words. And he hadn't been busy running a country at war. The thought left a bitter taste. That had all been for naught.

Aarinnaie put her hands on her hips. "You have that look like you're about to say something that's going to make me smack you. What?"

"Ilumat is young, inexperienced, ambitious. None of those are evil qualities. Does that make him wrong for Akrasia in Elena's absence? I don't know. He *is* her cousin."

"How can you not know? He took Brîn."

"If I had been a better prince, I would have held the city."

She snorted and shook her head, hands on her hips.

"He's ambitious enough to have murdered everyone of importance at the Citadel," Tyrolean said. "He's young enough to trust the Monoeans over his own countrymen. And inexperienced enough to think erasing centuries of House Khel rule is good for Brîn and Akrasia. The nature of a man does not destroy countries; his evil actions do."

"He's just another Akrasian. He may be no worse or better than the rest."

Tyrolean stiffened but Aarinnaie went on, fists clenched. "Elena's father conquered Brîn. He took Akhen Khel and killed the szi nêre and prominent bloodlords. He killed our grandfather and sent our father into slavery. He drove our people into Blood Bay like animals. Ilumat is no worse or better than his uncle; that's what Akrasians are."

Tyrolean shook his head slowly, his face drawn. "I cannot excuse all that, but I do know the King intended to leave Brîn as a mostly autonomous principality because he knew to do otherwise would destabilize the city and trade—bad for both Akrasia and Brîn. The intention was to place your father on the throne here. A fresh start with a new generation. But your father ran, disappeared to Monoea."

Aarinnaie's eyes narrowed. "To be captured and sold into slavery."

Tyrolean was shaking his head. "Princess, you can't believe all he told you—"

"Father was craven," Draken said firmly. "He was enslaved because he ran."

Aarinnaie glared at him. "And you're just like him, aren't you? A slave as he was? And now craven?"

"No. He was born in honor and threw it away. I was cursed from birth." His jaw was tight, his fingers gripped his sword hilt. "But I am no less Khel Szi."

She stared at him. He huffed a breath, and another, nostrils flared. She had watched his mother die by his hand, a woman unapologetic for sleeping with one slave and for birthing another. She had been the victim too, of culture and damned royal pride. He pried his fingers free of the hilt. This argument was getting them nowhere.

"It's all changed now. Sikyra—" He swallowed. "I want her to have a life. Maybe Ilumat as King is a way to give her that."

"All respect, Your Highness," Tyrolean said. "Sikyra is Princess, the rightful Queen if Elena is dead. As your life is not your own, nor is hers. You must protect her, not from the throne, but *for* it."

Listen to the Captain. Better for you to take back your power. Only then can you truly protect her.

Damn them. He fingered Sikyra's toy horse. "As you say, I'm known now. So how do I move about the city freely?"

"First, cut your hair." Aarinnaie met his gaze levelly, daring him to argue.

Customary during mourning, which was why he hadn't done. Cutting his hair would be publically admitting Elena was dead.

Ah, but you are not such a public person at the moment.

Draken nodded. "Agreed."

"Good. We need to make you look like you're a rogue mercenary again. Shouldn't be too difficult, eh?" A humorless smile and Aarinnaie strode toward the door. "I'll be back."

Draken pulled his knife from his belt and flipped it in his hand so it presented hilt-first. "It falls to you to corrupt me, Captain."

Tyrolean snorted softly. "I am a poor substitute for Aarinnaie, but I'll do my best."

◆ ◆ ◆

Aarinnaie returned with a bundle so heavy she fetched Tyrolean to carry it up the steps. Beads of rain dotted her damp cloak, and she dragged in a blast of cold and the thick scent of wet wool. "Dark in here, isn't it? Light a damned lantern."

"He made me put it out," Tyrolean said.

Draken rubbed his newly shorn head, grey-threaded locks scattered about his boots. The cool air against his neck felt familiar as a sharp blade. Tyrolean had also thinned and shaped his beard to the recent local style, low along his jaw and fuller around his mouth. Aarinnaie eyed Draken speculatively. "Tyrolean can have an alternate trade as a barber if rebelling doesn't work out."

"His blades are impeccably sharp," Draken answered. Thank the gods for his steady hand.

She tipped her chin at the clinking bundle Tyrolean had hefted into the room and dumped onto the cot, which swayed dangerously under the burden.

Draken rolled his eyes after untying the sack and peering in. It smelled of damp metal and old sweat. "Chainmail?" Poor man's armor, and the shirt had patches of rust and several broken links.

"You can't go about in expensive leathers and plate. It's a dead giveaway you've got coin, that you're associated with the Citadel. If you'd only go bare-chested like a proper bloodlord . . ."

"I'm not a proper bloodlord or anything like it," Draken growled.

"He can't," Tyrolean said reasonably. "If he takes a cut he'll heal. We can't explain that away."

"Right. So I got you these." She shifted the bag with some difficulty, Tyrolean grabbing the end. Chainmail and other items poured out: a moth-eaten gambeson, a tatty cloak, a worn, serviceable woolen shirt. "The Captain is right, by the way."

Tyrolean raised his eyebrows at Draken. "About?"

"As I waited for the shirt to be repaired I drank an ale at the inn next door. The taleteller there spoke of your healing ability." A mirthless laugh. "There are quite the load of stories about your escape circulating. Some think you can fly. Others think you can turn bodiless, like a ghost."

Draken shook his head, failing to see the humor. Especially with Truls's filmy gaze on him. Ghosts were real and no joke. His perspective shifted as Bruche pushed forward into his consciousness and turned his head to look at Aarinnaie. She was lighting a lantern. He forced his head away as the fire flared.

"But one I heard seemed to know you went through the tombs." She ran her tongue along her top teeth. "They must have interrogated Halmar or Konnon before—Well. Anyway. These are the best I could do on short notice."

"No. Osias said the men who helped me enter the tombs were captured and hanged in the square." Draken undid the laces on his shirt. "I assume there is a reward for my capture."

Aarinnaie nodded. "One hundred rare, alive. Fifty, dead."

How does it feel to know you're hardly worth keeping a bloodlord in wine for a year?

It doesn't matter. A hundred rare would be enough for many people.

Aarinnaie studied him, hands on her hips. "The beard fair helps, but it's not enough. Someone will recognize you."

"It's not to be helped," Tyrolean said. "It's cold and damp out. Wear your hood up."

"Inside?" Aarinnaie shook her head. "No. He needs something rather more drastic."

Draken wasn't sure what. Osias wasn't here to glamour him, and while ink was fine for war and had fooled the Monoeans for a little while when he'd had to go back there as an emissary, he couldn't walk about Brîn done up for battle.

Aarinnaie squatted to poke up the fire. The coals glared at Draken like the eyes of a bane. He turned his head away, squinting, to find Tyrolean watching him.

"Regardless of disguise, I need to see the Citadel." Draken pulled his shirt off and reached for the gambeson. It smelled worse out of the bag, but the fit was all right.

"Are you mad?" His sister gaped at him.

"Likely. But it's something I must do."

He let Tyrolean help him on with the mail shirt. Tyrolean buckled it up the back for him. Again, the fit was decent, but its weight would take a little getting used to.

"It's too dangerous." She swallowed. "And you don't need that in your head. You shouldn't remember them this way."

He had seen death before, aplenty. Countless men screaming on the end of his blade, pierced by his arrows. His father strung from Seakeep's gates. His wife hanging from a gamehook, gutted and bled out like a stag. He cast a glare toward Truls, who had arranged for her death, had taken her blood and used it to bring him here. "I do, actually. I must know what I'm up against."

He finished dressing, buckled his sword around his waist, and strode out into the damp daylight. The alleyway off the entrance was deserted but for rubbish caught in corners. Truls ranged ahead. Tyrolean had his hood up, and Draken followed suit. Even the meager light filtering through the thick clouds made him squint. Aarinnaie fell far enough behind to act as rearguard if needed.

You're going to have to do something about your vision.

The air felt chill and harsh against his skin, the dim light hot on his eyes.

He glanced over his shoulder at Eidola. The mountains, jagged shards of stone plunged into the low-slung clouds, flashed through his vision before he had to lower his gaze. The lower edges were clear and sharp enough he could fair imagine them drawing blood from the skies. It would be misty at the gatehouse to the realm of the unsettled dead, the sort of cold that seeps into bones. That damp air couldn't be good for Sikyra's illness. Had Osias managed to get her there by now? Was she crying for him? Did the Mance frighten her? She'd be missing her toy. His hand fell to finger the carved horse through the soft leather of his belt pouch. If he had only kept his daughter, he still would have the chance to disappear with her, make a life somewhere without all this danger and politics. He knew ships and the sea; he could have paid for a berth working as crew. They could be nations away within moonturns.

Draken almost stumbled over someone in his way, opened his mouth to apologize, but the younger man flicked his gaze over him, muttered an apology, and trotted out of his way. He was sundry, paler skin than Draken's with reddish Brînian locks, and smaller than Draken by half a head. A metal band encircled his neck. A slave then, on some errand for his master. Others skirted them as he stared after the slave. If Sikyra were captured . . . someone might enslave her because of her lighter skin mixed with her tight black curls. A pretty girl like her could be raised up for a brothel, make her masters a fortune . . .

"My lord." Tyrolean, voice quiet, hand steady on Draken's arm.

Draken swallowed the bile rising in his throat and forced himself to walk. Even under the shadow of his hood, he couldn't look up much without his eyes watering, so he focused on the cobbles at his feet, blackened with rain and dirt, fringed in tenacious green moss struggling under boots and hooves and the cold.

Brîn had succumbed to Ilumat so easily. Despite reports of violence, this day the people moved about their business as if it didn't matter who held the Citadel. Perhaps it didn't. He could claw his way back inside Citadel, kill Ilumat even. But the Akrasians would never accept a sundry bastard on their throne in Elena's absence. No wonder Ilumat had such an easy time of it. A pureblooded, landed cousin to the queen, in Sikyra's absence and with Elena declared dead, his lineage was absolute, undisputable.

You and Sikyra have more claim to the Akrasian and Brînian thrones than the one who did that. Bruche drew his gaze toward the Citadel.

Brînians moved in a quiet line before the wall, keeping their distance from several servii, who didn't seem to be doing much but standing around hurling the occasional insult. A hedge of ribbons and flowers divided the Akrasian guards and the Brînian people. Most of them looked like Sohalia leftovers; the best the people could come up with to honor their dying city-state on such short notice.

Draken stopped walking, a dozen paces back from the line of shuffling, grieving Brînians. He shifted his hand to his sword hilt and stilled, his throat tight. An odd quiet pervaded the road before the Citadel, broken only by an occasional cough. The familiar dome loomed over the other buildings, too lustrous under the shadow of clouds for Draken to look at for long. It had been home, but perhaps not. He felt a strange detachment from the place. But below . . . behind the gawking line of Brînians and sturdy guards . . . the heads of szi nêre dotted the spiked rail atop the stone wall.

Konnon, the dapples stark in his flaccid skin, lips gaping. One of his eye sockets hung empty, a streak of blood down his cheek, and his thick wavy hair was shorn. Maybe as a trophy.

Halmar . . . eyes closed, locks shorn. Someone had ripped the expensive rings from his ears and lips and brows. Blood had flowed freely, now russet stains on ash-black skin that even the rain and mists couldn't cleanse away. A dozen more, a row of familiar faces, szi nêre who had shadowed him, fought for him, jested with him, died for him.

Aarinnaie came up behind him and gasped softly. *"Thom."*

His chamberlain's Gadye mask gleamed with more verve than his dead, sightless eye. Draken fell very still, but for his hand tightening on his sword. He started to draw. Bruche chilled his arm and released the sword, shifting to take Aarin's hand in his. Draken grimaced in frustration. At least they hadn't taken Thom's mask. He'd known someone who had endured it and, bound to the body by ancient magic, ripping it away was among the worst of cruelties.

No. Not now. You'll have your revenge, but not here.

"Your hand is cold," Aarinnaie said at last.

"It's Bruche." The spirit's presence lingered heavy in his chest. Draken released her and turned without a word let Tyrolean lead him, blindly at first, and then with purpose.

A group walked ahead, speaking softly. Draken heard the words *Khel Szi* and almost stopped walking. Bruche pressed him on.

"Still loose then," someone commented. Another made the harsh Brînian grunt demanding silence. The familiarity of the sound struck Draken. These were his people. He'd already given himself over to them whether they wanted him or not, and there was no stepping back from it.

Sun cut through the clouds. Draken had to shut his eyes against the glare. He could barely see anyway for the tears. Tyrolean kept his hand on Draken's arm, guiding him. "Where are we going, my lord?"

"To build an army."

CHAPTER EIGHT

Aarinnaie fashioned a simple strip of loose-woven black linen tied round Draken's head into a mask so he could open his eyes and see in the light. It was only partially effective. To shield the oddness of wearing it, he pretended to be blind and let his sister lead him on the street. It wasn't all acting. Full daylight still forced his eyes to a tight squint and his eyelashes brushed the fabric annoyingly. He'd even taken to wearing it at night because the odd torch momentarily blinded him and it was frustrating for his companions to be without light.

In the dim tavern with the mask and gentle, ambient light from pierced lanterns, his vision settled. Tyrolean put his back to the wall, at a more private, corner table. Draken slid in next to him slowly, feeling his way because he wasn't supposed to be able to see. A full cloak concealed Seaborn tied securely to his thigh. Blind men had no use for swords but he refused to leave it. The blade on his wrist would draw less attention as it doubled as an eating knife. When the server set a mug in front of him he fumbled for it, hopefully convincingly.

Tyrolean reached for it, sipped, waited a breath or two, then pushed it into his hand. He still insisted on tasting for Draken, a habit he could give up if his disguise and the mask were any use at all. Though it might look as if Tyrolean was just taking some of his blind friend's ale.

For her part, Aarinnaie had never looked less a Princess. She wore a long tunic over trousers and boots, her hair braided up, a few curly sprigs framing her face. Gadye trinkets were woven in the braids at her temples. She didn't have a collar but her appearance made for a short jump to a bed slave. She perused the room before sitting across from them.

"They're staring, some of them. At you, Drae," Aarinnaie said lowly.

"Debility always draws attention." Draken could fair feel their curiosity. What was under the mask? A horrible scar? Did he even have eyes under there?

Truls moved between tables like a soldier hunting down a fugitive. He'd been quiet of late, but always moving, spilling anxious energy. Curious to watch the oblivious people shift or turn their heads as he passed. Draken reckoned he was falling in nicely with the gods' will, or he was so far gone off their path the Mance ghost had given up whispering to him. But Truls followed Draken always, as if he were the Seven's eyes.

His sister only shook her head. "All right. We're here. Now tell me why."

Draken kept his voice low. "Because here are my enemies."

"Some of them," Tyrolean said. He wore his hair down, stringy around his face, and tattered clothes. He'd put away his dual swords and replaced them with a good one on his hip. There were enough Akrasian camp followers on the streets that he didn't stand out by his mere presence. Most might assume him the master of two sundry slaves. That, they had decided, was a misconception they'd use as a disguise. Tyrolean just had to be careful about showing his face to anyone he knew. So far they hadn't frequented the better taverns where the new masters of the city did. Not that it seemed to matter. According to Aarinnaie, the better taverns were remarkably bereft of the city's new occupiers.

The tavern wasn't far from the Citadel. The last time he had been here his face hadn't been on a coin so he hadn't needed any disguise but to hide Elena's pendant.

"But the enemy I need most likes to come here," Draken said.

"Khisson?"

Draken nodded.

Aarinnaie set her mug on the table with a sharp thud. "Whatever you're thinking, it's a bad idea."

Last Tradeseason she had infiltrated an islander family working against Draken's rule. He and Tyrolean had stumbled upon them preparing to recruit Aarinnaie into their ranks by a fight, though he had the private impression that had they not arrived, such an initiation would involve something a bit more intimate than demonstrating her prowess with her knives. At any rate, he and Tyrolean had made quick work of the threat against her and blown her cover, to her consternation. But many of Khisson House still lived, most notably the bloodlord patriarch. By all accounts Khisson nursed a grudge against Draken as bitter as the ale in his mug.

"I know what I'm doing, and I know all about him. You weren't my only eyes and ears on the street," Draken said. She gave him a sharp look and he amended, "Just my best."

Tyrolean was on the other side of the table trying to hold back a grin. Draken failed to find the humor. "A sevennight ago—" Gods, had it been so recently he was still Khel Szi, ensconced in the Citadel? "—Khisson was seen in the city."

"Why? What would pull him from the Dragonstars at this time of year?" Most islanders spent Frostfall pursuing quiet endeavors at home, taking shelter from the coming storms. For that matter, so did mainlanders.

"An invasion of Akrasians and Monoeans, perhaps." Tyrolean barely sipped from his own mug, a sure sign he was nervy. "He might well recognize you, my lord."

"That's rather the point, isn't it, Ty?"

Tyrolean laid a neat stack of coins out on the table for the barmaid to see— some of their last, earned by selling off Draken's leather armor in pieces at the market. After a short wait, the barmaid stopped, eyed Draken, snatched up three more coins, and hurried off without a word.

Draken's masked itched. He closed his fist where it rested on the table.

Aarinnaie had argued vehemently against coming out at all. Now that she knew why they were here, she cursed softly. "Whether they're in league or not, Khisson is bound to turn you over to Ilumat."

Draken had Bruche to advise him on the finer points of the culture of Brî-nian vendetta and he agreed with his swordhand's assessment. "We killed his men, one of his sons. Makes it personal, if it wasn't before. No. He'll want to kill me himself if he can possibly manage it."

Tyrolean nodded his thanks to the barmaid as she deposited three fresh dented mugs on the table and scurried off.

"But you do have a price on your head and islanders are all about coin." Aarinnaie lifted the mug to her lips.

Truls had come behind Tyrolean and tipped his head as if listening to the conversation. Draken looked at his ale instead. A bit of something stuck to the inside of the cup. He picked at it with his nail and realized not only should he be unable to see it, his hands were grimier than all that. He sighed and drank.

"Draken." Tyrolean, low.

"Be easy, Ty. You don't need to taste for me. The only poison in this mug is dirt."

"No, not that. Khisson just walked in," Tyrolean said.

Draken pretended to turn his head to listen to Tyrolean so he could look. Bare-chested, a cloak sweeping behind, traditional loose-legged pants bound with a sash, though the bloodlord wore boots in deference to the wet cold. Enough chains round his neck and bands around his wrists and biceps to feed a borough of Brînian aged and infirm for a Sohalia.

He doesn't need your bounty, Bruche said.

No. He doesn't. Which suited Draken's plans just fine.

Half a dozen men followed the bloodlord. Narrowed eyes snagged on Draken and then twitched free. Maybe they considered him a good mark since he appeared blind, despite Tyrolean's lean, dangerous proximity. Or perhaps they wondered why an Akrasian and a blind Brînian were companions.

"I need a reason to go fetch him for you that won't raise brows, aye?" She was loosening the collar of her tunic. Aarinnaie hadn't much bosom to speak of—too slight and skinny. Draken had always thought her too young to be betrothed or considered an adult, though reasonably he knew twenty-five Sohalias made her well past marrying age.

The barmaid brought more ale. Tyrolean drained his cup and reached for the fresh one as Aarinnaie loosened her many braids from the leather strap holding them back, took up her new cup, and rose. With the Gadye trinkets woven at her brow and temples and her clothing, she'd easily be mistaken as sundry.

As her slight form moved through the tables toward them, Draken had a flash of what it would be for Sikyra, true sundry, to make her way alone in the world. His hand trembled as he wrapped it around his cup and brought it to his lips.

Aarinnaie laid her hand on Khisson's arm to get his attention, though he was already turning. Khisson stared, eyes widening. He said something and she responded, dipping her chin. Khisson said something else. Laughter broke out among them. Aarinnaie didn't smile. One of the men caught her arm and pulled her down to sit on the bench next to him.

Khisson rose and walked toward them. Three of his men followed. Aarinnaie was still held at the table. She grimaced but made no move to escape. Draken made no indication he could see as Khisson approached. Tyrolean shoved out the vacant bench opposite them with his boot. Khisson sat, slowly. His legs stretched out under the table so that his boots crowded Draken's. Lines creased his mouth and eyes under the yellow glow of the rusted lantern affixed to the wall over Draken's head. Not friendly lines. No smiles unless from a particular cruelty. His locks, thick and dangling halfway down his back, were dull compared to his shiny, clean skin. He was the darkest Brînian Draken had ever seen, his features sculpted and fine. Very pureblood, he assumed.

Ash dye hid the grey in his hair, dulling his locks. Of course. Draken resisted running a rueful hand over his own silver-threaded shorn head. He shifted his gaze under the mask to examine the others. Two of the guards surrounding them had muddied eyes. At first glance it might look like angry Mance eyes, but the whites were statically bruised. He knew that look. He'd seen it on Khisson's son. Addicted to eventide, the mad-spice grown downcoast.

"Thank you for joining me," Draken said. He tilted his face a little toward the others, still feigning blindness. His stomach knotted, wondering how long the disguise would work.

Having the man across from him, this man with a grudge, this man who hated him enough to keep up on his every move, made his hand desperate to draw Seaborn. A cold breath swept over the back of his bare neck. Truls, no doubt, watching Khisson curiously.

Draken eased a breath. "I know you. Your sons and men. I want to talk to you."

"All this ceremony over the whore? Pretty thing. Ten rare for the night and we'll have done with it."

Impatient, this one.

Bruche was right. But his guards sensed more, if Khisson did not. The others encircled the table, backs to the table and blocking Aarinnaie from view.

She can take care of herself. Kill them all in five breaths. Bruche's chill flooded Draken's trembling hands, resting on his knees. If it was meant to be soothing, it didn't work. It only made him long to draw his sword.

Truth, but I'd rather her not make her skills obvious just yet. Besides, he needed Khisson. Bruche brought Draken's hand up and he drank. His other arm came up to wipe his mouth on his sleeve. "It's not about the girl. Can I buy you a drink?"

"I'm never one to turn down a mug," Khisson said, tone ungracious. But he stayed. He was curious. Draken filed that away.

Tyrolean pushed back and rose. Went to fetch one. Khisson watched him, eyes narrowed. "Strange, a sundry merc with a fullblood Akrasian." He'd admirably resisted using a slur. Maybe trying to sort who answered to who, though Draken thought it was clear enough.

"The whole world has gone strange."

Khisson shrugged. "Wars happen and time runs on."

Draken acquiesced with a nod.

Tyrolean returned with the drink. There was a slight hesitation to Khisson's reach. A wince that didn't reach his face. Draken noticed it even with his gauzy vision because he had the same catch sometimes. Khisson was older than him, though. More battered. Scars crossed his chest. No matter how he greased his skin, the lines around his eyes and mouth were deepening. Crevices ever tougher to fill and hide, like the ones between peoples and ghosts and gods.

"I wanted your opinion on what happens now," Draken said. "Rumors say Monoea will take Brîn."

"Hm. We're naught but chattel to Akrasia since the old Khel Szi's time. This proves it gone, eh?"

Which Khel Szi? His ruddy father, or his grandfather who he'd never known, who Bruche had died protecting? A respected king, by all accounts. "Still. It makes a man wonder whether there is work to be had here or if I should move on. The Ashen won't hold with our ways, I reckon."

A humorless grunt. "Enslave the lot of us, more like. Akrasia did sell us for a song."

A bit more than a song. Khisson misjudged the effort to drag troops and weapons and the ram across Akrasia, of Ilumat's effort at organizing it. Was it a purposeful devaluation? "You don't sound too worried."

Khisson took a drink. "Let me see your eyes."

His lashes rubbed the mask as he blinked in surprise. So. Not fooled. Everything this man did was on purpose. Khisson was more clever than he'd given him credit for. Draken just hoped he wasn't going to make a habit of it. His jaw tight, he reached up and pulled the mask off. Lowered his gaze under the light. Blinked. Struggled to look up. To show them. He could barely keep them open. His pupils strained in the light.

Khisson hissed a breath. Reached out and grasped Draken's chin like he was an unruly child and lifted his face. "You're . . . What's wrong with you?"

"Aye. It's him." Tyrolean, his voice low. "And lack of respect will cost you dear."

Draken twisted free of Khisson's grip. "Magicked blind."

"By a Mance?" Khisson leaned back, too quick. His calm shattered. One of those who didn't hold with Mance or magic. One who saw his own ugliness reflected back by the necromancers.

"It doesn't rub off," Draken growled. "And no Mance did this."

"Who then?"

His breath was harsh in his chest. Anger twisted through him. "The gods."

"You're cursed?"

"As good as."

Khisson held very still. Stared. Draken lifted his head, squinting, to stare back at him with hot, watering eyes. He couldn't keep it up for long. He pulled the mask up into place. Immediately the heat faded from his eyes. A few tears dampened the fabric.

Khisson's voice strengthened. He was regaining his composure. "I should have known from the start. That whore must be your sister-Szirin. I'd heard about her. Unfit to marry any man."

There was no point in answering such a petty insult, so Draken didn't bother. He just hoped Aarin was ready to slice her way out of this if it came to it. Also, he wasn't certain how to phrase what he wanted from the bloodlord. A little panic edged into his reserve. Truls chose this moment to speak, not helping much.

the gods they come they come for you this man is one he comes

Bruche rumbled his unease. *What in bloody Korde is he talking about?*

Draken had no idea. Khisson grunted again. "Hm. You're not like your old da in talking. He didn't shut it for gods nor slaves, truth. But you've the stones to sit here with me, so speak."

Khisson tilted a look at Draken. He wanted Draken to ask, wanted him to say it: *You knew my father?* An intriguing question. If Khisson had known him, were they allies or enemies? Maybe his grudge against Draken went further back than he'd thought. Or maybe it only went as far back as Draken killing this man's son. But really, the *why* was an aside. A distraction.

Khisson shifted on the bench. One of his men turned his head, not hiding his attention to the conversation. Draken let his hand fall to Seaborn. Bruche's chill filled his fingers and arm. He was ready for Draken to speak, at least, even if Draken was not.

Draken filled his lungs with air. Released it before speaking so the words were calm, offhand. "I just wanted to know if you're still interested in killing me."

CHAPTER NINE

Khisson raised his brows, thin with age.

"It would be convenient for me to be thought dead," Draken added, fingers uncurling on the table between them.

A rich laugh. "It'd be a deal more convenient for me if you actually *were* dead."

"I'll remind you, you no longer have me on the throne ignoring certain of your activities. But you will again. I can be a valuable friend to you, Khisson, if you are one to me."

Khisson lifted his chin. It jutted, sharp, contrasting with his flat cheeks and forehead. "Or I can make fast friends with Ilumat with the gift of your body."

"Ilumat. Interesting he decided to move when he did. He's always been eager to prove himself, that one. What better way to prove yourself in Brîn than on a Dragonstar pirate?"

The lip curled further. Draken would lay his last rare that it was meant to hide Khisson's curiosity about Ilumat.

Draken added, "A sevennight of your time, my lord. It's all I'm asking."

"Khel Szi is a difficult man to kill," Tyrolean said very quietly.

"The heads of your szi nêre are on the walls. You're here with your Escort pawn and your sister. I think you seem not so difficult to kill."

"Have your men try me. I could do with some entertainment."

Khisson leaned forward, hands moved to fold together but didn't quite touch. The gnarled fingers flexed and curled. No imperfection of pain marred his dark face. Discipline or tonics. Draken thought he'd like to know which, since his shoulder and knee gave him little but trouble these days.

"I could kill you now, save myself the sevennight, *and* collect your bounty."

Draken schooled his face to show none of his alarm. It all made a bad sort of sense. "I *will* sit the throne at the Citadel again and you, my lord, will very much want me as a friend when I do."

"No. I am not convinced."

Bruche snorted. It reached Draken's throat. He coughed to cover it. "Why not? It'll be the simplest thing you do all Frostfall. Help make Ilumat fear me. Help him worry. And then you present evidence of my death to him. You earn coin and my undying gratitude. It's a win for you in all ways."

"Except you won't really be dead, nor in power. How will I provide evidence of your death without your head?"

Draken had no idea, of course. He traced a gouge along the tabletop, back and forth, back and forth. It curved and broke as if someone meant to graffiti glyphs into the wood but had gotten distracted. "That's for after you help me put the fear of the gods into him."

"How do I know I can trust you?"

"The Seven Eyes hold me to my word. I'll make certain Ilumat believes me dead."

"Short of your head, Akhen Khel would best convince him."

"No."

Khisson smiled slightly. He knew he'd touched a nerve. "You know I speak truth."

He did. He'd find another way to convince Ilumat. *"No."*

Khisson pushed back from the table. "I think we're finished. Good fortune to you, Khel Szi. You're going to need it."

Draken spoke a little faster. "Ilumat has no intention of letting go of the city. He doesn't understand us. And what Akrasian lords don't understand, they destroy."

Khisson's heavy brows dropped and he frowned deeply. It might have been his most honest expression all evening. "Why would you threaten him, then, if you've no plan to take the throne back right away? If you want to make him think you're dead."

"We will threaten him and let him think he has won, that I am dead. He'll put it to the other high lords—most are as young as he—that it was his conquest, no matter how it falls out. He must believe I am dead, though. They all must believe me dead."

Khisson's eyes narrowed. "So that you can strike him unaware."

"No. So I can travel through Akrasia unhindered."

"Akrasia is rampant with Ashen. Akrasia is lost. Our efforts are better spent here." Khisson hadn't actually risen from his chair yet. Bruche was very stiff and still inside Draken. Both their attention locked on the islander.

"I will use Akrasia to save Brîn. A sevennight, my lord. It's all I'm asking. Then you return to the Dragonstars a richer man with no one looking over your shoulder."

"If I agree, do I get to keep the Szirin?"

"Truth? You don't want her. She can be . . ." He tried to think of a charitable way to put it and gave up. "Annoying. But she can act as liaison between us."

Tyrolean eased forward. "Or I can."

Khisson looked at him. "Isn't that treachery?"

"I answer to the Night Lord. He outranks Ilumat."

"I understand your rank has been stripped."

This was news. "By Ilumat? Even my daughter outranks him. He has no calling nor right to strip me of my rank."

"And yet it's Kheinian servii guarding the Citadel now, is it not?"

Damn Ilumat. Draken's own fortress of servii was at Khein, gifted to him on the occasion of his rising to Night Lord, and brought here by lies, doubtless. But Commander Geffen Bodlean was loyal to Draken, had been since the war at Auwaer. "We both know where we stand and I've made my intentions plain. What I don't have is an answer from you. Rest assured, there are many other bloodlords who are happy to take Ilumat's coin and will cause me far less trouble."

"As you say. It makes a man wonder why you approached me."

"Ilumat is young. He is not stupid. He knows he won't be accepted easily by the Brînians. He knows of the resentment here against Akrasia. He knows despite my heritage most Brînians will rally behind me rather than a pureblood Akrasian. I have saved this city twice now, as well as Auwaer."

"The Palisade has fallen, rumors claim the city is worse than Reschan for crime, and you still haven't answered my question."

"If some bloodlord previously loyal to me brings him evidence of my assassination, doubt will fester. But you have a vendetta against me, one that is known to my House, to many Brînians. A ready few can advise Ilumat of your hatred for me. He will fair believe I'm dead if you're the one who tells him you killed me."

"And if you don't achieve the throne? If you fail?"

"Then I will be dead and you will have your reward in satisfaction."

Khisson searched his face. "You aren't quite the man I expected you to be."

"You aren't the first to say it. Are you in?"

A beat. Two. Then a nod. "Aye. I'm in. How shall we start?"

Behind Khisson, Trul's mouth stretched into a feral, broken grin. Draken wasn't sure whether to be pleased with the ghost's approval or wary of it. "With a deal of blood. Await my word."

Khisson inclined his head. "As you wish, Khel Szi."

◆ ◆ ◆

Aarinnaie's mean little bolt-hole was thick with Khissons, stinking of ale and sweat and damp leather. Khisson himself leaned by the door, hand resting on his sword. His presence was welcome as it seemed to keep the others subdued.

"That didn't take long," Draken said.

Khisson gave a slight bow of his head. "You are dealing with professionals."

Aarinnaie leaned opposite and apart from the others, arms crossed over her chest, weapons in plain view, her face guarded. The Khissons avoided her. She pushed off the wall to stand upright when Draken entered.

I don't like them knowing where you're staying.

So we find another place. Draken strode through them. They parted, giving him a path to the prisoner.

An escort was bound and wedged into the corner by the fireplace. Her greying hair hung over her face but she dragged her head up to look at the newcomer with bleary, bruised eyes. A thick gag bound her mouth, stretching it wide. She blinked rapidly up at him and worked her jaw.

Professionals indeed. As asked, they had brought him Commander Bodlean, of Khein fortress. A woman who answered directly to him. Or had, before Ilumat had stolen her.

Draken swore softly. "Geffen."

"She gave some resistance, Khel Szi." Khisson drew up to his elbow. "But she's sound."

"If a bit drunk," said one of Khisson's men. He had scratches on his face and neck. The others chuckled and nudged him.

Not too drunk, then.

"Be off. I'll seek you tomorrow," Draken said.

"You know where to find me?" Khisson asked.

"Lanehouse on Sea Road. Red door."

Khisson dipped his chin. "You have been watching me, Khel Szi. I am honored to have earned your attention."

Geffen's eyes widened. Not too drunk at all, then. She knew how dangerous it was for her to have heard that, for her to have her recognition of Draken confirmed.

"Your lodgings are not subtle and it is not for your honor I watch you." Half-drunk himself, he'd lost what little patience he had for false pleasantries. Khisson grunted but didn't make anything of it. Truth, with his sort there might be a payback later, but he could deal with it then. He waited until they all filed out before adding,

"Unbind her, Aarin, and let's see what she has to say. And light a fire, would you? Cold as a slaver's hold in here."

Tyrolean had scrounged a couple of benches from the pile of furniture to put on either side of the lopsided table. It rocked and thumped when Draken leaned his arm on it. Draken looked about, pried a bit of rock from the fireplace, and wedged it under the offending leg. He turned to find Geffen kneeling at the other side of the table.

He sat down across from her, easing down, not hiding his aches. Besides his knee, now his hip was stiff and sore. "Rise and join me at table. I'm sorry I've no wine to offer you."

She lifted her chin and studied him. One eye watered from the beating she'd taken; the whites were bruised and bloodshot, the black tattooed liner torn and crusted in blood. She lifted her hand, slow as if to indicate no bad intent, to wipe away the tears. She winced as her glove hit the tender skin. "You don't look the same as before, Your Highness."

"I don't imagine I do. How did you come to be here, Commander?"

"They captured me on my way to my lodging after—"

"I mean in Brîn."

"I was on patrol at Auwaer after the battle with the Ashen, and—"

"With a third of my Kheinians, if I recall."

"Aye, Your Highness. We were culled from cohorts at the front to come here."

"And the other two-thirds?"

"Some hundreds are at Khein. Baywatch, my lord. And in the Moonling woods . . . at the front." She hesitated.

"This is an interrogation, Commander," he reminded her. "You may speed things up by speaking freely."

"Odd goings there, rumors tell. Rumor has it Moonlings are afoot. Ready to join the war."

Oh. That was all. Right now Moonlings were the least of his worries. "Doubtless. How detailed were your recent orders?"

Her shoulders slipped down a notch, her darting gaze gave way to a regular pattern of blinking. "At first, only march out. Speculation all over the ranks, my lord. But Il . . . *Lord* Ilumat's Escorts didn't give us much. We marched hard to Crossroads, or where it had been. I thought it must be an Ashen attack."

Draken tensed. The Crossroads Inn had burned under his watch. Good people had died that day.

Not knowing why they marched is damned convenient.

Draken grunted his agreement with Bruche. Geffen took it as permission to continue. "Lord Ilumat met us then, talked to us himself. He said you're sundry, Your Highness."

A long pause. "Did he now." There wasn't enough air behind his words. Surely she noticed.

"He said you stole Brîn by trickery and banes, that you seduced the Queen and killed her. That you brought the Ashen here when you went to Monoea."

"So I'm a traitor." *That* was something not making the tavern rounds.

Softer: "Worse, Your Highness. An impostor."

"And what is the general consensus among your servii who came to Brîn?"

"Orders is orders, Your Highness."

"Not what I'm asking."

Her nostrils flared as she drew in a breath. "None like the Queen's seal and Khellian's sword in the hands of a sundry, my lord. Some never liked them in the hands of the Brînian Prince anyway. Ilumat and your heritage makes it fair convenient to discount you entirely, my lord. It's easier to hate someone when the powerful give you permission."

My lord. She was falling into her habitual form of more friendly address. A promising sign. "Any servii dare to argue with Ilumat?"

Her gaze dropped. "Two deserters."

"What happened to them?" Tyrolean asked.

"Hunted, hung, and bled out. They made us watch them 'til they died. Took half a day. Then we were marched hard to Brîn to make up the time."

Time? Draken frowned. What was a day or two? He hadn't had any plans himself that would affect the attack. Unless they thought runners would warn Brîn. Or someone else.

Aarinnaie had the same curiosity. "Trying to beat the worst of Frostfall? Some Gadye tell them a storm is coming?"

Geffen's eyes rolled toward her. "No, we were meeting a company here."

Draken shook his head. "The slaves who attacked the Citadel."

"Aye. We had more weapons for them."

He stared at her, leaned forward, blew out the candle on the table, and pulled his mask down. "What else? Did you see anything? Hear anything? You're commander at Khein. You ought to know something."

"Nothing, Your Highness."

He liked to think she was being forthright, which proved her potential loyalty to him. But with Aarinnaie in plain view with her knives and Tyrolean leaning against the hearth, he couldn't give her that much credit without her proving herself. He tipped his head toward Ty. "Do you remember who he is?"

She straightened, gave Tyrolean a nod. "First Captain Tyrolean, Royal Escorts."

Tyrolean spoke quietly. "Ilumat hasn't titled himself King?"

"Regent, my lord. Until things are settled, whatever that means. Heard it from his own self. Keeping tight discipline on us in the meantime."

That much was truth. Aarinnaie had been watching. The taverns should have been full of rowdy Akrasian servii fresh off the warfront, and maybe newly freed slaves, but they weren't. The new occupiers patrolled constantly, causing little mischief beyond helping themselves to lodging and food, and the Citadel was locked up tighter than a pirate akhanar's ale cask. Not that anyone would want to cross the mess of heads on the wall. "You got leave this night."

"I was disciplining a servii. Stopped for a drink after." A slight smile, a hint of Geffen's typical wryness. "Shouldn't have done."

"What are Ilumat's plans? Servii gossip. Rumors. Confirmed or not. I want it all."

She looked down at her lap.

"Geffen, I don't believe you've been formerly introduced to my sister, Aarinnaie Szirin. She has a fondness for quick knife work, which suits my needs as I am not a patient man."

Geffen's head turned with a twitch. Her throat moved with a hard swallow. Aarinnaie took a step forward, though she made no move toward her knives.

"You say Ilumat marched you from the front and now calls himself regent. You say he meant to meet a company of slaves here. Those actions have come to pass," Tyrolean reminded her calmly. "What else has he done? Is going to do?"

Her lips tightened. "He's holding a triumph processional."

Right. Again, nothing he hadn't heard or deduced. "When?"

"Khellian's full night."

Two nights hence. That didn't give them a great deal of time. He decided to test her. "There's no announcements, no criers, nothing posted."

"I think." She swallowed. Her eyes darted between them. "I think he's trying to head off trouble. Tomorrow the tale-tellers will be told. Scrolls pinned 'round. Some few nobles will be invited to the Citadel to feast."

Right. Keeping it quiet so the Brînians don't realize the Monoeans are going to take the city. They'd do a controlled announcement that left no time to dodge the axe aimed at Brîn's neck. With Ilumat the Regent on the dais, sitting in Draken's throne. Or maybe by then some Monoean would sit it. Not the priest. Another, important Landed perhaps. What he wouldn't have given to have killed all the Ashen when he was in Monoea, but the warships had already sailed. A burning itch crawled up his spine. The nearly insurmountable urge to move and fight roared through him—

Draken. You aren't finished here.

Truls emerged from the shadows to peer sightlessly at him, head tipped. Geffen's face paled, enough maybe she could feel his chill. Or maybe it was Draken's scowl.

He cleared his throat, eyeing the ghost and then Geffen. "And after the procession. After Ilumat officially 'takes the city.' What then?"

Geffen shrank back. "Your daughter. Is she living, Your Highness?"

Draken fell very still. "What about her?"

Geffen made a noise between a whimper and grunt. Her voice trembled. "Th-they must have found her, if they're announcing the triumph tomorrow."

"Is she dead?" Tyrolean pushed from the wall and strode closer. By the ghost, though he didn't seem to notice. How could the others not sense his crawling presence? "Is that what you're not wanting to say? They've assassinated the Princess?"

"No, Captain . . . Your Highness. Not that." Her eyes darted and settled somewhere on the empty air beside Draken, empty but for the ghost she couldn't see. "Ilumat is going to give her to the Monoeans. A trade for peace."

CHAPTER TEN

"You aren't being the least bit reasonable," Aarinnaie said. "It's not as if they can get to her." At Eidola, she meant, though she was smart enough not to mention Sikyra nor the Mance city up the nearby mountains in front of Geffen.

Draken didn't pause his pacing to look at his sister, who sounded angry enough to stomp her foot. Or slap him on the backside with his own sword; he wasn't sure which.

"We don't know that for certain." He never should have given Sikyra over to Osias. "This is Ilumat's doing, and his alone. No one else stands to gain from her death like he does. He'll have to die."

"Getting to him will be difficult," Geffen said. "Impossible."

"Tell me where he'll be and when."

She shook her head. "I'm not privy to his plans. But he's very well protected."

Draken snapped, his voice harsh, his hand on his sword. "You're meant to tell me this, aren't you? To use Sikyra as bait."

Paranoia will not serve you, Draken.

It's not paranoia if it's truth.

"No! You abducted me, remember?" Geffen shook her head violently. "Your Highness, you cannot go after Ilumat. You must not. They'll capture you."

Draken considered her, eyes narrowed. "Do you know for certain they have her?"

"I know he said he would have the triumph when he could turn her over to the Ashen, Your Highness. That I heard myself."

"Listen to the Commander, Drae," Aarinnaie said. "You'll never get close enough to kill him."

"And if he has Sikyra I'm supposed to sit back and do nothing?"

Aarinnaie's lips pressed into a thin line.

"I can't do that. I won't. Change of plan. We need to get to the triumph."

♦ ♦ ♦

Geffen told him all she knew, Draken was certain of it. Her good faith kept him from killing her outright and made him burn with shame at leaving her bound and gagged in the mean little room. But they couldn't spare someone to watch her. He certainly couldn't tell her there was a chance they all would die this day and she would never be found and freed in that case, not before her body rotted and stank enough for some local to investigate when warmer weather came.

"I'll give one of Khisson's men orders to free you by nightfall."

"Where are you going? What are you doing?"

Draken tightened the cords around her wrist and tied her to the iron firewood grate. It was bolted to the stone and held her fast.

"You know I'm loyal to you, Your Highness. I'll swear again. Anything. Don't leave me here. Please."

He gagged her, none too tightly, but enough to muffle her protests.

"Gods willing we meet again, you can swear to me then."

Her breath whined around the gag and her hollow stare drilled holes in his back. But this was for the people. And his daughter, because she was the rightful Queen. None of which filled the gaping hole his baby daughter had left inside him, the terror gripping his heart that Ilumat had her already, or the guilt at leaving Geffen at risk of dying such an ignoble death.

Brinian ways really have dug their claws into you. Bruche sounded impressed.

I don't know anyone of any race who finds starving to death, bound and helpless, a noble way to die.

The storm wind on Draken's cheeks filtered through his mask and made his eyes water, but the light was dim from the low-slung clouds and it felt oddly freeing to pass though Brîn without people staring at him because he was Khel Szi. Some few did look his way, but that might be his staff and pretended blindness. His likeness to his old self was changed enough to protect him from anything more than mild speculation.

Aarinnaie kept to his side, sleek and treacherous as a horned panther, pretending to guide him. She had her hair and neck covered with a scarf against the cold. Her breath came in quick grey puffs the breeze whisked away.

Tyrolean, swords on his belt and wrapped to conceal the distinctive hilts, moved in the same direction a little ahead and across the road. The Captain had taken orders to hold back from the attempt to kill Ilumat with his usual stoic obedience. They needed to hold him in reserve.

I already miss those swords of his, Bruche said.

I won't have him killing his own people, Draken replied.

Your people, too, Prince.

It was far too late to worry about him killing anyone. And who knew where things would stand when all the blood dried? Draken had already begged one known enemy for help. He had no illusions that Khisson was the only person in Brîn who wanted him dead. Favors could be called in even if he did achieve the throne again, leaving everyone close to him under threat. Khisson could demand more favors in exchange for silence and alliance. Some disgruntled Akrasian lord could accuse Tyrolean of treason if he had Akrasian blood on his sword.

Worry about getting the throne and city first, then worry about your friends.

Tyrolean looked at him from across the market, brows creased. Even in a plain homespun shirt he moved like a soldier. People would mark him as one of Ilumat's Escorts. Draken thought, hoped, he had the good sense to disappear when the attack started, futile as that was.

Half a dozen Khissons, the ones who were best with a bow, were to take position atop buildings. The rest, who numbered fifteen, would scatter across in the market in pairs and threes, placed to wait for the procession to pass by and make their move. One of Khisson's men would give the signal to be in position by dropping a rough celebratory banner down the façade on the building nearest where the procession would enter. That building was opposite from where he and Aarinnaie entered and remained unadorned.

The main cobbled thoroughfare open to carters and horses and foot traffic wound through hard-packed dirt patches where stall tents were usually set. People milled everywhere, obscuring the roadway. In this crowd the Akrasian procession might take quite a while to work their way through. Aarinnaie tugged his arm, nodding to a couple of Akrasian servii standing at the perimeter of the market. As he started looking, he found more. Many more, and not all in uniform.

"Ilumat isn't taking any chances," he replied.

His gaze kept straying toward the building where the signal would display, though Ilumat's procession hadn't yet appeared. There weren't anything like enough Khissons to stage a proper disruption in a gathering this size. He'd anticipated dozens of servii guards, not three hundred or more. He'd hoped the average Brînian would be more loyal to their royals, and stage, if not active protests, a silent one by not attending this farce of a triumph.

He slowed as they reached the center of Korde Market, partly because of the throngs of people and partly to make a good study of the area. It seemed half the city had come out to see this new lord who decreed Brîn reconquered by the Kingdom that already controlled it. Despite prejudice, fury over the coup, and lack of trust, no one seemed to be turning down Ilumat's wine. Draken couldn't recall ever seeing so many tapped barrels in one place, even in Sevenfel when Monoea had driven Akrasia from their shores. Perhaps Ilumat had found Draken's coffers after all. He'd certainly found his wine.

Fresh ribbons and conservatory flowers swagged railings like it was Sohalia Night. Wealthy merchants who lived in the buildings footed by their shops gathered on the balconies to look down on the festivities and debate whether the new arse sitting the throne at the Citadel would help or hinder trade. Boisterous, tense opinions drifted down.

Draken stalled as he reached a rope fence surrounding a cleared area. Stern servii placed every few steps guarded a few men still assembling a stage out of crate-wood. Truls appeared, filtering from the crowd to materialize within the ropes. He watched the men with obvious curiosity.

Speeches. Ilumat loves the sound of his own voice.

Draken nodded, agreeing with Bruche. That must be it. Not that anyone would hear him in this crowd.

Some few Akrasian bowmen crouched on rooftops, arrows on strings. Khissons would have to kill them to take their place. He wanted to go after Ilumat, to kill him. But the damned archers would bring any attackers down, certainly would if they were Kheinian. They were woodland soldiers, among the best bows in Akrasia.

"We needed more people on rooftops to take out the archers." He frowned as he spoke lowly to Aarinnaie. "I underestimated this crowd." And Ilumat's security efforts. Now he suspected many of the sundry in the crowd would turn on their masters if there were riot or rebellion.

He lowered his voice further and leaned toward Aarinnaie. "This is hopeless. No one can get close enough to him in this, especially once he gets to the stage."

"I will do it," Aarinnaie said with a sidelong glance. "I can get to him and get out again, too." Her body was tight, her face set into sharp lines.

Draken shook his head. "Not without getting shot."

"The Khissons will be on the rooftops soon, if they aren't already," she said. "They can cover me."

"What's to say they didn't look at this madness and reconsider? We may be alone here."

"Even so, you're right."

He couldn't joke. "About?"

She looked up into his face, and he looked at her, forgetting he wasn't supposed to be able to see. Her mouth pressed into a determined line and her chin jutted upward, but the sprigs of curls escaping her scarf trembled. "We can't let him have her."

He wished Truls, transparent in daylight as steam against a cloud, could put himself to use in killing Ilumat. He leaned down to speak in her ear, "If anyone can kill him, it's you. I know it. But I don't like it."

Aarinnaie swallowed and nodded, pulled away from him.

"Aarin," he said, letting his hand fall to his side. "I—"

"You'll see me soon," she said over her shoulder and melted into the crowd, falling away toward the middle of the market, slipping between revelers, barely touching anyone, largely unnoticed. His heart tugged at her childlike size. Bruche reminded him she'd saved his life more than once. Still, a discomfiting chill settled in his bones.

He kept moving, people parting for his breadth and tapping staff as soon as heads swiveled his way. The crowd thinned as he backed away from the stage, leaving more space to move about. He'd totally lost sight of Aarinnaie and didn't try to look, keeping cognizant that he was supposed to be blind.

Impatience began to flow through the crowd despite the wine. Gusts of wind tested nerves. The sky darkened as a low bank of clouds churned overhead. He looked for Truls. The ghost-Mance was near, slipping between and through people. A strange feeling of remembrance came over Draken. The night he'd killed Truls a sudden storm had rolled in. The Eros had risen and the moons turned blood red. He couldn't help casting a glance at the sky but no moons appeared, of course. This day the clouds refused to reveal the Eyes.

A low rumble rose through the people, sweeping from the narrow end. He turned toward the sound. No banner fell from the rooftop yet, so perhaps the procession hadn't passed by it. He scanned the building tops. Many had facades that made a sort of battlement to provide cover for a bowman. Some few had actual terraces, made for the gatherings that filled them. Most were empty, though he thought he caught a flitter of a shape on a couple. There, for certain. An archer dropping into position, a dark head peeking up.

About bloody time a Khisson turned up.

Anxiety grew with the storm. Mutterings swept through the crowd, broken by the rising gale rattling signs and rustling clothes. The air was damp, icy. Pickbirds flitted over the buildings. A poor omen, if one believed in such things. Over the tops of most of the heads Draken could see the surge of organized activity at the other end of the market. The procession gradually materialized as the crowd parted, pushed back by servii. Horses kept in near perfect step, green ribbons in their manes, cloaks of the Escorts fluttering. Armor and hair gleamed Akrasian black, dozens of heads perfectly combed and coifed, outlined eyes seeming distorted and too large at a distance.

The royal sigil embroidered in golden thread adorned the front of Ilumat's green tunic. That wasn't unusual; all Royal Escorts wore the royal sigil. But he also wore a bloody crown of sorts. Not a royal piece Draken had ever seen, but a jeweled band just the same. He had a hand up, waving, a benevolent smile playing on his lips.

Draken's hand tightened on his staff, wishing for a bow, but armor protected Ilumat's vulnerability to arrows. Ilumat was not a large man and he looked bulkier than usual. An arrow through the eye would take him down, but he wasn't at the right angle, he kept twisting his head from side to side, the wind toyed with everything in its path, and the cobbles would lead him even further astray of Draken's position.

The press of people toward the procession was convenient in that it gave Draken more cover. He couldn't help looking for Aarinnaie but she would be hidden among the taller people anyway. If he could reach the procession first he might have a decent chance at distracting them for her benefit. He could keep the guards busy with his sword while she plied her ugly trade on Ilumat. Bruche wordlessly wondered how many Escorts she'd have to kill to get to him. Draken judged it not so many; he paraded in a line only three abreast.

But where are the damned Khissons?

A storm-shadow slid over the market. Several faces lifted as cloaks flapped. The racket of the Brînian voices drowned out the shouts of the Escorts, though their mouths moved and their arms waved. Ilumat had enough sense to tell them not to draw their blades, or the horsemarshal did. They eased away from Draken, but not anything like as quickly as he parted the crowd and strode toward them. Voices of protest faded in his wake. Ilumat still had his arm up, but his face was pinched, pale. Draken felt another surge of satisfaction, until the lord turned his head and his attention locked on someone close by him.

Ilumat's lips gaped and then he shouted: a clear, high wordless alarm that pierced the noise on the street.

Aarinnaie. It had to be. Draken cursed and shoved ahead harder as the crowd shifted and turned like eddies at a river mouth. This time people did protest his passage; a woman he pushed aside cried out as someone else stumbled into her. He achieved the little pocket of free ground she left and drew his sword. The space grew as people backed away from him. Draken strained to see past them, past the parade. He saw not one mask. Were the Khissons coming from behind? Escorts converged on the other side of the procession line, which broke and curved as horses skittered across the cobbles. He kept moving but couldn't see,

until the flash of a Escort's sword caught his eye. Truls flitted ahead, weaving
through the throng, which was frantically backing away from the procession.
His sword heated in his hand. He wanted blood. Ilumat's blood. If Aarinnaie
were harmed in any way—

Someone grabbed his shoulder and pulled him back. He spun, sword lifted.
A hand batted the flat, knocking it aside. Draken met Akrasian lined eyes, a
hard face. Black hair falling loose of a usually perfect tail.

"Come, Draken." Tyrolean tugged on his shoulder.

"But Aarin—"

"Aye, Aarin. We must go from here."

He stood firm. "Where are the bloody Khissons?" There wasn't a mask in sight.
No flying arrows. No crowds screaming from a dozen swordsmen descending
upon the Akrasian procession. Just nervous, loud chatter around them.

"I don't know—"

"They agreed, damn them."

Draken. Hush now before they hear you. Draken chilled to his core—Bruche,
taking a measure of control to lead him out. "No."

Tyrolean, silent, firm, took hold of his sword and pulled it from Draken's grip.
His other hand tangled in the buckles of Draken's bracer so Draken couldn't break
free without twisting and maybe breaking his friend's fingers. Tyrolean tugged him
away from the tightening crowd around the parade. Bruche worked in tandem with
Tyrolean, forcing Draken's legs into motion from inside his body. Draken's jaw set
and his neck heated. He could twist his head around to look as they propelled him
away from the procession—he could do that much. The people nearby must have
believed Tyrolean one of Ilumat's Escorts for they parted readily enough. Did he
imagine the hissing whispers in his wake: *Khel Szi Khel Szi . . .*

Close enough. You must free yourself of this place before you're noticed.

But Aarinnaie—

You're no use to her imprisoned, or with your head on a spike on the Citadel wall.

The anticipated panic rose up then, wordless cries and shouts. Brînians surged
in all directions. Draken kept twisting to see and stumbled over Tyrolean's heels.
Bruche cursed. *Watch where you're going.* Draken paid him no mind. A servii
tumbled from a nearby rooftop; a Khisson in black and a mask rose behind
him. *About bloody time.* Draken stalled and Tyrolean cursed low as his fingers
twisted in his bracer buckle. He pulled his hand free of the bracer, speaking in
an earnest whisper. "You can't help them now. Let them do their work."

Faces turned toward them. Someone squinted. ". . . Khel Szi?"

Draken turned his head toward the voice; it had been his name too long
to disregard without effort, and he was distracted. A youngish Brînian with

his arm around a woman gaped at him. Dark eyes met his. Draken couldn't summon a denial. The man spoke. "It's him. I seen him at—" Voices clamored, drowning him out. Hands glided over his skin and armor, as if to confirm he was real.

"*Out*—I need out." He searched their faces for someone who would help him.

He sought any gap that might provide escape. But the people closed on him; hands gripped him. More cries rose up, further back in the crowd as the realization of his presence spread.

Tyrolean cursed and grabbed for Draken but people wedged in between them, forcing him back. Draken swung his fists but there wasn't enough room to get momentum. He drew only a few grunts. Weight pounded on his shoulders, his back. He used all his bulk to shove bodily toward Tyrolean, who kept shifting, ever out of reach. Bruche filled Draken's core with cold, ready to spring to action, but even their combined strength couldn't move all these people as they pressed in on him,

He lifted his chin, trying to get air into his chest. The sky blackened and churned with storm. He caught a flash of blade over the heads of the crowd— no. A faint glow against the shadows, shining in Tyrolean's direction. Bruche filled his legs and moved, heaving against the weight of citizenry. Days of inaction and not enough food took their toll. Pain knifed up the back of Draken's legs as his muscles strained. His heart thudded against his ribs. His bad knee buckled and he stumbled to the cobbles.

Draken, up. UP—

Whispers filled his head, hissing wet and cold along the back of his neck. Someone screamed, cut off by a gaping silence. The pressure eased. Magic. Time had stopped. The Abeyance—

No. They were still moving. The churning air chilled and he drew the thick scent of death into his lungs. Misty shapes of ghosts, more than just Truls, rushed through the people to settle around Draken. Ice settled his marrow and ached in his bones. No amount of violent trembling would shake it loose. His stomach churned at the reek of death. Gasping, people shied away, back. Bruche pushed up to see, turned Draken's head, forced his body toward Tyrolean. The cold ghosts surrounded him, parting the crowd.

The Captain waited, his face, lips grey as stained snow, eyes black as a lifeless painted icon. Seaborn glowed faintly in his hand, flared as Draken drew closer. It clattered to the cobbles as Tyrolean cursed, shaking his hand as if burned. Draken darted forward, spurred by Bruche, and swept up the sword.

Bruche took advantage of the distraction and pushed forward through the loosening outlying crowd. He turned Draken's head, searching a means of escape. Tyrolean had already pushed ahead, leaving several dozen people between them. His way was as good as any. Draken cursed and picked up the pace, shoving between people. Still, people strained their necks to see what these two men moving with purpose were about, especially the blindfolded one. Draken resisted the continual urge to turn back. Tyrolean and Bruche were right. Aarinnaie was likely captured. Maybe dead. There was no point in looking. He could only hope the Khissons on the rooftops saw enough to report her situation to him.

Khisson appeared before him, parting the crowd. He was a big man, his face contorted in a growl. Draken eased a breath. Between the two of them, they'd be able—

The blade came out of nowhere, flashing a perfect reflection of rooftops and sky at him before slicing into the tender skin under his jaw. It sank deep, bringing with it agony so consuming it made his head spin. He opened his mouth to scream and it spilled blood in a hot torrent down his chest. Draken succumbed to a weak, gagging cough as his knees crumpled. His head slammed hard against the cobbles and day closed into darkness.

CHAPTER ELEVEN

Draken's eyes fluttered and he shifted. His body snarled in protest, especially his bad shoulder, which he lay on, and the subsequent prickling of needles in his arm. His surroundings slowly registered. The canvas-clad side rail of a cot rested beyond his curled fingers. Aarinnaie's bolt-hole, dim from shuttered windows and dusty walls. He turned his head and groaned. His neck was stiff and sore. Tyrolean moved closer and helped him roll over, then up to a sit.

"All right, then?" Tyrolean kept his hand on Draken's shoulder. His sore one, which was worse than usual.

He shrugged him off, fighting to remember what had happened. A flash of blade. Khisson's ugly face. His hand went involuntarily to his throat. The skin under his chin was smooth but the muscles felt as if he'd slept wrong.

"Aye, sorry about that," Khisson said, sounding not sorry at all.

Draken lifted his head. Truls floated behind the bloodlord.

"You tried to *actually* kill me," Draken growled. Albeit not very fiercely because his throat wasn't putting much voice behind it.

"As soon as I realized people recognized you, I knew they had to see you dead."

It is a point he's making, truth. You enticed him with your death.

I enticed him with favors and coin. Draken growled and reached across his chest to loosen the straps on his mail. He needed it off. It was glued to his gambeson, which was glued to his skin with blood and sweat. Tyrolean brushed his hand away and undid the buckles for him.

"Sword?" Draken whispered.

Tyrolean gestured with his chin. It rested on the table in its battered scabbard.

Geffen had freed herself from her corner while they were gone, had managed to break the leash binding her to the heavy stand filled with logs, and scooted to the middle of the room. She lay on her side and watched them, muffled by the gag stuffed in her mouth and tied behind her head. Her arms were still secured and tied to her ankles. No chance of her getting out. Draken thought of her dying like that, should he have not returned. Worse than claw marks inside a cistern.

"Unbind her." He coughed. Blood droplets splattered his sleeve. It cleared his voice somewhat. He looked up at Khisson, then at Tyrolean. "Aarinnaie?"

Both shook their heads.

"When you're able we'll go to meet my men. I had some few with a vantage to see the Szirin's position." Khisson moved to untie Geffen, his big hands gentle.

As soon as she was able, she shook free of her ropes and rose, backing away from the bloodlord. Her fingers worked at the gag in her mouth and yanked it free. "Does this mean I can go?"

"No. You've seen me alive." There might be an advantage in her somewhere if Draken could make his mind capture the possibilities.

Khisson stared at her. Bruche chuckled low. *And no wonder. She moves like a fighter and could probably give him fair challenge.*

Aye, he's traditional bloodlord all right. Though female Brînian warriors weren't unheard of, traditionally women were regarded as useful for things other than fighting. But then, Khisson hadn't spent much time with Aarinnaie, and Draken would lay coin he'd not met enough Escorts to give the females among them enough credit for skill and training.

He looked at Khisson. "You took a fair risk. They could have captured me, and I wouldn't have been able to fight it."

"I saved you," Khisson growled. "The crowd had blood in mind and no mistake. Giving them what they wanted was a good distraction."

"How did you get my body out of there?"

"Oddest thing. Ground leapt like the very gods had us in a spice shaker. People seemed to lose interest in you after that."

Tyrolean helped Draken off with his chainmail—it took a deal of effort not to cry out as the weight tugged on his shoulder and neck—and dropped it onto the floor in a clanking heap at Geffen's feet. "There's water in the bucket. Rags there. Clean that."

She blinked at him. His tone brooked no disagreement, but she didn't hide her scowl as she dragged the mail to the water buckets.

Not up to the usual standard. Needs discipline, aye?

She'd been tied up for the better part of the day. Draken was willing to give her some leeway. He turned his attention to Khisson. "Had I woken in my own dungeon I might not be so conciliatory."

"The rumors proved true, but it took you fair long to recover."

"You cut a life vein. All the blood drained out of my head." Truth, he still felt woozy. He pulled Elena's pendant from round his neck. The chain was also crusted with blood.

Tyrolean took it and laid it next to the sword. "The people thought the shaking was the gods' displeasure."

"The people might be right, what with my being still alive." That brought up an interesting thought when twisted back on itself. Regardless, it could be damned useful if the people thought the gods were displeased with Draken dying. Later, after the usefulness of being thought dead had run out. He stripped off his gambeson, stiff from its soaking, and tossed it on the floor near the fireplace. It wasn't suitable for anything but burning. Then he stilled as the world spun slowly around him. His stomach twisted.

"Horses spooked," Tyrolean said. "The crowd panicked. Perhaps it gave the Princess a chance at escape."

Draken bent over, arm on his knee, and rubbed his hand over his face. Tyrolean carried over a bucket and set it at his feet. He splashed himself and scrubbed with the rag, splattering water everywhere and not caring. It diluted the dried blood and ran in rusty rivulets down his skin.

"I should go," Khisson said. "There are clothes for you since I ruined yours. I'll see you soon, Khel Szi."

Draken nodded. He didn't speak against until well after Khisson left. Scrubbing himself clean took a while. "How long was I out?"

"Long enough." Tyrolean sat on the cot opposite. "Your Highness . . ."

"I assume you have something to tell me I don't want to hear."

"I have something to tell you I don't want Khisson to hear. I went back to Korde Square."

Draken grunted, kept scrubbing. "You didn't wait for my recovery?"

"You were in the gods' hands, not mine."

"There's a comforting thought."

"However you feel about the gods, my presence certainly wouldn't assure you'd awaken. I had only a short time to find out what happened to the Princess."

Why *had* it taken him so bloody long to regain consciousness? He'd had more grievous injuries than his throat slit—bad enough once to break apart a ship and another to bring down the magical Palisade around Auwaer. But he just gave Tyrolean a curt nod to continue.

"She wasn't there—as well, the entire procession had disbanded. But the crowd spoke of her, and you."

"Fools all, out with it. What did they say?"

"She was taken away by Ilumat's Escorts—alive. That's as much as I could learn."
Silence.

She is worth more alive.

Draken grunted in response to Bruche. "If she's alive we have to get her out of there."

"Not a good idea, Your Highness."

"I still must see for myself." Draken gazed at Geffen, wondering what in Eidola he was going to do with her. She was scrubbing hard, glanced up. The scrubbing slowed. "If they kill her, they'll display her body."

Bring her. She could be useful.

In what way? She rubbed ineffectually at the chainmail. Water dripped everywhere, leaving a spreading brackish stain on the wood floor. It needed oiling or it would quickly rust.

As a bribe? I don't know. Just a feeling.

Draken suppressed a groan, though he was getting the same feeling. "Geffen."

Her eyes darted between them, the whites bright halos around the dark irises.

"Is there any possibility of your *not* betraying me at your earliest opportunity?"

Her jaw tightened. "I'm following orders."

"Whose? Certainly not mine. Not the Captain's. I've never seen such a poor job at cleaning armor."

"You don't need this mail. Magic keeps you alive." Her hands fisted around the rag, wringing pink water to drip onto the wood.

"This you knew."

"Ilumat is right about you."

"Aye? He is, is he? And what does he say of me?"

Her teeth gritted and her lips paled. She shook her head.

"I am the Night Lord and Prince of Brîn. No upstart Akrasian lord is going to change that fact."

Geffen picked up the bucket and heaved it toward them. Cold water splashed across the floor and cot. Tyrolean had to duck. Geffen darted for the door. Draken shoved into motion, his hurts biting into him. Tyrolean was faster, blocking the door. Draken caught her and hauled her back. She fought and emitted a rough scream. He clapped his hand over her mouth.

She bit him, hard. He jerked his hand away with a curse.

Geffen spat blood. "Let me go!"

"You're lucky I don't kill you." A tremor ran through the old building as the broken skin on his hand healed.

"Do it." She fought him more, and with skill, but he was stronger. "Do it! Coward!"

"SIT." He shoved her at the cot. The floor was wet, which made her slip awkwardly, but she got her hands beneath her. She spun to come at him again, but he stepped forward and pushed her down, his hands dwarfing her shoulders.

"Kill me."

He stared down at her, breathing hard. He was sorely tempted. The strain on his shoulder made him curse with pain. "Tell me why I shouldn't, Tyrolean."

"She is one of yours. Insubordinate at the moment, but she answers to you. Killing her without a trial is a betrayal of your lordship over her."

Draken's lip curled. "Such responsibility is not my favorite gift from the gods. But you . . ." His eyes narrowed at Geffen. "Your sort are why I do not reject it altogether. You are confused, but you must not fight the lord the Queen assigned you."

"The Queen is dead."

The words made him weary. Or maybe it was this sharp burst of activity so soon after dying. He released her and stepped back, thinking he could hardly tell her the ghost-Mance who had been right about other things insisted Elena lived. "Aye, she may be, but her reign lives on through me. Through her daughter Sikyra. Ilumat has a foothold, but he will slip. I'll be ready with Khellian's blade when he does. I have no wish to kill you. I'll return you to the Citadel if you wish it, no harm. But it will be a short and bloody stay."

She huffed up at him, nostrils flared. Blood—his blood—stained her pale bottom lip. Her tongue came out to wipe it off and her nose wrinkled. "Threats from sundry bastards don't frighten me."

Sundry bastard . . . He fell very still. She glared at him but some of the stiffness fell away from her.

"I am both. It is truth."

Maybe it was his low voice against the stillness of the room. Or the chill of dwelling ghosts easing from the shadows. She dropped her gaze.

Tyrolean sighed and crossed his arms over his chest.

She dared to search his face. He stared back, jaw set. She blinked first. "Ilumat said the Queen didn't know the truth of you."

Ilumat? How in Khellian's name had *he* found out? His eyes narrowed. "Just who are you, Geffen?"

Geffen held her ground. "Did the Queen know you're sundry?"

"No. But I never did her . . ." *Harm*, he'd been about to say. *But for Seaborn plunging into her chest by his own hand, the sickening reek of blood spilling over her armor and gown, the sensation of his blade catching on bone. The feel of her alive and soft and warm in his arms.* He stumbled back to sit on a bench. "Any children between us would be mixed race. She knew that well enough and she still chose me."

He hated the defeat in his voice but there it was, just the same. This was a losing battle. Twice he'd lost a woman he'd loved. Thrice, if he counted Sikyra.

Geffen's jaw was set. More grey threaded her hair than it had when they'd first met. War tended to age soldiers beyond all reason. She said resentfully, "Even sundry, you're a better soldier, a better man, than Ilumat or any of the other puffed-up lords who—"

"Who died on the edges of Ashen swords in Seakeep. Ilumat is all that's left."

She bowed her head in thought. At last she rose and saluted him. "I don't like you or what you've done. But no one else can bring Akrasia out of this war intact. So I will pledge to you, still."

Draken stared, then inclined his head in return, and winced at the catch in his neck. "Good. I'm taking you back now. I need you with Ilumat in case fortune joins our paths again. I would know his ambitions and his allies."

"My lord—" Tyrolean began, but Draken gave a sharp shake of his head.

"No. It's not up to you, Captain. Gather everything. We won't come back to this place."

There was very little, a small pack of food, his knives and sword, spare bits of armor. His pouch with precious few coins and Sikyra's toy horse. Geffen watched as he tucked everything carefully away and dressed in the fresh clothes brought from Khisson. Geffen didn't offer to help and he didn't ask.

Things had calmed out on the street and an icy night was falling over the city. Geffen walked alongside them, silent. He took note of her stance, the way she moved. Chin up, lined eyes taking it all in. Graceful, arms at her sides in loose fists as if poised to fight. Solid capability harnessed every step, and she wasn't afraid to say what she thought. He was sorry to lose her.

She'll be more effective on the inside, closer to Ilumat.

Unless he works out she's loyal to me.

Aye, but no point in mourning lost arrows. You always seem to find more.

Draken's armor rubbed without the gambeson despite having put on his thickest shirt, which was wool and itchy on the skin. He resisted scratching and kept a cautious eye alongside the others. Faint light glowed in most windows, shuttered against the damp air, the sort that soon would turn to icy rain. There was a marked lack of people.

They walked quietly, Tyrolean offering no protest even when the dome of the Citadel came within clear view. Something in his tone must have stopped him from questioning, and it was just as well. Draken had made another decision he wouldn't like.

CHAPTER TWELVE

T hey entered a torch-lit lane leading to the main gates of the Citadel.
Mist glossed the bright dome, which captured errant moonlight filtered
by the clouds. Draken said, "Stay here with her. I'll go look at the gate
for Aarinnaie and be back."

"My lord, I beg of you. Let me go. Or let us learn her fate from the taletellers.
You're of no use to her or Brîn dead."

"I have no army, Tyrolean, no fortress at Khein, no Citadel or szi nêre, not
even a collection of pirates on a ship to call mine any longer. I don't know if
Elena is dead or alive or if Sikyra is safe. But I still have a sister, here within
Brîn. If Aarinnaie is on that wall, I need to see for myself. I owe her that much.
Besides, Khisson killed me, remember? No one notices the dead."

Tyrolean held a long moment before giving him a minuscule nod and took
Geffen's arm. "We'll release you when we get back."

She went meekly with him back into the shadows. Draken wondered if she'd
scream or otherwise try to draw attention.

I hope not. I rather like her.

"You like anything on two legs," Draken muttered.

The lane was quiet and he'd surely be noticed, but if he kept to the shadows
with his hood up perhaps no servii would give him trouble. The wall still bore
their ghastly trophies. Surely the stench would drive Ilumat to remove them, but
as it reached his lungs, he wondered how gruesomely cruel the lord meant to be.

Friends. Lieges. Szi nêre and chamberlains and secretaries and slaves. Every
face was known to him. He studied each until his heart twisted into a hard knot
and his throat quit threatening to expunge rising bile. Truls, absent for the walk
through the city, flitted forward to peer into the faces of the Akrasian servii
guarding the gates. Lined eyes darted. Their greens looked too bright against
the stone walls. Draken's thumb worried the loose flap of leather on his hilt.

He'd seen what he'd meant to see, though, which was a distinct lack of Aarin-naie's body on display. It was less than reassuring. He knew one place she wasn't. That left many horrible places she could be. He started to turn but two servii strode his way, calling out to him. No bows in their hands, though surely there were some atop the small tower flanking the gates. Still, they had no reason to shoot him in the back for simply appearing and leaving, and soon he'd be out of range for an arrow to pierce his armor. He strode away quickly; he knew Brîn better than any Escort and could find a place to hide.

"Hie! You!" Boots thudding softly against the cobbles. Chainmail jingled behind him. "Stop!"

He started to run, forcing his bad knee to bear his jarring weight, though this sort of thing could quickly lead to debilitating agony. He cursed the gods under his breath for giving him the magic to cure himself of new wounds while ignoring the old. His lungs seemed in good working order, though. But his knee locked and pain stabbed up his thigh. Another step, Bruche rushed to numb it with cold, but he stumbled and landed on the knee. He spat a curse: *"Atu Khellian trese!"*

In bloody Moneoan. He groaned and struggled to his feet.

Pretend not to know Arkasian, Bruche suggested.

"Who are you? Why are you lurking round the Citadel after curfew?"

As fortune would have it he'd been chased down by servii who could speak passable Brînish. So much for that.

"I didn't know there is a curfew. I just returned to Brîn tonight and heard tale the Akrasians had taken the Citadel. I wanted to see for myself."

Behind the servii, Truls flitted toward the Citadel.

Two sets of lined eyes narrowed. "Brîn has been locked down since we took it. No one has entered or left the city without the Regent's permission."

First rule of lying: death is in the details.

The one who hadn't been speaking drew his sword and said in Akrasian, "And breaking curfew is against the Regent's law. Disarm."

He could fight them off. He could kill them easily . . . or Bruche could. But maybe they knew something of Aarin. "Is the Szirin inside?"

"What would a ruddy pirate like you care about the Princess?"

He was willing to wager this servii wouldn't know a real pirate if one slapped him on the backside with a broadsword. "I'm no pirate," he growled, drawing his own blade. "Insult me again and I'll show you your own insides."

Truls rushed toward him.

go let them take you go inside the citadel citadel go inside

Draken growled his agreement at the chattering ghost, but the servii took it as belligerence.

"You're going to challenge me? I've trained to the sword since I was barely toddling off my mother's skirts. Disarm before I do something you regret, pirate."

More servii headed their way, a half dozen if the torchlight didn't cast lying shadows against the mist. Heat rushed hard through Draken, fury that made Seaborn flare. He squinted, eyes stinging. It gave the servii a chance at attack. Bruche barely blocked the attack.

Khellian's stones. You have a damned deathwish. Bruche chilled Draken further until his whole body was under his firm control and cut down the servii with the sword. It happened so quickly Draken barely had time to blink.

The other emitted a strangled sound between fleshy lips—in that moment Draken realized how young they were, how inexperienced they must have been to approach him. The others, now closing in at a run, might have sent these two untried servii to harass the big Brînian who dared appear near the Citadel after curfew. Maybe as a damned jest.

Run, damn you. Bruche was trying to force him round, push his legs into movement. *They've no bows. You can make it—*

I can't leave her in there. You heard Truls. He snarled and wrested back control from Bruche.

You can't rescue her from inside the Citadel. Especially not alone.

I won't be alone. In that moment, with Bruche's help, he thought he might have a chance at fighting his way inside the Citadel. Truls still circled him and the gaping guard, raising a definite chill beyond the damp mist slipping through every seam of his armor and clothes. He still had Tyrolean on the outside, and Geffen. He trusted Khisson, despite his animosity, wouldn't betray their pact. It was a slim chance, but a chance just the same.

He attacked, a hard slash at the servii closest to him that probably only knocked the wind out of him, and pushed forward into the fray. They had swords too, but maybe they'd been ordered not to kill anyone else because they beat him with the flats of theirs and knocked his out of the way with a blow that seemingly came out of nowhere and wrenched his good shoulder. He was holding it too tightly, his whole body too tightly. Seaborn clattered away, flaring and blinding him.

"Wait!" One of them shouted, but the others were bringing him down. He struggled hard before submitting. They had him prone against the cobbles, a sharp rock digging into his cheek, someone's weight heavy enough on his back to make him gasp for air.

"Hie, stop. That's the sword! The bloody magic sword!"

Truth, the damned thing lay on the cobbles glowing, the traitor. Truls stood over it. Quiet now, having gotten his way.

"You're him, aren't you?" Hands hauled him to his feet. He struck out but they were on him in an instant, blows to the jaw to make his head spin, rough hands searching him for more weapons. They found the boot knives and the one at his wrist. But far worse than the blows and curses was seeing Seaborn in another's hand.

"I don't know what you're talking about."

There was a brief argument over bindings, of which they had none. Draken rolled his eyes. Guards unprepared to take prisoners? Whose servii were these? Certainly not from his fortress at Khein. He'd once sneaked inside there during a siege and they'd had a blade to his throat before he'd swung both legs over the battlement. But he wanted into the Citadel and also had no wish to be punched further, so he let them sort it out without struggling.

They grasped his arms and marched him down the lane and through the gates. He looked all around. The courtyard, usually peaceful and lush, was trampled by the many horses staked inside. His stables must be packed to overflowing. He gritted his teeth at the damage, and at the inclination to think of the Citadel as his.

But it is, by rights. It's your home.

Not helping, Bruche. Sentimentality would only interfere with his making an opportunity out of this disaster he'd brought upon himself.

The spirithand fell silent as he was marched past the steps and open doors leading to the Great Hall. Draken turned his head and peered into the torchlit round space. His breath caught and his steps faltered. Two dozen Akrasians milled about, but they parted to reveal Aarinnaie. It could only be her with unbound black curls and glimmering pale green robes draping her deceptively slim shoulders.

"Move along." A guard gave him a shove, but Draken growled and swung at him. The guard's head snapped back. Draken's fist stung. Another guard raised his voice, sharp words Draken was too busy pummeling the first guard to catch. Several guards rushed their way and dragged them apart. The guard backed away, hand clutching his face. Nose broken, if the stream of blood and sharp cry was any indication. Draken didn't see what happened inside the Great Hall as he was forced to the ground, face down in the churned, wet gravel path, a heavy man sitting on his back. Another's knees held down his legs. His stomach twisted from the slight tremble that ran through the ground as his bruises healed. The men on him made sharp noises of alarm as they registered the shaking ground. It wasn't enough, though, to give Draken leverage to escape them. He wheezed, all the breath squeezed out of his lungs.

"Is that a Brînian? Let him go!" Aarinnaie's sharp tone.

A deeper, more commanding voice answered. Draken couldn't make out the words. He struggled, but he was down. It sounded like Ilumat—

"What is the meaning of this? Who is this man?"

Definitely Ilumat.

"Caught him lurking round the gates, Your Grace. Tried to talk to him and he killed Servii Bedar outright."

Draken snorted. *"Your Grace." Gods, he's delusional and they've bought into it. He made noises about a regency, eh? What else would they call him?*

Ilumat's voice paired with the sounds of boots ringing out on the brightly tiled floor of the Great Hall. "You've let some pirate bloodlord interrupt the ceremony? I ought to put you all in gaol. Get him out of here."

Draken twisted his head so that the gravel dug into his cheek, but a foot pressed against his head. He couldn't see past Ilumat's fine boots and the steps leading up to the Great Hall. Aarinnaie's voice filtered out to him in echoes, intense protestations that didn't quite sound herself. They were quickly overcome by male shouts booming round the great hall. He twisted more, struggling against the weight on his back. He heaved, ignoring the wrenching pain in his shoulder, shoved off the man on his back, and used his good leg to lever himself to his feet. Someone yanked the back at the neck of his armor with strangling speed, but his eyes met Ilumat's.

The Akrasian lord stilled. Draken took him in: no armor or weapons, dressed in finely woven robes the same pale green as Aarinnaie's. "You're supposed to be dead," Ilumat said.

"Not for lack of trying." Draken was shoved down, hard. He grunted into the gravel. "You don't sound so surprised."

"I'm surprised you're stupid enough to lurk about the Citadel. But I've heard of your ability." Of course he had. Draken cursed inwardly. "You fools. This is Draken vae Khellian."

There was some shuffling of boots, some confused, apologetic noises. Behind him, someone muttered that he'd damned well told them so. "Khel Szi or Your Highness. Either suits."

Ilumat sneered. "You've been stripped of all that. Did the official scroll fail to reach you?" He reached down to grasp the chain with Elena's pendant and tugged so that it yanked Draken's head forward. Draken gasped in pain.

Of course it won't break that easily. Ruddy fool.

Ilumat pulled it over Draken's head instead, still with that smile that spoke of worse forthcoming. Draken stared at the pendant in Ilumat's hand. Told himself it didn't matter. He was still his Queen's chosen consort, the father of the Crown-Princess.

"I'm glad you're here. Aarinnaie has been a bit reticent. Surely she'll cooperate now."

"Reticent." Draken snorted, a mirthless smile tugging on his scarred lips. "With what?"

"Our wedding."

His insides went cold, and it had nothing to do with Bruche. "She never will agree to that."

"Ah, but she has. It's important Brîn is firmly bound to Akrasia, aye?"

"And my throne is an important step for you taking Elena's, aye?"

"It's essential if we're to beat back this Monoean threat." His eyes narrowed. "Of course, to you it may very well not be a threat. Brîn as of yet remains uninvaded."

"I'm no friend to the Ashen, not like you," Draken growled. He almost spat what he knew, but he couldn't betray Geffen. He might have need of her later. *One can only hope.*

Draken's mind reeled too much to react to Bruche's quip, and he only caught half the conversation. Aarinnaie, bound to this traitor? He'd bed her immediately, get her pregnant as soon as possible. Aarinnaie could do anything from kill Ilumat to take her own life. He had to stop this. "Your children will be sundry."

"As yours is."

"Sikyra is daughter to the rightful Queen."

"Bring him." Ilumat spun and strode back up the steps. A short cape edged in dark green ribbon fluttered from his shoulders. "Princess, your brother is here just in time. Shall we proceed?"

Two servii held his arms and marched him up the steps. Draken didn't fight them; they were taking him in the right direction now. Aarinnaie turned toward Ilumat, filmy robes matching his and concealing her slight form.

"You lie—" A sharp intake of breath cut off the word. "Draken."

Aarinnaie started toward him and stumbled with a sharp clinking sound. An Escort caught her round the shoulders and Draken realized her ankles and wrists were shackled.

"Those won't be necessary any longer, I trust. Unbind her," Ilumat said. "And lay that sword to Draken's throat. If she refuses, or hesitates in her vows to me, I'll take his head. Surely even your unholy healing cannot reattach it."

Draken frowned. *Unholy . . . ?* But Aarinnaie's chains rattled. "No!"

"Enough," Ilumat said. "Where is the bloody priest?"

"Just here, my lord." The gentle Citadel temple priest with the tender hands hurried forward. He stared at Draken. His mouth opened to speak. Draken shook his head at him. If he called him Khel Szi, Ilumat might well kill him.

"Your Grace," Ilumat snarled.

"This won't help you achieve the throne, Ilumat," Draken said. "I already am Regent of Akrasia, and I soon will be her King. It's Brîn I'm bringing to heel."

Aarinnaie stared as they forced Draken to his knees and pulled his head back, fingers wound painfully tight in his short hair. One of the servii held Akhen Khel to his throat. Even on this cold, misty night, even compared to Bruche's internal chill when he took over Draken's body, there was nothing so cold as a sharp blade against the skin. Especially one he was certain could kill him. He gritted his teeth. "Don't do it, Aarin."

She just stared at him, blue eyes wide.

He struggled but the blade bit into his skin. Blood trickled in a hot stream down his throat. "Aarinnaie. Do not do this."

She gave him a pleading look. "I have to. You cannot die."

"He'll kill me anyway."

She turned on Ilumat. "Will you?"

"Truth, he'll live if you marry me." A thin smile. "He'll be family after all."

"The bastard has no honor." The hands yanked his head back further as he spoke. "Don't believe him, Aar—" The blade tightened on his throat, cutting him off.

"If she refuses me, then you are of no use and I kill you both." Ilumat spread his hands. The long, wide sleeves draping his arms spread like wings. "As my wife I will cherish you, keep you from harm, give you independence as you earn my trust. Freedom or death, Princess. I can offer you either. You may choose."

"My death would be freedom from you, and marriage means certain death: yours. So it's not really a choice, is it?" she said. Ilumat frowned, obviously not liking how she twisted his words. She didn't see. Her gaze slid to Draken and locked there.

His heart twisted, a squeezing pain. He shook his head. More blood trickled down his throat. No trembling under his knees, no sting of healing. Just blood. Draken swallowed in his dry throat.

Truls drifted toward Draken, pushing his foul, broken face close to his. Beyond, though the misty shape, he could see Ilumat reach out and take Aarinnaie's hand, her unresisting but stiff. He wanted to protest, to shout at the ghost and at Aarinnaie. But she showed unfailing logic. They were outnumbered. Ilumat held all the power. And Aarin knew what Seaborn would do to him.

The Priest's attention kept straying to Draken. Maybe he still had his loyalty, but what good was a soft-handed old Priest? His voice trembled as he spoke. "Do you have the gifts, my lord?"

"Aye." Ilumat bowed his head to the priest as was expected and gestured to servants. One by one they brought the Seven Gifts to honor the gods: a cage of live bird chicks for Ma'Vanni, the mother. A knife for Khellian, god of war. A rich, folded, woven blanket to show the comfort of Shaim's peace. A bouquet of flowers, rich breads, and fruit to ask Agrias's bounty upon their marriage. A couple of proxy advisors to ensure Zozia's wisdom. Seven gold pieces to pay Aarinnaie's tax to Korde. Aarinnaie bore this procession of gifts stony-faced, not so much as nodding at the priests. Her gaze kept flicking to Draken.

Ilumat said the perfunctory words of commitment to Aarinnaie. She repeated them back woodenly, her gaze on Draken. He stared back, every swallow, every breath pressing the skin of his throat against the sharp edge of the blade there.

Ilumat snapped the marriage bracelet onto his own arm first, an engraved cuff of moonwrought with a locking latch. It would have to be sawn off. He snapped a matching cuff onto Aarinnaie's wrist. Draken closed his eyes, knowing the cold metal must feel like a shackle. They were married. Entirely proper and utterly heartless.

The pressure of the blade eased against Draken's neck. It was still there, though. Draken didn't move, held quite still. It was still close enough to slit his throat with a twitch and Draken didn't trust that Ilumat wouldn't give the nod now that Aarinnaie was his. He squinted at his sister. Aarinnaie stared at nothing, her face toward the throne and tilted down. The cowl draping her curls was stark against the riot of colors filling the torchlit Great Hall.

Gods, she looks the perfect bride. Bile rose as he thought of what came next for her.

Bruche had no quip, no quick answer. His was an anxious quiet. At last: *I worry more what comes next for you.*

Fools all. Draken couldn't conceal his apprehension or—admit it—fear. *Ilumat might very well need me. A trade or some nonsense. The Monoeans might like very much to kill me themselves.*

Bruche rumbled in his chest like a cat trying to soothe itself by purring. Both of them were thinking torture was more likely than death. There was no use speaking of it. Draken found himself slipping into that space between fear and thought, a place he had dwelled when his father last tortured him, when the Monoeans had beaten and branded him in gaol, while he endured hazing as a new sailor, the place where silent screams had echoed when his slavemasters beat him as a child. He barely felt Seaborn press into his throat any more.

Ilumat turned to Draken. His mustache was perfect, his clothes pristine. Draken wished for the mask to shield his eyes. He had to squint down at the Akrasian as he drew near. Ilumat's fingers, pale and clean, closed over the hilt of Seaborn and took it from the guard holding Draken. The guard replaced the blade with his bulky arm. Few men were as big as Draken; this one must have been specially chosen for the job of handling him.

"It appears we are now family, brother," Ilumat said.

Draken's jaw tightened. Truth, in peacetime a cousin to the Queen would make an acceptable husband for Aarinnaie. He had wondered if raising Tyrolean officially back to First Captain would make him a suitable match, since the two seemed to get on. But that had been before Elena had disappeared, before Monoea had attacked, before even Sikyra was born. That time was lost forever and this match wasn't good for Brîn or Aarinnaie.

Gods willing, it would be even worse for Ilumat.

Bruche tried to chill him as a warning not to speak, but Draken couldn't help himself. "I only hope you live long enough to regret it. Aarinnaie is not someone to be trifled with." A humorless laugh erupted from him. "You've really no idea what you've gotten yourself into. First Brîn and now this."

Ilumat paled slightly, if possible. Maybe he had heard the rumors of his new assassin bride. Whatever it was, Draken was glad to plant a seed of doubt in him.

"The gods do not fate well wives who do not come to heel," Ilumat said.

Draken stilled. Ilumat's last wife had died in childbirth . . . supposedly. "That hasn't been Akrasia's way for generations and you know it."

Ilumat twitched a hand at the guard holding Draken. "Take him away."

Aarinnaie made a strangled noise. It seemed to stop the guard. She moved toward Draken. Gods. She should be running away, not toward him.

He met her gaze. "Aarin."

She stopped.

He couldn't reassure her, couldn't tell her anything. His throat was tight. At least she was alive. That was all he had to hang onto.

Her face hardened as her narrow fingers toyed with the bracelet locked around her arm.

Ilumat strode to her and took her hand. It hung limp and defeated in his. He lifted it to his lips. "Come, wife."

His gentle tone made Draken's skin crawl. Bruche shifted uneasily within him. He was sworn to protect the Brînian royals and standing here doing nothing made him feel as if he bore a stone in his gut.

Aarinnaie didn't respond, didn't shift her gaze from Draken, until Ilumat tugged her along, a solicitous hand at her back as he guided her toward the private quarters. She walked without hesitation, her back stiff. A guard followed with a bright lantern, which stung Draken's eyes and made them water. He squinted that way as best he could, twisting his head despite the bright lantern light as they dragged him away, tears streaming.

CHAPTER THIRTEEN

A grim maze dwelled between thought and pain. An old armsmaster had told Draken everyone had one. To find the path back to thought took training. Experience. Long bouts of agony.

Draken was familiar enough with such pain. His earliest beatings had been punishments. Later, there'd been torture to get him to do something, like when his father hurt him until he took up Akhen Khel as a conduit to the gods. He'd had people try to beat information out of him, and he'd spent long nights in a Monoean gaol suffering at the hands of prisoners and guards alike when he refused to accept blame for his wife's death. He'd also spent much more time learning to deliver pain, and did it often enough if it served some purpose.

With all that, he'd never received or given pain without knowing the end game. It made it difficult to linger in the grim place. Anger and frustration kept intruding as Akrasian guards dragged Draken outside and bound him to a sturdy frame, his arms bound high over his head, his shirt hanging in tatters from his waistband. Torch posts stuck up from the bloodstained gravel in a haphazard circle as if he were the offering in some ancient death rite to Korde. The flames burned his eyes against the black of night. They started with fists, the brute who'd dragged him out and bore the brunt of his struggles taking the most turns. The blows made him swing back as far as the ropes on his ankles allowed, and while Bruche chilled him to numb the immediate sting, the spirit couldn't silence the thud of fist on flesh, the crack of his ribs, the grind of bone on bone as his bad shoulder threatened to dislocate. A shudder ran through the structure as his ribs knit.

He hung his head, eyes closed against the torchlight. There wasn't much to do but wait it out; no questions were asked and aside from a few rough chuckles and coughs the Akrasians went about their business of beating him senseless. Bruche's cold couldn't numb his nausea either, and it wasn't much helped by Truls wavering nearby or the balcony off Draken's chambers hanging overhead like a portent. Ilumat wouldn't have been able to resist taking them for his own and Draken's mind couldn't resist flitting to the horrors within.

When Draken lifted his head he saw a man watching from the shadows under the balcony. Clean. Long, light hair tied back. Sundry? But he had a sword strapped to his hip, and his broad shoulders and barrel chest promised strength and maybe some skill. Maybe a trusted slave guard then, someone raised up from illegal fighting pits. It could happen. Konnon, whose dappled head rotted on the Citadel wall, had been a sundry bed slave raised to the ranks of szi nêre.

I wish they'd cut you. Your healing would bring the frame down.

For all the good that would do him. Draken snorted. His assailant took it as an insult or sarcasm and hit him quick, thrice in the ribs and once on the jaw. It made his head snap back. His chest heaved as the courtyard and trees and sky wavered. The ground wobbled under his toes and the structure holding him up creaked. The men around him spoke in sharp tones. He tasted blood.

When he could lift his head again the man with the sword was closer. Just inside the circle of torchlight. It made him a deal more difficult to see. Draken lowered his gaze to the sword. The man rested his hand on the hilt as he spoke softly to one of the others. Draken's brows drew in. That scabbard . . . scraped and stained and battered . . .

Do you see it?

It can't be. Ilumat would never let Seaborn out of his sight.

Was that man at the wedding? He'd only had eyes for Aarinnaie. *I think he was at the gates, behind the invasion.* It was fuzzy, as if he'd more felt the man than seen him. Or felt the man watching. Who knew what the sight magic even was?

I don't know. You—

A fist slammed into his gut. Draken dragged his knees up, but the drag on his shoulders was unbearable. He let his feet drop again. Bruche encased him in cold and things started to fade.

Stay with me, Draken.

Why?

Bruche didn't have a good answer to that. Draken wished they'd hit him again. A few more sharp blows to the head would make everything go to nicely quiet.

The voices of the Akrasians pitched in alarm as the gravel shifted and rocked. A sharp chinking, *tick tick tick,* threatened to drag Draken back to full consciousness. He closed his eyes and swallowed. His throat was very dry. Water sloshed in a lopsided rhythm, not that of the sea but it put him in mind of water lapping the side of a ship. The shock of a cold splash twisted the sea and reality in his mind, but only for a breath. Draken sputtered and swung his

head, shivering violently. Water spiked with chunks of ice drenched his head
and chest. It ran down his skin in itchy rivulets.

Draken dragged his head up, blinking against the torchlight and the water.

"What's wrong with you?" A voice out of the light, a shadow that could talk.

Draken shook his head. Nothing. He forgot to speak. He licked the water
from his lips. Salty sea water.

Bruche settled in his shoulders and chest. *No, blood.*

Someone plucked a torch from a post and jabbed it closer to get a good look
at Draken. Draken winced and squeezed his eyes shut.

Rough fingers wiped across Draken's lips. "Seven take me, it's true. He heals
himself."

"I told you." Another voice answered. "I saw it at Auwaer. Brought the whole
Palisade down."

"The Ashen said it was bad magic, old Moonling stuff."

The Ashen? Why would these two ever hear something *they* said? Were they
the enemy or not? Bruche said, *Perhaps not, with Ilumat's "alliance."*

Anger spiked, colder than the air nipping at his wet skin. It dragged him
unwillingly back to full consciousness. "Fools all. You going to chat all night or
beat on me more? Whichever, bloody well get on with it."

They obliged, beating him nearly senseless. By the time they cut him down,
he was passive and hurting enough that he gave them no trouble. Even Bruche
couldn't stop the pain knifing up his bad knee from his thigh or making his
shoulder seize. He cried out when his arm came down. Blood ran down his
chin from his broken nose. They grabbed his bound wrists and dragged him
around to the servants' hall. It was blessedly dark and quiet. Someone walked
by, slowing to stare, maybe. Draken hauled his head up to look, curious if it
was the other man, the one with Seaborn. No. Not him. A woman. She was
Akrasian and vaguely familiar. Her skin was so pale she appeared to glow. Or
was she really glowing? Draken blinked but he was too bleary-eyed to work it
out. Truls wavered behind her, drifting back toward the corridor downstairs. As
if he were leading them.

The dungeons. At least he could see in the dark.

They dragged him down the steps, his feet bumping along behind, toes scraping on the stone steps. He couldn't fight them at all. His arms were numb with
cold and weak from holding himself up. Bruche couldn't entirely conceal the
further strain in his bad shoulder. Even the gods had never managed to heal it.

The row of cells were dusty and empty of life as the crypts, rotting reeds
rustling underfoot. They had to hold him up as one of them struggled with the
lock. It turned with a clang that sounded as if something broke inside and the

door swung forward with an unearthly squeal of metal on stone. They shoved him inside. He fell on his face when his arms couldn't get up in time to catch him. Agony bolted through his broken nose again. A sneezing and coughing fit overtook him, making it impossible to breathe.

When it ceased and he could lift his head, he was alone. Not much to see when his eyes adjusted to the pitch: a hole in the floor emanating the reek of waste, a wooden door strapped with rusted bands, petrified reeds under his body. His vision in the dark only carried as far as the stone walls and solid wood and metal door of his cell. The place stank of dust and sweat. Or maybe it was him. He shoved himself over onto his back. It took some doing. Beams crossed the low ceiling, strung with webs, glimmering in his night-sight.

"I'm wishing now I'd taken care to make the dungeon more inhabitable." Another coughing fit broke through a weak burst of maniacal laughter.

Draken. Keep yourself together.

Together. As if he were the sum of parts. But truth, it made some sense. Maybe he was no more than the dirty, sundry blood swirling in his veins. Or perhaps actions made the man. If so, he was anointed with the blood of violence. And what of Bruche? He seemed more ghost than man. They had been together long enough they needed few words. Their memories blended so well he could hardly tell the difference between their different women, the sensation of blade slicing flesh and sinew, echoes of voices and laughter and cries of fear and pain. Draken had even died once as Bruche had, blood spilling down his chest in a hot rush, stumbling to his knees without a thought, blackness closing in—

He woke with a start.

Truls lingered in a corner, lower than usual and quite still, as if sitting on a ghost-bench.

Draken raised a shaking hand to rub his face. "What do you want?"

the gods come kill them

"Bloody Seven." Not that again.

He rolled over with a groan, lay panting on his side for a while, letting the pain infiltrate. Acceptance was the first step to getting back on his feet. Upstairs somewhere were his wraps, the soaking salts, potions, and heat salves. But all the slaves who had cared for him were dead. He closed his eyes.

More time passed, a fog of blackness cut with shards of the odd grey of his night vision when he opened his eyes. He only heard his own breath, shallow and labored, and a trickle of water somewhere that made him desperate for a drink. Bruche was quiet, watchful. Truls waited.

"It doesn't matter if a god has come. I can do nothing from here," he said as if continuing a conversation. Perhaps he had been in his dreams.

If a god has come, perhaps he is here to help. You bear Khellian's name, his sword.
Truls shook his head, pale in the corner. It made his face blur. Draken swallowed, coughed in his parched throat. He should have licked the water they'd thrown at him from his skin. It occurred he might be left here to die, a dried husk. Too fitting. Too like his esteemed ancestors.

But Aarinnaie, she would live. Trapped like an animal, aye. Damaged, most likely. Clever, certainly. She could escape Ilumat someday. If they ever let her near so much as a table knife, she'd kill him. He hoped it wasn't tonight. It was too soon. Ilumat knew exactly what he'd done. He bore no love for her and would keep his guards close. Take some time to gain his trust; better, if she could manage to woo him, something Draken feared she had a lot of experience doing, she would get her chance. He knew his sister. She would never rest until Ilumat was dead. His fingers clenched. He longed with all he was for his sword and the chance to thrust it through Ilumat's throat.

We've finally done it, then. Turned you into a proper swordhand.
Draken's breath husked. He swallowed again. Spoke because if the oppressive silence seeping from the very stone around him went on much longer he'd go mad with it. "She'd rather kill him herself."

Aye. But you are her brother, her prince.
"There are no crowns in dungeons."

It's far too soon to go maudlin on me.
Draken sighed. He didn't even know how much time had passed since they'd dumped him in here. Long enough his pants and the tatters of his shirt had dried, along with his mouth and throat. Long enough Aarinnaie's marriage was likely consummated.

You think she will not fight him? Bruche asked.
"Does it matter? She will be raped just the same."

Is rape the worst thing that can happen to her?
Draken started to retort but he snagged on the question. He didn't have an answer. They both fell quiet for a while. Truls carried on staring at him. A faint stench rose from the pit in the corner. Draken hadn't made much use of the dungeons. The last people to sit down here were Ilumat and his men. He should have killed Ilumat when he'd had the chance . . .

A rustle made him twitch awake. He rubbed his face, listening. Boots scuffed the reeds in the corridor. He frowned. No clink of a key. Whoever it was couldn't get into his cell, then. Or was it just barred? He wasn't certain; he couldn't remember. If it was, maybe he could jiggle it loose somehow.

Maybe he'd imagined it but Bruche shook his head slowly, listening and sharing the wordless sentiment that the silence had changed. Draken couldn't put his mind to just *how*; but he felt a familiar pressure in his head and joints, as if a storm were brewing. He sought the memories, but his failures flooded over him like an assault. Maybe they'd brought Aarinnaie here to flaunt her. Or maybe she'd served her use and Ilumat would keep her in the dungeon . . .

The steps came closer. Stopped.

Draken sat very still, staring at the outline of the door in the dark. No flicker of torchlight shone through the cracks, it was just that odd grey murk of his night vision. Or there were no cracks. The Citadel was well-made for such an old building, and it stood to reason that the solid foundation, which the dungeons rested between, kept doors from skewing on their hinges. For the first time it occurred to Draken to wonder if some magic kept the ruining damp at bay.

The bar locking him in rubbed the outside of the door to his cell. Draken's fingers tightened to fists. He'd had some rest now and Bruche was ever alert, his chill filling his muscles with strength. Damn them, they might take him and torture him again, but not without some pain on their end.

The door scraped the floor as it opened. He hadn't noticed that before either. He stared up at the servii as she came into focus. Slighter than some, Akrasian. Even in his condition, even without Bruche's strength, he could take her.

But for the short sword at her hip.

She didn't reach for it though. She stood there, eyes shifting like she didn't know where to look. She couldn't see in the dark, then. Draken wasn't sure why he expected it. Bruche shifted within him. Truls had risen and drawn closer to the servii.

They were all uneasy. Logic said it was because the enemy stood in the doorway of his cell. But that shouldn't make his gut twist. He wasn't afraid of torture, nor death. Instead, he craved it. Freedom from his mistakes and violence, this bloody war, responsibility for those who didn't want him. The agony of loss. Fire and ice tangled in his veins. He didn't want to care any longer. He didn't want to heal himself anymore. He wanted the relief of blackness, and he couldn't get it even in the Seven-damned dark of his own dungeon. His fists clenched, muscles straining.

There was a way . . . if he could get his hands on that blade.

Draken!

He exhaled hard. *I can't do this any longer, Bruche. I'm just sitting here waiting to die and you and I both know how bad it could go if the Ashen control my magic.*

How would they do that? You wouldn't allow it, even should they capture you.

He swallowed. He couldn't say his daughter's name.

Bruche replied fiercely just the same. *That isn't going to happen.*

Gods, it was only a matter of time. Why was she just bloody standing there? He scrambled to his feet, using the wall at his back as leverage. His sore body caught him up with stabs of pain in the shoulders and his knee. "Come on, then."

The servii opened her mouth into a gaping grin. No flash of teeth. No tongue filling the bottom. His eyes flicked to her hands, narrowed. His vision sharpened as he stared. It picked out colors from the grey.

Her hands were crimson to the wrist. One of them held a small, bloody blade. He took a step forward. She lifted it up, held it on the palm of her hand, out to him. An offering of peace, despite the blood. He took another step.

Draken, no. Bruche filled him, held him still.

Draken could fight off his control, had done before under extreme need. It had surprised Osias that he could. It hadn't surprised Draken because he hadn't known to be surprised.

do not go to her

The clearest thing Truls had said. An order, and fully formed.

"What are you?" he growled before realizing what he was saying. *Bruche . . .*

The servii opened up her mouth with no tongue and no teeth. Screamed, ending in a scratchy, gawping squawk. No intelligence behind the sound. It disintegrated into a faint gagging whimper.

Still, the scream shuddered in Draken's bones. Real enough. And familiar.

A damned bane.

Silence clotted the air. How had one of the evil spirits gotten into the Citadel to possess this servii? His vision faded but for the bloody knife on the bloody hand. It was a gift, something to use to find relief. Draken pried himself from Bruche's control. It was like unfolding himself from a tight box. He burst forth from it with a grunt. The box still compressed his chest, though. No air in there. Soon it wouldn't matter.

His fingers closed around the blade. It bit into his fingers, pain a focus point. The smooth wooden handle was Oscher wood. Rare enough for Brîn. Oscher wood meant for a king: pale, pliant but strong. No, not just a king. A dead king. The blade was fresh and sharp as if just drawn from the fire and anvil and grinding stone. One of his ancestors had clutched this blade with the oscher wood handle in his still, rotting finger bones in the dark for generations . . .

Bruche sounded stricken. *How can you know that?*

He knew because he had seen it before in their escape through the tombs. Cold froze Draken's arm on its climb through the air toward his throat. His muscles strained, locked in ethereal battle. All of Bruche, all his strength, was in that arm.

Draken still had his other arm. He reached. Gasped the last of his air. Without Bruche's cold, he felt every strand of his shoulder muscles tear further. Bone ground on bone. He grunted. His bad arm fell and he opened his mouth in an involuntary cry, silent with no air behind it. Bruche leapt down his other arm and shook the blade loose of his fingers. It clattered to the rustling reeds and stone.

Draken's growl broke the silence. The bane in the doorway moved forward, grasped his arm, and pulled him down to pick up the blade. Her face creased with feral hunger. Draken stared at her, unresisting, as his fingers touched the knife. Bruche kicked in, straining back against the bane's otherworldly strength. She tightened her grip. A groan escaped Draken as his bones twisted from the inside out. A sudden thought struck him: if they broke his arm the healing could damage the cell enough for him to escape. Or it could collapse and kill him. At the moment he thought the latter preferable. Truls hovered behind the bane, useless, his edges shifting and reforming. Draken thought he detected fear on his misty face.

A white light cut the shadows spilling into the cell from the doorway. Draken had to duck his head against the sting in his eyes. The echoes of a Voice reverberated inside his chest, tearing pain inside. He gasped. Gods. Someone was trying to rip Bruche away. The swordhand dug in to Draken's insides with the claws of his soul. The bane froze, her fingers crushing Draken's wrist. He winced, tried to shake her off, but they loosened as quick. She fell forward, limp against him but still moving, pawing at him. He stumbled back under her weight. The light swirled quicker through the cell, ruffling over his bare skin as if he'd come through a fine web. It wavered through Truls, tearing away the beautiful, concerned features of life to reveal his gruesome, rotted skull. The bane crumpled to the floor without sound. Two pale arrows stuck from her back. Truls's face came back.

Draken was too shocked to feel relief.

"Be easy, Draken."

Draken swallowed, found he couldn't breathe very well. Bruche relaxed his hold so he could speak in a husk of his voice. *"Osias."*

The Mance glowed faintly from the powerful necromancy he'd worked to dispatch the bane. He looked at Truls, who retreated.

"You're making a bad habit"—Draken had to stop to breathe—"of rescuing me from dungeons."

Osias lifted his chin a little and his lips took on a wry twist. "Tyrolean sought my help."

"Tyrolean? How . . . ?"

"I gave him my pipe. Twine the smoke and it summons me."

What in bloody Seven did that mean? *Twine the . . .* Ah. His pipe had two bowls. He smoked two different leaves. "Where is he?"

"I came alone." Not an answer, but perhaps as much as Osias knew. Definitely as much as he would say.

"And Sikyra?"

"Safe in Eidola."

"She needs you there, damn you. You're supposed to be protecting her."

"She is protected. But she needs her father. Come."

"No. We have to get to Aarinnaie." He scowled. "You're a damned lantern. Can you snuff the light? I can't see."

It eased, though slowly. Osias rubbed the back of his hand on his chin. Not a gesture Draken had seen from him. "Aarinnaie Szirin is here?"

"Ilumat married her."

It was a rare thing to surprise a Mance. His glow had faded enough Draken could look directly at him. His eye color shifted rapidly. Various spirits, taking their turn to stare at the upstart Khel Szi, no doubt.

"She's more hostage than wife, of course." He came forward, grunted as a twinge in his knee caught him up. Bruche fled to fill it, easing the pain with cold. Someday he wished he could have a warm wrap and bath again. Someday he wished he could have a damned normal life. He was getting too old for this nonsense. He silently, gruffly, thanked the old spirit for his help. "I need my sister. And coin. And my sword," he added in a growl. "I'm not leaving without those three things."

He felt handicapped without his blade and he'd need coin to buy better loyalty. With Bruche's help he pushed past Osias to look down the corridor. All dark and empty, but Osias's slight glow still hindered his vision.

"Draken . . ."

"I don't have time to argue. I don't care about me. Aarin needs to get out." He bent to catch the old tomb blade up in in his hand—better than nothing—and led the way down the corridor. He had to glance back to see if Osias was following, the Mance was so silent.

Draken knew the way well enough but moved slowly. He realized the dungeon was so black, and his vision so seamless, that he had no idea if it was day or night outside. The top of the steps was barred by a door. He was trying to remember if there was a guard stationed there in his time, or if the door was simply locked. Most of the time his dungeon had no residents. More likely there were guards now, since he was such an important prisoner. He paused at the bottom of the steps and kept his voice low. "How long have I been down here?"

"It's the second night, past half-bell."

He rubbed his hand over his face. How had so much time passed? "Guards up there?"

"Dead."

Draken raised his brows. Excellent. "Right, then." He started up the stairs, moving with more assurance. There'd almost certainly be fewer people in the corridors at night. While the Citadel never rested under a Khel Szi's rule, the Bastion at Auwaer certainly did. Akrasians liked their sleep.

He pressed his ear to the door, feeling Bruche lean in. No sound, but the thick wooden door would smother much of it. *Just keep me in fighting shape*, he told the swordhand irritably. He needed Bruche to concentrate on chilling his sore spots. The joints were stiff, but pain would hinder him more. He reached for the lever, cringed at the snick of the latch. The door was heavy, and it was a slow push, but it wasn't locked from the outside. A crack of light pierced his vision. He ducked his head. Damn magical sight. The glow wasn't all that bright, though, just a sconce on the wall holding a single thick candle. The corridor was lined with them, but only this one was lit. He frowned at that. Odd.

They've no slaves to keep candles lit. They killed them all.

Draken's jaw tightened just as the door tugged and swung free of his grip. A servii stared at him, obviously expecting her compatriot who had been taken by the bane. But she recovered enough to rush him as she drew her blade. A mistake, even Draken knew, and one borne of a lack of training. One hand caught her arm, stopping the sword at about halfway exiting its sheath. His other caught her throat. It was the only vulnerable part of her armored form on such short notice. She stiffened, lined eyes round as he yanked her closer by the arm into his tight grip. Her lips parted. She made gagging noises.

"Are you going to make me kill you?"

Her head twitched *no*. He growled and released her throat. She gasped for breath and made a sound—not a scream but a gasping cry loud enough to filter down the dark hallway to ears beyond. He growled and slammed the grip of his bloody knife into her temple. He pulled back to do it again but Bruche stayed his hand. She fell limp, the sword yanking from its sheath as she crumpled. Bruche neatly caught the blade before it could clatter to the floor and handed it to Osias so Draken could haul her the couple of steps to the landing inside the door.

We should kill her, he told Bruche.

Don't you recognize her? She's one of yours, from Khein. Bruche thrust a memory at him, servii hauling him over the wall at Khein when he climbed it to help them during an Ashen siege.

Draken didn't answer. He'd been wrong, talking to Geffen the way he had. He was no longer Prince or Night Lord. Those days had passed.

The corridor stayed quiet as he strode across to snuff the candle. Darkness closed around them, but instead of dulling Draken's senses, it heightened them. His vision cleared. As expected, the Akrasians seemed to be sleeping. They could rely on their guards at the wall, the thick line of servii waiting to taunt the Brînians who dared step too close. He looked up and down the hall. Tiled. Dark. Familiar, but not. A shell of itself, of his memory, which was what? A sevennight ago? Two? He couldn't recall and fought down momentary panic. Bruche rumbled in his chest. *Focus on the thing at hand. Find the Szirin and escape.*

How?

One stride at a time. She'll be in Elena's quarters, don't you think?

"I hope leaving that guard there doesn't bite us in the arse."

Osias didn't answer. Draken led the way fair quick to the Queen's chambers. It was past his own and around a corner; the best in the palace. He hadn't been in there, or even gone so far down the corridor, since he'd returned to the Citadel. But as soon as he approached the doors he knew she wasn't there.

No guards. Then where?

Draken grunted, thinking. All was quiet. Too quiet.

"Perhaps she has gained Ilumat's trust," Osias said softly. He held out the servii's sword.

Draken gave him a look to hide that he'd nearly forgotten the Mance was with him and took the blade. Truls lingered nearby, useless as usual. "Or she's chained."

He pushed through the carved doors, sword first. A servii lifted her sleepy head from the bench in the antechamber. This time Draken took no chances. He lunged out with his stolen sword, which felt different—longer. Lighter. But it did the job. Blood jutted from the servii's neck. Draken stepped back—not that more blood on him would make a fair difference in his current state of unclean. Before her hand could lift to the wound, she slipped to the floor in a gasping, writhing mess.

Osias stepped forward, eyes stormy as the spirits pushed forward. The lines of his face took on a hard, ugly edge. Draken turned away. They couldn't afford another scream alerting anyone else to predators in their midst. A guard meant someone was here. Someone important. Like a princess.

Light pierced the interior louvered doors. Draken blinked and shoved through quickly, meaning to surprise any guards on the other side. The room was chilly, the only light shed from a guttering fire. No guards, but there was a soft form on the bed who lifted her dark head.

"Aarin."

She sat all the way up, clinking. Draken cursed under his breath as he strode toward the bed.

"Drae, behind you!"

He spun, sword and knife brandished, but the burly guard dropped in front of him with a thud Draken felt through his bare feet. No injury, no blood. He must've come from the far side of the wardrobe. Osias stood in the doorway. He lowered his hand and nodded to Aarinnaie. "Szirin."

"Where was that magic before?" Draken asked.

"It's not something I can often use. It draws the wrong sort of attention."

"It's about time," Aarinnaie said irritably. She lifted her arm. An iron chain led from the wedding bracelet to the bedpost.

Draken cursed as he examined the chain. "Are you all right?"

"Not as bad off as you, I think."

A grunt. "I'm recovered, as you well know."

She sniffled, but not crying. Just a runny nose from the cold. "I don't suppose you brought the key?"

"I don't suppose you know where it is?"

She shook her head.

"We have to do this the old fashioned way, then." The chain wasn't so thick and heavy, but too short for her to get further from the bed than the chamber pot set next to it. Draken nudged it under the bed with his foot; it stank. More anger. "How long have you been chained here?"

Her expression closed. "Since a little after the wedding. He let me move around this morning."

Draken dared to give her a close look. A bruise darkened her cheek. "He hit you?"

"I killed a guard and tried to escape. He wasn't pleased." A shrug, but a tad stiff, affected. "Get this thing off me."

He studied the chain. It wasn't nearly as thick as the wedding band, nor the metal anything like the quality. He held it stiff from the bedpost and sawed at it with the sword, leaving gouges.

"That'll take all night," she said.

"And the sword is my only weapon, save this." He pulled the bloody knife from his waistband and dropped it on the bed.

Osias came close to watch over Draken's shoulder. He held a candle, which made Draken squint. "I can help, I think."

"How?"

Osias gave Aarinnaie a thin smile. "Easier to show. Step back, Khel Szi. I don't think you'll want to watch too closely."

Draken obeyed, but too curious to not look. Osias took the chain and held it between himself and the candle, barely a handspan apart. The candle carried on flickering, as Draken had seen a thousand other candles do. But the room brightened. He turned to squint at the fire. No, still barely catching the log. Aarinnaie gasped. He turned back but only caught a glimpse before he had to slap his hand over his eyes: Osias, *glowing*. It was a clean, white light, like the Seven drifting across clear skies on a hot night.

A metallic smell emitted from the Mance and Draken could feel the heat growing. The chain clinked and Aarinnaie made a noise: a whimper, then sharper. The chain clinked louder, as if it had fallen. The heat faded and Draken peeked between his eyelids. The glow had faded. He cautiously lowered his hand. "Let me guess. Another trick that draws too much attention."

"Rather, aye." Osias dipped his chin and blew out the candle.

Aarinnaie scrambled off the other side of the bed toward the wardrobe and flung it open. She wore a nightgown, billowing, white, sheer. Most unlike her. Draken realized with a start it looked familiar. Elena's.

She came up with a tunic and leggings that were too long, but pulled them on just the same, turning her back to change her shirt. Draken couldn't help but look her over for bruising, but saw only a large mark over her kidney, which, truth, could have been from when she was captured or even before. "Too big but they'll do." She pulled slippers from the bottom of the wardrobe and snatched up the knife. "Let's go kill Ilumat."

"I'll be happy just to get us all out unharmed."

She stared at him. "Craven? You?"

He marshaled his temper. "No one wants him dead more than me—"

"He's my kill."

What had Ilumat done to her . . . besides the obvious. Gods, what if he'd gotten her with child? The heavy bracelet hung from her narrow wrist, dragged down by the shackle behind it and a couple of links of iron chain. They'd clink and bang into her hand and otherwise cause a nuisance. He came forward, tore a piece of sheeting off the bed, and wrapped it around her arm to tie down the loose metal.

His voice gentled. "Agreed. But there's no way to get to Ilumat without going through a wagonload of guards. That's not going to happen tonight."

She didn't respond, didn't look at him. Her jaw jutted out.

Oh I don't like that expression at all.

I just have to get her out of here as quickly as possible. "I need my sword and to collect some coin. Do you know where Seaborn is?"

"I don't know. I haven't seen it since that night." Her wedding night.

Draken nodded grimly. "We'll find it."

"Not the Great Hall. Ilumat would be too worried someone would take it."

"He wouldn't keep it with him, would he? In his chamber?" Osias asked.

Draken thought about it. "Not with the magic, no. At his heart, Ilumat is craven."

"The armory, then. We should check there."

Draken nodded, but before she could head for the door, he turned to Truls. "Make yourself useful. Is anyone lurking about in the hall?"

Aarinnaie gave him a look. "Drae, you're not still going on about—"

"I assure you Truls is quite real and present, Szirin," Osias said.

Aarinnaie didn't flinch or show anything but determination in her face, but she surely resented the ghost of the one who had trained her to be an assassin.

Truls, expressionless, drifted through the closed doors. In a few breaths he returned. Draken narrowed his eyes. Did the doors *move* when he glided back through? Truls nodded to him, stretched a wavering arm to indicate it was clear to go. Draken strode through. At this point he figured he could trust Truls as far as this went. The ghost had plenty of opportunities to throw him over, but hadn't. And he'd stuck close despite the gods apparently lurking nearby. Osias had stayed, as well.

The thought of gods watching him made him nervous, but he shoved that back and strode on down the hall toward the armory. They skulked back the way they'd come through the private chamber; the corridor would skirt the Great Hall, which could be tricky with all the open doorways; then down toward his study, which served his other purpose of securing some coin. The route might even provide an escape route, if it proved unguarded or at least as sleepy as the rest of the Citadel appeared.

Shallow grooves had worn into the tile floors down this older part of the Citadel. Odd how he hadn't noticed it before. Steps and odd graduations followed the elevation of the ground. Bruche wordlessly shared a little history, maybe hoping to calm his nerves. At one time, the palace had consisted of only the Great Hall with one corridor skirting it and rooms to the outside. It had been a public place only, with living quarters located elsewhere on the grounds. Before the city had been walled, before Brîn was a small kingdom or principality. Wondering how they'd managed to build the huge structure carried Draken all the way to the minor, interior armory. He frowned. No guard even here, at the armory? He shook his head and reached for the door.

Osias caught his arm, tipped his head toward Truls. The ghost slid forward and through the door. Draken heard his voice even before he reappeared:

empty empty empty

Inside, he stared in shock, pivoting slowly. The weapons were gone, with barely a scrap of metal to mark a forgotten rusted knife or a stack of arrows more suited to kindling.

Explains the lack of guards.

"Empty, indeed. Aarin, can you think of any other—" He pushed past Osias to look in the hallway. "Seven damn her, she's gone."

Seven guesses where she isn't, Bruche said. He didn't bother hiding his admiration of the Szirin, even when she was being bloody foolish. Draken had no illusions that killing Ilumat would be his ghostly szi nêre's first intention as well as his sister's. Royal guards were protective sorts and Aarinnaie was just . . . vehement.

You also know how foolish she is to try just now. He had to find her, and straightaway. Osias must have been listening in because he followed without comment. Draken gripped his sword, cursing Aarinnaie up one side and down the other. He never should have given her that old knife. *I'll kill her myself if the Akrasians don't manage it.* "Osias, I'll take you to the coffers. You have to get a sizable sum out. If I don't escape, keep it for Sikyra. It's her birth right."

"I think you need my help worse than your baby daughter needs the coin at the moment, Khel Szi."

"Just do as I say. I have to go after Aarinnaie and I won't risk you further." He took him in his study, familiar and yet cold and empty. Truls shifted erratically, which wasn't helping his own nerves much. He waved a hand at Truls. "Be still, ghoul. My own escape is for naught without this coin. I've bargained much to secure Khisson's help. I need him to take back the city."

Osias stared at him, features unaccountably smooth. Draken decided to take that as a good omen.

"Take back the city—?" Osias began.

"Aye. Khisson will sit the Khel Szi throne while I'm gone."

"Where are you going?"

"To find the Queen."

"But Ilumat has proof—"

"Hang his bloody proof. If she's dead, it's by his hand. But she's not."

"Because Truls says it?"

"Aye. And because you don't see her among the dead. Because Ilumat would have had a grand funeral and installed himself as King already if he had real proof. Because . . ." His voice graveled. "Because she can't be."

Osias gripped Draken's shoulder.

"You said once you would serve me if need," Draken said. "I've need, Osias."

"Aye, that I did." Osias let him go but his tone lacked defeat. "Show me the coin and I'll do as you bid."

He nodded and went back to the door to listen. No sounds. He frowned. He really didn't like how quiet the Citadel was.

Be easy. You know Akrasian ways of guarding. Remember walking the Bastion at night? No one on the loose but your sister that night.

And she was on the loose again, this night. *By now, surely someone has noticed I'm missing.*

You went two nights without anyone coming. Ilumat trusted you had no one to aid you.

Two nights. He hadn't realized. *Ilumat doesn't know about you and Truls.*

And he couldn't do a damned thing about it if he did.

He hadn't been away long, but coming into his study felt like a minor invasion. Someone had shuffled through the scrolls and trinkets. Draken didn't have time now to see if anything was missing; truth, he didn't know the value of any of the items beyond ancestral sentimentality. The maps on the desk were scattered; the chairs were moved since he'd last been in the room. He stared a moment. This was where he'd run Brîn with his confidants. Ilumat and his traitorous lords had taken his place.

He shoved his mind to matters of more importance: the coffers seemed undisturbed. He ran his hand first up to one hidden latch, then down to another, and then higher to the third. They clicked open quietly, well-oiled because of the vital contents within. There was barely enough space to walk between the back of the open shelves and the ones concealed behind them. His shoulder nudged a stack of thick leather bags designed for moving heavy coin. Baskets filled shelves, but mostly empty, depleted by war and dwindling taxes.

It was something a common man might not think of—Draken certainly hadn't as a career sailor and soldier—how war drains a country on two fronts. When people are at the front, they also aren't earning and spending in the local economy. The Akrasian crown was in even worse shape than Brîn. Another Sohalia and the soldiers would have to fend for themselves, which meant unleashing massive amounts of hunting and robbery on their people. Draken wondered if Ilumat knew, then chided himself. Of course he didn't.

Even though he'd been raised up to run lands, Ilumat seemed possessed of a stubborn ignorance.

At any rate, a bag of Rare was sufficient for his personal needs. For now. As for the rest, it would be here when he got his city back. Hopefully.

He grabbed up a thick leather pouch and gestured Osias in. "Close the door behind you and hold this."

"Fair dark as a cavern," Osias said.

"I can see you. Don't move."

He hefted a basket off a shelf and scooped coins out with his cupped hand, pouring them into the bag Osias held. The Mance seemed nonplussed, eyes wide; maybe the growing weight surprised him. "Can you carry it? We'll find a pack—"

Hush.

Aye, he heard it. Soft boot sounds. So did Osias because he froze, then set the bag on the shelf. It clinked softly. The hidden doorway was cracked, just enough to break the alignment of the shelves. Someone paying close attention could find it from the outside. Draken gritted his teeth. They'd have to die, whoever they were, and quickly. He couldn't afford to be caught, nor have them live to tell about the secret coffers. He wished for Aarinnaie about now. He also wished there were room for him to maneuver around Osias and go first, but there simply wasn't. He lifted the sword from where he'd laid it on the shelf and whispered with barely any breath: *"We'll fight through. Ready your bow."*

"Aye. Don't look."

Draken frowned. Don't look? Why? But the Mance just turned and put the bag on the shelf. *"Cover your eyes, Draken."* He started to glow, a sort of tarnished silver. But it pierced Draken's eyes like the sun. Soon he brightened. Draken could see the glowing through his eyelids and he felt a brash heat wash over him.

Korde, was Osias going to catch flame? He'd burn all the scrolls to ash with him. At any rate, there was no hiding now. The glow permeated the crack between the shelves. Draken heard shuffling beyond, even as he ducked his head against the hot light. He gripped the unfamiliar hilt tightly in his hand, knowing the balance was wrong, knowing he couldn't fight his best with it. Worse, he couldn't back the Mance if he couldn't bloody *see.*

There was a muffled shout and scuffling. No sound of a door but there wouldn't be; it had been kept sound and level over so many Sohalias. Then a sharp scream. Draken shifted forward, but he'd turned away from Osias and bumped into a shelf. Cursed. Another shout. The *thwup* of a bowstring. The echoless *thud* when an arrow pierces flesh and halts abruptly at bone. More screaming so the arrow didn't do its job properly—

"Come, Draken!"

Night vision painted everything in greys. Osias was gone—must've pushed his way out of the narrow coffers. Draken raised his sword and took three, four quick steps. The screaming servii lay clutching the arrow in his chest. Draken bent and swiped at the man's throat. The blade caught him above the collar of his hauberk. Four, no, six more poured into the room. Osias had a protected spot behind the desk and shot them as they came in. Oscherwood shafts could pierce boiled leather or even metal plate; these interior guards mostly wore mail. The next arrow knocked a lantern from a servii's hands. Its bearer shouted in pain and the lantern crashed to the floor, sparks and oil splattering as it rolled.

Draken cursed their shouts, which would draw more, and numbers, which felt overwhelming in the furniture-cluttered space. He ran at them from the side, dodging the haphazardly set chairs, leading with his swordarm. Osias was smart enough to let them gain some ground before killing the first two with arrows; doorways made for awkward sword fights. The third came in with a roar. She was good—very good—and bellowed as she went on the offensive. Draken wasted precious breaths parrying her strikes. The noise of the attackers and the dying would surely bring down the whole Citadel on them. He killed her at last. Luck, really; she risked leaving her ribs open to slash at his chest. Her blade caught his skin, blood hot and stinging as it hit the air. Bad move. His sword was at her low-line, beneath her ribs and coming up. She stumbled back, but he had his weight forward and stabbed deeper. She gaped at him, coughed. He yanked his blade back and she crumpled, spouting blood. In that moment he didn't know if it were he or Bruche in control, or if they'd found some balance.

The rest lay dead, bristling with white arrows.

The room shook as the sting of healing overtook him. He had to grab the back of a chair to keep upright. While he was regaining his balance, two more servii rounded the corner into the door. Draken didn't have the breath to curse. They came at Draken, young and nimble. *Gods, this is bloody hopeless.* He'd kill these two, and then what? More servii were on their way with this racket. There were hundreds of them in the Citadel. So much blood and hatred. If he died, it would all end—

His body fell cold as the grave. Bruche backed him away, putting him behind the chairs and the dead servii, gaining time and improved position.

The two servii split without a word, one climbing over the dead and the other cutting across the room toward Draken's goal, the desk. Osias shot an arrow in him. He paused, swaying back from the impact of an oscher bolt through mail, and kept coming. Blood spilled from the wound. He didn't appear to notice he was supposed to be dead or on his way to it. The other was shoving past chairs to get to Draken.

"Osias, a little help here . . ."

Osias's Voice thundered, shaking scrolls in their cubbies. Draken couldn't catch the words—was too busy watching the one closing on him, watching Bruche plan his defense from some shrinking place deep inside.

Both servii stopped. At once their limbs jerked askew, bodies twisting and thrusting in a macabre farce of a dance. Even Bruche stared. It went on several breaths, long enough for Draken to notice his hand tiring from gripping his sword. Osias's Voice raised in pitch. His beautiful face strained, all hard angles.

Truls glided forward, mouth open. No sound emitted; either he spoke in some death pitch beyond Draken's ken or it was a frustrated effort. It didn't matter. Whatever he did, or failed to do, twin sounds built in both chests of the servii, deep, guttural, screams bursting forth from their mouths and dying as abruptly. Both twitched violently and fell to the tile floor, soundless, motionless lumps of flesh.

Truls looked at Draken.

Draken looked at Osias. Blinked. Sniffed smoke. The fallen lantern had singed some lower scrolls.

"It took two of us," Osias said, wonder in his voice. "I've never . . ." For the first time, Draken saw his friend at an utter loss.

korde is come

CHAPTER FOURTEEN

D raken opened his mouth but couldn't decide which words to string together. He needed to know what questions to ask first. "What just happened?"

Osias started moving, shifting smoothly between bodies to remove his arrows. "Korde is here. Why do you look at me like that? I warned you earlier."

Draken gaped at him, then shut his mouth. "But you're hidden from him."

"Aye, as long as I don't work magic."

he is here he is here here

Osias talked over Truls's whispers, saying maybe more than Draken had ever heard him say in one go. "We have no time. I'll do as you bid and take the coin out. I'll hide it as quickly as possible. Think of a place and I'll go. You're right, we must separate. Korde will likely follow me—"

"Likely?" Fair nerve-racking, this gods-on-the-chase business.

And annoying when we've business elsewise.

"—As soon as I lose him, I'll return to Sikyra. I will move her. You must find Aarinnaie and bring her out. We can meet in Reschan." Osias started for the door, picking his way over bodies, pausing to remove arrows.

"I can't leave Brîn if I'm to take back the city."

"If Korde does not find me, nor achieve what he desires, he will be angry. Proximity to his wrath must be avoided."

"Osias?" The Mance kept moving. "Osias!"

The Mance looked up from working an arrow out from the ribcage and torn mail on a prone servii. *"What. Happened."* Draken pointed at the servii who had danced to their deaths.

"They were banes . . . of a sort. More powerful because they were controlled by Korde himself. I barely stopped them. Only with Truls's help . . ." Osias's pale brows fell, making worry lines Draken had never seen before. "I'll lead Korde away from you and try to lose him in the city."

"You act like he's a man."

"He is limited in this form."

"Form?" Frustration bubbled up in Draken like steam from the ground. This was untangling thornwood from rockweed. "What form? Earlier I thought I saw . . . a man. With horns—"

A brisk nod. "Khellian."

"I thought I was dreaming. The pain—"

"Draken, we don't have time for this."

"If some god comes after me I'd like to know what he's capable of."

Truls was watching them. By now Draken thought he'd warn them if someone were coming right away.

Osias released a breath that wasn't quite a sigh, but showed his impatience just the same. He lifted the heavy bag of coin. "They sense magic. Each have their own sort and are drawn to it. Korde's is mine; death magic. Agrian is healing magic and can find a Gadye without trouble. And—"

"And Khellian can find his namesake. That's what you're circling round?"

"Aye, Khel Szi." Emphasis on the name.

Draken's skin crawled. "You never thought to mention they can come down here to walk among us? It seems rather an important fact."

"They only come under great duress, though I have met Korde in Eidola."

"You've *met* him—?" As if for tea.

"They've come for some reason. Reasons that surely have more to do with more than you and me. Something bigger is afoot, my friend."

"Like the war, possibly?" He couldn't help the sarcasm.

"Perhaps even bigger. Something to draw their attention. Perhaps they feel threatened. Or that you are." He picked up the bag. "Where shall I leave this?"

Draken thought about it. "The last room, the one in the abandoned building by the back gates."

"Aye, I remember."

"Put it up in the chimney, over the flue." He cleared his throat. "And kiss my daughter for me."

The Mance nodded. His mouth tightened. "Take care and be well, my friend. I'll see you soon." He went through the doorway, glamour filtering him away from Draken's view.

Truls stared at Draken. Bruche shifted uneasily, knowing what came next.

He'll be in my quarters. I'm certain of it.

A faint, internal groan. *Of course. He couldn't resist.*

Draken sent Truls ahead and when he didn't return, he reckoned the way was clear. He paused at a corner where the wing to the Citadel business chambers met the rounded corridor that skirted the Great Hall to listen. No sounds. He held, wondering if Truls would return from scouting ahead. It'd be a handy thing to have a ghost scout, but so far Truls's help was inconsistent at best. But would the ghost sense Korde if the god was really walking around in the flesh? He had no idea of the god's abilities, nor Truls's—who obviously had helped with taking out the banes. And who knew what mischief Aarinnaie was finding on the loose. His sister acting on a death grudge wasn't a pretty thought.

Perhaps Korde's presence is why she is so determined to see Ilumat killed. Or Truls. He trained her.

Draken gritted his jaw. *You think his marrying her and raping her isn't enough motivation?*

Despite trying for a nobler attitude, between killing several attacking guards, his rising anxiety over meeting up with a vengeful god in the flesh, and worrying over whatever his sister was getting up to, he was nurturing a healthy dose of hatred for the Akrasians who had taken over his palace. Where were the rest of the guards? Ilumat had brought three thousand troops to Brîn.

What if they're rebelling against him?

By not guarding him? That's a damn subtle rebellion. Almost too subtle to notice.

Perhaps that's the point . . . The spirit sounded speculative. *Haven't you heard of similar? Soldiers who respond to orders too late. Surely some realize how incompetent Ilumat is. Perhaps they're trying to undermine him now.*

Draken could only wish there were something like that afoot. But for some reason the thought of that only raised his disquiet. If they rebelled against a high lord, with some—he had to admit it—claim to the throne, they'd surely never follow him or his daughter, two sundry bastards with naught but stolen names.

He started to step around the corner but Truls rounded it, flitting at him so quickly he encased Draken in a quick fog of cold. *they come they come*

Footsteps followed, boots ringing on the tile with authority, others following, and a clear female voice issuing terse orders. "No, I'll inform Lord Ilumat when we're sure he's secure."

He only caught a few words as he backtracked down the corridor, but it was enough. They'd be coming to find the servii he'd killed, to see if their valuable prisoner had been caught. The commander wisely decided to delay informing their volatile Regent until she had good news.

He went through the first door he found—Thom's chamberlain office. The latch caught and he winced at the noise, but he was able to shove on through and get it shut. He leaned against the door, searching the space for a way to bar himself in. No, of course a lock on Thom's door would be a great insult to his Khel Szi.

Good lad, Thom . . .

Bootsteps and voices closed in, overcoming his twinge of grief. Were they slowing? He tried to breathe but his throat closed around it, even his heart seemed to pause—

"Search every room. He's here somewhere. I doubt he'd leave without trying to free the princess."

"She's chained to her bed," another voice answered. "She's not going anywhere."

"Thank the gods for a small boon. Now if they grant me thorough servii—" Her tone was pointed but broke off. Boots quickened on the tile. Must've seen the damage and dead in the study.

It's a fair distraction, aye?

No. They're too close. But there were shuttered windows opposite the door, two of them. They would have to do, even with the likelihood of guards patrolling the grounds. He could climb the two-story private wing if he had to. He tried to think of the lay of the land just outside the office windows but couldn't. He'd rarely been in here, really only walked by. Citadel staff came to the Khel Szi, not the other way around.

Plain, battered work tables at a good height for standing, an old map tacked to the wall, chairs and stools standing sentry over a few scrolls knocked to the floor. The shelves looked mostly untouched. Akrasians had come through but apparently not found anything of value. As far as Draken's immediate predicament, the best he could come up with was a chair under the latch. He jammed it under the handle as best he could without resorting to kicking the legs to wedge it tighter. More footsteps and voices outside told him he'd be heard, and that he didn't have much time before the comprehensive search for him began in earnest. At best the chair would give him some warning if someone came through.

He strode to the window, the floor cold against his bare feet, and listened for a moment. Looked at Truls. "Check if it's clear."

Truls didn't move.

"What? Don't like the outdoors?" he muttered. Perhaps errant gods-in-the-flesh lingered in palace gardens.

He squeezed his fists to warm his fingers, undid the latch, and cracked the shutter to peer through it. Shrubs and trees crowded the ground; it was the more natural part of the garden and small woods on the palace grounds. Shadows reigned, broken only by the faint glimmer of light rain. Cold air swept over his chest. He could use something warmer to wear. It reminded him when he first landed at Akrasia in old rags that barely covered him. It hadn't been

Frostseason then. A cloak? A blanket? No. Just worktables standing in silence peculiar to the typical activity in the room.

He shoved the shutter open and climbed out, gripping the stolen sword in one hand. A thorn pricked his foot as he hit the ground. Hissing, he bent to pull it out as light flashed amid the trees. He stayed down, crouching under the open shutters, back against the smooth stone of the building. He picked out moving people, three at least, each with lanterns. He wished for a bow because, trees or not, he could at least set them on the run.

A thud jerked his attention to the room at his back. Someone was coming, surely. He shifted to a crawl along the cold dirt, fingers clasped tight around the unfamiliar hilt as he eased around the building. The occasional bones of a shrub scratched his arm as it made for meager concealment.

Bruche urged him irritably, *Pick up the pace. They'll be hopping out that window and coming after you in a breath.*

Unless they are subtle rebels, he retorted, just as surly. He was making for the corner but he had no idea what was around it. He had never come back here but for the very occasional stroll. Why would he? The cold ached in his bad knee and his shoulder fussed from crawling. Worse, the icy rain fell harder, shifting from mists to stinging by the time he reached the corner. He took meager shelter under a shrub but trembles overcame him. He gritted his jaw. If his teeth chattering gave him away he'd never live it down. Of course, he wasn't likely to survive the night as it was . . .

Enough. Focus. You're thinking like a bane got hold of you.

Draken shook his head and wiped rain from his eyes with a dirty hand. Optimism was a bit difficult to come by when crawling in the mud and rain at one's bloody palace with a horde of eager servii just behind. But he didn't waste effort in arguing, just poked his head around the corner to look. It was lighter ahead with torches under the dripping overhang, but the rain shaded his sensitive eyes well enough. No figures moved there and the doors were shut. Perhaps not so eager then. He smiled grimly and kept crawling, forcing each arguing joint on.

At last he pushed his back against the wall under the narrow overhang, gripping his sword in one hand and wiping his face with the other. Simplest would be to rush in right through these doors. He was steps away from his private chamber, just a corridor and a flight of stairs.

Enough thinking. He turned and pulled the door open. Stopped, squinted in the light. Voices filtered down the corridor, but no footsteps, nothing came closer. He eased the door closed behind him, shutting out the wet. His heart thundered in his throat. Cold, still air on his wet skin made him shiver. His

fingers tightened on the blade again. Bruche forced them looser, an easier grip
for easier killing.

Truls sifted upward, seeming to leave foggy bits of himself that faded and
reformed higher up the flight of steps. Draken didn't wait for him to appear
whole at the top but started after him, keeping his eyes on his own feet as
they landed. A shallow groove slanted the middle of each tiled step, bright
glaze worn down to hardened clay. But the stairs didn't creak or ease under his
weight. Draken listened, knew no one was coming, but Bruche lifted his head
when he neared the top. Truls waited, as expected.

Couldn't go on ahead and be useful, could he?

No need. There's no one here.

Bruche spoke truth. The corridor lay before him, dark and empty. His antechamber doors hung open. No sound, and then a low grunt, maybe a *ting* of
metal on metal. His antechamber was roomy and if the inner doors were shut
they'd mostly conceal sounds from within. But a few short, running strides
had him there, shoving the door open. Bruche had the stolen sword up, point
first through the doors as they swung open and slammed against the flanking
wall. The noise startled those within. Draken squinted at the movement in
the candlelight. Ilumat squared off with Aarinnaie, though their faces were
twinned in astonishment. Seaborn glittered in her grip. As she recovered and
swung, Draken got the sudden rush of ruthless insight that it was better suited
to her hand than his.

As he moved forward, Bruche shifted his blade up for leverage on the attack.
It was perfect: his form, the approach. Ilumat did his damnedest to always keep
his fight above his opponent's sword. It was a brash style and he was reputedly
better at it than anyone, at least better than anyone he or Bruche had ever
fought.

Draken stumbled over something soft and heavy, hands and knees slamming
the tile. The sword bounced from his fist. He looked back. A body, unyielding
under his ankles. *The bane from the dungeon.*

Draken didn't have time to think about it. A sword blade flashed, reflecting
candlelight that should be dim but to Draken was nearly blinding. He ducked
his head in a wince from the burn and felt a whoosh of air over the top of his
shorn head. Then a sharp clang and Aarinnaie shouted. Draken looked up in
time to see her drive Ilumat back two steps.

Ilumat grunted: frustration or fury, Draken couldn't tell. Aarinnaie really was
no match for him, but she kept him busy enough for Draken to find his feet.
He swept up his stolen sword and pressed in on Ilumat's swordhand, trying to
draw him away from her. Ilumat backed further, but it was just to improve his

balance. He attacked Draken in force. His sword was superior to the servii's weapon. The first swing notched Draken's blade as Bruche raised it to block, and Ilumat twisted his sword down and around Draken's too quick to see.

Bruche flicked the tip of Ilumat's sword away from his hilt and swung his around, trying to catch Ilumat's arm. He only snagged the wide sleeve of Ilumat's long sleeping tunic. It did set the Akrasian off-step, but not enough to halt a rebounding attack, a fury of blows even Bruche had a hard time managing, especially with the poorly balanced sword. Aarinnaie pressed in from the side again, diverting Ilumat's attention.

The doors to his antechamber slammed open and the air filled with shouts and cries. Draken raced toward Aarinnaie, struck hard at Ilumat's throat with his free hand. The Akrasian cried out and staggered back. Draken didn't wait to see if he was dead. He dragged Aarinnaie away toward Sikyra's chambers. She paused, grabbed up an oil lantern, and threw it back the way they'd come. Bright light flashed as it exploded, the reflection against the tiles ahead nearly blinding Draken. More cries from behind them. Bruche kept him stumbling forward.

Aarinnaie slammed the doors behind them and set the latches. The little-used far set of doors off Sikyra's room led to another balcony cloaked in overgrown branches from a sizable tree. They pushed through the doors and Aarinnaie leaned back against them. Tree branches concealed them, broad leaves slick. A heavy rain fell, dampening harried voices behind and below them.

Draken took his sword back, pressed the smaller stolen blade into Aarinnaie's hands, and climbed out. The tree made him feel like a stranded target, though he was concealed from all sides. He felt awkward and heavy in it, and it creaked softly under his weight. He found a place he could more or less stand, bare feet on a lower, broad branch, hands gripping another. Droplets showered him as leaves shifted. Branches had been trimmed up to clear the ground below. Getting down required a jump higher than he was tall. Draken hoped his knee could bear up. Bruche returned the sentiment to move cautiously and quit whining.

Aarinnaie climbed out behind him, sleek and nimble. Leaves rustled but she slipped between branches and started climbing down. *"Stable,"* she whispered.

Is she mad? You'll never get horses out of here.

Mad? No more than he. But Aarin wasn't called Ghost for small reason. He moved to drop his foot to a lower limb . . .

The balcony door creaked open. Both he and Aarinnaie stilled. Air locked in Draken's chest and soon started to burn. He eased it from his lungs, unwilling to risk a noisy, desperate exhale.

"Still can't see from that damned lantern exploding. Black as pitch out here. But they must have come out this way." A male voice, brisk.

Branches shifted. A female voice answered: "Climb down the tree, then, and find them."

"You climb it. You're littler than me. And I outrank you."

Draken narrowed his eyes so the whites wouldn't show. A rain started to fall, pattering against the broad leaves, splashing off them onto his head. Wind ruffled around him, ran over the top of his wet head and chilled his bare skin. Rain ran down his skin in maddening streams. He gritted his teeth.

The female servii snorted. "Blast the Seven. Maybe they already got down and tried the temple again."

"If they did, they're already caught. It's blocked and escorts are positioned there. They've got to be on the grounds somewhere if not right here in the damn tree. Go on, then. I'll notify Lord Ilumat and meet you below."

A hesitation and the servii started out on the same branch Draken had, grasping it with both hands and swinging a leg over the balcony. Draken looked down at Seaborn in his hand. The sword wasn't much use in a bloody tree. Aarinnaie lifted her knife. She'd have to strike quick and just right to kill the guard soundlessly. The dead made no noise, but the dying made plenty. *A dead servii will make plenty of noise falling from this tree*, Bruche growled.

At any rate, she struck too quickly for Draken to stop her. The servii turned a little, hanging onto the balcony rail with one hand and reaching for a branch with the other as she swung her other leg over the railing. Her stiff boot slipped on the wet branch. Aarinnaie reached out and shoved her with her fist. For a moment she seemed to hang, as if she wouldn't fall. Her lips parted. "You—"

Aarinnaie jabbed her in the throat with the knife, letting it go as the servii tumbled through the branches. Blood trailed after her, splattering on leaves. She made a dull thud as she hit the ground. Draken was already climbing down. Something felt as if it tore inside his knee as he landed and hot pain raced up his thigh. He hissed a curse, grabbed the servii, and hauled her behind the big tree trunk.

Aarinnaie dropped to the ground in a quiet crouch. She leaped up into a run, fleet through the shadows at the edges of the courtyard. Bruche rushed to chill the pain and Draken ran after her, albeit in a lopsided limp.

They skirted the courtyard, which helped Draken's vision. Soldiers were positioned by the gates but other than that the space was empty. A few trees and damp shadows hid their progress as they moved in front of the temple. He wished they didn't have to get so close—he raced up and grabbed Aarinnaie's arm and dragged her back. She had the presence of mind not to shout but fought him until she realized who had her. He pulled her back against a tree and gestured. Two Escorts stood under the overhang at the front of the temple. Their fishscale and pale skin glinted against the night. Aarinnaie shook her head and gave him a look.

He tugged her along the side of the temple, toward the back of the grounds. Trees were more plentiful there, providing cover from eyes and the pounding rain. He limped along as quietly as possible, which wasn't much with mud squishing between his cold toes and sticks jabbing his feet and scraping his ankles. He studied the small woods around them intently, but no movement penetrated the gloom. It struck him. He'd walked here often. There had been gardeners, animals scurrying underfoot, and birds calling. The animals had run and flown to escape. The gardeners had died on the edges of Akrasian swords.

He slowed as he came upon the back corner of the temple. Beneath his feet was escape, the tunnels filled with his ancestors. His hand crept up to sign the horns but he dragged it back down. The gods walked in Brîn. Such a sign might be a summons.

Aarinnaie lingered close as he paused, her warmth against his back. The rain eased as he looked around the corner at the darkened clearing behind the temple. Empty of servii. Still, every bit of him was sharply alert, every muscle ready to leap to the fight. It was dark, but all cleared ground. Tall buildings, mostly windowless, butted up against the back wall. On the ground there was not so much as a shrub for cover. He judged the temple fifty paces wide, and twice that to the stable. But escape hinged on not being seen. They couldn't fight off even a few servii, and those would let others know, and they'd be over-run. And then the stable . . . how were they to escape that?

He looked back at Aarinnaie and whispered, *"This is a bad idea."*

She shook her head. *"Go, Drae. I'll show you there."* When he didn't move right away, she shoved him. *"They'll come. Go!"*

He clenched his jaw; arguing wasn't going to help. But damn her, even as good as she was, there was no escaping the Citadel.

You must at least try.

He growled annoyance because Bruche was right. They'd gotten this far. He rounded the corner, sword up. The patch of bare ground behind the temple was clear and quiet. It wasn't as muddy back there as it was under the trees. A carpet of cropped, wet plants, softer underfoot, concealed the noise of their movement. He peered around the next corner. Torches burned by the stable entrance. He squinted against the glare but saw no guards. Horses crowded the paddock—Akrasian mounts, he assumed. He pressed his back against the smooth wall of the temple and looked at his sister.

"I don't see servii, but the slaves usually sleep in the stable, don't they?"

"They're all dead, remember?" she whispered. The words were like a punch to the gut but she didn't seem to notice. She shifted around him to look. "We're going in the back, through the paddock."

"You don't think we'll upset the horses?"

She shrugged. "I don't plan on upsetting them. Do you?"

Bruche snorted, amused.

He scowled at her and gestured her ahead. He hadn't ever walked through the stable, a sizable building housing dozens of animals. Horses had always been brought to him in the courtyard. He'd usually mounted about where he'd been strung on the scaffolding and tortured.

Aarinnaie walked smoothly and without much hurry to the fence. Draken followed, skin crawling with cold and apprehension, certain arrows would cut them down at any moment. Horses lifted their heads and snuffled at them. A couple moved toward the fence, maybe looking for a handout. She never hesitated. Simply walked to the fence and climbed over to disappear among them.

Clever girl.

Draken grunted softly. Too clever by half. He climbed, bad knee first, wincing when that foot hit the ground on the other side. He hoped none of the horses stepped on his bare feet. Besides hurting like a bane, his healing would shake the ground and terrify them into a stampede. Horses snuffled his shoulders as he shifted between them, and a strange calm fell over him. A dangerous calm. He kept moving, sword pressed to his thigh, using them as cover. He lost sight of Aarin, but by then he'd reckoned where they were headed: the door hanging from rollers that led from the low-slung wooden stable to the crowded paddock.

Aarinnaie started to slide the door open but it squealed on its track and she stopped. Every horse's head lifted and turned that way. *"Fools all."* Draken cursed under his breath. Servii could be in the building and now they had warning. He pushed through quicker to reach her.

Voices from within. Damn, damn, damn. He pulled Aarin around the side of the building. There was a narrow slice of ground between it and the Citadel wall, perfect for them to slide sideways into. Also perfect for a semi-competent archer to draw arrow at one end and take them out like snakes in a tunnel. The reek of rotting flesh drifted down from overhead; the Brînian trophies who had once been his slaves and guards.

The sliding door squealed again as someone opened it, and a voice hissed the horses back. Then quiet fell. Whoever it was must be studying the paddock. Draken lifted his sword to the ready.

"Must've been a bittersnake or something that riled them," a voice said.

Another hushed the horses. "Aye, well. Doesn't matter. They won't get out by horseback at any rate."

There was a point. Draken turned his head give his sister a look. What were they doing here? She grinned at him, teeth with a feral gleam, trusting he could see in the pitch between the walls.

Aarinnaie started edging down the gap between the wall and the stable. The wall was rough, scraping along his back. Damn, was it narrowing? Or perhaps it was his hard, anxious breath filling his chest that made it seem smaller. Faint tremors running through the ground under his feet as he healed the scratches wouldn't help much. He hoped she had a plan but he couldn't fathom what it might be. They were trapped and it was only going to be a matter of breaths before they were found and dragged out into the courtyard. He couldn't bear the thought of Aarinnaie getting strung up on that scaffolding—

Stop now. Those who expect the worst often get it.

Aarinnaie stepped forward and disappeared. He blinked and edged closer. A damned opening, tight. He tried to force himself through after her, but even his near starvation diet of the past couple of sevennight hadn't reduced his chest breadth enough to allow him passage between the log and a stone wall. Three horses were crammed into a stall and one stretched its neck to snuffle at him curiously. It was golden and unfamiliar. The horses, just the scent of them, gave him the same feeling seeing ships sailing from their moorings in Blood Bay. Old days, and some good ones, when he thought himself free. But he should know by now he was no more free than he had been as a child slave.

Aarinnaie emerged from between the horses, startling Draken. They didn't so much a snuffle at her arrival. He grunted and stepped back.

"Sh." She lifted her hand to her mouth to quiet him. It gripped a bloody knife. "Go through the paddock. It's clear."

He scowled at her but she disappeared again, so he did as she bid, edging back the way he'd come, blade held aloft. His whole body tightened, but no one saw him but the horses. He slipped around to the sliding door and stepped through, only to stumble over a body sprawled on the hard-packed dirt. A black-red stain surrounded it. The second time the dead had tripped him up this evening. Aarinnaie drifted past him to pull the door closed and set the bar.

"There," she said, as if finishing a household chore and moving onto the next one. She didn't even whisper, though her voice was low.

"As fine as these horses are, I doubt any of them can carry us through the courtyard, the locked gates, and a row of servii," Draken said.

"We aren't going that way." She moved past him to start untying a rope that hung diagonal from a beam to a post. It swung down. "We're going up. There's a hole."

"In my stable roof?"

"Not all the time. They patch it and I have to keep breaking it open. Very tiresome. But the weather has been fine until a few sevennight ago and I doubt the Akrasians have had time or inclination." She grinned.

She's enjoying this.

Aye, and I could kiss her for it. Bruche's return grin reached Draken's lips before he could shove the spirit back down. The thought left a faintly sick feeling in Draken's gut, as did the strong reek of horse urine. The Akrasians hadn't been managing the stable to Brînian standards.

Aarinnaie didn't appear to notice any of it, though; she was too busy shimmying up the rope ladder before it had quit swinging. At the top she slung a leg over a crossbeam and crawled along it. Draken followed along on the ground, shoulders tight, wanting to work out where he had to go before climbing up. Time was he'd shine up ship rigging without a thought to untangle a line, take down a torn sail, or shoot his bow at pirates from the swaying lookout platform. Time was he'd been a young man once, and eager to please. Now he just felt sore and old and wondered if all the fighting and pain and effort would ever really help Brîn or Akrasia or if he was just deluding himself.

A sharp bang against the courtyard door to the stable startled him and made the crowded horses shift against each other. It shifted on its rollers, but less than a handspan. Aarinnaie had barred it as well. Good girl.

A shout followed, and then another, as the Akrasians sorted out what a stable barred from the inside might mean. Overhead Aarinnaie grunted and he heard a creaking tear of wood.

"Climb up, Dra—Damn!"

He strode back to the ladder and put his bare foot on the bottom rung. It was wooden. So were the next three, but they were broken. "What?"

She crawled back along the beam and opened her mouth but before she could answer, a blinding orange light flashed across the moonlit hole she'd been so diligently enlarging. Then another, and a horse kicked and neighed. Similar racket started on the paddock door.

"Come, Draken! Wife! The search is over."

Ilumat, shouting. He sounded gleeful, more than a little mad. In a breath Draken knew why. A faint whiff of smoke drifted down to him. He swore, not bothering to keep his voice down. The Akrasians knew they were there and were willing to risk their finest horses to burn them out.

CHAPTER FIFTEEN

"Come down, Aarin." Draken didn't bother keeping his voice low. Sparks fluttered through the hole in the roof she'd been working on, pinprick stings against his eyes. She crawled along the beam toward him, but not all the way. "No. You come up. We have to get out of here."

The doors rattled. Voices shouted, now with purpose. Strategizing how to get inside. Horses neighed and jostled and kicked their stalls as they scented smoke.

"We're trapped here. They'll be climbing the walls to get in. We can't ride out. They are too many." Damn her, all things she knew. All obvious to a whipped dolt. He shifted from foot to foot. His free hand clenched and unclenched. He could open a door and at least die with his sword in his hand. It would be fast and ugly. Honorable.

Bruche chilled his legs, holding him in place.

Before Draken could chide him, or snatch back control, Aarinnaie hissed and scrambled back to the hole. Gods, a hand, a shoulder, a face. She snarled and stretched up to pull the servii down. He bounced off the beam and slammed to the aisle floor. The dirt-packed impact stunned him. Draken stared, then Bruche was moving him there. Draken lifted his sword and killed him, neat, quick, a body moving from breathing to not in a flash of steel piercing flesh unresisting to death. There wasn't even much blood, but the horses neighed in terror from this fresh spill. Fire and shouting and blood in their safe space was too much for even trained warhorses to bear. Panic spread through them. One of the stall doors swung out a little from a kick, snapping back on its terrified prisoner.

"Draken, damn you, son of a pig-sucking—" A shout interrupted Aarinnaie's curse. She swore again. "Korde take you, Draken, get up here!"

Korde very well might. She knew nothing about the gods come to earth.

"Why, only to climb back down?" Or get shot down.

"Come *on!*" She scurried like a rat back to the hole, grasped a strut between the beam, and swung up to cautiously poke her head up through the hole she'd made. Someone shouted. She snarled something unintelligible, ducked down, and her knife caught the firelight. Draken blinked. It was brighter, much. All in the span of a few breaths.

She must know something. Go.

Bruche sounded adamant, and more than a little impatient. Draken sighed, grasped the ladder, and started to climb. He had to muscle his way up past the broken rungs, arms straining. Bruche, annoyed, didn't rush to soothe the pain in his bad shoulder. The joint felt slippery inside his skin, like it could pop out with one more reach. He grimaced and grasped the rope with his opposite hand.

"What are we doing on the roo—"

"Sh! Do you want to announce what we're doing?"

They couldn't hear anyway. Too much shouting, too much terror. He could hear Ilumat, voice at a high, angry pitch. He climbed the rest of the way, feeling old and stiff as he held onto the beam with one arm. She gestured to him. The fire was hot here, sparking against his vision, filtering through cracks in the roof. It clogged his lungs, achingly familiar. They'll burn the whole city maybe . . . he climbed along the beam. It was a little wider than he had judged from the ground, but splinters prickled his palms and his knuckles where his fingers curled around his sword. Tiny tremors ran through the beam up through his knees as the skin closed tight around them.

When he reached Aarinnaie, she was standing, head and shoulders and chest out the hole in the roof. She moved, set her feet, body twisting just so, and the familiar thrup of a bow—maybe he imagined it through the screams of the horses.

"Where'd the bow come from?"

She ran out of arrows and threw it down. It skipped along the roof tiles to disappear over the edge.

There was no way but up and he didn't want her to stop shooting servii, so he nudged her supple boot. After a slight hesitation she leveraged herself through with her elbows on the roof, sliding from sight. Standing was a dangerous balancing act. He tried not to think of the broken body on the dirt floor far below as he rose and grasped the edge of the roof. The hole tugged on the skin of his sides as he pulled through, splintered wood scraping.

He emerged into billowing smoke. It made him cough, but hopefully it provided cover. Aarin crouched low on the roof, moving back, toward the middle.

He followed. Be nice if she mentioned where they were going, but he was pretty sure she didn't know either, just putting maximum distance between them and the men on the ground. The whole barn rumbled and there were shouts below. Draken wasn't sure if it was from his self-healing or a dozen men trying to break through the heavy wooden doors.

"Did you pull up the ladder?"

He gave her a blank look.

"Bloody Seven, Draken!"

"Where are we going?" They were birds on a rail sitting up here.

She jerked her chin toward the wall. Toward the street. Out. He shook his head. Spikes topped the wall, and it was piled with rotting trophies. The stench was another reason to be glad of the smoke.

"It's the only way. We have to. Hurry!" She started to crawl down the roof, feet first, her fingers gripping the tiles. A few broken pieces from the hole she'd enlarged tumbled past her as Draken slid over them.

Another arrow flitted past them, crackling flames, and Draken ducked. The smoke must be thick enough they couldn't really see them from below. She reached the edge of the roof, slipping and catching herself with her boot on the wall across the gap. Her shorter legs barely reached. Draken cursed under his breath and the shingles rattled as his skin closed around splinters and tiny scrapes. The heads on the wall emerged from the smoke, and the reek of them too. They were too distorted to recognize. He slid down to her and braced himself with his foot on the wall. Grimaced. She was right. The spikes weren't too high to climb over and they had to hurry before their route was discovered. He pushed off the roof, hung for a single heartbeat over the gap, and grasped an unbloodied spike between heads. The wind ruffled the hair of the head next to it and it brushed the back of his hand. The wall was rough, even sharp in places, but the soles of his feet had grown tough in the previous moonturns from going barefoot. He stepped over the row of head-topped spikes, trying not to inhale the stench or smoke, and reached out to her with his free hand.

She shifted, slipped a little more. His heart lurched, but she grasped his fingers, then strengthened her grip on his hand. She was so light, he nearly sent himself over the wall pulling her toward him. She caught another free spike and balanced there. Her jaw set in a stubborn tilt. "Go."

It wasn't a far drop, but high enough he hoped he didn't break his foot or something on the way down. Even magical healing might take time he didn't have. He dropped his sword down. It clattered into the bit of dirt and weeds growing at the base. Then he eased one leg over, groaned at his stiffness, and let the other leg fall. Reasonably, he knew his feet weren't too far from the ground.

But he had to grip the rail beneath a swollen, slack-jawed head, and blood had dripped down. The constant damp and bloodstains made the metal tacky. Bile rose. He chided himself. All the blood he'd seen and shed and spilled, and a little sticky metal could make his stomach twist like a writhing snake. Bruche rumbled soothing words and chilled his hand so he didn't feel it, but too late; the sensation would last a lifetime. His legs dangled sickeningly for a moment and then he dropped.

He stumbled back but managed not fall entirely back onto his arse. Aarinnaie was already scrambling over. He reached up and grasped her legs to steady her, lowering her to the ground. They were on the open street, mostly unguarded but for a couple of distracted servii because there were no gates in this section of wall, and someone would have to do exactly what Draken and Aarinnaie had done, crossed a spiked wall flush with rotting heads. The guards were just pointless bravado anyway. No one in their right minds would try to get into the Citadel with an Akrasian in residence.

Without a word, Draken snatched up his sword and they raced off, toward the center of Brîn. Draken wasn't quite sure why he took that route, except he hoped for more cover of people, of buildings. Also, it led any pursuers away from Khisson's strongholds and his own bolt-hole where Osias would hopefully leave the coin. He heard shouts behind them and threw his dwindling energy into a burst of speed. Aarinnaie ran as if she were born to it, drawing ahead and leading him around the bend in a road. He followed. She always knew where she was going.

He hoped.

◆ ◆ ◆

They snuck into Khisson's house through a back shuttered window, shivering cold, dripping with icy rain, stinking of death and sweat. The stench was probably what alerted Khisson's guards they were there. Two swords appeared in the darkened sitting room, close enough to nick skin.

Bruche snorted at the threat. Draken pushed one away with Seaborn. The two swords made a gentle clink. "T-tell K-Khisson I'm here."

It took some time for the bloodlord to appear, but in the meantime someone brought them warmed wine and blankets and stoked up the fire. Draken ignored the wine and kept as close to the fire as he could without standing in it, sword gripped tight in one hand, the ends of the blanket clenched around his shoulders. He squinted tightly against the light. The servant kindly lit some candles, which Aarinnaie snuffed as soon as he left.

"You're singeing the blanket." Aarinnaie finished her wine in a couple of gulps and pulled him back from the flames a half step.

"I can't stay here. I need clothes, a horse—"

"A bath first," Khisson said. He dipped his chin to Draken. "Khel Szi."

"The Akrasians are going after my daughter. I have little time to waste on pleasantries."

"Through the back gates to Eidola?"

Draken's eyes narrowed. How did he know where Sikyra was? But Khisson waved a hand. "I am not a stupid man. I also can send men to stop them."

"I don't know how much head start they've got." A dagger of fear caught him in the chest. What if Khisson took his daughter captive? Killed her. Bruche held him steady and Draken cleared his throat. "Aye, send them."

"Come this way. There're warming a bath for you in the kitchen. Clothes. Food. We'll plan after you're more comfortable, with your leave."

Fair enough. Even inscrutable Aarinnaie was wrinkling her nose and he didn't favor traipsing outside in his soaked rags. The kitchen was warm from the cooking hearth and steamy from the water. He stripped off his things, tossing them into the hearth.

Alone for the first time since the dungeon, he gripped the side of the metal tub with both hands and bent over, staggered by all he'd done, all that had happened. His friends, his people . . . his slaves. It had been slaves' heads they'd climbed over; that was a side wall, less trafficked than the front entrance to the Citadel. But his people, nonetheless. He could still feel the brush of dead flesh, smell the rot and smoke . . . he looked down at himself. He was stained with black patches of ash. Dried blood flecked off his skin.. He'd never be shed of it. Never.

He forced himself to step into the stinging hot water and sank down so that it covered the top of his head, blocking all sound and sight. Bruche let him sit in peace for a bit before easing him back up. Nasty bits of dirt and worse skimmed the top of the water. He ignored it and scrubbed all over with the bar of caustic soap and rough cloth until his whole skin felt raw and tight. Someone, a slave impressed with their guest perhaps, had left out a bowl of thatchnut oil. He stared at it for a moment before rubbing it into his skin. The clothes provided were warm and fine and fit well—even the boots served once he wound his feet in tight cloth strips and stuck them in. A long cloak topped it all, sized to his height. Must be Khisson's. He missed the weight of Elena's pendant and his own scabbard and belt, though. No scabbard was provided so he carried the sword back in his hand.

"I've been thinking on that." Khisson had a few sheaths laid out for him to inspect.

Draken found one that would suit and strapped it to his hip, saying, "I owe you more debt than I've means repay at the moment."

Khisson had left the room dark. The flames cast odd shifting shadows up his face, but Draken could see the dangerous glimmer of his gaze, the thick strands of grey infiltrating his locks now that the ashdye had worn off for the day. "Szirin has been telling me what went on at the Citadel."

Aarinnaie wrapped her opposite hand around the marriage bracelet and stared at the fire. An empty wine cup dangled from her fingers.

"This man Ilumat has offended House Khel and your patron god. I will see him put down." He glanced at Aarinnaie. "When I kill him, you will be free."

Draken didn't much like that look. Ilumat was what he was, and Khisson did nothing without gain. He was probably thinking Aarinnaie would make a fine wife for one of his sons, if a bit used.

"Ilumat is my kill," she said.

Khisson's brows raised, but he bowed his head to her.

"Aye, well," Draken said. "Ilumat is a slippery one. At the moment I'm more concerned with stopping them taking Sikyra hostage. First things first."

"I have a proposal for you, regarding your debt," Khisson said.

Well, you did bring it up. Both he and Bruche had been waiting to find out what Khisson wanted from all this risk and hard work.

"It's imperative we take back Brîn. You know as well as I do we're a bargaining stone with the Ashen."

Draken was quiet for a bit, considering the big bloodlord. "You're awfully well informed, Khisson."

"Aye, that I am, and I can wager with the best of them. I have connections among the other families . . . the ones Ilumat bought off. Each thinks they've got a chance at the . . . your throne."

Nice slip, that. Telling.

Sh. I want to hear what he has to say. "So you propose what?"

"I haven't told you it all yet." Khisson reached for a pipe. Draken shifted on his feet. But he was stuck here, barring fighting his way out and stealing a horse, and he wasn't ready to burn bridges with the bloodlord yet.

"I think Khel Szi said he hasn't much time," Aarinnaie said, her tone icy.

"He'll have time for this. Ilumat bargained away the lives of our people. The men and boys are to be enslaved to the Ashen, or as good as."

"To what end?"

"To rebuild Brîn in some other image." Khisson paused as he lit his pipe, letting his words sink in. He was smoking fine Gadye leaf, moist and pungent. Draken couldn't help taking a deep breath of it. It soothed his rough throat. Someday maybe he'd take up the pipe himself, if . . . *Don't even think it,* Bruche growled.

"The Ashen plan to dismantle it stone by stone and rebuild a new city, centered on a Moonminster temple the likes this world has never seen. They reckon this land is fertile for it, and with Blood Bay—"

"Fertile? Strange word."

"They use words like it all the time. Just off a bit, like they worship ruddy Agrian." No city dweller did. No soldier did. Agrian was left to the provincial farmers and herders. "But it's working. To hear the bloodlords talk, they're half believing these Ashen hail the gods' own coming."

Draken thought of the two gods he thought he'd seen and didn't doubt it. But he stayed quiet on that. "Why is Brîn such a good place to install this faith?"

"I think Akrasia has given them more fight than they expected. They consider Brînians ignorant barbarians, with minds ready to fill with some truth of their making. And there are our women . . ."

"What do women have to do with it?" Aarinnaie asked.

Khisson raised his brows. Grey had slipped through the black dye. "I thought you knew. Haven't you noticed the invasion is all men? They say women are not real people; no better than breeders, the thought goes."

When has he heard an Ashen say anything? Bruche said.

Aarinnaie snorted softly. She released her bracelet and refilled her cup with wine. "That couldn't matter less."

"It matters to the Ashen, and their plans for Brîn. They believe us coarse and that makes us more easily conformed to their sect. Also, in your blood runs Khellian's, so the better to mix with. It's surely why Ilumat took you to wife."

"You think Ilumat is conformed to their ways?" Draken asked her. Again Aarinnaie's hand strayed to her bracelet. She saw Draken watching and dropped it.

"We didn't speak much. I wouldn't know."

"I'd like to think the Ashen could be driven back from Brîn, if someone is here who knows how to handle things," Khisson said.

"Meaning you." Draken released a breath. "You didn't stop the invasion."

"Then we were caught off guard. I have people coming now, ready to fight."

"Dragonstar pirates."

Khisson stiffened, but he didn't protest the slur. "I will get you out of the city, free you to find your daughter. The Akrasians have used us for the last time. I will drive the Akrasians from Brîn, keep the Ashen out, and hold your throne for your return."

Aarinnaie snorted.

"You don't trust me." Khisson was so matter-of-fact Draken wondered if it was contrived.

"Why would I?"

Khisson drew in a breath that puffed his chest and made him seem bigger. "Khel Szi. It's a reasonable offer with heartfelt intent. And honestly, you don't have another. Your option is to try to escape the city on your own—unlikely— and leave Brîn to the Ashen to destroy. Without your favor as Brînian regent, I've little choice but to flee back to the Dragonstars."

"Regent? That's a high title for an island bloodlord." He didn't add pirate, though Khisson *was* a pirate. No sense in angering the man. He still needed that horse, and he wouldn't turn down aid getting through the gates either.

Speaking of, time does go on, Draken. Accept the deal and be off. Khisson in the Citadel is easier to sort than Ilumat and his Ashen priest.

Draken growled low. He knew no such thing. Khisson had an old vendetta against Draken. He had killed the man's son, after all—never mind the lad had attacked Aarinnaie and had it coming. Khisson's was no simple enmity to disregard, nor the man worth much trust. "Do not believe the throne is yours, no matter how comfortable it becomes, for you do not bear Khellian's blood. I or Aarinnaie will return. Your charge is to protect Brîn in our stead, nothing more."

"Aye, Khel Szi."

He wanted to say more, to tell the man to gather his warriors and to rush back with him and take the Citadel tonight while things were already in an uproar there. But fear for Sikyra won out. "I've an errand, so I'll be needing that horse now."

Khisson dipped his chin and bent his back in a bow, but it didn't hide the slight smile easing the harsh lines of his face. "As you wish."

CHAPTER SIXTEEN

E ven with as difficult a day—
Night, Bruche corrected.
—as Draken had had, he reckoned getting out of the city would be the toughest. The first challenge was lack of coin; it wasn't in the little safe room, and there was no sign Osias had been there. Draken could only hope he'd gotten out to Eidola.

Worse was leaving Tyrolean inside the city, but Draken didn't dare delay.

Khisson gave them clothes, coin, and tora ponies. The latter were short and sturdy and cranky at being sent out into the cold night. Draken had half a thought they'd been stolen, but he left it. Khisson had sent twenty men with him . . . who knew the islander lord had so many to spare? . . . and they cut their way through the back gates nearest Eidola, leaving the several servii guarding it in a messy pile of bodies.

Too easy. I don't like it. Bruche turned Draken's head to study the night.
Dying is always easy for those who do.
Dying shouldn't be so easy for the living, though.

It was a point, but Draken had just spent the better part of two sevennight under great strain. Now he was headed for his daughter with only a friendly town between them. The road to the farming villages were clear of people— live ones—at least. A couple of bodies sprawled off the road, a sevennight old if the bloat was any indication. The cold stink made the whole company raise cloak hems to faces. But they saw no Akrasians beyond the gate. Their business was inside the city and it seemed no point in risking challenges from outlying Brînians. Plenty of hard folk lived outside city walls, coaxing a life from the fertile valley soil and abundant woods nested at the bottom of the Eidolas, but they were every bit as loyal to their principality as city dwellers and islanders.

Neither Bruche nor Draken could look away from the giant mountain kingdom of the dead for long. They detected no movement on the craggy cliffs
spiking into low-slung clouds, and further up, into the night sky.

Aarinnaie rode close, whether as a guard or to be guarded, Draken didn't
know. She was uncommonly quiet and he wondered if the shock of the previous day and night and their nearing escape was catching up to her. But when
she turned her head, her mouth was relaxed and her chin lifted. "Are we going
through the village?" she asked, her tone making it plain what she thought of
that idea.

He shook his head. Khisson had agreed to get Draken out of the city but
he made no promises on chasing down any Akrasians who might venture up
to Eidola after Sikyra. They apparently had their own errands outside the city,
likely to meet their pirate soldiers. Draken did his damnedest to be satisfied
with the amount of help provided. Khisson's crowd of swift horses and armored
warriors would make a good decoy as the two of them split off, especially once
word of their escape at the gate took hold in the city. No one would expect the
Khel Szi and Szirin of Brîn to ride tora ponies.

The road breaking off outside the village toward Eidola was little more than a
path pounded into the tall lonegrass. It stood to reason; banes needed no paths
and most living avoided the kingdom of the dead. For a time he could still hear
the jingle of the horses' harness and the Khissons' mail shirts, but soon even
that faded into the godless time between moonfall and sunrise.

Draken felt his shoulders ease as he escaped the view of the Eyes. The world
around him sharpened without godslight piercing his vision. Eidola was closer
than he thought. He could see the fork in the road where they'd split with the
Khissons but not the horde of them any longer. Their ponies' harnesses had
been muffled with rags tied over chains and joints and over their hooves so they
walked along without much sound. It was silent, too silent. Even scents were
missing, no damp grasses or earth, no body odor or horse. No omnipresent
blood. The lack shrouded him but also drew him. He found himself nudging
his pony from a walk to a trot.

It feels . . . not like Eidola.

It was day and nearer to peacetime last you were there.

His pony stumbled, twitching Draken hard, and snorted its way to a stop.
Aarinnaie's pony bumped into him from behind, resulting in pinned ears.

"Khel Szi." Aarinnaie's hiss sizzled on the silence like a newly forged sword
plunged into water. "I know you can see but I barely can, nor the ponies.
Should we wait for some light?"

His gaze picked out blades of dormant lonegrass. Clods of dirt on the path. The black tips of his pony's light brown ears. "No." He urged the pony on, promising it silently to watch the path better.

She hurried after him, keeping close enough his pony pinned its ears back and swished its tail in irritation. "But it's so silent. Something is wrong."

"It's always quiet before dawn."

She huffed as if she meant to fill the air with herself, looking all around. Her head twisting was about to drive Draken mad. "You're not the only one who wanders the godless hours, Draken. It's never like this. Not so dead and still."

He sighed. "It's not so still with your yammering, is it?"

He instantly regretted his tone but she just snorted. "I'm telling you, this isn't right—you're speeding up again." She rode closer and grabbed at his rein. Draken tried to jerk it free but only succeeded in annoying his pony, who snuffled and tossed its head on its thick neck. It snapped at Aarinnaie's pony.

"Stop that," Draken said, kicking the pony on and tugging its head away from Aarinnaie.

"I'm telling you. This isn't right. It's . . ." A scream cut her off. She blinked and her pony tried to break back the way they'd come, snorting. It took her a few breaths to calm it. That she kept twisting her head around staring at the darkness with white eyes didn't help much. She stiffened, her lips parted.

"Aarin."

No response. She drew a blade.

He growled and caught her wrist. "What is it?"

She twisted free with remarkable strength, even for her. Her knife hand shifted up, not toward her, but toward him. He caught her wrist again. "What in Khellian's name are you doing?"

Her face was blank. She lunged at him with the knife again, slashing his arm. The ground rumbled, making the ponies shift on their big hooves.

A bane! This is a trap. Get out while you can.

Bruche tried to reel the pony around but Draken stopped it. Coldness threatened to smother his tongue. *No! I will not leave her.* "Aarin . . . Aarinnaie. Fight it off. It's me, Draken. It's me."

An itchy, scratching sensation filled the inside of his skin as a thick, suffocating chill crept over him. Not Bruche, not internal. Something trying to get in, something familiar and deadly. He had the sudden image of giving up. Elena was dead. Aarinnaie, as good as. His daughter was only fit for slavery.

Draken. Bruche's cold suffused him.

He blinked, Bruche's voice and surging control jolting him from his reverie of death and failure. He heard his own voice, sharp: "Aarinnaie. You're fighting a bane. Force it out. You did it before. Now do it again."

Banes sought out deepest, darkest wishes. For Draken, suicide. For Aarinnaie—she lunged at him again before he could guess. He shoved hard with his leg against the pony's side even as he shoved hard with his mind against what she meant. His pony sidestepped. She snarled but didn't chase him; the bane was biding its time. Draken looked around for anywhere to protect himself that wasn't completely away from his sister. Faces emerged from the dark. Was it his imagination? He blinked. They stared back at him, edged closer, mouths gaping, hungry for the evil in his soul. He had to get Aarin out of here, away. Someone had breached the gates of Eidola and released the banes.

He swung his pony around and urged it toward Aarinnaie's, though both ponies snorted and resisted getting so close. His voice sharpened. "Aarin, listen to me. We need to go."

She paid no attention to him but to tighten her grip on the blade and lunge for him again. He caught her wrist. Again. "I tire of this, bane. Release her."

A deep grunt was its only reply. Aarinnaie struggled with his grip but Bruche lent his strength and she couldn't shake free from Draken. He shouted in frustration.

no it protects her from the rest flee now korde attacks run

Draken didn't need to be told twice. He released Aarinnaie and snatched at her rein. "Hang on!" He had no idea if she'd obey as he wheeled his pony and kicked it, hard. Even his plodding tora pony sparked to a trot and then a gallop, muffled hooves thudding the ground. Aarinnaie's pony resisted being dragged along, but it finally burst into a lumbering canter. He kept them running past the trail to Eidola, past the lowland village, into the dark woods beyond.

A hissing wind swept round them, eerie cries in its wake. Aarinnaie's voice joined them. She jerked in her saddle, writhed, her face contorted. Truls burst through her and then flitted back over her head, arms outstretched. His hollow Voice seemed to swallow the others, wordless but powerful nonetheless.

Aarinnaie grabbed for her saddle. Panting, she moaned. "Drae—"

He choked out, still staring at Truls: "I'm here."

"Why did it let me go?"

"Truls."

"But he's—"

"Dead. And yet he's still with us. With me." He rubbed his rough hand over his face, calluses catching on his short beard. The ghost waited, quite still for once. "He freed you from the bane. He did it before, too. Helped Osias control banes in the Citadel." It was starting to make a horrid sense. The banes were free and had already achieved Brîn and the Citadel. There were so many and Brîn had no magic walls to keep them out, only the perserverence of his people. And then a worse thought occurred. If one possessed Ilumat, what would the young lord do? What were his greatest fears to act on?

"If they've escaped, then Sikyra . . ." Aarinnaie said.

Draken swallowed hard. "Aye. Sikyra."

Perhaps the Mance took her out, but in any case you aren't getting to her through a horde of banes.

Osias wasn't there. He was at the bloody Citadel saving my sorry hide. Gods willing, or not, the other Mance were able to protect her. He cursed under his breath, his chest clenching around his heart.

You need to keep moving, Drae.

Draken picked up his reins, urged the pony on, and looked back to see that Aarinnaie was following. She drew up next to him as they reached the crossroads and he took the wider road, the trade road that would link up to the River Eros. He drew in air deeply, thinking he already smelled the lowland damp that lingered around the Eros. Nothing followed but a faint greying of the sky stretching down toward land. *One good thing, the Akrasians have to get through the banes to get to you. And they don't have Truls to help them. Keep on, Draken.*

He let the pony walk. It huffed with each step, the noise ruining the muffled harness and hooves. The hardy creatures weren't meant for speed over long distances.

"Where now?" Aarinnaie asked.

"Reschan." It was the next sizable town. It was where the Mance might have taken Sikyra. He hoped.

She said nothing, giving no indication of her approval or not. He didn't look at her, didn't want to know. He couldn't do elsewise. His hands tightened on the reins as his questions wound through his mind. Korde hadn't attacked him directly. Why not? A bid for control? Or something else. Why not kill him and have done with it? He was the only thing standing between his daughter and the gods, between the Ashen and Akrasia.

An untruth. You're one man of many. Do the armies not fight?

"Do they?" He unthinkingly spoke aloud. "We cannot know whether they fight still." Winter had stalled the war, and Ilumat's move to take over Brîn and give it to the Ashen might well have halted it.

Once your daughter is safe you must see to the defenses.

His jaw tightened. "Safe" was an elusive concept. Aarinnaie and he alone on the road, one sword and a bow between them. He could provide no home for Sikyra on the road, always running from the Akrasians or Ashen. Perhaps he should have left her with her mother, with the Moonlings. They hadn't killed the babe when they'd had the chance. They'd kept her alive as a way to manipulate him. At the time it had infuriated him. This night, he'd gladly suffer manipulation and worse in trade for Sikyra's life.

CHAPTER SEVENTEEN

The nights grew chillier the further distance they put between Brîn and themselves. A routine developed between them as they traveled upland of the River Eros through the edges of the Grassland: Draken hunted up a meal with his bow; Aarinnaie cared for the horses. Most nights they ate sufficiently, digging into a couple of birds or tree rodents, maybe finishing with some berries. It was spit cooking, so there was no real way to boil roots for a side dish, though keeping closer to the Eros and its tributaries kept them in water all right. Copses of woods along the water gave them some shelter. But what worried him was Aarinnaie. Mostly silent, she went about her duties with her head down. She would sit watch when he asked. She slept and ate when he told her to. But other than that she did little but her assigned duties before rolling herself into her cloak. He had no idea if she ever really slept.

Draken sat one night about halfway to Reschan, thinking of Elena setting fire to Skyhaven. Lately it was more difficult to think of her as alive; he'd last seen her fleeing deeper into a burning forest, flames trailing from her fingertips. He bent his head, letting his neck stretch, trying to erase the image from his mind. Truls lingered nearby. The trees, under Shaim's and Elna's meager light, cast the tarnish of shadow over him. Aarinnaie was already rolled up in her cloak, unmoving, a slight figure with firelight glinting over her. He could sense her listening in the dark. She lay too stiffly to be asleep.

"I'll watch. You rest." He pushed to his feet.

He slung his bow over his shoulder and let his sword settle at his hip, glancing at her motionless figure before striding away. He wanted more for her than this slog toward the unknown, but this was what they had.

The land slept this night, with only the two waning moons and the shadows of the trees for company. His boots rustled the undergrowth. The trees were spread further apart and taller than the lowlands that stretched to the Agrian Range. He kept wary, but without real concern because he felt no threat. They had seen no one in half a sevennight. At length he leaned back against a tree, rather wishing for something to do. So when someone tapped his shoulder, he almost jumped out of his boots. He spun, drawing his sword despite that no attacker in his right mind would touch him to announce their appearance.

It was Truls, staring at him through empty, dead eyes, expression blank, body mostly formless. He slipped back, lifted a hand to gesture him on.

"You touched me?"

Again Truls made the gesture to move, ignoring him.

He seems to be gaining strength.

Aye. Perhaps. Draken didn't question further, being heartily sick of dealing with a ghost who gave him few answers. They didn't go far before Truls stopped and pointed, and when Draken saw why, his pulse quickened.

Firelight nipped at his eyes. He averted his gaze a moment and looked again, trying to force his gaze to adjust. His eyes only spilled tears for his trouble. He had to get closer and pointed to it and pantomimed taking a step. Truls bowed his head, but didn't indicate he would follow.

Wise one, that. Bruche had his misgivings.

Draken grunted and started moving through the woods, walking as softly as he could but wishing for Aarinnaie's skilled silence. Voices reached him, a sharp tone as if someone were reprimanding another. He stared hard into the dark trees, lifting a hand to shade his eyes against the bright spots of fire. Only a few of them. The smoke smelled old and damp, not fresh. His nose wrinkled and he blinked. The fires were close, unblocked but for the trees in front of him, perhaps thirty paces ahead.

Smoke scent filled his lungs as he drew nearer. The largest tent, swagged and tasseled, took up much of a clearing against the river. No Akrasian would have such an ornate thing on campaign. Monoeans, then. Important ones.

Draken crept closer, trusting the dark hid him from the encampment better than it hid the encampment from him, trying to count tents. Ten surrounding the commander's tent. Or royal tent. His fingers toyed with the loose tag of leather on his sword. A chance for him to rip out a taproot of the invasion, perhaps.

The rising pitch of an obstinate voice broke into his musings. "—prince any longer—"

"How *dare* you? You think some covenant with Korde gives you leave to disrespect my blood? My *birthright?*" Draken's breath caught. His cousin Galbrait, Crown Prince to Monoea.

A short, caustic laugh. "Where is your crown now, Prince? Or shall I call you 'king', though the gods see no kings among us."

Draken's nostrils flared. He knew that voice as well. The priest Rinwar, the one who had rallied the nobles of Monoea to take Akrasia by position of his old family, older money, and ancient faith. But why were they here?

"That is not true. My family has held the Monoean throne for centuries. If not by the grace of the gods, then who?"

"You ruled by the grace of our swords. But no more. Look around yourself. Step outside your spoiled mind and see. See who these men follow. See who the gods rely upon. Certainly not an upstart princeling with nothing to his name."

Breaths passed. Draken wondered if he actually heard the Prince's panting through the tent walls or if he imagined it. He knew his cousin well enough to know how he'd look: color high, jaw set, nostrils flared, chin up; the very painting of indignation, like a good prince was taught. Like a king employed right before levering some decree that took titles and heads.

Bruche rumbled his disapproval. *I know what you're thinking.*

Don't fight me. If I can kill Galbrait, it's a strike at the knees of this invasion. No matter the hard talk, they need him.

Galbrait knew it, too. His voice dropped into cold tones. "I am well versed in our kingdom's politics and social structure, Rinwar. You need a royal to sit the throne. I know you don't want me, and it's just as well since I've no desire to be your puppet. When you have my cousin, I will be free of this all, aye? But until then, I am Crown Prince."

Draken edged closer, jaw tight. Here, tonight, he could shatter this invasion. All he needed was to spill the blood in that tent.

"Not so fast, pirate." The words slurred but there wasn't anything soft about the steel edge pressed against his throat. Draken lifted his chin, tilting his head away from the sword. Whoever it was spoke passable Brînian, but no one from Brîn used the term pirate—not in a derogatory way, at any rate.

The blade nicked him. Draken leaned away and twisted. After a flash of pain, the ground rumbled under his feet. More than a nick, then. His assailant stepped back, lined eyes narrowed on him, ignoring the ground moving. Draken drew and swung. His blade thudded against a leather bracer as he brought his arm up awkwardly. Bruche held back with the wordless sentiment that he might be useful alive, but Draken's blood roared hot in his veins. Akrasians had taken Brîn, had murdered everyone in the Citadel. He recovered, backed a step, and went for him again. But the Akrasian was better prepared and blocked him with his sword.

It shattered as Seaborn's edge met it. The noise scratched through Draken like fingernails on slate. The Akrasian launched himself at Draken, eyes wild, fingers scrabbling for his throat, blade, grunting loud enough to warn his compatriots in the camp. Draken swung and cut off his arm above the elbow, then drew back to stab him through. The Akrasian gaped at him as blood poured out of him. Draken turned and ran, not waiting to watch him hit the ground.

Voices raised behind him as the camp roused to action. Soon the woods rang with shouts. Draken ran blindly, gripping his sword, ready to fight to the last, knowing only that he was steering away from Aarinnaie.

Moonlight filtered through the treetops, flashing into his eyes, surely lighting his path and turning his back into a target. The trees were too far apart for good cover, and the voices continued, keeping on him and never falling away enough to let him slow. His lungs and thighs started to burn.

By the Seven, Galbrait was a good tracker, trained in the Norvern Wilds of Monoea. Of course there was no way for regular Akrasians or Monoeans to know who they chased through the Moonling woods. They were unlikely to recognize him if caught.

But his cousin would know him. His legs pumped harder.

An arrow struck a tree with a thrum that ran all though him. Another whooshed past him into the underbrush. The Monoeans followed by foot, a dozen at least if the number of their sharp calls ringing through the night were any indication. They'd have reinforcements and he had only himself. And Bruche, who could keep him running some fair longer but not forever. He kept running, squinting against moonbeams shooting through the trees like flaming arrows into his eyes.

He picked out the stones of a wall ahead, though it made no sense. There weren't so many buildings along the river, some few farms and the village Khein with his great fortress, of course, but he was much too far yet from that. Most family buildings were made from overabundant wood rather than heavier and more difficult stone. He ran toward it. Maybe there was somewhere to hide.

Two high walls of a ruin formed a corridor between them. The river trickled between snow and ice behind it. Black as pitch inside, even for him. The ground sloped downward as he darted under the crumbling arched gateway. Underfoot, the soil felt springy, loamy. Fools all, they'd follow him here. It was too obvious. But he still heard voices so he kept on.

He had to slow as his eyes adjusted, straining against the black air, and when he'd gone two dozen steps, his hands out in front of him, he slowed and pressed his back against a stone. It was soft and fuzzy, startling him. Then he realized: His eyes cooled and his vision cleared, confirming his suspicion. Green moss grew liberally over the stone, and the tree canopy overhead blocked the moonglow almost completely. The cold damp of the riverside woods seemed to warm within the walls. No wind nor sound penetrated. He drew a breath, trying to calm his heart, still thudding from the chase. Ahead a four-legged stand with angled legs blocked the path. Beyond, the corridor formed by the stone walls went further than seemed right or even possible, having stumbled upon it in the woods. A rotting, lopsided sign dangled from the stand. Strands of moss hung from the corners and fuzzed the wood. He peered at the script carved into the wood but didn't recognize it.

Looks old, Bruche intoned. *Moonling or the ancients.*

Ancients?

Gadye.

He knew Bruche believed Gadye were the first settlers, but the Moonlings most certainly did not. But it made sense; the area outside Reschan, along the river, certainly was home to many Gadye. If this was some sort of Gadye stronghold, he wanted to keep on friendly terms with them. He didn't argue the point further, unsure if some magic at work could penetrate his and Bruche's private discussions. The Gadye had powerful sight magic of their own.

Voices startled him from behind, though he was half expecting them. Shouting, and a muffled answer from further away. Behind, faint moonlight lit the arched opening. He saw no one, but the voices tore through his calm. Darkness was safer. He edged by the sign and moved deeper into the tunnel, wishing for a bow.

A figure caught his eye far ahead. It appeared to dart around the corner at the end of the corridor. Damn. Someone got ahead of him? Or entered the ruins another way. This could swing wrong for him quickly. He slowed to listen. No footfalls. No voices from behind or ahead. Could it be most of the Monoeans had missed the structure? Or they were too nervous about coming inside?

Or is there some magic at work?

Draken scowled at the thought but the eerie quiet pressing on him made him suspicious. He edged past the sign and moved toward the corner. Turned the corner, sword first. Nothing but another long corridor, probably too dark for anyone else but him to see down. More moss. More thick leaves. The scent of earth, damp oozing from stone, a faint waft of rot, as from a grave. Another corner. He kept going, winding inward and then outward. The walking evened his breathing and he calmed some. One corner led to a niche and he backtracked, found another corner . . .

He stopped in the corridor. Looked the way he was headed. Turned his head and looked back. He tried to keep panic from edging in on him. That way led to Monoeans and Akrasians hunting him.

Be easy. You haven't made so many turns that we can't sort your way back out. And they don't seem to follow you. It's a good place to hide.

He turned and kept walking, kept turning. But even Bruche's anxiety grew. It was wrong, odd. Too far to go, too long walking inside some ruins that consisted of a few walls on the outside.

He turned another corner and stopped. A woman, bent and tiny, leaned on a staff ten paces ahead. Despite her stature, her face was clear, unlined. Her eyes had no pupils or irises, but were all whites. But her head lifted and her attention fixed on him.

"Draken vae Khellian." Her voice graveled through her throat.

His eyes narrowed and he lifted his sword. "Keep back."

"What danger is an old woman to you?"

"Old perhaps, but no woman." A Moonling? *The right size but no dapples. A member of another godsforsaken race he hadn't heard of?*

No. She's not from here . . . she's— Bruche spoke slowly and the word choked off. Draken felt his presence writhe and shrink inside him, as if he were tearing away the muscles from the inside of his skin.

He couldn't help grunting in pain. He stumbled to his knees but managed to grip his sword; only just. "Release him."

The sensation cut off, leaving him gasping. He sat back on his heels and scowled. "Which god are you?"

"Does it matter?"

"I like to know who I kill."

"You don't know the names of all those you've killed. You don't know a tenth of the names of those you've killed."

Truth, tossed at him like a tangle of nettles, and it stung. He eased to his feet, keeping his sword forward. "What is this place?"

She looked around. "My home. To you, it appears as a ruin. To me, it appears as it was, as it always has been. Murals of great deeds on the walls." She ran her finger over the crackling surface of the stone. Dust and plaster tumbled from it. "Warmth from fires. Laughter and the contentment that all is well."

Draken snorted. Nothing had ever been "all well" as far as he knew. "I see—"

"I know what you see." The voice sharpened to shrill and the pale face flushed.

Draken's eyes narrowed. Blood ran under that papery skin. *Things that bleed can be killed.*

Most things. Not you.

He wasn't so sure about that.

She swept the frail arm not holding the staff. The surroundings took on the pristine beauty she had described. Murals. Peaceful water sounds. The air warmed. Another sweep of her arm, including him in the gesture, and it all a ruin again, damp and still. "You're a fool. We've given you everything. Championed you. And you fight us at every turn."

Us? Ah, Eidola spare him. "Zozia. So it's true. But surely the gods are loath to muddy their boots on mortal dirt."

"You've proved difficult to find."

He lifted his sword. Blood had dried on it from the servii he'd killed but it still flashed in the dark, an inner light thirsting for more. He held, staring at her. "Why would you look for me at all?"

"All seek you, do they not? But not all have given you what we have. Healing. Darksight."

That's what it was called, this sight magic. Apparently given to persuade him to come to the gods' aid.

"A gift is no favor. Unasked for, they require no obligation."

"By the rules of men, perhaps. You still carry Khellian's sword, do you not?"

He still held it between them. "I fight with it when I wish. Kill who I wish. You certainly didn't give it to me." Still, a chill crawled through him. He was certain he'd seen Khellian there at the wall.

"Ah, the killing. Fond of it, aren't you? You even used our grace to that end, so that you may kill and kill and kill—"

"The healing." Draken shrugged, feigning nonchalance. In his bones he still felt the ship cracking beneath him, the great sweep of ocean up through the hull and deck. "What of it?"

"Agrian gave it to you. He is no god of death."

"What does Agrian want with me?" He narrowed his eyes in thought. "Wait. Scratch that. Who gave me the darksight?"

"Korde." The word was a snarl.

"You sound angry with him."

"Not him."

"Angry with me, then." What else was new? He grunted. "I've already proved I won't serve you all in the way you wish and—"

"Not all. Me, simply."

"I don't serve any of you."

"Why not?" Zozia sounded truly curious.

"Your battles are not mine."

"Aren't they? You've enemies upon your beloved shores now."

"They're my countrymen, all. In your quest to find a man to take your side you've found one of all sides." He edged closer. "Not only yours, that is."

Her face darkened, changed to something as turbulent and hard and ugly as any furious Mance.

Bruche rose in Draken. He darted forward in tandem with his swordhand and swung.

The blade swept through empty air. He spun to find the goddess behind him, still bent, her weight on her staff. She shook her head. Her staff whipped out and caught Draken on the side of his knee, his *bad* knee, of course, because where else would a god strike their errant pageboy? He stumbled with an emasculating yelp that died against dry stone and empty air. In a blink Zozia was gone.

He growled in frustration.

Bruche's sentiment: *Good fortune that's all the further it went.*

Draken didn't know if he meant the fight or his cry of pain, but Zozia was the wisest god. She had to be. She was smallest, the one most shadowed by the others. She meant to do something by pulling him here; he had no illusions he had stumbled upon this fortress ruin by accident. She took advantage of the chase, of his killing that servii runner in proximity to dozens of Monoeans . . .

He blinked and climbed to his feet, wincing on his way up. "I'm a ruddy fool."

"Perhaps not as foolish as you thought."

He turned slowly. The goddess leaned on her staff, head bowed. He cursed inwardly.

"Why didn't you kill me when you were at my back? Why talk at all?"

"We do not want you dead."

The healing. The godsdamned healing that shook foundations and took down war galleons. "No, I don't suppose you do."

Ask her what she does want.

Draken didn't answer his swordhand, but limped closer to the goddess. "Why did you start this war?"

"The magic is splintered. The races hide the fragments. We must make the world whole again."

Draken stared at her. Looked around at the ruins. "To make *your* world whole again, you mean." He didn't bother to lift his sword. She didn't bother to keep distance between them as he came closer. "I'm not your plaything. I'm certainly not your champion."

"Who do you fight for, then? I can give you more than war, Draken. You want peace. That is the truth. Wisdom is the path to both. Khellian has no peace, not even Mother—"

"There is no peace in truth." Only hatred and pain.

"What about in family? Your wife. Your daughter. Your Queen."

Draken cursed the hope flaring in his heart. "You lie. You don't know where they are."

"Ah, but Korde does." She smiled at Draken's wordless stare. "Your true master, before Khellian stole you from—"

Korde? Korde might well have murdered his daughter by releasing the banes. He growled, pure reaction. Magic surged through him, moonlight piercing his dayblinded eyes and carving a path through his veins to his heart. It stumbled to a pause and magic burst forth into his limbs. He thrust the sword up and drove it home. It slid through Zozia as if she were no more than heavy, damp air. The momentum dragged him closer to her. Her mouth opened in a silent shriek that echoed in his mind. But she flickered like a flame around his blade and fluttered away into the air like black mist. He panted, watching the mist fall where she had been. He slumped, exhaustion clawing at him from the surge of magic running through his veins.

Draken.

It was a moment before he could answer. "I know. I . . ." His voice broke off and he lifted a shaking hand to his face. "It's not real. She was just imagery, magic. I don't know. But I didn't kill her. I can *not* have killed her."

For what seemed a long while, his mind fell empty. And then, creeping in, selfish homesickness. For the first time in a long time he wished he could throw down the sword, return to his simpler life in Monoea, and know nothing of this. The world was so still he wondered if he might make it truth.

But no, black mist covered the flats of his sword. And Elena and Sikyra. Aarinnaie. Osias and Tyrolean and Halmar and everyone who had died in his name. He looked around himself, his jaw tight, and the crumbling stone walls faded to nothingness—or rather, into rustling woods, chill damp, and fading shouts of Monoeans searching for a fugitive who could end this war, if they only knew the truth. But there was no peace in truth, and now that he knew what the gods were about, there could be only war.

CHAPTER EIGHTEEN

Truls met him outside of where the ruins had been, lingering at the edges of a thick batch of trees. The ghost-Mance waited silently, staring with his black eyes at Draken.

"I killed it."

Truls did nothing.

"Her. I killed her. Zozia." Draken gestured back toward the ruins . . . where they had been. He lifted a shuddering hand to his face. "You knew about her. You knew she was rebelling against the other gods."

Another long stare.

"That's why you're here. Why you came to me . . ." He gasped, realization dawning. "That's why you rebelled against them in the first place . . ." He cursed. "You're rubbish at rebelling. As bad as they are."

Truls made no reaction, just turned into the woods to glide between the trees. Draken wiped the black dust off his sword and sheathed it before following.

Truls led him along, and he watched the trees absently as he walked, thinking of as little as possible, staying quiet, only pausing when he found some of the little twine and wooden sigils travelers used to mark their way and message each other in the Moonling Woods. One of the moons carved its path through the night and after a while he realized Truls led him along the edge of the light. He couldn't help but feel as if it were searching for him, whichever of the Seven it was.

Not Zozia, not anymore.

Truls moved faster as time got on. Snow broke the intermittent darkness, lacing the trees and limp leaves overhead, brightening patches of the woodland floor. Draken followed wearily, knowing he left a trail. But it couldn't be helped. The air was cold, full of damp that seeped into the bones, and the mists shaped themselves like wisps of ghosts in his darksight. He couldn't help but think of banes and steeled himself against them, though he worried for Aarinnaie after the episode by Eidola. He would blame Ilumat, but he was certain it had been Truls who had left her soiled with a darkness he couldn't hope to eradicate with simple brotherly care and love. At the Citadel she had been full of wrath and drive. And now he had left her alone and was following the damn Mance through the woods . . . woods he wasn't even supposed to be in, blast it.

He thought back over the evening, and it took on a sinister meaning. The guard who had attacked him had been an Akrasian. He'd been too busy fighting off the attack to process the incongruence of an Akrasian attacking him on the edges of a Monoean camp.

Truls kept on, peering back with his blank face at Draken as if to make sure he still followed. Snow-crusted undergrowth crunched beneath Draken's boots. He tried to listen beyond it but tried not to worry too much about pursuers or some other unsavory sort hearing him. He'd gotten far from where they should possibly have ranged. Much further than he should have gotten, damn it.

Hold.

Draken stopped immediately at Bruche's word, eyes narrowed. The moons had traversed the sky while he walked. They lingered directly overhead, lighting the scene around him too much for his comfort. Others could see better in the light and his vision was verging on worse, though it wasn't light enough to tie on his mask. He squinted all around himself, Bruche resting cold in the muscles of his arms.

Crackling sounds, like thin horn-pane snapping, or frozen grasses and twigs. What? Had the ghost-Mance led him into a trap? Someone flitted between trees in his darksight. Truls gestured to him.

Draken eased Seaborn from its sheath. A glow lit the area around him. Now . . . *now* the sword chose to light. He was beginning to think the blade did have a sort of sentience. *Better to make me a bloody target.*

Perhaps . . . Bruche fell silent as Draken followed whoever it was. No point in hiding the blade. He was already given away and likely he'd need it before long. He moved closer, making noise but not caring.

An Akrasian with a long tail of black hair and two swords pointing up over his shoulders . . . The man spun, reaching to draw, but froze when he saw Draken.

"Tyrolean?"

"Draken." A voice deep with relief.

"Where have you been?"

"I? You're the one who got left in Brîn."

"I came as soon as I could. Khisson told me your path. I wouldn't have caught up with you but for your delay."

Delay? "I ran into Monoeans. Rinwar and Galbrait."

Tyrolean gripped his shoulder. "Thank the gods you escaped."

Draken shook his head, confused. "I ran . . . but they didn't catch me. Why did you think they did?"

Tyrolean studied him a moment. "I assumed, since you've been gone two nights."

That was it. "Two . . . What? No."

"What happened? Did you lose consciousness?"

"No. Galbrait was at an encampment, arguing with the priest Rinwar. And a . . . scout found me. I killed him and ran." And then he'd met the goddess Zozia and maybe killed her but he couldn't be certain without seeing her moon . . . or not.

Tyrolean gave him a look but didn't press him. "Come. I'll take you to the Princess."

When they arrived at the little camp, the moons had dropped in the sky. She ran at him, fists up. "Where have you been?"

"Visiting enemies and gods." He caught her fists before she could pound his chest with them and pushed them down gently. "The gods are at war. One solicited my aid."

A grunt from Tyrolean. "You didn't think to mention you've become a mercenary again? Bit of an advancement, eh?"

"Quite. With a pay raise. She offered me my daughter and the Queen. A lie, I'm certain of it."

"What did you say?" Aarinnaie said.

"Er. I lost my temper. Rather." They both stared at him, wide-eyed. He shifted on his feet and looked away. Tyrolean was very devout. "I might have killed her with Seaborn."

"You killed a *god*? Which one?"

"I don't know if I killed her. She disappeared. Or dissipated, rather."

"She?"

"Zozia. But I can't, really. I mean, she's a bloody *god*—"

"The Wise One? You killed Zozia?" Tyrolean stared, then his gaze flicked upward. Looking for a tiny moon.

"I don't know if I killed her, all right? I think she's rebelling against Ma'Vanni at any rate." He held Tyrolean's gaze, then shifted it so that the fire didn't flicker at the edges of his darksight. "And she didn't sound like she was alone in the effort."

"Who?"

"Korde might have come up in conversation."

"And us without our Mance," Aarinnaie said. "Osias would sort this."

Draken grunted. He had Truls but didn't like to bring him up. "Regardless, I'm not helping any god with anything."

Tyrolean sat down on a fallen log they'd pulled by the fire. "I think we stay on the same path. Setia will protect your daughter. If anyone can possibly get her to Reschan and under Va Khlar's care it's her."

"Because she's Moonling and has the Abeyance." She could travel quickly within the Abeyance, if she could hold it long enough.

Tyrolean shook his head. "Because she is sundry and has been a slave, and there are no more resourceful creatures than sundry slaves."

◆ ◆ ◆

In Reschan, child beggars fair tried to climb their ponies, little fingers tugging at their saddles and boots while ragged, defeated adults coughed around alley fires. No Escorts or servii policed the crowded streets. Ice laced the air and stung his lungs. He thought of his daughter, chest rot worsening in the cold upper floor of an abandoned building, and his throat tightened. Where was she now? Among these people? Or worse.

They were a bedraggled and exhausted threesome standing at the gate of the utilitarian Baron's castle in Reschan. It sprawled through the middle of the town, brown stone walls grimy at the edges with rubbish and windblown dirty snow. Short towers anchored the structure.

Draken didn't dare announce who he was in case of Akrasian rebellion in the city, and he wore his mask. Aarinnaie assured him no one would believe it if he claimed to be Khel Szi anyway. The air was cold against the back of his neck with his locks shorn and he pulled his cloak hood up against it.

Beyond the castle walls, the market did thin business, chary patrons moving between stalls tended by worn keepers. It contrasted greatly to his first visit here where the sun had beat hot upon his back and the market had been so crowded he and Tyrolean could scarcely move without treading on a lady's skirts.

Tyrolean spoke to the guards. With his lined eyes and calm demeanor, he was the most respectable of the bunch. Draken shifted his weight, resettled his hands on his pony's reins, and gritted his jaw against speaking.

You're used to ordering your way through already, eh?

Fair truth, if he wanted to admit it. The guards were already casting him odd looks. And how he must appear: filthy, hair shorn and beard ragged, a rag around his eyes like a blind man. All of them looked disreputable. Their clothes were plain and they wore no armor, just swords slung over their cloaks. It had been serviceable enough stuff when given them by Khisson, but a sevennight in the woods had left them all tatty and stinking.

Whatever Tyrolean said got them in the door all right—some nonsense about bringing messages from Brîn—and inside the courtyard, swept clean and out of the wind at least. They dismounted and Draken looked around, though he didn't expect Va Khlar to come meet him in the cold, not knowing who had come calling at his gates. Bruche relaxed for the first time in days, reassured by the strong castle walls around them. So Draken didn't notice the drawn arrows until they were already pointed at them.

A captain stepped forward. He wore Escort greens but he was no fullblood Akrasian. His eyes weren't lined, for one. Gadye braids sprouted from his head and even his chin, though he had no mask. Astute, clear eyes studied him. "Who are you, really?"

How did he pick you out as leader?

Maybe it's the mask. He thought a moment and then sighed and removed the scrap of fabric from his face. The sun made him squint and his eyes water. "Khel Szi of Brîn."

"You're too light-skinned to be the Pirate Prince."

If he'd been able to open his eyes more than a sliver he'd have rolled them. "Nonetheless, I am he."

"Where's the Queen's pendant, then?"

"Stolen. I was captured in the coup at Brîn. Briefly."

The sundry Gadye captain stared at him. "Rumor has it the Prince is *dead* in the coup at Brîn. I've been assured dozens of witnesses saw you die."

Figures. "A convenient rumor for Lord Ilumat. Conveniently for me, I still live. Fetch Va Khlar and he'll confirm who I am."

"His lordship isn't here."

It was tough to pry Va Khlar from his beloved Reschan for any reason, even meeting with the Queen. "Where is he?"

The Captain curled his lip and gestured. "Move along. This way."

Draken hadn't been to the dungeons here before, though he'd put Reschan's nobility in them once, using his newfound power as Night Lord. Aarinnaie snarled at a guard who tried to take her arm, but a soft word from Tyrolean stilled the tussle and they all moved along without protest. When Va Khlar thought to take a look at his new prisoners, they'd be freed. Of course, who knew how long his errand would take?

But they weren't taken to the dungeon. The captain installed them instead on the top floor of a squat tower with slits for windows that allowed arrows to fly out and cold air to sweep in. His men shackled one wrist from each of them to the wall and left them, though they also left wine to hand.

Draken eased down to sit, his knee aching. Having his arm hanging from a shackle didn't do much for his bad shoulder either.

"What's happened that Va Khlar would imprison visitors? Even if we weren't who we are, this makes no sense. We posed no threat." Tyrolean ran his loose hand through his hair, sweeping it back from his forehead.

You shouldn't have claimed your own name.

Perhaps not. But by the Seven I thought I'd be known. His men have been at Brîn with him.

"It's difficult times," Draken answered Tyrolean aloud. He struggled to pull his mask up over his eyes with one hand. Finally he turned so that he could use two. The room smelled of wet stone and a coming storm. He could well imagine lashing rain slipping in through the arrow-slits in the stone. After a sevennight of sleeping on the ground he wondered if he'd ever be warm again.

Sorry. That bit I can't help you with.

"It's too bad we don't have Osias."

"If he'd stayed with us from the start, we wouldn't be chained to a bloody wall, now would we?" But Draken's words lacked bite. He was tired, exhausted to the bone after running from Monoeans and Akrasians during the day and avoiding the godslight at night.

"I don't know." Aarinnaie had remained standing, and was straining to look through one of the slits that counted for a window. Not that Draken thought there was anything to see. But her shoulders were tight and she paced as far as the short chain would allow, bouncing on the balls of her feet when could go no further. Tyrolean kept his feet, looking bare without his twin swords and the one on his hip. He alternated between watching Aarinnaie and the door.

She's young and energetic. You just rest.

Draken ignored Bruche. "I doubt even that annoying captain downstairs wants to challenge us . . ."

"I wouldn't be so certain. Something is off. I've spent time here and . . ."

Surely she isn't still enamored with the old baron.

That upstart that attacked me at the Crossroads?

Aye, that's the one.

As far as I know he's still in a cell here somewhere.

Waste of good magic, if you ask me.

That was an accident.

No it wasn't. You'd have never gotten out of there alive if I hadn't—

"Don't look at me like that!" Aarinnaie was staring at him.

Draken shook his head, mystified. His eyes had glazed as he'd talked to Bruche, reliving the memory of enacting Seaborn's magic on the old Baron of Reschan. A man who had once fancied his sister. "I was just remembering . . . things."

"Urian was a good man, just trying to protect me and Reschan. It's not easy to be Baron of this filthy city."

Certainly, he was a good man, Bruche said. *Good men try to kill you all the time.*

"I didn't say anything about Urian."

"You thought it!"

Draken lifted his free hand to rub his brow. "No. Bruche did. I'm more interested in what you have to say. Different how?"

She narrowed her eyes at him but apparently decided it was a serious question. "The way they tricked us to come in. Why let us in at all? I think that captain knew very well who you are when he first saw us. I wonder if he was under orders to capture us if possible. Or at least keep a wary eye."

"Truth, they mentioned the coup," Tyrolean said.

"There's no reason word wouldn't reach here by now. It's been nearly three sevennight."

"Longer," Aarinnaie said. She pushed her braids back from her face. "But I still don't like it. Their guard is up, obviously, but they still let us in. I think they believed you are who you said."

"It makes sense. They kept us together in something obviously not quite the regular dungeon," Tyrolean said.

"Maybe they're trying to keep us away from other prisoners," Draken said.

"Definitely the rest of the castle." Aarinnaie resumed trying to look out the slit but gave up with a sigh. "Urian kept a sizable court here and Va Khlar does too."

Draken grunted. "All I recall of Urian's court is a bunch of frips in silks tittering behind feather plumes. Va Khlar won't have kept them, and the current crop will surely follow his loyalty to me."

"Doesn't seem like it, since they locked us in irons right off," Aarinnaie said, tugging futilely at hers.

"Perhaps Va Khlar has suffered a coup too, then," Tyrolean suggested.

Draken's attention snapped to Tyrolean, though the words were delivered mildly. The Escort Captain went on. "There is no reason why the coup at Brîn wasn't coordinated with others. They had some of your troops from Khein. They surely could have taken Reschan, maybe Auwaer, perhaps even Algir and Septonshir."

Must be from the Ministry of Morale, that one.

"Thanks, Tyrolean. I can always count on you to make me feel fair better."

Aarinnaie straightened, lifting her fingers to her lips to quiet them. Footsteps in the corridor, a short struggle with the bolt, and the door swung open.

"Va Khlar," Draken said with relief.

The Reschanian trader-turned-Baron stood in the doorway, grim as ever. Grey light from the arrow slits revealed his scarred face, the one distorting his eyebrow and cheek, lending him a permanent scowl. He looked harder and leaner than the last Draken saw him. Not uncommon for war and Va Khlar always wore tension like a badge of honor. He held Seaborn in its battered scabbard in his hand.

"Your Highness. I'm honored to have you visit." Va Khlar strode forward, keys rattling in his hand, to unlock Draken's shackle.

"You could have bloody well fooled me," Draken growled, but they clasped arms and then hands, each meeting the other's eyes. The unlikeliest of friends made over the death of a child, Osias had once claimed, and it wasn't far off the truth.

Va Khlar moved to unlock the others. "Sorry. For your protection and all that."

"How do you figure?" Aarinnaie asked.

Va Khlar dipped his chin to her. "Princess. I'll explain your unconventional reception, shall I? While we have a meal below in private. Come, Your Highnesses, Captain. You look like you've traveled fair distance."

Or perhaps a bath first? Even I can smell you.

Draken ignored Bruche, but Va Khlar did take them to rooms to bathe and change clothes. More borrowed clothes. Draken didn't know why he cared, but he did. He missed his loose trousers, boots fitted just to him, and the reassuring weight of Elena's pendant resting against his chest.

Simple fare was laid in a comfortable sitting room where a warm fire blazed. Candles and oil lamps lit every handspan of the place. Draken lowered his head and squinted as he eased down onto a bench. "Can you put out some lights?"

Va Khlar ignored his ungraciousness, waved the slaves off, and shut the door behind them before moving to pour out wine. "I expected you, though hope waned as time went on. How did you manage it?"

"You first," Draken said, resettling his mask over his eyes.

Va Khlar dipped his chin and handed him a flagon, and poured two more for the others. "I've spies here, Akrasians who'll wag tongues to Ilumat. I wasn't *exactly* under orders to capture you, but I thought it best to make it appear that way. My captain, who I trust, was under orders to lock you up here. Not to imprison you, but protect you."

"So he knew who we are?"

"Aye, he suspected." A soft grunt. "But you lack the Queen's pendant and you wear a mask. If you mean to disguise yourself, you did a fair job of it."

Princes don't apologize; the first lesson drummed in him by Thom. "I've developed a . . . condition."

"He can see in the dark now," Aarinnaie said impatiently. "Magic sight."

Va Khlar, blurred by the gauzy fabric around Draken's eyes, turned his head to study Draken.

"Darksight, the gods call it. Where is my daughter, Va Khlar?"

Va Khlar sat across from him and put his hands on his knees with a long sigh. Draken's heart chilled. "I don't know. I received a message she was to be brought here. As time went on, I thought it impossible you escaped the city—"

"Who? Who brought the message?"

Va Khlar shook his head. He didn't know. "Then when she didn't appear day after day, and I heard Brîn was to be given to the Ashen, I assumed she was caught or waylaid. Who had her, Your Highness?"

"The Mance. Setia, to be specific. They'll be travelling together."

Va Khlar's usually ruddy cheeks paled.

Draken shook his head. "What?"

"I thought it didn't signify until now." Va Khlar lifted his head. His scars stood out against his pallid skin. "Someone attacked a group of Mance in the woods by the Eros."

"Setia?" Aarinnaie asked.

"Just Mance proper. Five of them." The words emitted from his tight jaw. "Downstream but close enough to the path here we've little doubt their purpose was Reschan."

Little doubt . . . "You didn't ask them where Setia and Sikyra is?"

"Couldn't, being they were all dead."

CHAPTER NINETEEN

Draken thrust himself up from his chair. "There is little magic that can touch the Mance. How did they die?"

"Looked to be the regular sort of way; stab wounds to the heart, mostly. Plenty of defensive wounds, as well. A few arrows spread around but I think they barely had time to take aim."

Gods, it made no sense. "No Setia?"

"I'm sorry. We looked everywhere for survivors."

"Obviously not *everywhere*." Draken paced while Va Khlar watched, silent. "I must go there. Look for evidence."

Va Khlar shook his head. "My men have already cleaned it up. We couldn't leave Mance to rot in the woods."

"The bodies?"

"On their way to the sea, Your Highness. I thought the fewer who see them, the better. It's a sharp blow to confidence."

"When do you think it happened?" Aarinnaie asked. "Tell us everything."

"Couldn't have been more than a night before I saw them from the looks of things. No evidence of the attack beyond the dead Mance. Not so much as a man's bootprint."

Aarinnaie sniffed, probably at the word *man*, but Draken shook his head at her. Her face shuttered; back to discipline. "This is madness. I've seen Osias fight. I've seen him stop hundreds of arrows."

"More than once," Tyrolean said. "This is a . . . devastating complication"

Draken had pushed past shock right into fury. An attack on the party that surely escorted his daughter. Killing Mance when . . . He blinked and looked up at Va Khlar.

"Your Highness?" Va Khlar said, chin tilted at an inquiring angle.

Draken shook his head and strode to the window, shoving the drapes aside and opening the shutters so that the cold breeze stirred the fire, making it snap

171

and snarl. Below, people rushed about on business of their own. No one looked up to those who were warm in the Baron's castle.

Va Khlar cleared his throat. "There's something else."

"Another attack?" Aarinnaie asked.

"No. An invitation . . . a standing invitation. I received it three sevennight ago—"

Around the time of the coup, wasn't it?

Grimly. *Aye.* "From who?"

"That's just it. It had no name. And that's not the only odd bit. It's not for you, Prince Draken. It's for Captain Tyrolean."

Draken looked at Tyrolean. "Who do you know in Reschan?"

"Or more importantly, who knows you're here?" Aarinnaie added.

Tyrolean shook his head. His fingers had tightened to fists. "I've some few acquaintances from my stationing here, but no one leaps to mind."

"Someone has been following your movements," Aarinnaie said, looking none too pleased. Draken thought it might be because she wondered if it was another woman.

Draken snorted. "Even your future movements. The message arrived before we had even thought to leave Brîn."

"Whoever it is wants you to meet him at The Mace Inn on the Eros which-ever evening you're available," Va Khlar said. "It's all I know."

Tyrolean's lip curled. By his expression Draken guessed the neighborhood wasn't a nice one. *Can I trust him, Bruche?*

A beat passed. *No. There is profit to be had by keeping your daughter from you. Unless you know for certain, have proof he isn't involved in this . . . by Korde, he even shoved off your asking to see where they died. And now this invitation.*

It had to have been Korde that killed the Mance.

You don't know that for—

No one else has the power over them, not even Ma'Vanni. Do you think Va Khlar knows about the gods walking among us?

A hesitation. *He might. He's behaving oddly.*

If so, Korde might have my daughter.

Again, you don't know that. You must discuss this with Osias.

If only. *Va Khlar was—is—my friend.*

Before you were known as sundry, he was. When you had power, he was. Va Khlar is friends with whoever will make him coin and power, especially now.

Draken felt as if a weight on his shoulders had deflated all his strength and hope.

Let him think you ignorant. Let his prejudice blind him to your capabilities.

He wasn't really sure what that meant, but he turned to face the room. "Whoever attacked the Mance has my daughter and Setia. They can't have gotten far in a day. Likely they'd come here . . . Sikyra was ill and may yet be. Va Khlar, put out word among the healers in the city."

"Aye, Your Highness. If you need help with guards or coin . . ."

"We've rare enough to pay for information and a reward for her return. And I'd just as soon not draw so much attention to myself."

Va Khlar's brows dropped, probably wondering where he'd gotten it and where the money was kept now. In their things that had been taken from them? Draken could fair see the blades sharpening plans in his mind. Next stop for the trader-Baron, the baskets where the guards had dropped their belongings.

◆ ◆ ◆

The markets were shutting up for the day and truth, the stallkeepers looked so harried and worn and, if he cared to admit it, hungry, he doubted they would have noticed a sundry with a baby . . . or anyone else for that matter. Tyrolean perfunctorily asked a few questions but returned shaking his head.

It was cold out on the street, but night had fallen enough Draken didn't have to wear his blasted mask. Like Tyrolean said, there might be a few coins about with his face on them, but nothing like in Brîn.

"I've been thinking," Aarinnaie said. "What if the mysterious meeting is from Setia?"

Tyrolean said. "But that would only be if she came straight here after taking the baby."

"Setia wouldn't come to some ruddy inn and set up a covert meeting."

"She might, if there were no other way. If there were danger. Or if she had warning," Aarinnaie said.

Patience, Khel Szi. Sometimes she has a good idea. Bruche kept his gaze firmly on Aarinnaie. A less than sisterly opinion of Aarinnaie seeped through their bond.

Draken grimaced inwardly. *First Tyrolean, now you.*

"We'll go there and see if this person arrives," Tyrolean said.

She shrugged. "It'll be useful to find out what happened to the Mance."

It was a point, though the last thing he felt like doing was lounging around an inn common room or a rowdy tavern. His body, every part of him, ached to find his daughter. He couldn't do that drinking watered ale and listening to tellers spin tales.

Perhaps not, but you have no other options at the moment. Likely, Setia is in the city—

No. Likely she held by whoever attacked the Mance. Or worse. He looked at Aarinnaie. "How well known is it that Mance do not die when they are 'killed'?"

By Tyrolean's raised brows, he guessed not very.

"I wondered if you knew since you managed it with Truls," Aarinnaie said, turning and leading them to gods knew what sort of place. "It's not a secret, exactly, just something that doesn't come up very often."

Draken got a whiff of grave scent and turned to find Truls lingering at his side. He frowned, wondering where he went when he wasn't following and interfering with things. The ghost was quiet. Damned awkward asking him if he knew anything about Setia, his daughter, or Osias in front of the others. Did he know who planned to meet them? Surely the ghost never appeared without reason, even if Draken had a tough time working out what that reason was.

He thought of Zozia and wondered if he'd actually killed her. He hadn't seen her moon in the night sky since, but he'd lost track of the phases. He'd found it difficult no longer spending his nights on the open seas.

This night carried clouds and the sting of icy rain. And why shouldn't foul weather follow him here? If snow was ankle deep in the Moonling Woods, where snow rarely fell, he might as well be as miserable as the troops he'd sent to fight there.

Draken. Bruche came forward, stalling his stride. *The snow. It must be the gods' work, aye?*

Now that Draken thought about it in so many words he rather assumed so. Tyrolean glanced back at him, curious. He started walking again. *It doesn't matter.*

Aye, but it does. It tells us at least one god is on the Monoean side of things.

I thought we knew that already. When they aren't fighting each other, they're trying to drive us mad.

Hardly on purpose, I think. It's their nature, aye? And ours.

Whatever. I think they're using Akrasia and Monoea to war amongst themselves.

Hm. The spirit was quiet while Aarinnaie searched out a table, didn't find one, but returned with drinks. A quick glance showed only the roughest traders frequented the place, the sort that cared little for clean-swept floors or quality ale, so long as the drinks came cheap and regular. The erratic rhythm of conversation set him on edge and the scent of malty vomit assaulted his nose. At least the place was almost dim enough for his darksight, making his mask unneccesary.

You're already on edge. Drink. Bruche lifted the cracked mug to his lips. But deep inside the chill that was Bruche, thoughts slithered like errings under

Draken's consciousness. He sighed and drank. When Bruche had it all worked out, he'd say so.

"He's here." Tyrolean was already headed for a table with a lone Akrasian man sitting there. Older and with a capable air, the man rose at the Captain's approach.

"Tyrolean."

Draken's eyes widened. Aarinnaie snickered. Tyrolean held out his hand and the two exchanged grips. "It's been a long time, Wes." He gestured to Draken and lowered his voice. "Draken, Khel Szi of Brîn, meet Weswick. My brother."

"Half-brother, youngling." His greyed brows raised as he took in Draken, and then dipped his chin to Aarinnaie. "And the Szirin, I presume." His Brînian wasn't flawless, but comfortable.

Draken nodded, accepting the courtesy. "I wasn't aware the Captain had a brother."

"Ah, well." Weswick waved a hand in dismissal and dropped back into Akrasian. "I'm a bastard from our father's war years. The family doesn't like to mention me."

Tyrolean snorted softly. Draken sat so they all would, sliding his long leg over the worn bench. "We've that much in common, then."

Weswick dipped his chin again. "I'd heard . . . rumors of your parentage, of your history. On the road, as it were, as you are now."

"Rumors on the road often prove true," Aarinnaie said.

"Aye, Princess. It's what I've found as well. I assume you heard of the . . . unpleasantness with the Mance on said road."

"You are very well-informed." For a brother he'd never heard of. Draken gave Tyrolean a sidewise glance as he spoke.

"It's my living to know, isn't it?" He glanced at Tyrolean as well. "You really haven't told them about me?"

"Your name hadn't come up." Tyrolean drank and added, ale shining on his lips, "My brother sells information."

"Are you in the employ of the Queen?" Draken wasn't privy to all of Elena's machinations. There hadn't been time to learn them all even if she had trusted him enough to share.

"No. I simply sell to whoever pays the most."

"Which has been who, lately?" Aarinnaie asked.

Weswick glanced around, but their voices were already low. "The local trader-Baron. Lately."

Draken grunted. "What do you know about the Mance?"

Weswick's eyes narrowed. "I see no coin."

"Consider me good for it."

"Aye, it's what people say when they aren't."

"*Weswick.*" Tyrolean's voice was a whip. The table next to them quieted and glanced their way. Whatever Tyrolean had been about to say, it died in his throat. He swallowed, his lip curling a little. Instead he chose a generic: "His word is binding."

Draken leaned forward. "What do you know?"

"They died by spear. Your friend Osias was not among them, nor his companion." He worked his jaw as if it were sore, as if it had just been hit with a fist. Draken didn't find the future possibility too far off the mark. "The Mance are dead in the way we die. Gone to Eidola as banes, most like."

Draken stared a shade too long. "You can't know all that for certain."

Weswick lifted his chin. "Logic, my prince. And keen observation from long practice."

"What did you observe?" Draken growled.

"Beautiful Mance bodies sprawled on cold ground, bled out and lifeless." He looked pleased, whether by their deaths or at delivering the news, Draken didn't know.

Next to Draken, Aarinnaie's breath hissed, covering whatever noise drawing a blade from her wrist sheath caused. It flashed in the corner of his darksight.

Draken wasn't in the mood to be baited. "How did you see all that?"

"I know enough to follow trader-Barons when they leave their castles, don't I?" His fingers curled as if he were holding tight to something. "I've more, too. You're as fortunate as the tales tell."

"If that were truth, dozens of heads wouldn't be rotting on Citadel walls." Draken rose, the bench scraping the dirt floor. "I'm finished here."

Weswick sighed. "No need for dramatics to lower the price. I'm a reasonable man."

"This is not a negotiation, brother. This is him at the end of his patience." Despite their attracting some notice from nearby patrons, Tyrolean's gaze was steady, fingers relaxed on the pitted wood table. "Please. Draken. Stay. I'll see he talks."

Bruche studied the man through Draken's eyes. Greyed, worn features no different from a thousand others. *Is he so desperate for money? Or something else.*

I don't care.

Ah, but Tyrolean does.

Draken clenched his jaw and sat again.

Weswick drew in a breath. Examined the table between them, eyes narrowed. "I knew about Ilumat's plan. Well, I had guessed."

"How?"

"He sent me as a messenger to Khein. They were far from happy to hear from him. I reckoned something more was afoot than sending more troops to a quiet front."

"And you didn't come warn me instead?"

"I hoped I was wrong." Weswick's voice dropped. His pale skin flushed. "And they held me at Khein until their troops departed."

"They must be the first who managed it," Tyrolean muttered.

"That Geffen is clever." Draken cursed inwardly. Why hadn't Geffen told him all this? "Unfortunately I made the mistake of thinking she was loyal, as well."

Weswick leaned forward on his forearm. "No. She told me she was threatened. Her husband, an Escort, is being held somewhere."

"They threatened to kill him?"

"They threatened to cut something off him every day she didn't comply, starting when I sent off. It took her two more days to decide to send troops, though she sent a messenger straight back to Ilumat." He shrugged. "Which, no, before you ask, I didn't know about all that. She had me told when I was released, once the troops had a four-day head start."

Draken considered hard whether to ask his next question, but in the end he couldn't *not* ask. "Ilumat said he had proof the Queen is dead."

The corner of Weswick's mouth twitched. It was some breaths before he answered. "While I waited for the preparation of Ilumat's message, nearly a sevennight, someone arrived with a wrapped body by night. It was all whisked away. Later, when I had heard more, I thought it must be her husband . . ."

"How did you see all that?" Aarinnaie asked.

Weswick shrugged. "Information and intrigue do not sleep. Nor do I."

"Whose body was it?" Draken said, vaguely surprised he could speak at all with his throat so tight.

"I never found out, Highness. But Ilumat's claim of proof of the Queen's death worries at me like a thorn in the foot. I'm loyal, I am."

"What would he show? Her head?" Aarinnaie said.

Tyrolean gave her a sharp look.

"It doesn't matter. If he actually has proof that he would have shown it by now." Draken gave Weswick a grudging nod. "You've more than earned your coin. Make arrangements with Tyrolean to be paid."

"But there's yet more."

Draken exchanged glances with Tyrolean.

"What, Weswick? Tell it all," Tyrolean said.

Weswick's manner changed. He blinked rapidly, glanced around the tavern, and tapped his fingers on the table thrice before stilling them. "Not here."

"Right, and let you lead us off into some trap?" Aarinnaie shook her head. "Come, Drae. We've got it all out of him already."

"No." The word was sharp, followed by a hissed, "Highness. Please."

"Come to the castle, then," Draken said.

Weswick hesitated. Bruche wondered if he actually worked for Va Khlar or if that were a boast or lie.

Likely truth, Draken replied. The trader-Baron was notorious for his tight grip on all things Reschan. "You're under my protection," Draken said. "No harm will come to you at the castle."

"Besides, think of what you might learn." Aarinnaie tended to goad people when curiosity got the better of her.

An effective tactic, Bruche noted admiringly. Apparently so, because Weswick relented with a curt nod.

They were admitted back into the castle without the previous arrival's threats and fanfare and settled in an alcove off the great hall. Draken summoned Va Khlar. The Baron took his time in coming and slaves brought wine and bread. Weswick didn't sit, but watched the entrance to the hall, stiff enough to bounce a blade off. Draken was better able to examine him here. His clothes were worn but once had been fine; his boots scuffed from travel. His eyes narrowed as he considered what this meant. Draken knew enough of Akrasian politics to know even a bastard son of a well-off, established military family would probably have advantages and expectations others wouldn't. And yet Weswick wore no visible weapons and did not bear the telltale broadness of shoulder from a lifetime at the sword, nor the lopsided cant to the body frame the bow bestowed on archers.

Perhaps he has found information to be weapon enough, Bruche suggested.

Draken doubted it; surely it was easy enough to kill a man with dangerous information, which begged the question: How did Weswick survive while so apparently physically defenseless?

Powerful friends.

Draken suspected one of them strolled in as he exchanged thoughts with his swordhand. Va Khlar in the castle as Baron suited him, strangely. A smile cut his usually cryptic, scarred face. He wore the expensive clothes, chains of office, and grandiose surroundings as if he had been born to them. Perhaps there was a thinner difference between decrees made in castle great halls and threats made in back alleys than Draken believed.

Va Khlar slowed his pace, staring at Weswick, then letting his gaze slide to Draken. Tyrolean rose. "My Lord Baron, this is my brother Weswick."

There was a slight edge to the word *brother*. Uncharacteristic of Tyrolean to warn someone, or behave with less than perfect courtesy to a lord or superior officer. From Tyrolean's tone, the tightening of Va Khlar's scarred expression, and Weswick looking rooted to the spot, someone needed to be.

"Sit, the lot of you." Draken had the urge to rise, but knew if he stayed seated, it would keep him leading things. He let a little princely annoyance taint his words. "I assume you've met Weswick."

"Aye, Your Highness. A herald of sorts. I admit he's not one I like to find on my doorstep in trying times." Va Khlar moved to take the chair nearest Draken. The others followed. Aarinnaie sat quietly for once, watching. "Nor one I expected to find with you."

"He was our mysterious meeting," Draken said. "He's had some interesting things to tell us."

"Oh?" Va Khlar reached for the pitcher of wine. No evidence of nervous trembling curled his fingers. But then, it wouldn't. He was adept in trading in lies, stolen goods, and violence. But the twisting of his scarred brow and a narrowing of the eye beneath it, and the way his attention seemed riveted to Weswick rather than his prince, set Draken's teeth on edge.

"And he claims to have more," Draken said. "I suggested we come here to finish our conversation."

"It's sensitive then?" A muscle twitched in Va Khlar's cheek, hollowing it.

Weswick rubbed his tongue along the edge of his teeth. "It's about the Queen. She is alive, Prince Draken."

Draken's throat felt as if it were closing. "I thought we discussed this before."

"It's not a safe truth for any to know. For her, for perhaps any of you."

It made sense, damn him. But this proclamation set Draken on sharp edge. It didn't help that Truls materialized from the shadows, head cocked. He didn't speak. Draken noticed Weswick watching him stare at what appeared to be nothing. He cleared his throat. "How can you know this?"

"A collusion of rumors often tell truth."

"And where do these rumors claim she is?"

"In the Moonling woods, headed for Brîn. For you, Highness."

"That will take her right through the front," Draken said. Or by Galbrait and Rinwar, depending where they were headed.

Truls moved, catching his eye. Draken felt a chill, caught a whiff of death scent. It struck him that Truls stank when he wanted Draken's attention dragged to something, or *from* something—

Aarinnaie had moved. Draken missed it. She struck, quick as a viper, a knife pressed under Weswick's chin. The skin was soft there, grey and sagging. His hand flew up to grip hers. It was wrinkled and spotted but still dug into her skin. She tipped his chair back and braced her heel against the stone wall. The blade tightened, sinking into an aged fold on the man's throat. He kicked, but only served to nudge the table. Va Khlar rose and shifted nearer to Weswick and Aarinnaie, hand on his hilt. It looked a ceremonial blade if the jewels and engraving were any indication, but even such were sharp.

"You're lying," Tyrolean said, sounding almost offhand. But then, he didn't know of the evil eating at Aarinnaie's soul.

Draken rose and spoke sharply. "Aarinnaie, stand down—"

She cut Draken off with a low, threatening hiss and a tightening of the blade. A shadow flickered around her, and Draken's vision shifted from color to the varied greys of darksight.

"Get her off me!" Weswick coughed, a wet gagging sound. A bit of spittle sprayed from his mouth. A trickle of crimson penetrated the creviced shadows under his chin, sparking against Draken's vision.

An odd effect . . . Draken blinked and his darksight faded. The room was dim enough to accommodate his vision without the mask.

Tyrolean sat still in his chair, watching her assault his brother. "Where is the Queen, Wes? The truth now."

"Damn it, Tyrolean." The Akrasian was closest to Aarinnaie, but doing nothing. He didn't know the danger she posed. He considered this a threat to get Weswick to talk. Maybe a little torture. Draken started to edge around the table. "Answer and she'll let you go. Aye, Aarinnaie?"

She didn't glance up at her name. Cold fear seized Draken.

Noisy pants from Weswick. "Algir! She makes for Algir."

"Are you quite certain?"

"Aye!"

"Who else knows?"

Weswick squirmed, trying to dislodge her arm with his wrinkled hands. "I've told no one. I'm no traitor!"

kill him kill him kill him

"Then talk," Draken growled, ignoring Truls's whispers. "The truth, mind you—" But her blade flashed down and disappeared into Weswick's chest as Va Khlar spoke.

"Aarinnaie!" Draken rushed around the table toward them.

It was too late. Weswick gagged and sputtered crimson. More blood spilled over Aarinnaie's arm. She released him with a shove. He tumbled to the floor in a death spasm. Blood drained from his mouth and his chest in slow, tepid pools against the stone.

Tyrolean rose, his face grey, fists clenched. She looked up at him. Blinked. Her face crumpled. She backed away from Weswick and Tyrolean, shaking her head wordlessly.

"Tyrolean." Draken looked from his friend to his sister, not knowing who was in worse shape.

"I didn't mean . . . I was just." Aarinnaie blinked down at her bloody sleeve. She swallowed hard.

Her eyes were too big in her face, her bloodied hand and wrist too narrow for a killer. Draken reached for her hand but she drew away, arms pressed to her sides. He wanted to hold her, to remind her it was Truls's doing, that the spirit surely manipulated her even now. Of course Truls had conveniently melted away into the air.

"She killed him in cold blood. We all saw it. You must lock her up, Your Highness," Va Khlar said, making Draken wonder just whose favor he was currying. Not his, certainly. Maybe trying to save his own skin since he'd uttered what amounted to an order, even if as Szirin, Aarinnaie outranked him. Before Draken could answer, a slave approached on soft feet. His soft clearing of his throat startled them all.

"My lord." He stared at the bloodied Aarinnaie, voice quivering. "A M-Mance is at the gates, b-bidding entrance."

"Fools all, let him in!" Draken strode around the table and took Aarinnaie by the wrist. "Send him to my chamber. Come, Aarinnaie."

◆ ◆ ◆

Aarinnaie changed into a loose gown brought by servants, and Draken washed her hands for her, and her neck and face of the blood splatter. She kept her face turned aside from him. It reminded him of the first time they'd really ever talked. She'd been a prisoner for attempted assassination of the Queen. He'd meant to manipulate her into compliance so she would give him the name of whoever held her leash. Instead, she'd manipulated him. Clever girl to have found out so much about him prior to their arrival at the Bastion; clever for her to understand the information from Draken's fellow prisoner meant something. And clever Truls, who had molded her into a murderous image of himself.

The ghost had made himself scarce. Just as well. His commands during Weswick's death hadn't fled Draken's notice. He couldn't help but wonder if Truls was still pulling her strings. Maybe it was her Truls was here for, not him.

Aarinnaie perched on the edge of a hard chair, her hands pressed between her knees. She finally looked up at him with wide, stricken eyes. Was that an affectation? She *was* clever. He'd just been thinking it . . .

She must be doing as he taught her.

"Will you lock me up as Va Khlar said?" As the trader-Baron had once done before turning her over to Draken.

"It's getting tougher for you to control." Not quite a question.

Aarinnaie swallowed and averted her gaze to somewhere near his knees. Nodded once.

"Perhaps you should be, until we can work out what to do."

She didn't move but for a slight tremble. "There isn't anything to do for it."

"You don't know that."

"Mast . . . Truls told me. When he yet lived."

"As he would." He stepped a little closer. "Aarinnaie—"

Unlike her shoulders and Draken's stomach, her voice was steady. "You'll do what's best, Khel Szi."

He highly doubted that. "Very well. Get some rest."

Draken didn't have to seek Osias for a private word. He was in Draken's room. The Mance looked thinner, a little frail. He was also in the throes of a full-on necromantic trance. Five shimmering shapes stood before him, speaking in wavering sounds that held no words Draken could make out. Draken stilled as realization came over him. These five were the dead Mance.

At one particular phrase, Osias hissed a breath. His Voice rumbled through the room, thrummed through the vast distances and tight places where Bruche melded with Draken, deeper than marrow but outside his skin, in some language Draken didn't know. He could track reverberations, like waves on the sea, traveling through the room. He pulled down his mask and stared.

More soft answers, weak and fading. Osias stretched out his fingertips to encompass all five. Webbing flowed from his hand, shackling the dead to the living world. They solidified again, but shied as if resistant. It was a moment before Osias spoke again. Draken braced himself against flinching, but Bruche clung tight to his insides, icy against his ribcage. Every echo strove to rip Bruche from him.

No Setia among them. Draken's heart stalled. But maybe she would not appear here if she were dead. Another thundering question. The ghost-Mance all shied again. The atmosphere in the room thickened. The fire flickered down, suffocated. Draken wasn't breathing or he'd be gasping for air. They didn't want to speak. He knew it in his bones, in the magic thrumming through him, in the darksight that showed him these ghosts. He wondered where Truls was in this. And what he knew that he wasn't saying.

A word, it sounded like, but muffled. Just one. Osias must have believed, because he waved a hand and the ghosts fled through the shutter slats.

The fire crackled and caught again. Draken dragged air into his chest and squinted against the glare. For a moment he just breathed.

"Khel Szi." Osias moved to block the firelight with his body.

"I hope you learned something."

Osias's gaze met Draken's with clear eyes, the crescent moon above them black against his silver skin. "They were killed by Korde and a handful of Moonlings working the Abeyance. That held them still in order for Korde to act."

"Sikyra and Setia?"

Osias just looked at him, arms hanging limp at his sides. "I am sorry, my friend."

A thick woolen silence fell between them. His heart seized. Draken sank to his knees, fingers gripping his knees, vision blurring into a dull grey so that even darksight faded away.

Sikyra.

Her voice. Her smile.

Every fear, every horror he had imagined crashed down on him. His life splintered into two parts: when Sikyra lived, when even the possibility of her lived. And now, a remnant of the former. An existence of futile memory. He lowered his head into his shaking hands, silent and still as the Abeyance.

◆ ◆ ◆

Draken listlessly wandered the polished stone floor, extinguishing the oil sconces in his room. Heat from the fire stretched long fingers through the slight draft coming from the bolted shutters. The headboard was carved with religious symbols surrounding the Seven in Sohalia phase. The bed looked inviting, piled with fine fabrics. He would find no rest there.

"The slaves say there was a murder," Osias finally said.

"Aye. A messenger who had it coming." Had blades spilled the blood from Sikyra's tiny body as it had Weswick's? He swallowed back bile.

"Who?"

It took Draken a moment to recall what they were talking about. "Aarin. She's out of control. I'll have to lock her up." His voice was flat. His heart was already too wrung, even as unfair as it was to his sister.

Soft cushions bolstered the benches by the hearth, one of which Osias commandeered. His nails made irritating scritches as he cleaned the twin bowls of his pipe. The smell of Gadye weed rose up as he packed them, sharpened as he lighted it with his fingertips and smoke filtered through the air. Usually intoxicating and soothing, it had no impact on Draken this night.

Despite his placid movements and the calming nature of the smoke, Osias's voice was fierce, sharp. "She would never recover from such betrayal of her faith. You are her last ally, her family, and her Khel Szi. She has driven all else away."

Such a betrayal would break you, as well. You need her more than ever.

"Your swordhand speaks truth, my friend."

"She cannot bear it—this desire to kill." His voice broke.

You must leave her be. What will come will come.

I tried that and she's married to Ilumat, who took her to his bed and did only the gods know what to her . . .

She knows. And she alone knows what she can bear.

"Perhaps it is you who cannot bear it? She is not a child, Draken. She is a grown, thinking woman all her own, and it is done. She doesn't need you to save her from this."

Draken mastered his voice. "Aarin said there's nothing to be done."

"It is old magic Truls used on her. Not just training, but necromantic soulwork. A bane splint."

Draken narrowed his eyes and frowned, an intense look of concentration to mask his baser feelings of grief and terror. Osias went on: "The part of evil that binds it to a soul. To rip it from her would unravel her. It's as much a part of her now as Bruche is of you."

He imagined long claws or spiraling antennae burrowing into Aarinnaie. "I think I see it in my mind's eye. This cursed sight the gods have given me."

Osias nodded. "The splint strengthens with her every kill."

Draken released a breath between his teeth. "I lost Bruche once. It wasn't so bad. Perhaps . . ."

"But he returned, aye? Followed you until he could join you again."

Can't bloody stay away. Death is boring.

Osias smoothed his hand over the front of his pale grey tunic. His face took on the hard planes of truth. "Even were I able to separate them, the splint would seek her, hunt her."

"So kill it."

"It cannot be done."

"Aye, it can. With a damned magic sword."

Osias shook his head. His voice gentled. "Not even Akhen Khel can destroy a bane splint, not without killing Aarinnaie, and I certainly cannot. The best she can do is to forgo spilling blood altogether. With time it will weaken its grip on her."

Draken shook his head, trying to shake away the words, his fears, the pressure that wanted to explode into pain behind his eyes. A knock sounded before he could answer. "Come!"

Tyrolean stepped inside. "I searched my brother before sending him to the deadcart. He had a deal of coin on him." He poured some from a bag out onto his palm. Draken's cousin, King Yssef of Monoea, stared back at them from the golden surfaces, a neat beard covering his very dead chin.

Draken cursed. "He was a ruddy traitor, then."

"Aye. Your Highness, I'm afraid we cannot trust anything he's said."

Truls caught his eye, melding into wisps of smoke escaping the flue. Draken turned away. He hadn't had time to even hope Weswick was telling the truth before Aarinnaie had killed him.

His gaze skirted Draken for Osias, who nodded. Tyrolean released a slow breath. "What's happened?"

"Sikyra is dead." He wondered if his voice sounded as hollow as he felt. Quiet passed between them. Before Tyrolean could offer condolences and draw up ruddy tears or the like, Draken went on. "I have to find Elena. She must be told."

Even though he had no idea how he would explain how he had sent their daughter away to her death.

She won't take it well, Bruche said.

Draken ignored this vast understatement.

Tyrolean cleared his throat. "Speaking of the Queen, her heading through the woods along the front makes sense if she's headed for Brîn. It's the quickest route."

"Weswick also said she was going to Algir," Osias said. "Who knows which is truth? We're no closer to catching up to any of them than we were."

More silence for a bit. Draken had nothing to offer, couldn't drag his mind to the implications of Weswick's lies.

"Logically," Tyrolean said, "If Wes was lying during our entire conversation—if he was paid by the Monoeans to keep her whereabouts secret—she is going to neither place." Draken shook his head, confused. Tyrolean lifted a hand. "Hear me out. We'd have had word if she was at Auwaer. She wouldn't go back to Skyhaven and the Moonlings. Which leaves . . . ?"

"Downland to Khein?" Draken said, finally catching on. "To the coast?"

"Too close to the front," Tyrolean said. "She'd have been seen, I think. And the coast is harsh during Frost, especially this one. No one is traveling by water now."

Osias huffed on his pipe. "Upland, then. Septonshir."

"But why?" Draken asked. "How can the Septs help?"

"They're too reclusive to attract much attention from the Monoeans, and they prefer Elena to Kings. Septonshir might make a good place to hide," Tyrolean said. "Especially if she knows about the coup in Brîn and presumes you dead."

"Then that's where we go." There was some relief in the decision, even if it was the grimmest trek he'd ever embark on.

"And Aarinnaie?" Osias asked.

"I'll speak to her about not killing any longer."

His sister had curled on the bed, blankets pulled up against the chill. She was awake, staring at the fire. Draken put his back to it. "We're leaving first thing in the morning."

She said nothing.

He should smooth the covers over her, stroke her hair. She needed comforting. But there was a wall of stoicism around her. "Will you come?"

She shifted to look up at him. "Will you have me?"

The thought of all she'd been through, their father, Truls, the bane splint, and Ilumat . . . it all tore at him. But he had to tell her. They could discuss her bane splint on the road. "I need you, Aarin. Osias brought word of Sikyra." His voice broke over her name.

She blinked up at him. Soulful, tearless eyes. "I'm sorry. You don't know how sorry."

He knew the strength in that small body, in that mind he'd only just gotten to know. She had resisted his every effort to coddle her, to discuss all that had damaged her, all that had made her weak.

Because it hadn't made her so weak after all.

"Get some rest," Draken said. "We leave at daybreak."

CHAPTER TWENTY

Afierce storm tormented the grassland plains upland of Reschan, along with anyone who dared cross it—except, of course, Truls and Osias, who were immune to the weather. Draken's pony kept his ears flattened as he leaned into the wind and he kept trying to shield his face in the rump of the pony in front of him. Aarinnaie took to calling him Bumpus.

Draken had forgone a thick saddle for a blanket in hopes of sharing the tora pony's shaggy warmth. He couldn't say it made much difference, but maybe it did keep him from freezing. The leather pants, thick woolen shirt, and undershirt under his buckled cloak helped, some, but the frosty air found ways of sneaking in. They all had scarves of wool tied around their faces and thick mitts on their hands. Draken's shoulder and bad knee ached from the tense position he'd held against the wind for the past two days. Their only saving grace was a lack of snow.

Before they'd left Reschan, Va Khlar had gifted him with a new mask: a finished strip of wide-weave linen with padding around the edges to hold it away from his eyelids. The glare of white, cloudy skies meant he wore the mask constantly in the day.

Aarinnaie always held her gaze just shy of his face, as if he might change his mind and start questioning her about the bane splint, her training, and Ilumat. But the constant wind dulled his curiosity, and he sank deep into silent grief. The four travelers spoke little.

Truls led them, and Draken doggedly followed, more from lack of determination and the assumption he was in on their plan to find Elena. So far Truls had not led him too far astray.

When Draken had envisioned the upland plains from maps in Monoea, and later as Prince, he had imagined it a flat stretch of deep grass as far as the eye could see, dotted with grazing herds. But the ground rolled underfoot into hills and valleys. Rock formations jutted up; the remnants of an ancient sea, Osias claimed. Draken and Bruche privately doubted even *his* spiritkind went back so far to have seen this land underwater, but some of the scrubby plateaus resting on sharp cliffs did look suspiciously like islands.

The dried grasses held pockets of ice and snow, but Bumpus rode the occasional slip without breaking stride. His plodding pace was so incessant Draken wondered if he would ever stop unless made to do so. At last Truls led them down a steep incline, waving his arm at them to follow before he disappeared completely. It was for the best; the Mance's silvery cloak was a beacon on the plains and with the country in upheaval from the war, they didn't know who they might meet. The skies were cloudy but Draken had no doubt the Seven—or Six, as it were—were looking for him.

Draken followed, leaning back as Bumpus plodded and slid down the grassy hillside into a long, deep crevice that was more grass at the bottom. Long, dried grasses wavered over the top, rustling and making a tunnel effect. Tyrolean and Aarinnaie followed and they gathered in the space. It was wide enough to walk at least three horses abreast and faded far off under the glare of clouds and misty, fading daylight. At least they were out of the worst of the blasted wind. It was enough to drag Draken from his fugue.

He pulled down his scarf. "What is this?"

"The Silent Trail."

"That's myth," Aarinnaie said.

"No, Szirin. I assure you it isn't." Osias gave her a slight smile.

Draken wondered if Osias ever got annoyed that Aarinnaie claimed to know the absolute truth of everything until proved otherwise.

No. I'm fair certain that only plagues you.

Draken grunted and concentrated on adjusting his scarf. The air was still cold even out of the wind. Red streaks marred the tops of Tyrolean's cheeks. "All right. I'll bite. What's the Silent Trail?"

"It was used to populate Septonshir and then further to Algir, though the trail hasn't worn as deep there. It is old and well used through the Grassland."

"Why silent?"

"Because you can hear and see anyone coming for miles on the plains, if you listen closely enough. As the trail wore down the ground, it cut the noise travelers make."

Truls, for his part, kept gliding ahead. He paused and looked back at Draken, then kept on. "I'll go ahead to scout," Draken said, staring after him.

Bruche signaled his silent disapproval, but didn't speak.

Osias looked from Truls to Draken. "I think you should rest, aye? Have a bite."

"I know you mean well, but—"

"One cannot live on anger and grief alone, friend." Osias sounded friendly enough but his eyes were slipping to storm.

He glanced at Aarinnaie. Hatred seemed to keep her going well enough. Having the bane splint seemed to be a bit like having another being inside her, perhaps, which reminded him . . . "Something I've been wondering, Osias. Did your power increase with the death of the other Mance?"

Osias was still a long moment until he nodded.

"You have all their power?"

"I don't yet understand the breadth of it."

Bruche was listening closely. *If that's true, you and your sword might not be the only thing that can kill a god. But would he do it?*

He rebelled once, removing the fetter.

Aye, and now perhaps the gods avoid our Mance.

Osias surely heard their conversation, but he turned away. "Go take your walk, my friend."

Draken shook himself. "Right. Best make camp here. Can't see how a fire will hurt down in this gulley. The wind will disperse the smoke."

He swung down from Bumpus, who needed a rest and, truth, wasn't fleet enough to get him anywhere much quicker than his own legs would. He untied his sword from the saddle, bound it around his middle, and strode off into the gloom before anyone could protest. Truls floated in his periphery, no help at all when he nearly stumbled right into a Monoean sentry. The man was just turning slightly away from Draken, staring into the darkness. Draken held, not breathing. His dull grey armor was shadowy, even to Draken's darksight. For the first time that struck him. If Korde had a hand in this army, had he armored them to shield them from Draken's darksight? Regardless, he could see the gleam of a seax gripped in one hand. The bracer on the other arm made him fair impenetrable, if the man knew his business.

Draken's sword, though oiled at Reschan, clung to the inside of its damp sheath. Draken stood in the man's line of sight, but darkness still cloaked him. One move would break through even regular night blindness. He considered and couldn't see another way.

Instead of drawing, Draken stepped forward and tried to catch the man's throat with his arm. The guard turned just as he made his move. His eyes widened and mouth opened. He emitted one wordless grunt before Draken's fist caught him in the jaw. The man staggered back. Draken followed, caught his throat in the crook of his arm, and squeezed. Killing in this position wasn't easy, but Draken had size to his advantage. The guard gagged, spat, struggled.

He twisted, shifting to try to bite and scrabble for his weapon. Draken turned his head away. He punched and flailed at Draken. The fists pounded his ribs, but it didn't cause enough strain to make him let go. Draken caught his wrist in his free hand and pulled, tightening the grip. The struggles faded and the man fell limp.

He had no thought to letting the man live and in this Bruche was in agreement. He held him, counting under his breath, then lowered the slack body to the ground to feel for a pulse. The vein had fallen still and Draken caught the twin scents of death flowing from the body. Draken yanked the helm and hood from the guard's head. A hairline of pale hair, no slant to the eye. Dark remnants of an oily ash mark on his brow. Whatever they used certainly stained the skin well enough. A Monoean. Draken stepped over the body and held, wondering if he should go on, return and get help, or simply retreat. But he couldn't make himself leave this opportunity to find out more about the enemy.

He walked as the gully gently curved, blade held in front of him. To his swordhand, rock outcroppings grew from the ground and broke through the grassy walls in spots, obviously having diverted the road. They blocked most of the moonlight, letting his eyes relax further. He slowed his pace and moved as silently as the dried grasses would allow. There'd been a guard, which meant someone or something important nearby.

As he came around an outcropping, a ray of moonglow made him squint. No, not just the moons. He dropped to peek over the edge of the gully, leaning against the slanted, grassy wall. Fires dotted the ground beyond, sparking against his darksight. He dared a glance upward, and had to close his eyes for a few breaths. Khellian and Ma'Vanni. War Phase. No wonder it was so bright.

Within the protection of the rocks, two rows of pointed tents materialized in his darksight. The wind nudged the fabric walls, though within the protective rocks it was considerably less than even where he stood in the gully. To one side, horses stood in tethered clumps, nosing the ground. The smell of cooking meat drifted up, which would have made his stomach ache with hunger if he wasn't only two nights from Reschan with relatively plentiful and fresh provisions.

Soldiers moved about, speaking in low tones that barely carried to his ears. Apprehension shrouded the camp. No huddled groups groused, gamed, and drank around the fires. It was all business. Cooking. Feeding horses. Walking the perimeter.

Curiosity itched under his skin. But magic or no, he was one man. Even with the others they only were four, and he'd guess this camp outmanned them tenfold. He cursed under his breath. Fools all! He should have questioned that guard before killing him.

Be easy. Think. There are guards, aye, but not so many. We've not seen one walk by us yet. Might there be a way to sneak in to eavesdrop on the tents or conversation?

When the fires are damped. There was enough wind to necessitate putting them out before bedding down. It just meant waiting.

Aye, and come in through the horses. They'll give good cover.

Draken made his way up the slanted, steep wall, slipping several times on dried grasses into the more recent ruts that scored the bottom of the gully, and listened rather than using his darksight. He still wore the mask; the Eyes watched closely this night. Still no Zozia. Perhaps she was dead after all.

Something rustled the grasses over his head. He eased down on the slanted wall of the Silent Road and winced as the grasses shushed beneath him. Bootsteps, sounding relatively idle, moving over his head.

"All quiet, sir." Monoean, docks accent. Conscript, then.

"So it appears. Not afraid to say this business makes me nervous."

"Are the royals settled in, then, sir?"

Draken pursed his lips. Royals? He couldn't possibly have had the good fortune to run into Galbrait a second time. But the conscript had clearly said royals. Plural. There were no Monoean Royals left but for Galbrait. Nerves clenched the back of his throat. Unless they meant Elena. Settled could be camp jargon for "secured."

Surely not, Bruche said.

I have to go in now. What if she's captive here?

The two Ashen moved away. He held until their footsteps mostly faded, until his own movements would be counted among the myriad other sounds on the plains, and he eased from his hiding spot and walked a little further until he heard whickers and the soft thud of hooves stamping.

He climbed a little way up the embankment top. A small forest of horse legs met his darksight, the scent of fresh manure and the tearing of grass. He pulled down his mask and hauled himself the rest of the way up, waiting on his knees, staring all around. A couple of horses turned their heads and shifted their hindquarters, but most were intent on their grain.

Of course he smelled of horse himself, and of sweat and the outdoors, like their riders. He eased among them, murmuring gently. They made way for him. He felt almost jealous; he'd like a real horse instead of the tora pony Bumpus.

Ah, but the pony suits a man of your status, does it not? An exile and prince now fallen from grace?

Very amusing. He had no laughter in him but appreciated Bruche treating him normally.

Draken moved parallel to the camp between the animals, keeping a watchful, albeit squinted eye. The damned moonlight made him feel as if someone were carrying a torch over his head like a beacon. At least the wind and animal noises covered his sounds.

Beyond, the tents poked up, and from this vantage he saw a taller five-stake tent encircled by the others. There might be the army commanders, and perhaps these "royals." Gaining proximity to it was going to require a better trick though. Fires still burned all around. It would be deep in the night before he had the chance. He melted back further, until his back was against the rocks sheltering the animals. He ran his hands over it and frowned as he found crumbling lines. Mortar? He turned his head to study it. An ancient wall rested against the rock outcropping. Maybe it had been a stable once, or a home. Or an inn to feed and lodge the long ago upland exodus.

What sort of people are the Septs?

Bruche gave an inward shrug. *Matriarchal. Reclusive. I've never met any but the sundry slaves marketed from there.*

You make it sound as if they breed them on purpose.

Perhaps they do. I've heard they are traders to give Va Khlar fair fits. I think they well know the value of their own flesh.

It irked, but slavery was a problem for another day. He watched the camp for a while but gradually shifted to a squat and then a sit. He thought over what he'd seen: few guards despite the "royals" within, and neat, hastily built fire pits. Nothing indicated a protracted stay. His best guess was they had arrived yesterday or the day before and were scheduled to pack up in the early daylight hours and move on immediately. But to where? And for what purpose?

The horses dozed, snuffling, stamping occasionally. The moons glided slowly across the sky. Ma'Vanni dropped behind the great standing rock, which the highlight of moonglow made look imposing. At length, deep night swept over the plains, his knee grew stiff from the cold, and he removed the mask. The wind still made the sparks dance from puddles of eye-searing coals. If he avoided them his darksight evened out and he could pick out the shadows of men easily enough.

His shoulders tightened as he finally emerged from between the horses. About twenty strides separated him from the nearest tents. He couldn't run or even walk fast. Men stirred slowly at night within a moving camp, only rising for duty or to relieve themselves, moving as if worn from long days on the sword or in the saddle.

The sound of cantering hooves made him startle and step back within the horses. Damn damn damn, they'd be bringing more animals this way. But he had to know who these late newcomers were. Outriders, or a rear guard? Or visitors.

A voice rang out, mindless of the sleeping camp. "I hope this isn't a waste of my time."

It chilled Draken far beyond what the wind had done. *Oklai*, Bruche whispered.

The Moonling had threatened him when he refused to free the slaves of Brîn outright. She had shifted from once saving his life to doing her damnedest to destroy it in the time he'd known her. Her diminutive stature belied the power and magic she held.

A much taller figure dismounted. He spoke in a voice locked tightly inside Draken's memory. A voice he'd never forget. "I would not lead you on a fool's journey, my lady."

"Majesty," Oklai answered, her voice chill.

Bloody Galbrait. Truls had found his cousin twice. Draken's fingers tightened on his sword. It would almost be worth it. He would be overcome, but he could surely kill both traitors before their guards cut him down.

Nay, hold. Information is the better weapon here. What you learn could be the death of them, aye? All of them.

Truth, and the thought of Elena held his blade as well. She deserved to hear of their daughter's fate from him, and he longed for her as well. With her, he could share his grief, even if she would surely blame him. And only he could understand her. He owed her that much.

It took a moment for Galbrait to reply, and his voice was dry. "Of course. Your Majesty. I forget we are of a rank."

"You're not King yet, child, nor are you a Prince if your own country won't have you. Well? Take me to him, then."

Galbrait held a moment, maybe holding back the comment that Oklai's country hardly named her Queen, so their rank was in accord after all. But at last he walked stiffly at her side toward the center tent. Their guards followed, and a pale, flitting glow.

Truls, following the enemies. He behaved strangely, though, stopping as if he'd hit an invisible barrier that Oklai and Galbrait passed through unheeded. Truls stilled for a moment and then vanished.

No help from the ghost, then, as they disappeared inside the central tent. Typical. No one stirred among the conscript tents, but the Moonling war party would see him if he approached from this direction. Draken cursed inwardly and eased between the horses away from the Escorts.

Best to come at it from behind anyway, but he had to wend his way through more tents. Once he was among them, he found it wasn't difficult to stay concealed. They were nearly as tall as him, and beyond some snoring and coughing, the camp was quiet. It obviously relied on their perimeter guards. Good. He drew his blade, mercifully dark, and eased down to a squat between the side of a conscript tent—emitting at least three varieties of snores—and the main tent.

He sorted the voices. Oklai, the Moonling warrior who fashioned herself Queen of the Moonlings, though they were subject to Elena. Galbrait, deferential in his familiar, Monoean-accented Akrasian. Rinwar, the younger brother of a Landed Lord Draken had killed in Monoea, a priest who liked to call himself a General, his accent thicker. No matter the language, he never sounded anything but confident.

And an unfamiliar, cold voice that rattled Draken to his core. "I assume you're here to renegotiate."

"Truth, our arrangement for the Agrian Range seems paltry when compared to your need," Oklai said.

Galbrait cleared his throat. A warning, maybe? But Oklai went on. "You cannot take these lands without Moonling magic."

"We will give you what your people want once you've done as you said you would."

"Perhaps a little more reward is in order, my . . ." Galbrait faltered as if he didn't know how to title the owner of the cold voice.

"'My lord' is sufficient." Amused, but with an edge that honed itself on souls. "The Moonlings have been of great aid to us, my lord," Galbrait said. "The soldiers you make are even more so."

Draken frowned. *The soldiers you make* . . . It wasn't a Monoean turn of phrase.

"Time does go on," Rinwar said.

"Agreed," Galbrait said. As he went on, his words strengthened. "Word of the Queen's movements are reaching the most common ears. It encourages the Akrasians. The last village fought us hard."

"But it did succumb."

"Nearly a hundred more followers, my lord."

"If I can find Elena, we can use her as bait," Oklai said. The cold voice remained silent. So did the others. Oklai went on with what Draken considered a great deal of bravado. "She seeks the Khel Szi, does she not?"

"Those are the rumors," Galbrait answered. "She travels to Brîn."

"It stands to reason, but in spite of the Reschanian trader's attempt to claim the opposite, his guards told me he had elite guests at his castle. The Khel Szi and three companions."

"Va Khlar could not be persuaded to cooperate, then," Rinwar said. "A pity."

"Not even under pain of death," Oklai replied.

Draken bowed his head. Truth, Va Khlar had few honorable ambitions, but he was a close, valuable ally. A friend.

"Could they have missed each other, Draken and the Queen?" Galbrait asked.

"Likely. Keep to the villages. We need to build our army more than some Akrasian outliers need their Queen. She matters naught to this war."

All the while Bruche's discomfort had been growing, a wordless plea to retreat. But they didn't know how this conversation would resolve. Draken had only got a taste of strategy . . . not enough to use against them. He'd only learned two things of value: They believed Elena was alive and on the move, and the Moonlings were using the Abeyance to help the Monoeans.

Bruche didn't reply in so many words, but he urged him to go while he could get away safely. Draken tipped his head up to look at the sky. There was more to learn here. But it was nearly moonset, the darkest of night, and the best time to escape. His companions would be wondering where he'd gotten to. His jaw tightened. Damn him, Bruche was right. He rose, grimacing at the cracking in his knees. Held. The voices continued in the tent, Oklai insisting the magic was worth more than the Agrian Range. The Abeyance, the Moonling's ability to stop time, had proved to be a valuable weapon. Draken thought she had a valid point as he stole between the tents back toward the horses.

Once among them, he turned his head and looked at the large tent, torn again between escape and doing something. So many enemies in one place. Galbrait, his cousin who had betrayed him. Oklai, who had taken his Queen and his child and held them captive, who had said in not so many words that she had killed Va Khlar. The Priest-General Rinwar, who had stabbed him in the chest with his own sword and brought down ancient walls. And that cold voice . . . someone new. Someone else in command.

He could cut the head off the invasion here. He might even seek revenge for Sikyra and Setia, since Moonlings had helped Korde kill them.

But it brought him no closer to Elena. He would die here and she would have to face Sikyra's loss alone. He retreated back to the old wall by the horses, his back against the crumbling stone. His fingers toyed with the leather flap on his sword grip.

I need to kill them.

Draken, you are one man. See reason.

I am one man with darksight, a man who cannot be killed.

You don't know that.

He did. He'd tried enough times. *I have a sword that kills gods. I surely can kill a few men and Moonlings.*

You don't know that's all they are.

Draken sighed. Bruche was right. That voice had felt different. He tried to think back to how he'd felt when speaking with Zozia. He'd been too surprised and apprehensive to notice much else.

But Oklai would ride out. Perhaps Galbrait would ride with her. He clenched his jaw as resolve took hold.

The problem would be catching up with their ponies. But the camp was still quiet and if they separated at all, he could take them out one by one. A voice niggled at him that he could still strive to ally the Moonlings. Surely some of them were more reasonable than Oklai. But a bigger part wanted her dead, gone from his life. She'd once done him a good turn, but abducting Elena and their infant daughter had far overshadowed it.

I'm more concerned with how you'll kill them without going down yourself. Besides, Galbrait may be of use yet. He knows things.

Not nearly enough. It was Rinwar he needed for information, to put this invasion to rest, but he'd learned the last time he'd gone up against the Priest not to underestimate him. This was a much smaller camp than Rinwar had kept at the siege of Auwaer, but as Bruche's incessant nagging reminded him, he was only one man. He fingered his sword hilt thoughtfully, and then it hit him. Of course.

He had the advantage of darkness, but the disadvantage of time. He thought back over the conversation. There'd been no offers of hospitality; not even an exchange of drinks or gifts, or pleasantries, for that matter. The Moonlings would surely soon mount their restless ponies and leave. He had a few breaths to decide and move. Soon the sun would stain the horizon gold.

He'd spilled so much blood since his exile. His first act on Akrasian soil had been to beat someone bloody. Not killing that man had nearly cost him his life. He wouldn't make the same mistake again. He slid the bow from his shoulder and lifted a little to string it.

Footsteps behind him. He stayed crouched in the deep darkness between tents, barely breathing, gripping his bow in one hand and his sword hilt in the other, ready to rise and spin and draw. They paused. Could someone see him between tents or . . . he turned his head slowly, hoping his neck didn't crack the way it usually did. A form took shape at the end of the little corridor made by this group of six tents; a soldier, his back to Draken. He appeared to be messing with something on the front of his armor, head down. He cursed low in Monoean about a broken strap.

A flitting pale flash appeared beyond. Draken's eyes narrowed. Truls, flickering into view and then out as if someone had extinguished a torch. The soldier looked up. Swore again, but his tone was questioning. He started off the way Truls had gone.

Draken released the breath he'd been holding and rose, turning to find a soldier climbing out of his tent, ducked low under the flap. Draken strode between tents, weaving through them toward the open plains rolling off between the two rock outcroppings. The wrong direction from his friends' camp, but he'd lay a thousand rare this was the way the Moonlings would ride. This way led back to their ruined home at Skyhaven.

Truls appeared again, having ditched his curious soldier. He gestured. Draken didn't pause to think. He moved toward the ghost, who lingered near four thick quivers leaning up against each other like the three-pole tents the Novern wilders used. Draken nodded to the ghost, grabbed a handful of arrows, ten or so to supplement the ones on his back, and kept moving. His back trickled sweat despite the cold wind sweeping over him as he escaped the encampment and emerged between the two great rocks.

The shadow of a boulder nudged his darksight. He made for it, cursing his limping run. He'd strained his knee beyond redemption for this night. But the stone provided good cover. He knelt—half fell—behind it and just breathed for a bit while he stared back the way he'd come. Motion . . . someone searching? No. A regular guard he'd just missed. And then a larger contingent: ponies and riders in a thick clump that spread out as they emerged between the rocks and darkness of the camp.

His jaw tightened and he rose just enough to string the bow. He set his arrows on the ground and ran his fingers along one, checking feathers and straightness. All of this he did by feel because he was too busy watching the group of Moonlings. They were close to the ground. No man of tall stature rode among them; no Galbrait. Poor fortune. He hissed softly and nocked an arrow.

Oklai would be in the middle, protected. As soon as one of her guards fell, he'd have to fire very fast to get her, and even then, getting away might be a challenge. They'd raise an alarm, blow a horn or scream or some damned thing. Maybe even work the Abeyance. It wouldn't be difficult to figure out where the arrows came from. But he had to risk it. He thought of going to Skyhaven to retrieve his family. Oklai's face when she'd spoken of his child as if she were no more than a thing; a bit of coin or a valuable oddity to hold as collateral for a bad loan. Elena, as she had shifted from relief at the sight of him to apprehension when she realized the Moonlings had no intention of letting her go, to determination to help Draken carry their child to safety. The sight of her throwing flame from her palms, screaming at him to run as she burned Skyhaven to the ground in order to provide him and Sikyra an opportunity at escape.

An escape for naught, for the Moonlings had caught up with his daughter and helped Korde murder her. How would he ever make Elena understand? He didn't understand himself, there was no explaining it unless he believed in destiny, which he bloody well did not. He had made the decisions that led to their daughter's death, and his presence with Elena could provide her no comfort. And truth, dying here this night, at least trying to achieve some justice, appealed more than living to explain himself to Elena, trying to give her comfort that she surely would not want from him.

Only a sliver of Khellian remained on the horizon, easier to see from behind the rocks with the great plains stretching toward its light. A great gust of wind buffeted his body and left still air in its wake. Khellian winked out and the greys of his darksight filled this blackest time.

His body fell into a position as familiar as breathing, string drawn to cheek, legs braced to give him stability. Even with having to adjust for weight and draw, a Moonling tumbled from her horse and he had another arrow on the string as quick. As a war tribe, they weren't stupid. They turned as a group toward him, leaving only one behind to see to their fallen comrade.

How can they see in this pitch? Bruche wondered.

Draken grimaced and shot again. Despite the arrow in his shoulder, the Moonling kept his seat. Draken had another arrow on the string, throwing two more Moonlings off their ponies.

As one, the clump of galloping ponies turned to head out to the plains, steering away from him, upland.

Why do they run? He thought it would be obvious he was alone, or at least that they far outnumbered their attackers, just by virtue of the arrows.

They can't see you and you fired quickly. You've more advantage than you thought.

Or they've got somewhere to be in a hurry. He watched the fleeing Moonlings leave their dying comrades behind, satisfied. Now they knew how it felt to be on the run, to fear hidden enemies who might strike at any time.

Bruche hesitated. *This is revenge, Draken, not battle strategy or even justice.*

They took Elena. They're allied with the Monoeans. With Galbrait. They are traitors.

But are they traitors when they never proclaimed their loyalty to you?

It was a fair question that made his blood run hot with fury. *Oklai proclaimed her friendship once, and then stole my family from me. Galbrait knelt to me and then betrayed me. They are out to break this country. For that, they will pay.*

CHAPTER TWENTY-ONE

"Where in Khellian's name have you been?" Aarinnaie jumped up, startling the horses and making Tyrolean snort softly awake. The sun was just greying the black skies. Shadows over the Grassland made it reminiscent of the sea. Osias stood apart, out of the light of the fire, an arrow on the string. He gave Draken a nod but kept his attention on the trail behind them.

He sat on the ground by the fire, glad for the heat. A pot boiled a little water with sweet-scented tea and wine. His scarf wrapped around his fingers to protect them from the hot metal, he poured himself a cupful and sipped. It warmed his bones. "I found a Monoean encampment. They had visitors in the night. This is quite good, by the way."

"It was meant for the Captain." Aarinnaie stood over him, hands propped on her hips. "What visitors?"

"Lady Oklai and her war party. And Galbrait."

"Prisoners?" She frowned when Draken shook his head.

"No. Guests. Allies. I was able to catch part of the conversation. The Moonlings are helping the Monoeans raid villages and farms, to secure their hold on Akrasia. They're trading magic for the Agrian Range. I'm not sure of Galbrait's role other than as a puppet king for the Ashen."

She sank down onto her heels, staring at him.

Tyrolean was listening because he rolled over and sat up, rubbing his hand over his face. "Why did they meet in the middle of the Grassland?"

"It was a very secret meeting, I think. The priest Rinwar was there, and some other. I don't know who it was." His voice dropped and he suppressed a shudder.

Tyrolean shook his head. "I'm surprised you didn't rush in and try to kill them all."

He shrugged. "I did manage to shoot some Moonlings with a bow as they rode away."

"And you survived it? One against a whole war party?" Tyrolean asked.

"It was dark and I was well-hidden." *And lucky*, Bruche pointed out. Draken grimaced. "And lucky. Our path will take us right by them. Morning patrols will find a dead guard and several dead Moonlings. We need to get on with it, and give them wide berth."

Tyrolean leaned his arm on his upraised knee, annoyingly *not* getting up to saddle his pony. "Vigilante action is against the Queen's law, Your Highness."

"I take your point, Ty. But I'm no longer Prince nor Night Lord." And Elena, if or when he saw her, had no reason to restore him now that Sikyra was dead. Whatever love and affection she shared with him would be lost to grief, he did not doubt.

"You can no more escape your royalty than you can your own skin, my friend," Osias said.

Draken grinned, and by Osias's widened eyes, it must have looked garish on his face. "Ilumat did a damned good job stripping me of it. I have no Bastion, no crown, no Night Lord Pendant, no daughter, no Queen. My connection to the royals of Monoea is destroyed as well. I don't even have a bloody horse. I might have royal blood but I am a common man again, common as I was in exile, common enough to hunt and kill those who attack my people."

"My people," Osias echoed faintly. "Those are not words of a man in exile."

Draken grunted. "Don't make more of it than it is. My time to lead is over." He had only one certain intention now, something more certain than chasing the cold trails of his Queen. He had to kill Galbrait and Oklai. He fingered the loose flap of leather on his sword. *And maybe a god or two while he was at it.*

Setia had once asked him if he was happy, during his early days in Akrasia. Content, he'd answered. Now there would be no contentment in killing them, but a sort of relief, maybe.

Aarinnaie toyed with her knife. "I welcome the opportunity to kill Monoeans."

Draken sucked down the rest of his tea, avoiding the topic and Osias's sharp gaze. He hadn't spoken to her of forgoing killing yet. He was out of the mood with revenge on his mind. "Saddle up, you lot. We've a distance to ride today."

◆ ◆ ◆

Draken pulled his mask off with relief the next night. Even with the nightfall chill, he was glad to have the air on his face. The world turned to the crisp, many-shaded grey as he shifted from veiled vision to his darksight, and the winds had subsided during the day so that riding with the sun on their backs was almost pleasant.

The terrain had shifted as well, cut through with tributaries and ice-laced ponds. The endless rolling grasses gave way to larger foliage, clumps of shrubs and copses of trees. Every now and then they saw a deserted house, sometimes burned, often left with doors and shutters banging in the winds. They approached none of them, guessing what they'd find. It seemed more Monoeans had swept upland, cutting through the Grassland like a scythe, leaving little life in their wake. Livestock from paddocks or fields were missing, butchered to feed the Monoean army.

For Draken's part, and his friends', they were nearly out of food and hungry. They rarely saw the small deer, wild horses, fowl, or hares populating the Grassland. Fresh water kept them going, and nibbles of the last of the dried stuff in their packs. Not even any silver fishtails flashed in the shallows under the ice, which was too thin and unreliable to venture upon.

Sighting a farm with some life to it ahead brought cautious hope for a bite and maybe bedding down out of the weather for a night. It was a lonely place, a cottage with sloped roof, a similar barn, a dirt paddock, and a small pond. Quiet. Too quiet. But as they rode closer, Draken's darksight picked out a man plodding between the barn and the house, stopping when he apparently saw the newcomers.

He was bulky in the way farmers are: barrel-chested and broad, but gone a little soft during Frost. Lined eyes, so full-blooded Akrasian. Unsurprising. Most of the herders and horse traders out here were full-blood, even this close to Septonshir.

He leaned on a shovel as he eyed them, and had a long knife strapped to his belt. At length he dipped his chin to Osias. "Well? Fair odd lot, aren't you?"

Osias introduced himself. "I and my friends would appreciate shelter for the night. The barn suits."

"Why would a blind man carry a sword?"

Draken didn't like the wry twist of the man's mouth.

"It is his sword," Aarinnaie said.

"Not got much use for it, has he?"

The shutter at the peak of the roof by the corner of the house moved, pulling tighter. Draken's eyes narrowed under his mask. "I can hear where a man stands. Fair enough to strike. Will you share space with us or shall we move on?"

"Not bloody Ashen are you?" This he addressed to Tyrolean.

Tyrolean shook his head, confused. "Of course not. We are on war business."
He lied smoothly, though perhaps it wasn't quite a lie.

"Reckon I'd best let you in, then. I'm Nolarth."

Osias gave him their names, though he used Drae and Aarin, and they dismounted and let the ponies into the paddock. While Draken moved to the
fence to lay Bumpus's blanket over it to air, Nolarth came up behind him.
Draken knew because he smelled of herbal soap scent. With the rain and sleet
filling water barrels and less to do around a farm in general in cold weather,
Draken imagined baths were in good supply. He longed for one himself.

"You move about fair well."

"I'm not entirely blind," Draken admitted, turning to face him. Bumpus
nipped at his hand and he smacked the pony's nose lightly. "Why did you
question our loyalty to the Crown?"

Nolarth squinted past him into the night. "Best to get inside, aye? Nightfall's
not safe on the Grassland."

Draken turned his head to watch the horizon.

Nothing. No army or such, Bruche said.

Though if some came, they'd make for good killing.

Nolarth had a wife, Finid, inside the house, but no children. Hadn't been
married but a few moonturns. While there was no overt affection between them,
he seemed gruffly kind to her and she seemed easy enough with him. She wasn't
any older than Aarinnaie, seemed timid of the men, and studied Aarinnaie
curiously whenever it appeared she didn't notice, which was most of the time.

Aarin kept her bracelet covered with a thick woolen wrap and stared into the
fire from a bench near it, the line of her body tight. When offered food, she ate
methodically and only after encouragement from Tyrolean.

Too long without spilling blood.

Draken feared it was so. He turned to Nolarth. "Have you seen evidence of
the Ashen?"

"Naught but what I hear." He sat with a pipe, which Osias moved to light for
him with his fingertips. Nolarth stared, then blinked. He puffed a few smoky
breaths before speaking. Dishes clinked softly in the background as Finid set
them aside and joined them. "Went to Larse's farm to help fix his fence. He'd
heard tell of farms raided. Livestock. Stores."

Draken nodded. "We've seen evidence of the same. Monoea has thousands of
men on Akrasian lands. It takes a deal to feed them."

"Aye. Rough hunting this Frost."

"We've not seen more than a hare or a few birds for a sevennight," Tyrolean
said, leaning forward with his forearms on his knees. He sat as close to Aarin-

naie as he could without their touching. "But we were hoping the bulk of the army hadn't moved so far upland. Last we knew the front was around Auwaer and lower into Moonling Woods."

Nolarth nodded. "Aye. What I've heard. But there's more. Some rumors tell the women and children were left dead and the men taken."

Draken frowned. That was usually the opposite of how it went.

Osias sat up straighter. "Taken? Why? Any soldiers among them?"

"Farmers up here, and herders." Nolarth shrugged. "Dunno the why."

Osias and Draken exchanged glances, but they had no answers for Nolarth, with his tense voice and deep pulls on his pipe. The rest of the evening passed slowly with stilted conversation and long silences. Aarinnaie, at last, was given a pallet on the floor by the fire. Draken, Osias, and Tyrolean went out to sleep in the hay stacks of the barn.

Osias was quieter than usual and moving slow. Draken wondered if it had to do with Setia's absence. He'd once said he'd given her some magic to survive with after a life-threatening injury, and it was that which bound them. But a necromancer fueled by hundreds of spirits probably had given her spirits rather than magic per se.

As he did you, Bruche said.

The gods couldn't have given me something really useful, like terminal warmth? Draken sat by a cracked shutter in the hay loft, staring out at the night, wrapped tight in his cloak and thoughts, neither of which served to dispel the cold.

I think the ability to heal any wound is quite enough. Besides a magic sword and the darksight. And ME.

Draken sighed. He tired of wearing the mask. Of never achieving a restful darkness. By day, the sun assaulted him, and by night he could not escape the shadows of death and life. That was why, despite his bone-throbbing exhaustion, he bid the others sleep. He alone could see enemy coming.

Bruche stilled within him. *Speaking of.*

Aye. Man-shaped shadows lumbered through the dark grassland right toward the farm with impeccable timing and chilling accuracy. "Tyrolean."

The captain hadn't been sleeping too deeply because he only had to say his name once. He crawled up beside Draken and hissed a breath. "Ten?"

"Or a dozen, aye."

"I'd best get to the house," Tyrolean said.

"I think they're likely to attack there first," Draken agreed in a whisper. "Nolarth looked like he could handle himself around a spade or knife, eh?"

"Aye." Tyrolean started to climb down, stopping to wake Osias. Draken readied his arrows. He'd fell as many as he could once they were within range, but he was running low after his ambush on the Moonlings. He'd have to find or make more after this. Osias set himself by the doorway to shoot any attackers who got closer. Truls shifted nervously on the dirt floor.

Do you suppose they won't attack? Maybe they're just looking for shelter as you were.

"No. They'll attack." Draken rose to string his bow. He settled back down onto one knee with an arrow nocked, his gaze on the clump of men. Moonlight glinted on weapons. Monoeans, had to be.

He drew his arrow and sighted down it, head tipped, drawing in a deep, steadying breath. His eyes narrowed and he cursed. Shadows wove between them. He said it under his breath just as Truls announced it:

banes

"Could have bloody told us sooner," he hissed at the ghost. No matter. He had a necromancer to subdue the banes, providing Osias had the will and strength. He drew and fired into the clump. Nocked, drew, fired. Nock, draw, fire. A rhythm made comforting by long practice. They kept coming at the farm, toward his arrows, as if he needed any indication they were actually driven by banes.

He reached down and his fingers found only an empty quiver. He cursed softly, snatched up his sword in its scabbard, and scrambled for the edge of the loft, throwing himself down the short ladder. Osias was already rushing out of the barn. Draken moved swiftly to catch up. Magic or no, the Mance had no sword.

Magic makes a fair weapon . . . there, Draken! As they passed through the doorway, one of the bane-ridden . . . *Akrasians?!* rushed him. Draken blinked and struck just in time to block the shovel coming at him. It was a clumsy attempt; just the handle banged his arm. The man's lined eyes stared unblinking as he died. But another came at him, stepping right over the first. This one had no weapon, no armor, just hands held up like claws, an inhuman snarl twisting his face. Draken grimaced, but killed him with a slash across the throat. Despite being far too used to it by now, bile rose at the thick splatter of blood. He forced it back and strode for the house. The others had already smashed through the door to get at those inside and a raucous noise filtered through the wood and shutters: shouts and wordless grunts and snarls. Clouds swirled overhead, concealing the moons. A pelting rain began to fall as Draken raced for the house.

Inside was bedlam. Finid fought with a kitchen blade, clumsy and screaming in terror as she did so. Aarinnaie was silent, more frightening than the banes in her skilled efficiency. She slipped inside the guard of one man and killed him by stabbing him hard in the chest, then spun and gouged the throat of the one coming at her from behind. Her banesplint flared like a beacon and Draken wondered as he joined the fray if it maybe *was* a beacon of sorts to the other banes. Nolarth had one on the ground, slamming his head over and over against the wooden floor. Another Akrasian crawled onto Nolarth's broad back, hands tangled around his neck. Osias glided to the farmer first, his magical Voice roaring through them all with words Draken couldn't understand but a tenor he certainly did. The Mance had his hands outstretched and the baneshadow on Nolarth's back pulled from within his skin, scrabbling for its host. But to no avail; the bane flew to Osias's hand and was crushed to stinking mists. Draken stared. Knowing necromancy existed was one thing, but actually *seeing* it . . .

Pain brought him back. A bane slashed at him, slicing through the skin of his back. He whirled to kill it. The man crumpled and the bane tried to flee. A seax clattered to the floor.

"No—I'll stop them. Don't kill them," Osias shouted, even as Aarinnaie attacked another. Tyrolean shoved off the one he was fighting and strode to her. He put his arm around her waist and dragged her back. She tried to stab at his arm but his bracer stopped it.

The cut on Draken's back stung deeply and then started to close, the house shuddering.

Osias bellowed in his Voice and at once the bane-riddled Akrasians slumped to the floor, black shadows misting up into a foul wind that threw open the shutters and door but soon cleared the room of stench. It was too late. They were too injured and bled out before they could be helped.

Draken leaned on the table, panting as his skin finished closing. He lifted his head to look at Nolarth once the house stopped shaking. He'd probably knocked nails from their holes. "You must go from this place."

"But we've nowhere."

There was no sleep for them that night. They helped Nolarth burn the bodies in a fallow field, saddled their horses, and rode away.

Osias lighted his pipe as they rode. The smoke trailed forward to Draken on the wind at their backs. "There is no place for revenge in this war, my friend. The army must be mobilized again. You must find the Queen."

◆ ◆ ◆

It was two nights before they stopped longer than it took to fill their canteens and let the ponies graze a bit. Their pace had slowed and Draken knew they'd have to have to sleep soon. This one, or next. He couldn't keep driving the ponies like this. They, at least, needed to eat and rest. The day dawned sunny, which made the others relax a bit, but stung Draken's eyes so that even with his mask, he had to tuck his chin most of the time.

The grasses deepened, and more tree branches arched overhead, naked from Frost. Draken stared. He hadn't seen trees such as these since Monoea. The Moonling Woods didn't shed its canopy, and most of the trees in the forests flanking the Eros outside the city of Brîn proper had needles. He thought of the tree arching over the ruins of his cottage in Monoea, his throat thick. He'd led so many lives since then. Endured so many losses.

The castle itself had been overrun with Ashen as they escaped Monoea and he wouldn't be surprised to learn all of Sevenfel was ruled by the Moonminsters. What would it be for the cities to lose half its workforce, women sequestered at home and all the young men brought here to fight and die on foreign soil? He gritted his jaw against the shreds of sympathy. Monoea was the enemy, and there was no turning back to it, blood or no.

"Drae."

The single syllable made him lift his head. Tyrolean . . . using no Highness or Khel Szi. Hissing sounds carried further distances than any. Bumpus eased to a stop behind the others, tail swishing across the dried grasses long enough to brush Draken's boots. Truls stood ahead, as usual. This time he pointed in the direction they were going as if to gesture them on.

A scent carried to him: cold, salty, rank. He frowned. The sea?

No. Fish. Salted for storage. They're Sept.

A heavy hoof stamped. Draken squinted. Travelers in a wagon, flanked by six mounted Monoeans in their grey armor. An older man sat on the wagon seat with his hands up. Must be the arrows the Monoeans pointed at him. A woman in a miscellany of armored leather stood between the wagon and a Monoean who had gotten to his feet. She had Akrasian features but no lined eyes. The Monoean was an officer, if his tone could be judged. Authoritative and haughty.

An attacker who loves the sound of his own voice. Excellent.

Is there any other kind? Bruche moved his hand to Seaborn, tied to Draken's saddle.

What are the chances there are people in those wagons rather than fish?

Sons, most like. They send their sons to villages to sell.

To sell the sons? Draken shook his head, confused.

A low chuckle reached Draken's lips. *No. The sons go to sell the ruddy fish.*

"Come, then." This must be something Truls wanted them to interrupt, as he kept pointing at the wagon. He urged Bumpus on, dropping the reins to untie his bow from the saddle and nock an arrow. The Monoeans' backs were to Draken.

As they moved closer, the officer grabbed at the woman. The man on the wagon stood, reaching for something. An arrow caught his arm. He screamed when the arrow stuck, blood pouring out. The officer had the woman by the hair and around the neck, shouted at the screaming man to shut it.

Draken urged Bumpus on, but the best he could get from the stubborn pony was a trot. Instead he reined up, swung down, and ran the distance himself. In a breath, Aarinnaie ran ahead of him, slight enough to slip between blades of the dry, feathered grasses.

Despite the commotion right in front of them, the Monoeans noticed the new arrivals and turned. Another arrow flew, slicing Draken's shoulder as he tried to duck it. The ground trembled with his healing, and the warrior woman in the officer's arms struggled. Draken was just reaching him, ready to forgo formalities and cut him down, when she twisted in his arms, raised hers to chop at the thick hand holding her hair, and took him down at the knees with a swing of her leg. A blade appeared out of nowhere—armored skirt? bodice? thin bloody air? Draken had no idea—and it was resting tight beneath the man's chin before another arrow flew or word was spoken.

The wagon driver sank to his seat with a whimper.

"Do these men value your life, Ashen?" The warrior woman spoke in the clipped accent of a breathless Sept.

Draken strode closer. "I value it. For information."

Behind him Tyrolean and Osias covered him with more bows. Aarinnaie stopped by the woman who held the man and stared down at him. Her fingers gripped her knife tightly.

"Hush, you," she said to Draken.

Draken spoke in Monoean to the officer and his soldiers. "Dismount, the lot of you, unless you want to watch him bleed out."

The Ashen soldiers blinked.

"You're . . . *him*," one said. "You've the magic."

Draken didn't deny it. "Off your horses."

They did so. The Sept man in the wagon shifted, holding his arm.

The woman spoke loudly, as if trying to reclaim control of the situation. "Disarm, you lot." The man under her blade opened his mouth to speak. No one moved.

"You heard her," Draken said.

Weapons thumped to the ground and they all knelt, hands within view.

The officer gaped up at him. Draken took him in. Beard trimmed. Clothes clean. He cursed inwardly. Not too far from a camp, then. He might be of use for questioning. Someone also might come looking for him when he didn't return straightaway.

The warrior slit his throat. He gagged and fell forward, blood spreading in a gruesome pool across the crumpled grass. Another arrow, this time a heart shot. A gasp and the officer was dead.

Draken gaped at the woman. Fury bit through his shock. One of the soldiers started toward his weapons, but Aarinnaie darted toward him. Two slashes and he was down. Gasping and moaning. Not dead, but soon.

"Aarin, enough." Brînian this time.

She obeyed, nostrils flared.

The Sept woman ignored the three soldiers, who stared at their dead officer and the soldier Aarinnaie had cut down. She stared at Draken instead, shifted her gaze to take in Tyrolean and Osias. Her eyes narrowed. She turned her head toward Aarinnaie. "Who are you?"

A quick frown furrowed Aarinnaie's brow. No one talked to her. She was a ghost, and liked it that way. Except when she didn't.

"Travelers," Draken said. "Headed for Septonshir."

"And rescuers, where none are needed." The woman whistled, high pitched ending in two low notes. The grass all around rustled and a dozen women rose from it, running fleet toward them, bows in hand, tightening a noose-like circle around them.

Draken felt his mouth twitch. He raised his chin. "I see that," he said dryly. He scowled at Truls, who had surely realized the Sept had more warriors with them. "Thanks very much, Truls. I'll be certain to return the favor."

The warrior woman gave him a veiled look, maybe considering the condition of his right mind. She finally settled for: "Do not speak unless I bid you." She lifted her chin to Aarinnaie. "Can you not control him? The others are silent."

Didn't she know a Mance when she saw him? An Akrasian warrior? Draken gritted his jaw. Aarinnaie was breathing hard. She filled her lungs. Exhaled. Looked at Draken. "No. He's got a mind of his own. Enough for a dozen men, actually. Are we prisoners then?"

Again the appraising look, over each of them. A few of the women who had appeared were busy killing the last three Monoeans.

A slight smile crossed the warrior's pale lips. "Guests."

CHAPTER TWENTY-TWO

After the grunts of the dying Ashen faded off, faint cries pierced the air upland, sounding like distant children screaming as if whipped. More Monoeans attacking? "What is that?"

Their captors ignored Draken, just bound his wrists. He shrugged free of them and demanded again, "Who is being hurt?"

"Fool man." The warrior woman swung aboard her horse. "Get on that horse. You are delaying us."

Draken was given a real horse—one of the Monoeans'— but was hardly able to enjoy it with his hands tied to the saddle. Tyrolean endured his binding quietly. Osias was allowed to remain untied due to his status, but was treated brusquely as the other men.

Draken fought and earned sharp jabs to the temple and gut for his trouble. The woman knew how to use a bow for more than shooting. The bruising made him feel woozy for a bit, but quick enough his magic took hold and eased the pain. The horses skittered across the shuddering ground but the strangers didn't know to attribute it to him. The bindings were tight, cutting off the circulation to his hands. But the worst of it was their taking his mask. Or, well, yanking it down so the woman could get a good look at him. Draken's eyes were forced closed by the sun, which seemed to burn straight through to the back of his skull. She grunted. With some effort, Draken lifted his head to meet her gaze. She nodded, seeming to take it as submission or some damn thing.

Bruche chuckled.

Their ponies were tied in a line and led behind the rest, ears pinned at Bumpus, who of course kept trying to shove ahead.

For her part, Aarinnaie rode ahead with their captors, chin up, ignoring Draken and the others. Truth, Draken hadn't realized she had it in her to be diplomatic enough to fit in, though the opportunity to snub him probably made it easy. The first real lake appeared soon after they started, smallish from what Draken could glean from quick glances. They skirted it and headed for another, crossing a low bridge of fine stonework over a tributary that joined it to the previous. A stone roadway continued between the two. Draken's maps had always shown Septonshir with symbolic seven lakes, smaller than the sizable mountain lake Skymarke nestled against the Agrian range. Draken saw now it was a region of mostly waterlogged ground with paths built up to traverse it. Despite the cold, flocks of white birds swooped and screamed over the ice, seeking patches of uncovered water. Here were the cries of the beaten children. No wonder she'd called him a fool.

Trees and shrubs started crowding the banks of lakes, channels, and ponds, high enough to block much view. They crossed a few shallow rivers, following an increasingly obvious trail, until they reached a lake big enough to appear on Draken's maps. It was vaguely round but for a curved slash of land on the far side where a village rested. Trees skirted the village and lined the shores. They and their horses were hustled onto barges crewed by four burly, silent men each who hauled them on a sledge across the ice.

Damp seeped into his bones the deeper they got into Septonshir, aching in his old injuries. At least his hands weren't tied behind his back; that always wreaked havoc on his shoulder. When the group walked off the barges to rein up before a long, low-slung, log building, one of his guards untied his hands. Draken swung down. His knee gave way as he hit the ground, and he had to grapple for the saddle with his numb hands. He cursed and tried to concentrate on their surroundings, shooting squinty glances all around. Two men were atop the longhouse, patching the reed roof. He saw no one that looked particularly like guards beyond the party who had brought them here.

Aarinnaie strode to him to help him up, her strong, small hands tugging on his bicep. "Are you all right, Khel Szi?"

He sighed when the guards turned their heads at his name. He hadn't yet decided whether it was a good idea to announce who he was. He gave her a frown to which she didn't respond and the guards led them inside the door of the longhouse. The warmth inside was stuffy but welcome, and it was even better to be out of the daylight. Clean-swept, hard-packed dirt made up the floor, beaten into near stone by generations of feet.

The walls had been plastered neatly, little peaks looking like the lakes must on a windy day. Log pillars as big around as Draken supported the structure and braced the roof overhead. Men and women sat on mats honing weapons, repairing and creating household items, and tending the three round hearth fires spaced at intervals along the center of the long room. Typical winter work for a clan who'd stored enough food come Frost. Curtains divided off a few spaces, maybe for sleeping or private pursuits, but most were drawn back.

The woman who seemed to be the leader of the raiding company led them toward the central hearth, flanked by an aged man and woman hunched in fine, large chairs carved over with animals and fish. The woman turned to stand before the fire, hands clasped over her leather armor and metal-plated kilt. In this light Draken could finally get a good look at her. Grey threaded through her hair, which was braided and looped short on either side of her head. A worn hilt stuck from the scabbard at her side. She studied Draken openly as he nudged ahead of his sister to take the lead. Her pale face was stiff and her shoulders looked tight as a drawn bow. The older couple studied him in turn but soon shifted their attention to the others.

And Truls stood behind them, grey against the firelight. The black holes in his face held Draken's gaze as surely as if a thousand eyes stared out from his wavering form.

Perhaps they do. There is much we don't know about the ghost.

One of their guards dumped a rough canvas bag in front of the old woman's seat. It clanked with their confiscated weapons.

"Why do you come here, Khel Szi?" the younger woman asked.

Draken's brows raised before he could stop them. "You hold the advantage over us, my lady. Perhaps an introduction before interrogation?"

"You come to us and from so far. I should think you know who we are."

Draken had worked out toughness would go further than diplomacy with her. "I know little of the Sept beyond what limited experience I've got with the sundry slaves from here."

The woman spat on the ground. "Rape-get or worse. Why are you here, man?" She spat the last word like an insult.

Before Draken could wonder what was worse, the old woman in the chair lifted her head. The loose skin under her chin trembled a bit on her thin neck but her eyes were quick and her voice clear. "Courtesy, Tirnine, is a sharper weapon than many."

The warrior woman's lip twitched. "Aye, Mother. I am Tirnine, and my mother is Jonine, Oxbow Clan Leader." She tipped her head to indicate the old man. "Her consort Sulvan. We know who you all are."

Without missing a beat, the old woman Jonine added: "But we don't know why you are here."

Draken tried to slow the interrogation by dipping his chin politely. "We mean no harm. We merely come seeking Queen Elena, and to provide warning, and aid if need."

"Not here. Take your weapons and go."

Bruche snorted. *Gentle old ladies, my arse.*

Just how cut off was Septonshir? "You do realize the party that attacked your travelers are part of a much larger army?"

"We are reclusive, not blind. As you are."

Draken met the clear blue eyes—not dark like his and especially not the brown-black of Akrasians. Despite their facial features, they did have their own blood then. Still, it was odd to see such a pale face without the black lines encircling her eyes.

Osias stepped forward. "If I may, my lady? Khel Szi is not blind. His eyes are sensitive to daylight. You have heard no mention of the Queen by your scouts or visitors?"

"It is Frost, not Trade. We've few visitors this time of year, only Ashen and Akrasian raiders. If she is here—"

"Akrasian raiders?" Draken's voice was sharp.

Her gaze slid to Tyrolean. "Them what like him."

"What of the Moonlings?"

"Them what only interested in their mountains and the salt beyond. Not these lakes."

It took Draken half a breath to work out what she meant by *salt*. "Septonshir lakes run to the sea, do they not?"

"Aye, but forests and stone hills wall us from the salt."

"Mother, the world comes. We must embrace it—"

Jonine turned her steely gaze on her daughter. "It is our way to keep to ourselves."

Draken broke in before they could continue what looked like a longstanding argument. "I care not if you keep from others. I care only for my Queen, who is reported to be here, in Septonshir. If not your clan, then another. I will search them all if I must. So have you heard such a thing?"

Jonine made no response.

Tirnine's jaw tightened. "The prisoners spoke of the great lady seen by the Lilia clan. This you know. Would you lie outright to our Queen's consort?"

Draken cleared his throat before the spat could go further. "Prisoners . . . I assume Monoeans?"

Silence for a beat. Jonine shifted closer to the edge of her seat, the consort Sulvan looked from one to the other, but Tirnine held her ground. "Akrasians. Searching for their Queen."

Sounds like a promising lead.

"Where are they now?" Draken asked.

"Dead."

"I hope you had a good reason to kill them."

"Them what infected."

Infection and illness was expected with the front lines dug into the snow this Frostseason and thousands of Monoeans bringing strange plagues to their foreign shores. Anyone leaving those lines would carry those illnesses. He'd yet to hear of a deadly plague, though.

"No. You mean they were infected with banes," Osias said.

Tirnine nodded, and after a deep breath, Jonine dropped her chin in accord.

Draken stared at the Oxbow women, then turned to look back at Osias. It struck him all at once. Gods, the Mance were all dead but for him. No one guarded Eidola. And could they have stood against Korde at any rate?

"Do you see now why we keep to ourselves?" Jonine said.

Draken shook his head. "That's not how they shift from one person to another. They don't rely on contact between people."

Jonine sniffed and looked away. "They require only a dark heart," Tyrolean said, drawing her attention again. "And a weak will."

A chill climbed the back of Draken's neck. Tyrolean didn't know that Draken had been possessed by a bane, had nearly killed himself under the influence of one, and it had only been Osias's quick action that had saved him, and Bruche's resistance against later attacks.

"Dark-hearted, aye. Them what were. Writhing in chains like animals. One even bit me."

"What did they say about the Queen?"

"Were looking for her. Thought she was with the Cove Clan but the Cove wouldn't let them near."

"Take us to Cove Clan lands and we'll see to our own passage inside," Tyrolean said.

Jonine barked a soft, rough laugh, her age slipping through. "Don't let anyone near, them what live on the Cove."

"We'll trade for guidance there," Draken said. "What do you need?"

Tirnine's gaze flicked over him and for a moment he wondered—and Bruche hoped—if she was going to ask for a night together. "You have precious little what we want. We take care of our own."

If you'd smile once in a while, you might get bedded more often.

Truth enough, he had little else now but the armor on his back, his sword, and a decent bow gifted to him by Va Khlar. The villagers looked well enough, few coughs and no crying cut through the bustle of winter work. He almost asked if anyone needed killing nearby but Osias pushed forward.

"You want to be secluded?" he said. "Left alone by invaders and others?"

"And the banes," Jonine said, eyes narrowed to slits among the wrinkles.

Osias touched his fingertips to his forehead, flanking the black crescent moon marring his sharpened features. In the quiet light by the fire he had taken on a sinister air. None but Draken seemed to notice; they all watched him with wide eyes. All but Jonine, who held her posture of suspicion.

Not one to cross, Bruche said, and Draken agreed.

The Mance's hair slid forward over his shoulders. Silvery, glowing, enticing— once Draken blinked away the idea of killing someone in trade for passage to the other clan.

"I can make it so," Osias said.

◆ ◆ ◆

The moons hid, one behind thick forest, the others behind the horizon, as Draken rode the barge back across the water. Against the others' protests, Draken insisted on taking this journey alone. Finally he convinced Aarinnaie there was danger letting her so near Akrasians because Ilumat would surely want his wife back. Once across and under the thick tangle of naked tree limbs, he let his eyes open wide with a sigh of relief. The trees were shifting black shadows against the brighter night and Draken's darksight turned the lake into opaline pools. Woods gradually filled in to flank the path, and normal night sounds of prowling animals and the cold breeze creaking the trees. At least he tried to tell himself they were normal sounds.

Bruche's hand kept straying to Seaborn's hilt. Finally Draken allowed it to rest there, the spirit chilling his arm. For his part, he tried to consider if Elena were there, tried to prepare himself to say the words which would surely devastate her. He would have to admit his part in Sikyra's loss.

Aye, ever the martyr. Blaming you will surely make her feel better. The swordhand snorted.

Knowing why may help, at the least. Sikyra's death was his fault. This close to Elena, to telling her, he realized he'd spent far more time apart from her than in her presence, and he had no idea what she would do when so grief-stricken.

Bruche just settled in with quiet disapproval. It was an argument they'd had before.

They walked a long while on the path. It narrowed and Draken kept a sharp eye to their surroundings. Truls drifted along, weaving between trees. Or through them, Draken couldn't see which. He made no gesture to Draken, or indicated the way. He followed now.

Something twitched in the woods to the offhand. Then another something. The unmistakable creak of a drawn bow. Four people emerged into his dark-sight from the shadows, hooded and armored.

"Who are you?" came the demand. The sentries were a mixed group, gender made indeterminate by similar sets of broad shoulders and bows.

Tirnine started to speak but Draken urged Bumpus forward, his mind already made up. "I am Khel Szi of Brîn."

No immediate reaction from the cloaked figure, like a flying arrow, which he took as a good sign. He added, "I come seeking Queen Elena."

"You come to the wrong place, Khel Szi." Stiffly courteous. All right, he'd take it.

"I have it on good authority she is on Cove lands."

"Oxbow told," the Cove guard hissed. The guards around them tightened and more bows creaked. Draken twisted in his saddle, counting. Eight. More than he'd thought. There was movement in the forest beyond. He wondered if getting stuck with arrows and his subsequent earth-shaking healing would startle Bumpus from his plodding pace into a trot. He wasn't exactly eager to find out. Healing or no, arrows *hurt*.

"I have no quarrel with you, and I mean no harm. Just take me to Queen Elena," he said. "Please."

"You'll come. As a prisoner."

Draken lifted his hand clear of his sword. "If it gets me to the Queen, excellent."

There was a rustling behind Draken, and a muffled command. He turned to look, feeling skittish. A tall, slim, cloak-draped figure emerged from the trees crowding the road. He fell very still, watching. The figure paused and his eyes picked out the details: lined eyes, a certain tilt to the mouth, black hair tied back into a knot.

But it was her voice, a gasping desperation, that tore something loose inside him. "Draken."

He slid from his horse and strode to her, gathering her in his arms without pausing to look her over again. She leaned against him, wet cheek pressed against his. He ran his hand over her familiar, narrow back, and his shoulders eased. He felt at peace for exactly one breath, which he spent on her name: "*Elena.*"

"Where is our daughter?"

CHAPTER TWENTY-THREE

"We must talk." Draken set her back and looked at all the guards. "These people are yours?"

"Mercenaries, working on promised coin." She gazed up into his face. "Where is she?"

"Sikyra." His eyes were hot, her pale face and heartrending eyes burned into his darksight. He cleared his throat. "I called her Sikyra, after my mother."

"Sikyra." She said it slowly, the accent off. It was a foreign word, after all, and she knew only basic Monoean greetings and phrases of courtesy.

"Sikyra," he repeated correctly. "Kyra for short. Aarin calls her that."

"But you said you never knew your mother."

If that was the biggest lie that caught up with him today, he'd consider himself fair fortunate. "We met. Briefly. Elena, we need to go talk somewhere privately. Not here."

"She is well? Tell me that much."

A hollow space grew below his sternum, yawning wide for his daughter. *You cannot tell her. Not here, not like this.*

Bruche was right. What could he say but the truth as he wished it, not as he feared it? He shook his head, not daring to lie with words. "We must talk," he repeated.

Elena searched his face, then nodded. "Fetch our horses," she instructed her people. "We'll go back to the village."

We must be close, then.

It stood to reason. He couldn't imagine Elena straying far from a stronghold at night. It definitely wasn't safe, with banes flitting about. He turned his head, found Truls lurking near the rear of the group. Just as well. Perhaps he'd be of some use.

"Did you know I was coming?"

"There were some vague rumors. Nothing to substantiate. I hoped," she answered. He helped her mount her horse and instead of riding Bumpus, he walked by her side holding his reins.

The forest thickened and the path narrowed until he thought it would disappear altogether. The scent of fish wafted on the air, warning of water ahead. The land spilled wide into a rocky beach fronting a cove. The trees had obviously been cleared and used to build the cottages on the lakefront because they crowded back round the lake beyond, stretching out like a sea quieted by ice, glistening under the moonlight. A couple of huts rested on the ice, far out. He studied it all silently, trying to think of anything else, trying to put off the inevitable.

Without seeing to the well-being of the others, Elena took Draken's arm and started him toward a hut set apart from the rest.

Royal command shrouded the woman he loved like clouds over a moon. He followed without comment, ducking under the low lintel into a cramped cabin. He gave it a quick glance, noted the dirt floor, the straw, wool-covered pallet piled with furs. Not lodging Elena would be accustomed to. Even the Moonling town at Skyhaven had been cleaner and had planked decking underfoot . . . that is, before Elena had burned it to the ground.

You don't know what she's been through since then, Bruche reminded him. *This might be luxury.*

He only wanted to take her into his arms and comfort her, feel her lean against him again. But she opened her mouth to speak and he knew it would be more questions about Sikyra and so he rushed in with a diversion. "Where have you been all this time?"

"Seeking to build up the army. Everywhere I go, I find I am assumed dead and I must explain who I am anew. I've never gone anywhere before and not been recognized. Not been Queen."

"You are still Queen, Elena. Mine, and Akrasia's." He wasn't so certain about Brîn. "What will you do next?"

"Rejoin the main force and march for Auwaer to protect it."

"Perhaps it is best you go sooner, rather than later. Unfortunately, the Monoeans also suspect you're in this region."

She twitched an impatient hand, not asking how he knew that. "I'll have you with me. Where is our daughter?"

His hand shifted to his sword hilt and his jaw tightened. He lowered his head. "I sent her with Osias after Brîn—"

"Monoeans took Brîn. I'd heard."

"No. Ilumat took Brîn and gave it to them." He said the words before he realized perhaps now wasn't the best time for such bluntness.

"Ilumat is at Auwaer awaiting our reinforcements. He barely survived. He told me he thought you were dead. But for some rumors . . . I barely dared hope. *Where* is Sikyra?"

"You can't trust Ilumat. He's ly . . ." Her dark gaze drilled into his, cutting him off. His pulse quickened and his mouth felt dry. "I sent Sikyra to Eidola with Osias. There was no other safe place. We were in hiding; she was ill." He had to stop to breathe. Saying it all aloud brutalized him worse than any sword could. "But the Mance were forced to flee Eidola."

"With our daughter?"

He nodded. "Eidola was attacked. We think Korde freed the banes. But when we met in Reschan Va Khlar told us the Mance were all dead. They didn't find the baby or Setia. I'd hoped they were just taken hostage but Osias summoned the dead Mance and they told him . . ."

Elena's fingers flared with fire. The shock of it cut off his words. He tilted his head away, closing his eyes. An instinctual gesture against the sting.

Steady, friend.

The magic and darksight didn't matter. None of it mattered. "If it could be any other way, if it could have been me, I would trade my life. She was—" His voice broke and the rest husked out. "Bright and loving. A joy—I wish—Gods, Elena, I wish you had known—"

Her shrill anguish cut through him. "Stop! Just stop talking!"

Draken obeyed. Her eyes were too bright and glistening, endless black caverns of grief. They looked—felt—all too familiar. The hollowness he'd been feeling yawned wide and spilled out his pain. He tried taking a step closer to her. She shied back.

"The Mance is wrong," she said. "She is not dead."

"Elena, I was there. She's gone." His voice snagged on the last word.

A woman in constant motion, the very air around her stilled. "You gave her up to them."

He'd tried to prepare himself, but her words felt like a spear had pierced his chest. His eyes heated, but no tears threatened. He had been here too many times, failed all too often. He felt dried up as the dead grasses he'd just rode through to deliver this revelation. He closed them and lowered his head, a single nod. He hadn't known what else to do. But he was a Prince and a father. He had no excuse.

"She's alive. She has to be."

"Elena, she's not—"

"I am your *Queen*."

A beat. "Your Majesty. There would be some word, some rumor to chase. I would have found it if it existed. She is dead."

"I'll find her myself if you're too craven to try."

"You aren't listening to me. Sikyra is gone. All that's left to us is to rid our lands of the enemy."

"Enemy? You think I don't know what you are? You are the enemy! You went there and brought your people back to conquer us."

"I did not bring them back. They manipulated me, tricked me. I swear on all that is holy, on Sikyra's life—"

"You lied to me, as I handed our daughter to you, to her . . . death." Her voice broke on the last word.

"Your Majesty, I didn't—" He stopped. "Not about that. Not ever about her. I loved Sikyra. She was my only link to you and she was nothing but a joy."

Tears fell freely. She wiped at them with her sleeve. The dust and grime smudged her face. "You don't deny you are Monoean?"

His heart pounded in his throat. Here it was then. The wrong blood. The wrong man. All of it had led to Sikyra's short life. "Who told you?"

"My cousin, my new Night Lord, who fought for Brîn and lost it to the Monoeans, and nearly lost his life. All this while you *ran*. While you threw away my daughter!"

Ilumat, again. He rose into Draken's life like the reek of soured milk ruining fine silk. He was taking Draken's life. His city. His sister. Now Elena. "I am a half-blood. Sacrilege, an abomination. No better than banespawn. So was our daughter, for that matter. Is that what you want me to say?"

No, Draken. Tell her all Ilumat did.

In that moment Draken knew protesting Ilumat would only make it worse. In a way, in many ways, he was glad. He was so tired of fighting all the right battles all the wrong ways. "Do as you will. Execute me for a traitor, if you can manage it. Gods know they've tried. Gods know how I have longed for death."

"Give me the sword."

Draken, no.

He drew without hesitation, flipped it in his hand so that he caught it by the blade. It cut the soft join between his thumb and forefinger. Blood dripped over the sword and off his hand.

"Kill me. This alone will do it," he said quietly.

Fools all! Can't you shut it while you're ahead?

She was carved of pale moonstone, molten hatred rippling beneath the surface. The sword gleamed in her hand, fire flicking along its blade. But there was more. A shudder in her gaze.

Fear.

Fear of the damned ruddy gods.

"Get out."

He held out the sword further. "Take it. Cut me down. One last favor."

"No. You will live and suffer as I will." She stared at him, her face set, then turned her back on him, a graceful, heartless shift of body and mind. There was no fire in her for him. He wondered if there ever had been.

Numb, he re-sheathed his sword and turned to duck back out under the lintel. His chest was too tight to breathe, heart squeezing all the blood away, chilling him from the inside out. No. Bruche. Dragging the cold air in as he seized control of Draken, forced him to breathe and stay upright.

He paused, his hand gripping the frame. "Beware the gods. They war among us. They hunt me. I think they hunt you, too."

What had started as a stab to the heart had become a wearying deep ache and the hot press of anger. Something he could live with. Not live well, but enough to avenge his daughter. The gods could bloody wait for whatever plans they had in mind for him. He let the swordhand have free rein over his body and guide him away.

CHAPTER TWENTY-FOUR

This time the Ashen died in eerie silence. Truth, most still slept as Draken's blade struck, but after it was done, as he wiped Seaborn with a scrap of torn tent canvas, the stillness seeped into his bones.

It's always this way, the quiet. You're too busy killing them to notice.

Draken lifted his head and his darksight stretched across the encampment, picking out slow movement: Aarinnaie making her way through the bloody wreckage. Tyrolean already stood panting softly next to him, blades crimson. Gadye-made swords for royal guards, never intended for raw vengeance.

Tyrolean bent over a dead man for a few breaths, hands propped on his knees. "My lord."

Draken turned. Tyrolean gestured with his sword at the dead man's face. Draken had to shift around the body to see it. He stared. Thick black lines tattooed around eyes that stared into nothing. He nudged the man's cloak hood aside with the tip of his sword. Tightly shorn hair capped his head, not bound back in a tail like most Akrasian men wore theirs.

"He had one of their weapons." Tyrolean bent to retrieve a very typical, plain seax.

"Another bane," Draken said. But this was the first they'd run across in their attacks since leaving Elena.

"Aye." Tyrolean thrust the seax into the unmoving chest amid the other stab wounds still oozing stinking blood. Draken gave Tyrolean a close look, but he only cut away some of the hem of another Ashen's cloak and straightened to clean his blades. Not a scratch on him, as usual, while Draken's healing from taking on a too-alert guard had trembled the ground throughout the attack, waking a few enemy before he could manage to kill them.

Draken stripped off his bracer and wiped his face with his sleeve. "Hunger is getting to you, Captain. You never used to be out of breath." Now they never had enough to eat.

221

"I keep asking you to use my given name . . ." Tyrolean inhaled deeply, sounding a bit raspy. ". . . and you keep not using it, my lord."

Draken grunted, tired of their ongoing argument. "Elena didn't get the chance to decommission you, so I call you by rank. Speaking of, you don't have to do this. She would take you back. I didn't tell her you were traveling with me."

The silence seemed to close tighter around them, something he could see with his darksight . . . a sort of dull grey void. It was his first time speaking the Queen's name since she'd turned them out four sevennight ago. Draken concentrated on looking through the silence for any glimmer of a god. They came round sometimes, drawn by the blood. But he saw only Truls, drifting about studying the Ashen they'd killed. All male. All very young. Like the squad before this one, and all the others that had come before. They massacred at least two such encampments a sevennight.

"And you are my lord, so I'll call you such," Tyrolean said at last.

"Even if I'm only here to find my cousin and kill him for betraying me?"

"Even so, my lord."

Draken sighed. "Any sign of him, Aarin? Or do they mock me once again?"

"No Galbrait and not much in the way of food," Aarinnaie said as she jogged up to them.

Draken just gave her a curt nod. He'd run across Galbrait twice. It shouldn't be so difficult to find the man unless the gods had decided to use his cousin to toy with him. Draken nudged the body of the servii to show her the lined eyes. She snorted softly but offered no comment.

If the Ashen were getting hungry, they'd be sloppy and desperate, which made men much easier to kill. Regional Akrasian farms had been robbed of much of their livestock to feed the invaders, and they'd started hunting the grassland horse herds running wild on the prairie. But Draken knew from recent experience they were difficult to catch, and smart, too. One scent of people and the herds made themselves scarce. Maybe this lot hadn't roved the countryside killing locals like so many of the other small Ashen bands they'd discovered.

"I did find this." She grinned and tossed him a small bag. It clanked with Monean gold. He nodded. They'd be able to eat a fair long while on it.

They'd drawn further upland to the far edges of Septonshir, hunting out these Monoean squads. Osias said there were tiny villages scattered on the rivers and creeks streaming inland from the lakes. A day's ride downland and they'd meet the tributary of the River Eros where it faded into bubbling groundwater and treed swampland. A small town rested there but rumor had it—if the dead souls Osias had summoned could be believed—that it was completely overrun with Ashen. It was from there they staged these raids, which were perplexingly unlike typical Monoean tactics.

What Elena's troops were doing, Draken had no idea. He couldn't think too hard on it—on any of it. He only got angry when his thoughts drew too close to her. But he warmed to the idea of running into Ashen at inns. That could mean fights ahead of them, and maybe against important people. Maybe he'd find Galbrait. "The locals will be hungry enough for gold, I expect."

"Aye. The Akrasian army is melting rare and common for arrowheads." Tyrolean spoke in a tone of finality and looked around at the dead men sprawled about, his face hard. "Coin is closer than the Brînian mines."

Mines that were nearly dead. But Tyrolean was losing interest in the conversation. "Aye, Captain. Pray your piece and then we'll go."

Draken turned to his sister. The shadow only came over her in the night, or maybe it was there all the time, revealed only by his darksight. The bane splint. Darker. Stronger every night from all the blood they drew.

If you hadn't taken her, she would have found a way to kill Ilumat by now. And Elena would have had to execute her.

Bruche was right. It didn't make it any easier. Draken gestured to his sister and led her a little away, into a copse of trees where they'd left their packs. He let her drink first from the poor wine from his skin.

"Are you all right?" he asked.

"Don't start." She wiped her mouth with her bloody sleeve and looked around. "Where is Osias? He's usually met us by now."

Draken nodded to Truls, who headed off to where Osias stood guard. At least the dead Mance was making himself useful in a practical way lately.

Tyrolean joined in short order and they followed the ghost's trail back to Osias. He'd kept the ponies in a gully, part of the Silent Trail where the sides had weathered and worn it shallower. But as they approached, Draken's eyes narrowed. A party of riders gathered on a rock field stretching over where Osias should be, but from this distance he couldn't make out their armor and uniforms. The last moon was just dropping below the horizon: Elna with her black spot. She was gentle on his eyes.

He slowed and knelt, staring, willing himself to see, fingers nocking an arrow from habit. Tyrolean and Aarinnaie paused in his wake and knelt by him.

"Akrasians? Or Ashen?" Aarinnaie whispered, keeping low. He was the only one who could see anyway.

"I don't know who they are," Draken muttered. He drew and sighted down the arrow just in case.

Gradually his vision stretched and sharpened. He hissed a soft breath. "Ashen."

"Not from here. We'll have to get closer to pick them off."

They'd have to, for if the Monoeans ran on horseback, they'd lose them on foot. The three of them belly-crawled slowly through the grasses, Draken peeking up occasionally to see that they were still there. Their four ponies had been led up out of the gully. No sign of Osias. Glamoured then. Draken prayed to Khellian he'd stay out of the way of the arrows. Or better yet, divert them.

A dozen men, another Ashen raiding party. Again, it struck him how odd this action was compared to the tactics he knew. They'd worked that way in the Black Guard, but it had been elite, confined to specific duties. To work haphazardly across a war zone in small, secret groups didn't feel like Monoean way. It felt more like . . .

Moonling ways, actually.

Draken frowned. *Damn, you're right.*

It was a stupid tactic. With so many men, the Monoean army could sweep across the plains and destroy all in its path, especially with Korde turning their hapless victims into bane-ridden killers, and particularly if it had a Moonling contingent to work the Abeyance. Stopping time proved a very effective weapon. But then, maybe it stood to reason, the Monoeans adopting Moonling ways. Perhaps these unpopulated Grasslands were considered a waste of effort and only a small portion of the Monoean army had been sent out. Perhaps Korde had driven his Monoean army to other, more fertile battlefields. After all, the Monoeans sought to reinstill the Moonminster Faith, and that would be most effective in the cities. Surely the Moonlings would be happy to destroy the cities that had enslaved them. But none seemed to realize, the Ashen invaders, the Moonlings, even the Akrasians, that the gods made pawns of them all in their own war. The Monoeans were allied with Korde, the god of death. Surely that meant he would see them all die . . .

Someone tugged on his boot. Aarinnaie. He'd kept crawling while discussing things with Bruche and had gotten very close to the Monoeans. They spoke quietly, studying the little encampment Osias had made. Half the men had dismounted. Arrows might hold them at bay for a few breaths. He glanced over his shoulder at Elna. She left only the faintest glow at the horizon. The others wouldn't be able to see at all in a moment.

He pushed up to his knees, counting on the Monoeans' distraction and the darkness to shield him. He fired as he rose, and a figure tumbled from his horse. Another arrow, and shouts. The Monoeans shifted, knotting together in the dark, scrambling for their horses. Tyrolean and Aarinnaie joined him, arrows soaring like pickbirds in rhythmic clumps. Draken pushed to his feet and ran toward the enemy, still firing. Shouts echoed across the grass. Bumpus and the other tora ponies whinnied and trotted away, stubbornly dragging the shouting Monoean holding them.

He fired through his final two arrows and dropped his bow to draw Seaborn. It lit the area in front of him, making him a target. He snarled a curse and raced on. Any arrows he took would have to be pushed on through his flesh later. Right now he had Monoeans to kill.

A rider spun within the pandemonium, reached out and grabbed the reins of another, dragging him along. Both shouted at each other; the strains of argument reached Draken without his making out the words. The closest Ashen had started their ululating war cries *"Il Vanni masacr!"* blocking any meaning from the other shouts. Fury flared and he growled as he struck the Ashen between helm and shoulder. His cries dropped off abruptly.

Bruche forced Draken's attention past the newly dead man toward the two riders. *Galbrait.*

It couldn't be. Was it? Yes, there. The gold torque gleaming about his neck. Draken couldn't risk letting him go. He reached another Ashen and slashed. The Ashen, clad in their grey metal plate, parried with his bracer and fought back with skill. With a sword instead of a seax.

No ordinary Ashen, these. Bruche slipped fully into place, taking over the fight and leaving Draken in dispassion. Two strikes and he drove the sword through the Ashen's throat, shoved past him. By then Tyrolean was there, his swords clanging on armor until they found flesh, and Aarinnaie with her long knives, stabbing.

The Prince!

Galbrait was getting away. Bruche cut his way through another Ashen and Draken raced for a horse, threw himself on it, and kicked it to a gallop. He thought Aarinnaie might be calling after him but he couldn't stop to look back or wait for aid. Catching them without an arrow was unlikely at best. But his horse, happy to flee the fight, stretched out and thundered over the dried grass. Trepidation at losing the man who had betrayed him and eluded him twice gnawed at Draken. He felt every nuance of the uneven ground through the horse's gait, but he whipped it on, leaning low over its neck.

Draken's darksight stretched ahead of his quarry to a bluish glow, faint color against the mass of whirring greys. A chill encased him; Bruche whispered rare fear. The swordhand tried to slow the horse but Draken refused to let him take command. The horse's nostrils flared with a crying neigh as it tried to slow. It had seen it: Korde or whatever god was chasing them now.

The two horses ahead balked. One rider was thrown. Galbrait looked back, his pale face imprinted on Draken's vision, and whipped his horse. But it was enough, only just. They ran nearly abreast, Draken trying to steer his animal into his prey. Galbrait swung wide and gained ground again.

"Damn the gods, you are mine!" Draken roared the words, uncaring whether Galbrait heard. His mount threw on a final burst of speed. But just as Draken was edging up on Galbrait, his horse's bit on a level with Galbrait's stirrup, his horse stumbled. Violently, and with a terrible scream.

Draken was thrown forward over the horse's head. In a moment of clarity, Draken's and Bruche's minds melded. Draken twisted up as he flew through the air, arms stretching, catching at whatever he could. His swordhand banged into Galbrait's back plate. A collective snap and pain lanced through his fingers. His offhand, though, snagged the Prince around his neck. Awkwardly and hard enough to send a searing jab of pain through his shoulder, he slammed into the Prince with enough force to tumble them both off the racing horse. He crashed onto Galbrait's armored body as they hit the ground, jarring his bad shoulder.

When do you ever not land on your bad shoulder? Maybe that's why it's bad, eh?

Draken shoved himself to his knees with his offhand and looked back. Galbrait wasn't moving. But the extra rider ran at him from behind with a sword. Draken had to roll aside of Galbrait and fend off blows with the armored bracer of his offhand. He cursed inwardly, wishing he could draw Seaborn. The Ashen had lost his helm, an easy vulnerability even Draken could take advantage of. But with broken fingers Bruche couldn't help him draw the sword strapped to his back. It was trapped between him and the ground. In a moment the Ashen's blade would find his flesh. His mind flashed to a ship he'd taken down with his healing. That would shake everyone off their feet. But Draken couldn't risk taking such a brutal injury, not now, when he was so close to exacting his revenge. First he would bleed Galbrait for his betrayal of their family, and then they would hunt Ilumat, Elena and the Queen's law be damned—

The hard ground trembled beneath his knees, rattling the dried grasses and teeth. Draken cradled his broken hand against his chest, grunting in pain as the bones knit. His attacker tripped to one knee. His gaze darted from Draken's face. Before the pain was quite finished, Bruche rolled him to his side and drew Seaborn. Draken climbed to his feet. The blade glowed blue with godslight against the black sky, flashing as Bruche stepped Draken forward and swung before the Ashen could open his mouth.

Galbrait groaned. Draken sank back to one knee, in pain as Bruche receded. He stared at the young Prince . . . the rightful King of Monoea . . . coming awake on the hard grassy plain in a foreign country and wondered again at the machinations that brought them all to this point.

"Damned bloody gods. Wasteful bastards." Draken reached down and slapped Galbrait's cheek with his gauntleted hand . . . the one *not* still stinging from breaking and healing inside twenty breaths. "Wake up, Galbrait. It's time to die. I wouldn't want you to miss it."

The Prince's eyelids fluttered. His brow compressed into a frown. Draken glanced back over his shoulder toward the camp. Too far to see. He had to count on the others having killed the rest of the Ashen. He lifted his sword and pressed the point under Galbrait's chin.

The Prince twitched back from the blade with a semi-conscious grunt but Draken let it follow, let it prick the skin deep enough to leave a scar.

Galbrait groaned, tried again to escape the blade, tried to knock it away with his gauntleted hand. Draken shifted the blade, poked the end deeper under his chin.

The Prince's eyes opened and he stared upward at the black sky overhead. "Draken," he husked out.

"Where is Rinwar and the other commanders?"

"Rinwar is dead. You killed him."

"The priest, fool."

"Oh. Him. The Meek One, he calls himself." The lump in Galbrait's throat bobbed beneath the blade.

"Ironic, considering what he does daily to my country," Draken said.

"I don't disagree." Another harsh swallow, and he coughed, making the obvious effort not to move. "What do you want from me?"

"I want their location. And then I want you to die."

"You're not giving me much incentive to help you."

"It's not meant as incentive. It's a statement of fact. You are dying shortly. If you want it quick and painless, then talk. If you want me to enjoy it overmuch, then don't."

"I haven't seen them in many sevennight."

"You saw them at an encampment on the Silent Trail, downland of here. You. The priest. Moonlings. And someone else." The encampment was disbanded. They'd moved on. It had been the first place he'd gone after leaving Elena.

"It's too late. I'm speaking truth. The Priest has given himself over to something that cannot be forsaken or defeated."

"Not good enough. I'm looking for specifics, Galbrait." Draken heard rustling behind him, felt the faint thud of hooves. He turned to make sure it wasn't a Monoean rescue company. Aarinnaie, Tyrolean, and Osias on horses and leading the ponies. A bound prisoner bounced on his stomach across Bumpus's back. A rope tied him to Bumpus's neck. Bumpus ran along with his head up and ears back, straining on his lead as if protesting every urgent step.

Galbrait moved; Draken heard it rather than felt it. He spun back as Galbrait rolled away from his blade and started to push to his feet. Frustration bit at him. He followed the Prince with the sword. Galbrait tripped over some grasses and fell back to his knees. Draken thumped him hard on the arse with the flat of his blade and sent him sprawling. "Say goodbye, Galbrait."

"Draken," Osias said.

"He won't talk. Maybe the one you brought will be more cooperative."

"Wait," Osias said. "We can question them both."

Draken ignored him, strode forward, pressed the tip of his sword to the bare spot at the top of Galbrait's spine . . .

Osias tried again. "Draken! No!"

Draken put some weight on the sword. An agony of spasm assaulted his back from bending over at the odd angle. He froze in pain, stopping the progress of the blade.

Galbrait grunted. Softly he said, muffled by grasses: "I know where your daughter is."

CHAPTER TWENTY-FIVE

No quickness or desperation in Galbrait's voice. Just simple words shaped into a lie, but they stayed Draken's hand just the same. He hated the surge of hope in his heart. Hope made a man weak, sloppy.

Bruche?

Death can make people say many things. Some truth, some lies. There is no way to know for sure.

"My daughter is dead."

"Could you move your blade? I'd be able to concentrate better if I were upright."

Draken shifted the sword back a handspan. Galbrait sat up gingerly and turned to face him. His gaze flicked back to Tyrolean and Osias, who had dismounted and gathered round. Aarinnaie hauled the prisoner off Bumpus. He hit the ground with a sharp grunt and struggled in his bonds, but she kicked him and he stopped moving.

"Tell me your lies before you die. A story to entertain me," Draken said.

"She and the Manceling . . . that Moonling half. They were brought to the same meet where you claim to have seen me."

"I did see you, with the Moonlings and some ruddy Ashen," Draken growled, but a growing unease filled his chest.

"The Moonlings were there to take Sikyra. A trade for favors done."

"What bloody favors?"

"I don't know."

"I can fair guess," Tyrolean said. Galbrait's gaze flicked to him. Tyrolean's voice had no expression, the same since they'd left Elena.

"When did they take Sikyra?"

"That night. But I heard later someone attacked them. They got away with her, though, only just."

No one moved, but Draken felt their attention on him. He held still, trying to force himself to breathe, to stop his heart lurching. Gods, he could have killed her—

You didn't know. Bruche was a soothing rumble in his icy, locked chest.

Ignorance would not have left her any less dead.

Galbrait says they got away. Your daughter lives.

We don't know that. He's lying.

Ask where they went. See if it's even plausible.

It could be a ruse. Galbrait had tricked him before, had fooled the entire Monoean royal family into believing he was a victim rather than instigator, and they had died for it. All but Draken.

Galbrait's horse, over its fright from the chase, wandered near. Galbrait waited quietly, rumpled, dirty, and sitting stiffly in his armor.

"Where are they taking her, and why?"

He answered without hesitation. "At first thaw a ship will take her back to Monoea."

"Why?"

"Her blood is yours, yes?" Galbrait dropped into Monoean. "They want her on the throne."

"You're King. The rightful one, if not deserving."

Galbrait dropped his gaze. "I've no magic. I'm old guard. A heretic, they say. The only reason I'm still alive is because I helped them."

The arguments against the credibility of his claim stacked in Draken's mind. "They need you. They need your support. My daughter is foreign and you are last of the family that ruled for generations."

"No! Your daughter is the last of the generation," Galbrait said.

"The Moonminsters are stealing the power of all the women of this land. This makes no sense. They are to be only mothers, like Ma Vanni. This I have heard. I've seen who the Ashen kill, and it is not the men."

"It is not untrue. They want your daughter to birth a new race of Kings." Galbrait lifted his chin. "I'm telling you, Draken. She is alive. And I know where they are taking her."

"Watch him, Tyrolean." He stepped away with his sister and Osias, putting his back to the sun. "Well?"

"He's lying."

Draken sighed. "I know, Aarin, but how much are lies? If he leads me to Rinwar, I can kill him."

"If there is even a chance she is alive, you must go," Osias said. "You must inform Elena and seek your child."

"And Setia."

"Aye. And Setia." Osias held his gaze without a flicker of threat crossing the irises.

As honest as a Mance can get, Bruche said.

"Does she even have magic, Osias? I was not born with mine."

"Aye, you were. You were born to take up Akhen Khel. Someday the sword may light for her as it does you. Or, it will not."

"In which case they'll kill her," Aarinnaie said.

"They won't know," Draken said. "I have the sword."

Sometimes he wished he'd left the damn thing on the bottom of the ocean when he'd had the chance. Of course, it had been Bruche who recovered it, not him. He stared past them as the Grassland were brought to life by the sun, muted by his mask.

"His story makes sense. If they do want Sikyra for her magic, Galbrait's support would be invaluable in her smooth placement on the throne. He could formally abdicate for her."

"She's just a baby—"

"It doesn't matter," Draken said. Aarinnaie didn't blanch at his tone, but he drew a breath. Snapping at his friends and sister served nothing. "The first sign of magic, they'll turn her into a silked, gilded slave."

"Take Galbrait to—" Osias began but a shout and jingle of tack interrupted him. They spun to see the prisoner upright on Galbrait's horse and galloping away. Draken cursed and ran for his bow, remembered he was out of arrows, and didn't bother running for Bumpus. Tyrolean had the presence of mind to keep all his weapons on him; he shot but missed.

Draken looked around at the placid tora ponies, munching dried grasses as if nothing had happened. "Don't waste your arrows, Ty."

"You are no longer in charge of knots, Princess," Tyrolean said.

Draken blinked at him. He shook his head a little and went back to Galbrait. Gave him a solid kick in the breast plate. It didn't do him much damage but knock his wind, but it was satisfying. Draken stared down at him as he lay gasping on the ground. "Mistake to let him take your horse."

"I didn't—I—"

"On your feet. You have a long walk ahead of you. Good fortune for you the ponies keep a slow pace."

As they checked tack, shoved Galbrait out front of them where they could keep an eye on him, and rode out, Aarinnaie said lowly, "Where are we going?"

Draken didn't answer. Aarinnaie wasn't going to much like it.

◆ ◆ ◆

As they neared Cove Clan lands, they were ambushed by Oxbow riders. No arrows flew but bows creaked and blades slipped from sheaths. Tirnine looked extremely displeased to see them.

That's you. Making friends wherever you go.

Draken sighed and dismounted. He had to look up at them from Bumpus's back anyway and he needed to keep close to Galbrait, make certain he didn't do anything foolish.

"Tirnine."

"Khel Szi." Her lip curled.

He ignored that. "Is the Queen still at Cove lands?"

"Not as like. Them what got their own war to fight, and we got ours."

It took a moment to parse the meaning from her dialect. "Then we'll go. I have to find her, and quickly."

"You what started up fights again. Cove killed my people."

Draken shook his head. "Why?"

"We brought you to her, aye?"

He took a step closer. A bow creaked. Galbrait looked from him to the Sept warriors surrounding them. Draken stopped, lifted his hands. "Don't shoot me. It'll only startle your horses."

"The Queen ordered it. We knew where she was and wanted it secret."

The air fled his chest in a rush. He cursed, but soundlessly. Surely she wasn't so upset with him to make a stupid mistake that would leave two clans at war . . . She'd left *him* alive, after all. And there was Sikyra to consider. Anxiety itched at the back of his neck. He dragged air in, just enough for a few words. "You didn't go after her?"

"She's gone. Cove Clan what did the killing anyway." Her eyes narrowed. "You come make it right."

Draken gaped at her. "Me? How?"

"Not much caring. You talk to them. Make them reattribute it."

He frowned at her misuse of the word, though her meaning was plain, and reached up to rub his eyes. His fingers found his mask. The daylight stung his vision even with it. "I don't have time for this."

"You what come to us, aye? The gods bring you. You make time."

The gods . . . he didn't doubt their complicity. He sighed. Looked at Osias, Tyrolean. Aarinnaie was uncharacteristically silent, her head bowed. Maybe trying to contain her violent proclivities for once.

"Damn it, no." Truls caught his eye, flitting and frantic, bright in the sunlight. He looked like a torch illuminated against the shadowed woods. Beyond him, a figure darted away into the trees. Draken stared, ignoring the sting of sunlight.

"My lord?" Tyrolean, interminably calm.

Draken nodded and strode back for Bumpus. "I'll come, Tirnine. You may have one day, no longer."

Tirnine poked a finger toward Galbrait. "And him?"

"My cousin. He's no harm to you but of value to me."

Tirnine spun her horse without a word and led the way back along the river, water just breaking through the ice with an early thaw. A reminder the fighting would heat up with the weather, and how painfully little Draken had done to stop the invasion.

You were hamstrung by Elena, but fathers have a penchant for saving their children.

Do they now. I don't really feel like one of those fathers at the moment.

Galbrait shifted to walk near Bumpus. When he spoke he was a little out of breath. "Why are you helping them?"

Draken growled. "They think I'm their Prince and this is what Princes do, if you've forgotten."

Galbrait snorted softly. "Thank you for saving me from their arrows. It's almost as if you've some sentimentality left for your old family."

"Don't flatter yourself. The only reason you're still alive is because you claim you can take me to my daughter."

He's not entirely wrong, is he?

Bruche, I don't need you as my conscience.

I think you do if the past few sevennight are any indication.

Draken snorted, a sound identical to Galbrait's if he cared to admit it. *You've killed plenty, and with less reason than I've had.*

I don't deny it. But not for revenge. You've been clamoring for it since Lesle died.

And I'll have it too. He kicked futilely at Bumpus's sides, shoving him into a slow trot and forcing Galbrait to pick up his pace. Truls lingered in the shadows of the woods lacing the lakes. Draken saw no more signs of whichever god was tracking him now.

When they arrived at the crosspath that would lead to Cove Clan lands, he drew up and looked at his companions, beckoning them close so he could speak softly. "I'll go on alone."

"Dra—"

"No, I won't hear an argument, Aarin. I need someone to watch the prisoner here. The Cove may think him valuable or dangerous, or both."

"We will see he stays well protected until he is in Queen Elena's hands, my lord," Tyrolean said.

That was the assurance he needed. He turned down the path and walked on alone. If Truls followed, he didn't know. Despite daylight flickering onto the path through the canopy, normal forest sounds, and the cheerful chatter of melting creek water running over rocks, he couldn't avoid imagining arrows flying or someone rushing him with a blade. He could hardly be the clan's favorite person.

Even anticipating attack, six armed men materializing from the trees startled both him and Bruche. They wore thick braids down their backs and furs against the cold. The spirit drew Seaborn, which glowed uncomfortably into Draken's eyes. He shoved his will forward and his arm down.

"Why do you come?" one of them demanded.

His Akrasian was proper and hardly accented. Draken tipped his chin down, slightly. A gesture of respect, not compliance. "I've come to broker peace between your clan and Oxbow. I take it Queen Elena is gone?"

He had some faint hope she remained, that Tirnine could have no real idea what transpired inside lands she warred with. But the guard nodded. "Some sevennight. Come, my lord. My clanmaster will speak to you."

He didn't sound happy about it, or nearly enough surprised to see him, but they hadn't turned him away. Draken urged Bumpus forward and they walked their horses around him. He felt oddly short, and it made him think of Setia. It had been some nights before he'd considered her at all, and he was ashamed. Osias must have thought of little else since Galbrait had told them Sikyra lived, though he didn't speak of her.

They emerged from the tree-clad path as the birds quieted around them and the day had fallen enough for Draken to take down his mask. If the consort guards noticed anything wrong about his eyes, they didn't indicate it. When they dismounted, so did he.

The clanmaster sat crosslegged in front of a fire. The guard who spoke to Draken strode ahead to kneel by him. They spoke and looked at Draken, who sat on the ground across the fire from him and held his stiff hands out to the warm flames. The air chilled sharply as the sun fell. The guard backed away, standing with his back to a wooden hut, hand on his sword.

The man was rotund, his great chest and belly rising and falling with heavy, labored breaths. Ritual scarring marked his cheeks and throat, pink against his flaccidly pale skin. Draken hadn't met him before; Elena hadn't given them time. But he was curious: he'd been told all the Sept clans were matriarchal. Nevertheless, he dipped his chin to the clanmaster, who returned the gesture in kind.

"Draken vae Khellian of Brîn."

"Khel Szi." The words were a little wheezy.

"That remains to be seen."

"One is born Khel Szi according to the gods' wishes. It is not a prize to be taken or given."

Draken, however, well remembered Elena putting the crown on his head. Brîn was subject to Akrasia and the Crown. But he didn't argue, just nodded. "Call me as you wish."

"I am Feslar, Khel Szi." He offered no title or honorific, and as Khel Szi was considered a name, Draken went with it.

"You don't seem surprised to see me, Feslar."

Feslar's eyes swept the area behind Draken. Considering the circumstances, Feslar's nervous glance was a normal enough response with a potential enemy in their midst, but it made Draken's spine crawl just the same.

"I came alone," he said.

"Aye," Feslar said. "And why do you come?"

"To broker peace . . . The Oxbow Tirnine's idea, not mine."

"Oh? And how does the Oxbow force Khel Szi to broker peace?" Again the visual sweep.

"The usual way. At spear point." Draken resisted glancing over his shoulder. "What's this about? Why did you kill the Oxbows? Their help to me caused your clan no harm."

"The Queen required her presence stay secret."

Odd way to word that. Bruche silently agreed. "So she ordered you to kill them."

Again the crawling feeling of unease. Draken held back on asking what was really going on and waited.

"Not in so many words."

"Then why?"

Feslar's lip twitched.

I don't like this, Draken.

Draken didn't much like it either. He gave into his urge to look around. At first glance, things had seemed normal. But now that he really looked, he saw what amounted to a deserted village. Beyond the guards who had escorted him in, the buildings were quiet. No smoke filtered into the night beyond the fire at his knees. No cooking smells. Just the sound the lake lapping its shores and the nervous breathing of the man across from him.

"Where is your clan?"

No answer.

Draken shifted on his knees, ready to get to his feet. "Are they attacking Oxbow? Is this a distraction?" He didn't stop to think how Feslar might have orchestrated such a thing . . .

"No. I sent them away to safety," Feslar said.

Bruche murmured, *How did he know you were coming?*

"Because you had word I was here?"

Feslar's eyes darted, and he shifted. The effort made him wheeze, which took some time before he could answer. "Of course not. It's a dangerous time."

Draken released a breath. "The war, then? Plague? Gods, man, speak plainly."

Feslar shuddered, visibly shuddered, his jowls trembling over his thick neck.

"You're frightened. Of what?" Draken said.

"I am not craven."

"Fear and cowardice are not the same." He was feeling plenty of fear himself at the moment. This man had grown old and fat leading a clan of warriors. He'd learned to pay close attention to such leaders when they were nervous. "I would never accuse you of cowardice. I don't think your people would tolerate it from you. And the Queen trusted you enough to let you host her. I suspect it takes a deal to frighten you."

Direct questions seemed to only lead to evasion; he let the words trail off without it.

Feslar settled, oddly, shoulders slumped and breathing slowed. Almost a submission. His wheezy voice turned to a whisper. "We did not choose to fight. We did not decide to kill the Oxbows."

Draken leaned forward. "Aye, I'm aware. The Queen—"

"No. Something else." Feslar's eyes locked on him and Draken missed the sensation of someone watching his back.

Bruche felt it, too. *Something else well could be.*

Feslar fell quiet. It took a few breaths before Draken could fill it. He tried to keep his tone conversational. "I have seen some damned odd things since the Monoeans attacked Akrasia, and before. Unexplainable things."

"Magic."

For the first time, Draken wondered if the Sept had any, and how it manifested. "Beyond even that. I carry a sword that gives life as readily as it takes it. I can heal myself with magic. And I can see well enough that these creatures are different."

Feslar nodded slowly. Either his breathing had stopped or his wheezing had suddenly cleared. His chest still rose and fell.

Draken's voice felt hollow and his words too quick. He pressed on anyway, sensing an opportunity to test the man. "Someone murdered the Mance, all but one. They are necromancers, filled with the strength of many spirits. They command the banes. I have been under the control of a bane. It is no small thing and the Mance were strong. I wonder who could do such a thing, kill Mance."

"The Lord God Korde."

The whispered words had no ire or fear in them though; only reverence. They prickled over Draken's spine on their way to his mind.

Draken swallowed in his dry throat. "You are not Feslar."

CHAPTER TWENTY-SIX

Nor was he Korde. Even so, Draken didn't wait for a response. He shifted and drew, shoving to his feet with his good leg. The other knee still ached, damp, cold, worn from riding. He didn't pay it much mind and Bruche rushed to chill it with his presence, erasing the pain.

Whoever held the clanmaster in thrall didn't move.

"You're no better than a bane, holding this man captive. Which one are you?" Draken said. His mind sifted through the possibilities. Shaim who had tried to make peace. Agrias, who might have chased him. His eyes narrowed, trying to sort through the moon phases. Who had been missing? He'd avoided the Eyes and so hadn't kept track . . .

"You seek which god you have betrayed." Aye, the wheezing was fair gone, as if it had never been.

"I never asked to be liege to any of you."

"You are an earth-crawler. You are in liege to us whether you want it or not."

Draken's fingers tightened on the sword. "You call it betrayal. I call it freedom."

Even as the name left his lips he knew it was wrong. The god shook his head, an irritating smile playing on Feslar's pale, fleshy lips.

"I killed Zozia. Shaim is a god of peace. Khellian and MaVanni still ride the skies. So—" Draken's eyes narrowed and he forced strength into his voice, though the notion of speaking to another god made his skin crawl. "Agrias. But you're all about the land and food and animals. Why do you have your fingers in this?"

"You use my land, my living world, to heal yourself. Every time you do so, you break a little part of what's mine."

Of what's mine? Was Agrias claiming the whole of the earth and stone? "I didn't ask for it. I didn't ask for any magic."

"No. And you have been most ungrateful. I am here to take it back."

I've a feeling the only way for him to take it back is to make you very dead. Bruche lifted Draken's arm and reset his grip on the sword. He came around the fire. As he did so, Agrias lifted a knife. Instead of shifting Feslar's heavy bulk to strike at Draken, the god turned the knife on his own body. The edge of blade sunk into Feslar's chest and started to slide down the skin, slicing it off in a neat, if bloody, wide strip. The big man didn't so much as flinch.

The sight stayed Draken's blade; even Bruche held. "Stop! You'll kill him."

The god carved another strip of flesh from Feslar, baring white fat and marbled muscle. Blood ran down, harsh against Draken's darksight. "And how do you intend on killing me? You have to go through him to get to me."

"Why are you doing this?" He had to force the words through painfully clenched teeth.

Agrias didn't answer. Something squiggled amid the blood, shifting beneath it, causing gruesome, bloody ripples under the raw flesh.

Fingers. Bruche's voice was more awe than horror.

Pale fingers, like sunless dirt slugs, broke through the thin strands of uncut muscle, emerging bloody as a newborn horror. The god had hidden *inside* Feslar. Not a bane, but like a parasite. It split through Feslar's chest and leapt at him, gangling fingers and arms stretched for him, a pale, writhing thing so pale it had never seen the sun. Draken didn't think, didn't hesitate. He shifted his weight and slashed. Seaborn struck the creature—wrinkled and hairless with wide, white eyes and limbs unfolding like a spider's. Rank-smelling dirt sprayed from the wound, worse than gutter sludge in Reschan. Agrias screamed inhuman shrieks that burned the mind. Even wounded, the god attacked, fingers scrabbling into Draken's stomach, tearing and ripping his skin. Draken gasped in agony and fell back with Agrias on him. His sword tumbled away. The god's tearing fingers squeezed Draken's throat. He couldn't pry them off. The great rend in his stomach started to knit, a confusion of pain as the edges tried to find each other from the inside of his torn gut. The fingers squeezed tighter. Black sludge filled Draken's vision. Ghosts twitched in his periphery. He reached out for his sword, throwing his arm down flat across the rough ground. He found the edge, cut himself, but dragged it closer. Still holding it by the blade he stabbed sideways into the god.

The body writhed over him, jerking like a doll on strings. The grip weakened. Draken dragged in air and threw him off, shoving to his feet, mindless of his bleeding hand and the healing pain in his stomach. He struggled closer on his knees, stabbing again and again until Bruche grasped control of his muscles from the inside, cooling his limbs and his ire. The dirt roiled beneath, tearing grass roots and upending the stones encircling the fire. It spread out in waves until the body of the god was in several pale pieces. His blood sizzled softly as it drained onto the ground. Dusty, stinking smoke rose from it. It dried and sank deep into the bare dirt.

Draken's palm stung like nettles burned inside the cuts, and there was nothing for it. They didn't heal. He growled and tore the scarf from his neck to wrap around the wound.

The entire ground to the trees and the lake was furrowed in circles as if great bladed plows had run through it. Draken stared at the ruined god, panting while the black sludge-blood dripped from his sword.

"Do you think Agrias is dead?" he asked Bruche between pants.

Aye, you did a fair job of it.

Guards had edged closer, but none made to draw. He looked up at the nearest one, guessed what they'd been dealing with, and straightened his back. Soreness had set into his shoulder alongside the cold. His chest still lifted quickly with breath. "How long has he been behaving strangely?"

The man swallowed hard enough Draken heard his throat work. "Since the Queen left. He said kill the Oxbows." He paused. "And his own sons and daughters."

"Where is the rest of your clan?"

"Attacking. Children and elders I sent off to our old camp, upland that way." He pointed.

"You didn't obey . . . ?"

"Something needed doing, my lord."

"Well done. You're now clanmaster and you should . . . *what?*"

The guard sputtered. "My lord, I'm just a guard. I cannot . . ."

"Something needs doing," Draken repeated grimly. "And you're the only one to do it. Proved by your actions. Fetch your kin back from attacking Oxbow and then fetch your children and elders."

The guard looked down at his clanmaster, reduced to a bloody heap, slashes gleaming crimson under a rising moon. Draken glanced up. Khellian. For a long time, the only sounds were his heavy breaths, until the regular forest and lake sounds surrounded them again.

"Was he really a god?"

Draken gave a tired nod.

"We should. Ah." The guard blinked wide eyes, eased back from Draken and the clanmaster. "Hide. We need walls and—"

"Walls cannot stand against the gods, and there's no hiding from the others, so don't bother trying. Bring your people home and with a little good fortune, your part in this is done."

"And you, my lord? What is your part?"

"I don't know yet, but I've a bad feeling it's just begun. Now. Tell me where my Queen has gone."

◆ ◆ ◆

Draken leaned against Bumpus as he spoke with Tirnine, who had rushed out to see him as he rode into their village. It had been a long night rounding up the Cove warriors and explaining things. Then he had to speak with Oxbow to get *them* to stop the fighting. It was a tremulous peace, which he hoped would hold with the Cove clan being so busy retrieving their children and elders from their hiding spot. At last he trudged to the longhouse to speak with his own companions.

"You survived." Aarinnaie raised her brows but didn't get to her feet like Tyrolean did when he shoved aside the curtain strung for privacy. Fire warmed the space, and Osias's pipe and good food smells, though it was quiet and mostly empty at this time of night.

Draken nodded them both and lowered himself to the floor with the fire to his offhand to keep the glare from his eyes. His sore knee made annoyingly loud cracks as he sat. "It was easier than I expected."

Bruche's snort reached his lips.

He shifted his attention to Osias, who sat quietly in the shadows, a little apart, smoke twining from the dual bowls of his pipe. The shadows carved his face into ugly lines.

"Agrias is no fighter," Draken said.

A puff of smoke filtered up into the still air inside the longhouse. "No. I suppose not."

"Agrias . . . what did he want?" Aarinnaie went back to sharpening her blades, apparently unmoved that Draken had killed another god.

"To take his magic back. Apparently he gave me healing." *His own,* Bruche added. "Aye, Bruche is right. He gave me *his* healing."

She shook her head, mystified. "Why?"

"Korde made him do it, I suspect. Apparently there was some notion of turning me against Khellian. Something about my bad attitude."

Galbrait snorted softly. "Surely not that."

Draken shook his head, too weary to snap back at him. "At any rate, the guards know where Elena went and now so do I."

◆ ◆ ◆

A day and a night of hard riding left Draken trembling with weariness and half-asleep in the saddle, but Elena was where she'd told the Cove Clan she'd be, entrenched in a sizable camp outside one of the larger villages resting on a river streaming upland from the mountainous Skymarke Lake. It was wide and shallow, and it died into a thick, wet, cold marsh that took half a day to trudge through, but the army had found dry land on the banks of the river. Tents spread out across the trampled grazing lands under copses of scraggy, Frost-wrecked trees. Draken thought he saw the merest hint of green shading the land. He wasn't sure if it meant Newseason was nearly upon them or if it was some trick of his darksight.

He felt like a drifter riding up to the sharply armed Escorts and servii, days off a bath, more time in the saddle than he cared to admit, beard scruffing all their chins but Osias's, and the shaggy tora ponies coated to their hocks in mud. They were challenged, and sorting out their identities took some time since Draken had no pendant to show. "Tell the Queen I have news."

They were shown to a tent, one big enough for dignitaries. That was confusing, to be treated so, but Draken nodded to the servii who brought them, asked for some wash water, and put in a request for an audience with Elena. But no amount of negotiation kept them from taking Galbrait off to a makeshift gaol. The Prince looked back at them, a protest on his lips, but Draken scowled at him, silencing it. He couldn't deny the relief of having someone else look after his cousin for a bit.

"I wonder if they'll rough him up," Tyrolean said.

"He can take it. Besides, he has it coming. The Queen might do much more."

"No. He's too clever," Osias said. "He won't tell where your daughter is until he's certain of his freedom."

"Aye, he learned that much from his father." Gods, how he wished for Yseff now. His cousin hadn't been the best of kings, but he'd been a decent man.

The others cleaned up quickly and went off to find something to eat. Maybe they sensed his wanting to be alone to gather his thoughts. A camp maid brought a cloth and a bucket of water, dipping into a curtsy. He dipped his fingers in once she'd gone. Cold, of course. He wasn't *that* honored of a guest.

Draken undid his sword harness and laid it aside, then stripped to the waist to scrub off the road. He ran a cloth over his head and face. His beard had grown in thick. He had no body slave to shape it into something decent, so he edged his knife blade on the strap and shaved it off, wincing at the occasional sting. The tent poles rattled slightly as the minor nicks and cuts healed.

He wiped his face with the cloth again. It came away grimy and a little blood-stained. He dug into his pack for a shirt, but a rustle at the entrance to the tent made him look up.

"Elena." The name unwound from his lips without bidding, without thought.

She let the tent flap fall shut behind her, her dark eyes on him. She didn't reprimand him so he didn't offer a correction, just straightened, his clean shirt in his hands. Her chill gaze left him struggling not to cringe. He knew how he must look to her: an aging and battered man, scars lacing his dark skin. Rough. Corrupt. Heathen.

"You lit no lantern."

"I don't need it. The gods gave me darksight. I can barely stand the glow of the moons." He pulled his shirt over his head, trying to hide the slight tremble in his hands.

She glanced behind her at the open tent flap, admitting only the faintest moonglow. Elna, perhaps, or Khellian's crescent. "The moons are irregular. Not as many shine in the night sky."

"That's because I killed two of them."

"No wonder they curse you. I understand you brought a prisoner."

"My cousin. Crown Prince Galbrait of Monoea." He dried his damp hair, taking the time to sort his words. "He claims Sikyra lives. He claims to know where they're taking her."

Silence. "'They' who?"

"Moonlings. A trade with the Ashen for land and autonomy. They are transporting her somewhere to give her to the Monoeans."

Elena lifted her chin. "They want to make certain she is dead? This makes no sense."

"No. They want her on the throne. She bears royal Monoean blood—"

"She is sundry."

"Aye. Monoeans aren't nearly as picky about mixed blood as Akrasians are. Besides, they want her magic. My magic. And maybe yours. I expect the Moonlings mentioned what you did to Skyhaven to the Monoeans."

Elena hissed a breath.

Draken hurried on before she could accuse him of some further wrongdoing against their child. "They believe she has magic. I've seen no evidence of it but she is very young. And maybe you passed on Truls's magic as well." Who lurked in the corner, his silhouette sharpening as Draken said his name.

"You believe she lives now."

"I had my blade at his throat. He knows if he's found false I'll kill him straightaway. He's young. He doesn't want to die."

"I'll have it out of him." She turned to go, cloak snapping behind her.

"Elena!"

She turned, her queen's mask lacquered into place.

"Your Majesty, I know him. He's far out of his depth. The Ashen used him to kill his family, promised him a throne, and stole it back from him." He didn't know if it happened just like that, but he needed a simple story to keep the Akrasians from torturing and killing him. "Bring him. We'll talk to him together."

"Do not presume to advise me."

A hesitation, during which he beat down the urge to snap back at her. "This is a respectful request, my Queen. I think I can get the information from the lad well enough, and perhaps secure his help against the Ashen."

"How will you do that?"

"Point out the many ways they have betrayed him."

"He betrayed you, as I understand it. Giving you over to that priest, nearly killing you."

She was much better informed than he'd realized. "He betrayed me at the sword point of his countrymen. Not his choice." A complete untruth, but he needed the lie for now. He had to keep Galbrait from harm. "Treating him well will garner his trust and respect. We need that trust if we're to find—"

A raised voice, sharp in anger, cut him off. Aarinnaie. Elena turned and ducked from the tent. His mouth pressed into a hard line, Draken followed. Someone gripped her arm—some Akrasian in clothes too fine for a battle-camp. Someone whose combed and oiled black hair he recognized with a cold heart.

Easy, Draken.

"Ilumat. Unhand my sister."

"My wife, you mean to say." Ilumat did as he asked but spun on him. Obviously Draken's presence was known to him. Draken wished he'd had the same courtesy. "I merely asked her to dine with me."

"Demanded, more like," Aarinnaie said. "As if I could tolerate your disgusting presence for even a moment—"

"Manners, my sweet," Ilumat said. "We are in the presence of the Queen."

"Aarinnaie is fresh off a long road," Draken said. The only thing keeping his temper was Bruche, chilling his arms and legs so that he couldn't lunge at the fop without tripping over himself. "I'm certain exhaustion is affecting her tone and judgement. Perhaps tomorrow she will be better company."

At his pointed look, Aarinnaie turned and went into the tent. Draken eased a breath. "You wish to speak with Prince Galbrait, Your Majesty?"

His words had the intended effect on Ilumat. The lord's brows fell. "Galbrait, here? Did he turn on his people then?"

Wouldn't he like to know.

Aye, he would.

"I'll have him brought to my tent," Elena said. "Come along, Draken."

Draken groaned inwardly. She sounded like she was directing a child. But he followed, Ilumat trailing along. Draken wished for Osias and said so when they reached the privacy of her tent. Elena nodded to a young sundry Moonling slave who looked vaguely familiar. Fortunately, only a few cutwork lanterns flickered from hooks on tentpoles. Draken didn't think Elena would appreciate his wearing the mask.

The tent wasn't for sleeping, but for making war. A stack of rolled maps rested on a wooden folding table, weapons hung on a rack, and a cushioned chair rested on a low dais covered with rugs. Two Escorts flanked the dais, their dark eyes following Draken as he entered. Draken didn't have so much as a boot knife on him since the Queen had caught him at his ablutions, so he ignored them.

Elena moved to sit on the chair, her chainmail clinking softly. Ilumat shifted to stand near her. He flipped one edge of his cloak back over his shoulder to show his hand resting on his swordhilt. It was then Draken saw the Night Lord pendant . . . or the chain to it, hanging round his neck. He'd known, of course. But the air punched from Draken's lungs as if someone had gotten in a direct shot right beneath his heart.

Galbrait came in chains, shuffling the short steps his shackles allowed. His wrists looked raw from the ropes Draken had used, and fresh bruising stained his jaw. His armor was missing. His undertunic and trousers were sweat-stained and wet to the mid-thigh, leather boots black with wet from two days of fighting his way through the marsh on foot. A ripe, damp odor rose from him. He rubbed his runny nose on his sleeve, and stared around at all of them, looking as stricken as Draken felt.

Elena straightened her back. Ilumat looked at Draken and back at the Prince, eyes narrowed.

Draken, speak.

Draken cleared his throat. "Courtesy would be a good place to start, Your Highness. You stand on the land of this Queen and in her presence."

With his arms shackled back and his ankles held so close, Galbrait would have to fall rather than kneel, so the Prince dropped his chin. The Escort at his side shoved him down to his knees anyway. Draken recalled grimly the first time he'd met the Queen and been treated thus.

"I come here to help, Your Majesty," Galbrait said.

"No, you came at swordpoint," Elena said.

Draken clenched his jaw. Not the way to garner Galbrait's help. "Tell the Queen who has our daughter."

"I told you. Moonlings. With their help, Korde murdered the Princess's Mance escort and gave her to them. Not that I saw it, mind you. I'm repeating what I've been told."

Osias came in, rustling the tent flap, lending a cold white light to the golden flicker of the lanterns. Galbrait turned to see who had come in and the Escort poked him in the side with the grip of his sword.

"Not this gods nonsense again," Ilumat said.

Of course she told Ilumat. He is his Night Lord.

I'm aware. But he knew what Bruche meant. "What else do you suggest killed six Mance, my lord?"

"We've got a Mance here. We could ask him." Ilumat turned as odd a gaze on Osias as Draken had ever seen. People generally ranged between adoration and repulsion when confronted with a Mance. Ilumat loitered somewhere near haughty.

Osias took a step forward, eyes swirling into storm. "It takes something rather more powerful than an ordinary mortal to kill one of my kind, if you recall, Your Majesty."

"Like a magical sword?" Ilumat sniffed. "How do we know Draken is not responsible for their deaths, then?"

Should have seen that coming, Bruche said.

"I've never quarreled with the Mance. We are allies. I trusted them. I gave our daughter to them for safekeeping."

"Didn't work out quite the way you expected, eh?" Ilumat cocked his head.

"Rather like your giving Brîn to the Ashen, Lord Ilumat?"

Ilumat's face greyed with anger. "Brîn was taken. The Ashen *betrayed* me."

"Odd. At the time it didn't feel like so much a betrayal as an answer to an invitation," Draken said.

Galbrait was watching with interest.

"Enough." Elena, irritated as only a Queen can be. "At the moment I'm only interested in the whereabouts of my daughter."

You can take Ilumat on later. But in the meantime he had to keep between Ilumat and his daughter's whereabouts. Ilumat had every reason to see Sikyra safely out of the way, or better yet, dead.

Draken twisted his head to crack his neck, trying to ease the stiffness. "Galbrait. Do you believe Korde is helping the Ashen?"

"They believe he is."

A subtle truth. Draken thought fast. "Why did the Moonlings take Sikyra?"

"To exchange her for land once the Monoeans have taken Akrasia. The Ashen want her as Queen in Monoea."

Queen Elena leaned forward. A subtle difference in posture, but to Draken, who had watched her and admired her, it betrayed a carefully concealed hope. "And where will the exchange take place?"

"I don't yet know. But I know where I can find out."

Draken growled under his breath. Galbrait fair knew where they were taking Sikyra. He just refused to say. Playing his game would best ensure his cooperation, but beating it out of him was tempting. Gods, so tempting. "Which is?" Elena asked.

Galbrait lifted his chin. "I daren't reveal it. I'm young, not stupid. I know my life lies in the balance of your daughter's well-being."

Elena drew in a breath, breast rising and falling with finality. "You'll surely understand if I keep you under guard."

"I expect nothing less, Your Majesty."

"If you cooperate, you will come to no harm under my care." Elena looked at Draken as she spoke. He felt the prickle of . . . not guilt. But the sort of discomfort from being found out.

Galbrait lifted his chains. "Are these necessary?"

"We shall see, aye?" Draken said. He was in no mood to guard his cousin all night. Nor the next.

Galbrait swallowed, flicked his gaze between the three of them. Nodded.

The Queen gestured to have Galbrait taken back to wherever they were holding him. Draken dipped his chin to her. "If that is all, Your Majesty . . ."

"Draken."

He turned back to her, waiting. His shoulders were stiff, tight.

"Is it true you've been killing many Ashen?"

"While searching for Galbrait, aye."

"You knew Galbrait had word of Sikyra."

Perhaps it is time for the truth to serve, Bruche said gently.

"No. I sought to kill him for his betrayals."

"Not exactly behavior becoming a prince—"

Draken forgot himself. "I am a free man with no commitments, and it's not exactly a lawful place, Akrasia these days. Khellian's balls, at least I'm doing *something.*"

"Are you suggesting I'm not?"

"The Monoeans are still here, aren't they?" Even as the words came out of his mouth he wished he could take them back.

Bruche groaned. *Now you've done it.*

"Lord Ilumat." Her voice lashed through Draken's. "All of you. Leave us."

"Your Majesty." Ilumat bowed his way out without protest.

Apparently he's clever enough to know when to hold his tongue.

Elena leaned back in her chair. Despite Draken's heavily bloodstained recent past, she showed no fear of him. "All you've done is kill a few Ashen at random."

Enough lies, enough death, enough injustice. Draken had nothing more to lose. "Not random. Opportunistically and strategized. Common enough in war. And I've learned things, truths, even if you don't like the sound of them." He'd brought her Galbrait, hadn't he?

Her chin lifted. "And now you know why I took your titles."

"Because you can't take bad news from your advisors? No, my Queen. We both know that has nothing to do with it."

"I gave you my daughter to keep her safe." Anguish wound through her words. The urge to hold her twined with the urge to shout her down.

"*Our* daughter," Draken said, though he couldn't get much air behind it.

"You lied to me. You told me she was dead."

"The Mance said it was so."

"You tried to keep from looking for her."

"What? No! I would nev—"

"She belongs with me. I am her Queen. She inherits from me. As you say, you're rather busy with killing to raise up a princess."

She hadn't made him leave, even though he had accused Galbrait, even though he was stripped of titles and rank, even though she was obviously, and rightly, furious with him. "I won't fight you for her. I would never do that to her. But if she lives, I will find her." He'd already pushed this far. It was hard to keep his mouth shut now. "I want Ilumat to leave Aarinnaie alone."

"That is outside my will. Their marriage belongs to the gods now."

"He's lying to you."

"He has no reason to do so."

He held onto his calm tone like a man scrabbling to hang onto a cliff. "Doesn't he?"

Her fingers curled around the arms of her chair, pale skin whitening further. "Ilumat has done nothing but be a friend to me, support me. We have known each other since we were children. You're nothing but a common mercenary best suited to killing with that damned sword of yours."

The truth in that stung. "He lies to you. Why don't you see it?" But he knew the answer as soon as he asked it. Grief, fear, hatred for Draken. He would have clung to the familiar if the situation were reversed. He had tried, gods he'd tried. The only thing that had driven him when he'd first been exiled to this godsforsaken country was finding his wife's killer, as if it might somehow redeem him and restore his old life.

Elena lifted her chin. "Prove his lies, then, if you insist."

Draken shook his head. His word was worth nothing; Aarinnaie's even less. Gods, it was a futile argument. "You're right. I'm best suited to killing, not advising Queens. But Galbrait knows I'm more than capable of giving him a slow, painful death if he crosses me. I do believe he knows where Sikyra is. Let me take him and find her."

"I'll go."

"Your Majesty, he won't cooperate with you, not like he will me. And you have a war to fight."

"As you say, I'm not much good at it."

Not fair, tossing that stone back onto the board. Bruche sounded more impressed than sympathetic.

"At least let me come with you. Galbrait won't cooperate unless I do. I know him." An outright lie. Galbrait might submit under torture and tell them all sorts of bloody things.

"I'll allow it. But never forget the child is mine."

"I don't see how I can forget with you reminding me of it every other breath. Your Majesty." He gave her a stiff dip of his chin and strode out without waiting for a formal dismissal.

CHAPTER TWENTY-SEVEN

Draken avoided the Queen as they rode out and on subsequent nights as Galbrait led them upland. Ilumat made it easy, riding at her side, hand never straying far from that blasted brass-chased sword of his. He kept a cohort of guards around them as well, to insulate them from the servii on the march. Draken plodded along toward the rear of the line, keeping a lookout as best he could from Bumpus's low back, for they rode with the Agrian Range at the edge of view to their offhand. The mountains grew by the day. Nothing like the dagger-shaped peaks that made up Eidola, but enough to remind a man riding a tora pony of his insignificance.

Ach, you're a morbid one, Bruche finally said as they quit the saddle for the night and Draken was brushing out Bumpus's thick wiry fur and staking him to graze under some trees. The swordhand had been quiet, also watching, but sitting in a sullen funk deep within Draken. *Can't you be cheerful rather than ride along on this pony like you're on sleepweed? You don't even chat to the others at night.*

I do what needs doing.

But how about a song?

Draken snorted and looked for his sister. She was cornered by Ilumat, again. The lord kept trying with his wife, and Draken had to admit he hadn't been unkind to her since they had started on their journey. It was just the original unkindness of making her marry him at swordpoint that annulled all subsequent decency. He made his way over to them but was waylaid by an Escort with a familiar, lined face.

"I've been waiting to speak to you, my lord," Commander Geffen Bodlean said.

"Commander." His eyes narrowed and he didn't offer his hand in response to hers. How had she escaped Brîn? "I'm no longer a lord. Not even a servii."

Her grey brows drew in over her lined eyes. She lowered her hand. "I'd heard. There are plenty here who will follow you, including me."

"That's treason, Commander."

"Aye. It's also truth." She sighed. "I know we didn't part on good terms. May I speak with you about it?"

He glanced back at Aarinnaie. She was saying something biting because Ilumat bore a tight smile. Draken could hear her voice but couldn't make out the words.

"I need to go to her. Later, then. I'll be—"

Geffen signaled past Draken. He turned to look. An Escort behind Draken nodded to Geffen and approached Ilumat, speaking quietly but interrupting just the same. Ilumat scowled and strode off with her.

Draken twitched a grim smile. "What was that about?"

"Some help. And an offer of more."

"What sort of help?"

"Whatever returns the Princess to her family and rids Akrasia of these damned Ashen, my lord."

"Have you forgotten I took you captive in Brîn?"

"No. Nor have I forgotten how you led us to war at Auwaer and that you are the rightful Prince and Night Lord." She lowered her head in thought. "Ilumat is no leader and I fear he is worse, a traitor."

"Right. The Ashen."

"He turned on them, wanted Brîn for himself, and they responded in kind. We barely escaped."

"How well is this known?"

She shook her head. "He claims he simply lost a fight due to being outnumbered in an attack on Brîn."

"Keep quiet on this, Commander. And don't do anything stupid. I'm not in the Queen's favor and I wouldn't see you out of it."

"Aye. I've been around far too long to get caught at insubordination. All will be well, now that you're here." She nodded to Tyrolean, who had eased toward them. "Captain. Good evening." She melted off into the crowd of servii and escorts readying camp for the night.

"What was that about?" Tyrolean asked.

"She wants to help." Draken pulled down his mask and let his gaze follow her. Truls didn't shy from her. "And she's not a god, so there's that."

"Good."

Draken raised his brows at him. "Tyrolean, you surprise me. I assume you're rather disappointed not to have met any yet."

"I'll leave the diplomacy to you, my lord."

Draken snorted. That hadn't worked out so well in the past, or really, ever. But his heart felt lighter anyway. "Come. It's time Galbrait tells us where we're going."

The Prince had been released from his chains but sat with a servii guarding him. Not too close, Draken noted. He was gaining some trust, then. Probably a good thing.

A pretty face and a sweet tongue. Unlike other princes we know.

Draken grunted inwardly. "Be off," he said to the servii, who hesitated.

Tyrolean gave him a crisp nod and the servii touched his fist to breast and left.

Tyrolean shrugged but a slight grin tugged at the corner of his mouth. Until he switched his attention to Galbrait. Draken wondered if he remembered Galbrait giving him a little bit of a challenge over Aarinnaie while they were in Monoea. Not that it mattered now.

Galbrait sat with his legs folded in front of him and his hands resting on his knees. He wore no armor still, and no weapons, of course. Someone had given him a tatty, stained cloak and he had the hood up over his greasy blond hair.

"You look sound enough," Draken observed in Monoean.

"Two meals a day and a horse to ride. I'd like to brush up on the language but they're not much for conversation, these Akrasians."

"They're under instructions not to speak to you," Draken said.

"From the Queen?"

"From me."

His pale brows rose. "I understood you were stripped of all rank and titles."

Draken knew Galbrait had fair command of the Akrasian language. Still, getting caught in the lie surprised him. He shrugged to hide his sudden fear Galbrait would refuse to tell him anything. "Where are we going, Galbrait?"

"As I said, to find—"

"No. I think you know where my daughter is and you're not saying because you fear we'll have no use for you and kill you."

"The thought has occurred."

"Queen Elena no doubt plans your speedy death as soon as we know where the princess is. I, on the other hand, do not."

"Why not?"

"Because you are my kin and heir to the Monoean throne. Which makes you of use to me."

That threw the young Prince. He frowned.

"You're clever. Think on it. After you tell me where we're going."

Galbrait stared at him. Draken held his gaze, unmoving. If he bent now, he'd never have it out of the Prince, or it would be too late.

"Why wouldn't I just lie?" Galbrait asked.

Draken gestured to his mask. "Because I'll know if you do. A parting gift from the gods, before I started killing them."

Galbrait cursed, buying that lie. "They're right about you, the 'Minsters. You are godsworn."

"It doesn't matter. I'll die before I let the Ashen use me again. And you're certainly dying before I do. You might turn that thought over. Now. Where are they going with my daughter?"

"Algir." Galbrait looked down at his grimy hands. "As I told you before . . . as soon as thaw hits, ships will take her back to Monoea."

Perhaps not the whole truth. But it was enough to go on. He rose and walked away. Galbrait called his name but he ignored him.

"We've got a sevennight," Tyrolean said once they'd reached relative privacy of their tent. Osias sat repairing arrows, shafts and feathers on a bedroll. "Two at best. Thaw comes early this year."

"Aye. And we've got all this to muddle with." Draken waved a hand, indicating Elena's blasted, plodding army.

"We're making good time, considering," Osias said.

"Not good enough—" Draken growled, but was interrupted by Geffen. She ducked into their tent without a word to them. Draken and Tyrolean exchanged glances as she sat cross-legged on the canvas floor; servii tents weren't big enough to stand up in. Her mail clinked as she shifted to salute him, an incongruous gesture within in the casual stance of the meeting. "My lord. I've just come from the briefing on the front. Reschan was taken by the enemy in the last sevennight."

Draken hissed a slow breath. The wood-walled trade city wouldn't last long under assault, this he knew. But he hadn't expected it so soon. "Va Khlar? I'd heard he was already dead."

She nodded. "Aye, and every other noble in the city."

The urge to hunt and kill Korde filled him with shuddering certainty. It was the only way to end this, lest the god turn all of Akrasia against itself.

If you leave now, Sikyra will be lost.

So I am to choose between my daughter and my country.

There is no choice.

The tent flap rustled. Aarinnaie stepped in, slight enough to barely have to dip her head, and stopped. "I didn't expect this."

"Nor I," Draken said. "Join us."

"I have to hide from Ilumat. He's just come out of a meeting with the Queen."

"Aye. We were discussing that." Draken told her about Reschan. She was quiet for long breaths. Draken had nothing to add. In the intervening silence, Truls appeared, kneeling in the corner, crowded behind Geffen. She shifted and he wondered if on some level she sensed the ghost-Mance. Draken could smell him in the close quarters.

"You should go. Find troops. Get them to Reschan," Aarinnaie said.

"There are none to take. They're all at the front, protecting Auwaer, I assume."

Draken looked at Geffen, who nodded slowly. "Except some five hundred held in reserve at Khein."

"The Monoeans are closing the gap between Reschan and Brîn, I take it?"

"The Queen has decreed the protection of Auwaer is paramount," she said. "On Ilumat's advice."

"I don't think it's just Brîn Monoea means to secure." The Ashen owned Brîn, after all, thanks to Ilumat. "It's Eidola."

"There's no breaching those gates," Geffen said.

"There is with no Mance to protect them. The last living one is here with us."

She stared at him, but there was nothing left to discuss. The Queen had hamstrung him from fighting Akrasia's greatest threat: Korde and the banes. He'd have to do that on his own. Instead, he moved on. "Is there much fighting around Auwaer?"

Geffen's mouth tightened. "It fair holds. But there are odd reports . . ."

Draken took a leap. "Of Akrasians fighting alongside Ashen."

She stared. "How did you know?"

"I've seen it. Does the Queen believe?"

A pause. "No."

And why would she, having not seen it? It is too horrific a thought to take under advisement.

The first time I met her I brought news of a bane attack. She ended up believing me then.

One attack is one thing. An army of bane-riddled soldiers is quite another . . . But her reaction is a good thing.

Why?

It shows she trusts no one else either. That still leaves room for you.

"And Ilumat?" Draken said abruptly. "What does he say?"

"Lord Ilumat thinks the rumors are based only on a very few servii converts to Moonminster Faith, my lord," Geffen answered.

Not an "I told you so" Draken wanted to evoke in Bruche at the moment. There was no satisfaction, only thousands dead at the feet of a disbelieving Queen.

"You have people at Auwaer?" Aarinnaie asked Geffen.

A dry smile, stretched thin on a face that had seen too much bloodshed and dreaded a future of it. "Lord Ilumat does, Princess. I simply go where I am told."

Aarinnaie twisted the bracelet around her arm, turning it so the facets of metal and carvings flashed stinging light against Draken's darksight.

"Aarin. It's a bad idea."

Innocently: "What is?"

"Whatever you're thinking."

"I might as well use my marriage to our advantage." Aarinnaie dropped her arm with the heavy marriage bracelet and turned back to Geffen. "Can you draw up orders to move some Kheinian servii to camp outside Reschan? I'd like to make a safe pathway for my brother and niece to get home to Brîn."

"Brîn is lost," Geffen said.

"Not forever. Not with troops to take her back." Aarinnaie gave Geffen a sugary smile. "Will you write the orders? I'll carry them if you do."

"That is treason."

Traceable treason, Bruche said.

The sort people got tortured and hung for. But . . . Aarinnaie had a point. And he lived in fear of her going dark on Ilumat. Best if they were apart as much as possible.

"Letting Monoea win the war is worse treason," Draken said.

"I wasn't aware there was a moral scale of treason," Tyrolean said.

"Reschan is an enormous loss," Draken said. "Besides being the kingdom's trade center, it means a third of Akrasia is potentially under Ashen control in only half a Sohalia. Galbrait just told me Monoea is now headed for Algir. As soon as thaw allows, they'll set anchor in Rimeguard, collect Sikyra, and probably release more troops on us."

"They'll set a noose around Auwaer," Tyrolean said.

"Can you believe Prince Galbrait?" Geffen asked.

"I can, aye." Draken didn't offer more, though every time he met her gaze, hers skittered away. He wondered what rumors Galbrait had spread practicing his Akrasian. Perhaps that Draken could see through lies? That would be convenient.

Geffen shook her head. "My troops will rally to you, my lord. Not your sister."

He gave her a smile cold enough to chill burned meat. "She is Lord Ilumat's wife and of a rank with him. Greater rank, if Brîn still counts for anything."

"Everyone knows women are subordinate to male heirs in Brîn."

"But not so in Akrasia. Nor Monoea, if they're trying to set my daughter as Queen. And Brîn is not under her own control."

Geffen studied him, and his eyes, and shifted her attention to Aarinnaie. "You'll need an escort."

"I'll go," Osias said.

Draken turned his head, surprised.

"The Queen would have made use of me if she wanted. And I think I'm better off with the Szirin, don't you think?"

Draken nodded in relief. Osias would keep her from doing anything too foolhardy.

The next morning as the Akrasians broke camp and the troops stretched out over the grassy marches, Aarinnaie, Osias, and an Escort hand-picked by Geffen fell behind until Draken glanced back and they were no longer in view. Even should Ilumat notice in time for him to catch up, he would be hard-pressed to work out where she was going.

"Have you ever known Aarinnaie to not get her way, Captain?" Draken asked at length.

Tyrolean shook his head. "No, my lord. Never."

"Good enough, then."

Bruche chuckled mirthlessly. *As good as it's bound to get.*

CHAPTER TWENTY-EIGHT

The next evening found Draken sitting with a mismatched collection of servii around a cooking fire awaiting a meal. He toyed with Sikyra's horse, wishing he had a bit of sand to smooth the rough spot on the tail. His muscles were weary from another long day plodding along on Bumpus.

"Looks a meager meal." A servii leaned over the pot and reached for a ladle.

The cook smacked her hand away. "Aye, well, hunting wouldn't kill you."

"Naught to be found on this Grassland but Ashen," she said, backing off with a good-natured grin. They'd had a skirmish earlier that day and left the Ashens' bodies strung up on trees for carrion and a warning. That bit hadn't sat right with Draken, but he said nothing of it then or now. The Queen had given the order and even Ilumat hesitated at contradicting her during these long, hard days on the road.

Another packed an old cracked pipe with eventide and lifted his blackened eyes to her face. "Should've cut their cocks off to toss in the pot."

"It'd take a bloody lot of them to feed us," she retorted. It amused Bruche, causing even Draken to quirk a grin.

Ilumat strode to the fire and glowered down at Draken. "Where is my wife?"

It took most of Draken's will to not let his smile widen. "Hiding, I imagine, my lord. She's none too keen on marriage, if you've noticed."

"You did something *with* her."

Draken snorted. "She was wandering off for days at a time well before I came along and if you'd bothered to get to know her before you married her, you'd have realized she's not going to stop for the likes of you."

The servii had fallen silent around them.

Ilumat's pale face whitened further, his lips in a tight line. His hand found his sword, curled around the engraved hilt. Draken didn't move. Seaborn was slung on his back for ease of sitting, and he wasn't about to make so grand a gesture as reaching for it. As hot as his temper ran whenever he considered

Ilumat, as satisfying as it would be to spill his blood, Sikyra was worth staying the urge.

"You will speak to the Queen with me," Ilumat said.

Draken didn't move. "She may send for me any time she likes and I will attend her."

"Now."

Draken had a retort ready on his tongue, but Bruche silenced him. He sat still a moment longer, trying to contain the anger flaring through him. Bruche gently chilled him all over, taking subtle control. The swordhand levered him to his feet. Draken sighed and let Bruche guide him, staring at the back of Ilumat's perfectly coifed head. How in Korde's name had he managed baths on the march? He knew Elena had servants with her, but surely not Ilumat . . .

In that he was wrong. The lord had two sundry body slaves. One of them was dumping out said bathwater as they walked by. His dark eyes followed Draken.

He knows you.

Everyone seems to.

Ilumat marched right up to the Queen's tent and was admitted without a word by the guard. Draken hesitated and then followed. She was eating, but put down her knife as they entered.

"Forgive me for interrupting your meal, Your Majesty," Ilumat said with a bow.

She nodded to him but let her gaze rest on Draken. He stared back a moment before realizing she must be waiting for him to kneel, though he'd once been given dispensation not to. He lowered himself stiffly to one knee, reminded unpleasantly of his early audiences with Elena and Reavan . . . who had been Truls under glamour.

It'd be convenient if Ilumat could be proved false.

It doesn't matter. Elena isn't interested in truth. She's only interested in seeing me pay. Which he had no doubt would happen once Sikyra was found safe, and doubly so if she weren't.

Always making with the good cheer, you are. I often wish you would be more grim and cynical.

Cynicism has kept me alive this far.

My mistake. I thought it was me.

"Draken did something with my wife," Ilumat said.

"Did something?" the Queen echoed faintly. Her tone gave Draken some hope but Ilumat kept on.

"Killed her. Sent her away. I know not. I only know she is not in this camp."

Draken shook his head but a glance from Elena quelled the motion.

"You disagree? She is in camp?" Elena asked.

Draken sighed. "I do not disagree, Your Majesty. She is fair gone."

Ilumat stepped forward, just shy of stomping his boot on Elena's fine rug. "Out with it. Where is she?"

Draken kept his attention on Elena, her impenetrable mask of royalty, and tried to ignore the stone weighing his stomach. "She has her way of disappearing, this you know, and I have never controlled her."

"You deign to tell the Queen what she knows?"

"Queen Elena knows much of Aarinnaie. I daresay almost as much as I do. Certainly more than you, my lord. Of course, nearly everyone knows more of Aarinnaie than you."

"She is my wife."

Draken snorted. Bravado under Elena's dark stare. "A formality and one you hardly prepared yourself for."

"Enough." Quietly, but Elena silenced Draken.

He bowed his head, then lifted it. "She left. She fears for Reschan, my Queen. She fears for Brîn. She fears I will have no safe path to take Sikyra home, nor home to take her to."

Elena's lined eyes narrowed until they appeared shadowed from brow to cheekbone. "Her fears are misguided. You will never take Sikyra anywhere again."

"Our daughter needs me."

"Only long enough to see her safely to her mother's arms," Ilumat said. "Your usefulness will end in that moment."

"As yours ended the moment you gave Brîn to the Ashen. Never forget, Ilumat. They do not take nobility as prisoners, only the common soldier. Nobility get their throats cut."

"Then you should be safe enough in their hands when it comes to it," Ilumat retorted.

"Do not let him bait you, cousin." Elena set her knife down. The scent of fresh-cooked meat filled the tent. Draken's stomach clenched in hunger. "You spoke with Galbrait today. If he said nothing of use, I shall let Ilumat try his own methods."

Draken's jaw clenched. He'd wanted the chance to tell her alone. It was dangerous information for Ilumat to have, if he didn't already. There was nothing for it, though. Ilumat stood rooted as if his claws had unfurled from his boots to grip the very earth he stood upon.

"Algir," Draken said. "The Ashen plan to mount a new offensive there as soon as thaw allows ships to land. And the Moonlings hope to trade Sikyra there, to send her to Monoea."

"Why the Moonlings?" Ilumat asked.

Draken ignored him. "You've seen their magic, Your Majesty. You know it firsthand. It was only your quick thinking that allowed you to defeat it when they held you captive."

Reminding her of that time was a gamble, and one he lost.

"It matters not. We will march on it and put to the blade any person who dares threaten my daughter."

Draken couldn't help believing he was included in that statement.

After he was dismissed from likely for the last audience he would ever have with Elena, he went back to the fire and sat with a sigh. There was a slight lull in conversation, a few curious glances. But other than that, the servii were more interested in eating than the doings of royals. He ate his cold food and started walking the camp. Servii nodded to him, and one, rosy-faced from hacking wood, even started to salute before his compatriot pulled his arm down and whispered a few words. Draken made no acknowledgement he saw.

Is it so curious they admire you? You led many of these soldiers in the battle of Auwaer. After a long time of quiet, Bruche's low voice inside his head startled him.

I nearly fell there. He'd been captured, stabbed, and thrust into the Palisade. Galbrait and the priest Rinwar had used his healing against him to bring down the magical wall around the city. It lay there still, rubble of seeming nothingness in chunks and black dust.

But you didn't, nor did you allow Auwaer to fall. It is in Akrasian hands yet, and the Queen has you to thank whether she likes it or not.

He snorted and kept walking, wondering how his sister fared. There was no sleep for him that night, so he joined the patrols, watching with his darksight. There had been a few attacks on them, and already he saw Ilumat's fearful influence. They were guard heavy, enough to make for tired indifference late in the night and leave too many exhausted during the day marches. Draken kept circling the encampment slowly when he realized they perked up a bit at his presence. It wasn't enough, though, because Ashen slipped through as the last moon was dropping.

Draken's darksight sharpened as pitch fell over the Grassland, but it was the gurgle of a stabbed man that caught his attention. He rushed for the sound, Bruche drawing Seaborn, but the guard was blue-faced and irretrievably dead while the Ashen loped between the tents. Draken followed, bellowing an alarm. A few sleeping servii rolled from tents and rushed to defense, but there had to be a dozen or more. Shouts broke out from across the encampment, thirty tents away. Draken's heart sank. This was a multi-pronged attack.

"To the Queen!" Draken shouted even while he ran for where Galbrait slept under guard. They were already at him; Galbrait's guards fought those who would kill or rescue him. The Ashen were expertly brutal and quick with their seaxes, and had learned the less obvious weaknesses in servii armor kits. Two of his guards fell before Draken could reach them.

Draken had the advantage of a rear approach and knew his enemy's weaknesses. He slipped Seaborn between grey plates and severed muscle and, catching a rib, focused on detail rather than the broad scene. The Ashen didn't scream, but lurched free and turned to face him. Then Draken caught the trailing shadow of a bane. He snarled and slashed at the man's throat. The Ashen tumbled at his feet. The last servii standing took out the other two guards in a driven, expert move that warranted a promotion if Draken had been in a position to give one. Instead he nodded to her and ducked into the tent, bumping heads with Galbrait. Pain lashed through Draken's cheekbone, but he hauled the prince up and out by his bicep. "Move."

"Where!?"

Draken didn't answer. He didn't know. Bruche had an idea though, and directed him toward the center of camp. Toward the Queen. He stashed Galbrait in a nearby horsemarshal's tent, not daring to broach hers.

All told, three dozen enemy tried to recapture Galbrait. In the process, eight servii lost their lives. Ilumat cursed their incompetence, but Draken thought it relatively few, especially when he saw the bodies. Some dozen of the attackers were Akrasians, unarmored. He stared down at them, bile rising at the violent waste. They wore the plain clothes of farmers and traders. Nothing marked them as soldiers but their wounds. Three were captured.

The bane-riddled Akrasians had little interest in the Queen and even less in being interrogated, and yet Ilumat gave it a go in a voice pitched to keep everyone in camp awake. Draken's jaw clenched. The captive Ashen growled in their shackles like animals, trying to lunge through the trampled grasses at anyone who moved, teeth snapping. Servii milled about, trying not to look like they were watching too closely.

"Ruddy bit me, that one did," a servii nearby said. She lifted her arm to show them her ripped, bloody sleeve.

Two brawny servii held one of the snarling Akrasians down on the ground. Ilumat stepped closer. "Where is your commander? Your encampment?"

The Ashen struggled with inhuman grunts and snarls and tried to stretch and bite, but the servii held firm. Draken sighed. He knew what it felt like to be bane-ridden. There was no reason in these men. "They're bane-ridden."

"You were at Brîn during the Battle of Red Moons, my lord?" Not quite a question, but the servii with the bite looked at him expectantly.

Draken raised his brows. He hadn't heard it called that before. At length he nodded. It was no secret he'd been there when two entire armies tried to slaughter each other. Albeit his view had been limited by a particularly uncomfortable position on the ground with his arms and legs trussed. Galbrait gave him a curious look but Draken didn't explain.

"You might as well kill him," Draken said. With no Mance to release him, it was hopeless. He was too far gone.

"He is Akrasian," Ilumat said.

"He is nothing better a dead man." Draken tried to keep his voice down, but disapproving murmurs rose around him, spurred by his statement. Akrasians were nothing if not fiercely loyal to their own kind. "Kill him and have done with it."

Ilumat's nostrils flared. "No man wants to die."

"No. But these are not men any longer."

Ilumat drew his sword. Draken's fingers twitched. Was Ilumat coming after him? But the swordsman turned back to his captive and held the sword point close to the man's chin. "Tell me the answers to my questions, traitor, and I'll spare your life."

Draken's stomach turned as the black spirit flowed through the barrier of skin and then snapped back within its confines. The bane turned the Akrasian farmer's head to look at Draken, then lurched the body at Ilumat's sword point. It jammed through the man's throat without giving Ilumat time to react. Blood spurted all over the lord's fine clothes. He stepped back, breathing hard, pale under Draken's darksight. The serviis' cries of shocked dismay battered Draken.

Draken cursed and turned to go.

"Don't leave my sight. This is your fault. This is—" The rumble of excited conversation swallowed Ilumat's shouts. Draken kept walking. Ilumat and the Queen were blind in a far worse way than he. Korde would only keep attacking, a diversion that not only slowed them from catching up with the Newseason melt and Sikyra but one that brought the death and mayhem Korde desired. He glanced up at the edge of Ma'Vanni, sliding over the horizon into the deepening dark before dawn, taking her usual path with ambivalence despite all that transpired below.

CHAPTER TWENTY-NINE

The Wall of Algir had broken.

It crawled up into the cold, overcast sky, matching its greyness but for the two great rents in it, as if a godhand had torn stones out and let them crash into rubble below. From careful listening, and by Tyrolean's estimation, it wasn't recent enough to attribute to the Ashen, which left many questions. Speculation ran through the army like a bout of sour-gut from bad water. No one suggested the Moonlings. Their diminutive size had everyone fooled against their formidable power. Draken was alone in his suspicion because even Bruche disagreed.

Even from well outside the city, ocean winds swept down over the rugged, rocky steppes to the Akrasian encampment . . . the final one whence they would launch searches and attacks. They were a bit warmer, thank the gods, with signs of Newseason coming on. It had been three sevennight to drag the reluctant footsoldiers to Algir and now that he was here, his worry increased tenfold. There was no sign of Aarinnaie or his soldiers at Khein. She should have moved far quicker than Elena's army, even with the distance she had to travel. The Kheinians were all on horseback and she had promised to travel light. They should be here.

Unless they had been waylaid by attacks from the Ashen. He cursed himself for sending her and even Bruche didn't try to disagree.

Exhaustion, dwindling food supply, and increased patrol duties had the whole army on edge. As Draken walked through it the day after they arrived, taking shadowy glances through his blindfold toward the great broken city wall and castle ruins rising over the city and port, he noticed how poorly their encampment was set. Instead of customary neat rows, the tents were staked haphazardly and sometimes with makeshift poles and ropes fixed with knots.

Tyrolean walked with him and Truls drifted behind. Draken saw the ghost-Mance so often he hardly noticed him now. After the incident with the bane,

263

he had hardly slept for watching each night, and Geffen had put her distance between them. Just as well . . . she must know he was a dangerous ally to have, in more ways than one. Draken's mood turned surly and tense. This close to the city, all he wanted to do was rush in. Holding himself back for even half a day was agony.

"I need to speak with the Queen," Draken said.

Tyrolean shook his head. "Is that such a good idea, my lord?"

"My daughter is in that city. I need servii. I need to go after her—" A party riding out toward the city caught his eye. He stared at them, the riders and hills and city beyond hazed by his mask and the stinging late daylight. His strides lengthened for the Queen's tent.

He expected not to be admitted, but she allowed them. She stood quietly by her maps table, Ilumat by her side. A lantern illuminated the pale, exquisite planes of her face and her armored form.

Draken said nothing, nor did he take a knee. Tyrolean did, at Draken's side.

"It's time for me to go in and start to search, Your Majesty." Her title bit into what little calm he had left and came out clipped.

"It's already done," Ilumat said. "No need to fret."

"Lord Ilumat suggested sending a party of our best horsemarshals to the city to begin a preliminary search. A dozen just rode out. Perhaps you saw them."

Draken's jaw clenched. "I saw. What do they hope to achieve, exactly, my lord, with their swords and uniforms? Announce the search to her captors with banners and criers?"

"They will be subtle."

Draken shook his head. "The enemy will be watching for threat. We walk a precipice with her future and you send strangers . . ."

Elena flinched. Draken steeled himself against mirroring it. He had been cruel to her before, to spur action. Truls moved closer to her. She reached up and rubbed her arm, maybe feeling his ethereal chill.

Draken followed the ghost-Mance's progress rather than looking directly at Elena. "Prince Galbrait and I should go. He knows his people and their ways."

"Your people, too," Ilumat said.

Draken ignored that. "The Prince has led us here. Let him lead me the rest of the way to our daughter."

"The Queen well knows your reliance on this foreign prince, which is why she is taking my advice on finding the child," Ilumat said. "I am her Night Lord. Not you."

you go go you must attend her . . . Truls seemed to flicker, edges fluttering. Maybe it was the damned lantern.

Draken tore his attention from the insistent ghost. "I am Sikyra's father."

"Blood only. You've no rights to her," Elena said.

It was a moment before Draken could speak, before his voice sounded at all normal. "If they go into the city asking pointed questions the Moonlings will be alerted to our presence and intention."

"They've only gone to see if the ice has thawed."

Draken snorted. "A dozen horsemarshals riding into Algir on an errand better served by a lowrank servii will notify anyone paying attention—"

"The city is reportedly held by Monoea but they aren't guarding the wall. They also will approach the baron to ascertain the truth of the situation, and to seek the Princess." Elena delivered this with grudging confession.

"This is a mad plan. You should have let me go," Draken said.

"We can do far more than you alone," Ilumat said. His back was rigid, his hand solicitously resting on Elena's lower back.

Anger surged. "I'm not known in Algir. I've no rank, no connection to the royal houses, as Queen Elena has made abundantly clear. I'm—"

"A vigilante," Elena said. "You're no better than the enemy. The last thing we need. You got us here. Now back off and let us do our work in finding my daughter."

"I alone realize the true threat. You two are blind—deliberately, I assume—"

Elena's voice shook with fury. "Leave us before I bind you in the center of camp for a whipping."

"You're only threatening me because you know I'm right."

"Get out!"

Even Truls startled.

A steady hand on his back. Tyrolean.

Calming whispers in his mind. Bruche.

Draken complied without another word. He strode back for his tent. Tyrolean hurried along at his side. "What are we doing now?"

"I'm going to get my daughter."

"Do you think the Queen will allow you to leave?"

"She can't stop me and she knows it." If she whipped him in the middle of camp, his healing would send the tents tumbling and startle their horses into fleeing.

"But how do *you* know?" Tyrolean ducked under the tent flap with him and took a knee under its low roof as Draken bent for the rest of his knives and a pack. The oiled canvas blocked enough daylight that Draken could pull down his mask.

"She would have arrested me if she means to stop me," Draken said, grabbing up his last blade and strapping it on his wrist. He didn't have time to work out why she was only threatening him, not stopping him. "Fetch Galbrait, will you?"

"And if his guards challenge me?"

"Pull rank. Kill them. I don't care. We need him."

Tyrolean held a moment, but, a muscle twitching in his cheek, he ducked out.

You take advantage of him, Bruche said.

He accepts the consequences of friendship with me.

And Galbrait?

He may know where the meeting is to take place, and when. I think he hasn't been honest with me, not entirely.

What will you do with him at the end? When you find Sikyra.

Draken closed his eyes. Felt himself sway. *I'll keep my word to not kill him, and nothing more.*

By extraordinarily good timing, a couple of outriders returned to report to the Queen and Ilumat. That would keep them occupied while he rode out. In short order, Tyrolean returned with Galbrait, who walked unbound. He must have been kept in his tent since they had arrived in the dark of night because he turned his head to stare at the leftover pieces of wall jutting up into the evening fog.

"Aye. That's where we're going." Draken started walking for the horses. Tyrolean and Galbrait followed.

"You think they're there already?"

"Sikyra and Setia, aye. The Ashen, I've no idea. But Ilumat has sent in troops. I don't trust they'll pave a safe path to my daughter." He found Bumpus milling among the horses in a makeshift rope pen and slipped his bridle over his ears. The tora pony stretched his mouth wide in a grimace as the bit settled between his teeth, then tried to close them on Draken's shoulder. Draken thumped his nose and led him to the others.

"You can ride him," he said to Galbrait. "His saddle is just there. Mind his teeth."

He'd be damned if he was riding a tora pony into Algir to fetch back his daughter. By the time the first moon paled the night horizon, they were half the distance to Algir and Draken had long since removed his mask. Truls flitted alongside the party until he balked and turned his blank, soulless face toward them. Draken's blood lit with alarm.

The familiar reek of spilled blood and released bowels drifted on the air ahead. Crimson-stained green uniforms, horses tumbled, bodies sprawled. Over the massacre loomed a black shadow, stark against his darksight.

Bruche chilled, rising to the threat.

"What is it?" Galbrait, steady on the pony. He leaned forward to peer into the darkness but Draken got the idea he couldn't see anything.

Draken swallowed, his chest hollow with fear. His horse snorted and stamped, tried to turn back, away, escape. The scent of blood spooked her, perhaps. He circled her and brought her back around to face the carnage, a mindless motion that served to calm them both. His hand was already on his sword hilt.

Truls had disappeared, which confirmed what the black shadow was. "Show yourself, Korde."

"Here?" Galbrait drew up next to him. His hand moved to his side but they'd not given him a weapon. Not that ordinary weapons, maybe any weapon, could kill the god of the dead.

"Can't you feel him?"

The Prince shook his head, even as the rest of the light seemed to fade from the world. Then a flash, which made Draken drop his chin. Galbrait gasped and Tyrolean uttered a rare curse.

Draken forced his burning eyes up, watched through streaming tears as a flicker of shadow against the dim night took on the shape of a looming figure topped with leering, gruesome, asymmetrical visage. The glow was the sickening green of mossy sludge. The edges were fluid, shifting quick as river rapids. More figures took shape within the glow. Dozens, shifting and jostling for position, looking as stormy as Osias's angry eyes ever did. The glow raised up in the air at least the height of a half-dozen men.

Bumpus backed several steps, snorting and snuffling. Draken's blood chilled. Galbrait slowed the pony, still looking all around for threat.

He can't see Korde.

And Bruche only saw it through Draken. He grimaced and drew his sword. It gleamed like a soft-spoken threat. Only Khellian rose enough to see his soldier fight below, and the Warrior's Eye was a sliver.

"Tyrolean."

"My lord?"

"Hold well back. If I fall, warn Elena."

"You can't be killed."

Draken looked down at his hand where thin white scars crossed his palm. His own sword had made wounds that wouldn't heal. One of his last secrets, one Korde undoubtedly knew. The glow off the blade stung his uncovered eyes. And while Seaborn had killed two gods and he had showed bravado in talking about facing down Korde, he walked into this now with nothing but weaknesses and uncertainty.

No words now, just a chill wind shifting grasses and bones, hissing like Frost through iced sails. It whipped his cloak and caught at the flat of his sword. He reached up and unclasped the cloak, let it fall on his horse's rump. Then he slung a leg over and slid to the ground. His feet stung from the cold, his knee gave way, and he gasped, gripping his thigh in an effort to keep himself upright. The horse skittered away and Draken had to throw a foot back to not land on his arse. By the time he looked up for Korde, the greenish shadow was so near the stink of death sank into his bones and his blood froze in his veins. Bruche lifted Seaborn but it felt ineffectual and small. The fluctuating form of the god resonated through Draken's darksight and made his stomach turn. With it came stinking winds. He retched, falling to his hands and knees in the dirt.

Of course the god of death would know how to turn magical gifts of life against him.

That wasn't his only trick. Korde's wind tugged at this clothes and swept around the scene of death. Bones trembled along the ground, scattering and reforming. *Rising.* Wrong shapes . . . but still they rose lopsided and clanking. Fingerbones gripped hilts of the weapons they'd wielded in life.

What binds them?

Necromancy. The bastard god has made a dead army.

A dead army, aye, but one he'd have to fight through. In perfect tandem he and Bruche lurched forward, thrusting with body and blade. The bones tore his skin and the fog of necromancy bruised Bruche, but slashes of Akhen Khel scattered them. Bruche's control fluctuated. A thigh bone flew through Korde. The god stilled as if wounded. Draken was under no illusions what they'd do to himself. He already bled from a half dozen cuts; the ground already trembled with his healing. He feared the bones, should they make a mortal wound, could tear a hole in Bruche's consciousness.

Agony stabbed through him at the thought. Full of battle-rage and terror, he hadn't realized how badly the bones injured him. Percussions of healing exploded from him. He squinted in surprise as violent waves rippled through the bones and the very air. They shattered to bits, and the bits shattered to harmless dust, floating out in concentric waves.

There go your only weapons.

He drew his head up to glare at the god. He growled and rushed forward. Nothing held him now, no bones or grave dust or fear. He slashed at Korde, who didn't seem to move, didn't seem to notice Draken was suddenly in front of him until his sword sliced his leg in two.

Except it didn't. It made Korde's form waver slightly, as if the breeze had caught at his smoky form. Draken swung again and again. None of the extra figures, the spirits that made up the god, fell. They just kept shifting. Korde reached down with a great hand and pierced Draken. Squeezed. Pulled. He shuddered and gasped, trying to grab and cut at the god's arm. His hand and sword went right through it.

His darksight squeezed like his heart, the world narrowing to a grey pinprick. He made noise—he must have, a guttural cry devoid of enough breath to make it carry far—

He could feel Bruche separating from inside his soul. Korde was tearing him away and Bruche could do nothing but scream. Someone shook the ground. Fresh agony pierced him. Gods, his body was trying to heal itself even as Korde ripped his heart from his chest—*Bruche? Bruche!*

The healing seemed to reject the god's attack. The hand withdrew from his body. But an icy grip on the back of his neck, ethereal fingers winding round his throat. "No!" he husked out the word and lashed out, haphazard with his sword.

It slashed through trailing black edges like a broom sweeping through fine ash. The god barely moved, didn't laugh or make a sound. Again Draken slashed. Instead of cutting the black mass apart, the god started to take shape, to bind himself together into something resembling a human, something familiar. Draken's mind clawed for whatever Korde reminded him of. It seemed important. But the memory hid itself.

Korde's other arm . . . it was in the right place if not quite the right shape . . . swung through him. It ran through Draken like an icy sluice of sea water, clogging lungs, stealing his air. He yawned for breath, throat desperate to swallow, lungs tight and empty. Nothing. Nothing.

Ethereal laughter ran through him like shards of metal, the glint of a thousand deaths amid his grasping for life. Despair filled him, but he cut through it like a drowning man splashing at roiling sea for a raft. He gasped for breath and none came.

A piercing scream reverberated through him, shaking the ground, the air, more than any of his healing had ever done. The pressure on his throat released but a great flash blinded Draken, twin daggers of pain from his eyes straight through his skull. He fell back, his sword clattering to his side, and the world closed in tight.

CHAPTER THIRTY

Arumbling shudder ran through him, dragging him back from darkness. And voices. Several frantic, one demanding. Bruche's low, deep inside, weak. Gradually Draken's hurts made themselves known as well as the spirithand's. He drew a breath. Coughed and curled up on his side. He felt like his skin had been scraped off his bones, as if pokers filled his gut. Bruche; the recollection of death come upon him. Gods, no. They had flayed him alive with Seaborn, tortured him for his loyalty to Brîn. It had happened again just now, and even so, Bruche had refused to leave him.

Be easy. Rest. Draken soothing Bruche for once. Gradually he lay flat, letting his spine settle back into place. Beneath his back the ground thudded with what sounded like a thousand hooves and boots. Beyond, those voices, more insistent by the breath. He couldn't be bothered to open his eyes. It all felt very distant, until a hand shook his chest, right over his heart.

"Drae? Draken. There you are!" The voice was soft, almost a whisper.

Draken flinched and pried open his eyes. "Aarin . . ." A wet gasp.

"Stay. Rest." She crouched on her heels next to him, a fighting knife in one hand, her other still shaking him. The shaking ached all the way through him to his back. No. Not quite right. The hooves shuddering the ground, shadows against his darksight, and overhead, stinging Khellian rose to fully examine his failure. Korde he didn't see, but he still smelled the rot and decay, still trembled from him near. The Eyes glowered down at him, storming the skies and drawing the wind.

A deep rumble joined the cacophony. A Voice. Words he didn't know, some language he might have heard before but couldn't fathom. Bruche shoved the name into his mind. "Osias."

"Aye." Aarinnaie turned her head. White fire seemed to glint deep in her dark blue eyes. She squinted and lifted her arm to her brow. "He was. I don't know what he is now."

Draken summoned his strength from some forgotten cavern of will and pushed to a sit. Something white and glowing stung his darksight. He ducked his chin and fumbled for his mask where it hung around his neck. And stared through the mesh, tears streaming at the sting.

Overhead the skies roiled with brilliant stinging colors, streaming and banking across the entire sky. Draken pointed but Aarinnaie didn't see. She had her chin tucked to her chest, eyes closed.

Within the white flame he made out a slender figure, silvery white, robes and long hair wavering within the brightness. The sting in his eyes lessened as his mind started to catch up with what he saw, and he pulled the mask down. A thousand eyes took shape within the glow, drifting around the central figure like moths to a flame. Gradually Draken found he could let the glow fill his darksight. The world took on edges, still cast in greys but sharper than before. Shadows materialized into shapes. Rows of soldiers . . . *his* soldiers . . . uniforms he recognized. Kheinian bows and swords, Brînians, even braided Gadye, all on their knees before the glowing figure. Hundreds strong. The Eyes and the new harsh light glittered off chains of rank and caste.

And then the memory, the familiarity struck Draken. Korde had made the Mance in his own image.

And Osias had remade himself into Korde.

Aarinnaie gasped. "Your eyes."

"What of them?" His voice was hoarse.

"They're silver . . . like a seashell."

Tyrolean stared. "Iridescent."

Osias. He swallowed hard and struggled to stand.

Aarinnaie took his arm and Tyrolean caught his other. Together they lifted Draken and helped him limp forward past the army of bowed heads and bodies. His body was stiff and battered, muscles moving like tough sinew under his skin. But he found the more he looked into the white fire that Osias had become, the easier he could bear it.

Bruche reached for the figure, pulling him along, drawn to Osias. Draken felt it, too; the dead god strengthening the dead. Truls drew near, glowing, too. Everyone living kept their heads ducked down, arms over their heads, eyes closed.

"You . . . how . . . ?" Draken stammered to a stop. His throat was very dry.

RITUAL, AS WITH BRUCHE. SIMPLE, REALLY.

Necromancy. Simple. Draken bowed his head, shook it. Osias sounded much the same . . . and not. "What now?"

FETCH YOUR DAUGHTER. The fiery form lifted his head toward the sky. *AND I WILL FETCH MINE.*

"Your daughter? Osias . . . Damn you. Talk sense."

ELNA YET LEADS THE MOONLINGS ASTRAY.

Draken blinked. He had never paid attention to the gods' family tree, never thought it mattered. Gradually his confusion cleared and the truth emerged. The last rebel god, working unknown to him. Draken felt very stupid, and very, very weary.

Truls disappeared into Osias's light. The other dead Mance did as well. And banes . . . all drawn to him. Draken watched the blurs of raw power speed through the air toward their new god. Osias absorbed them and grew brighter.

"Damn you, Osias. It wasn't supposed to be this way. What of Setia?"

Draken found he was able to pick out pale eyes within the bright form. Peaceful eyes, no storm. Just light. *SEEK HER. WE WILL SEE EACH OTHER AGAIN.*

A silvery, fiery arm reached toward Draken. He steeled himself against shying away. This was his friend. His good friend. Perhaps the best he'd ever known.

Osias's hand was warm as it took his. Solid. Draken met those eyes, startled, and felt the thousand souls staring back at him. Despite it all, Osias's beautiful face was at peace. The last of the wind whooshed upward. The sky cleared to let Khellian shine down, clear and pure, untainted with hatred and blood. The moon-storms were gone.

A breath later, so was Osias.

◆ ◆ ◆

It took until daybreak to reorganize the troops to march on the city. Stricken by the transformation of Mance into god, they milled about until Aarinnaie and Draken took them under firm hand. His horse had fled along with many others. The tora ponies remained, including Osias's mount, a squat, solid mare. Draken reluctantly took Bumpus back, who greeted him with bared teeth.

"How long until they start tattooing themselves with Osias's moon and painting their skin silver?" Draken asked Tyrolean.

"Doubtless as soon as this business in Algir is done," Tyrolean answered.

"And you, Ty?"

"I rely on all the gods, my lord. And their chosen defender." A grin quirked his lips.

Draken snorted. "I didn't do much but almost get killed by Korde. Osias did all the heavy lifting."

"Do not underestimate the distraction of your death. I watched what happened. Korde didn't mean to kill you, he meant to enthrall you. But I think he couldn't enter your skin and stay. Whatever magic the other gods have given you, it repelled him."

"I feel like I was run over by a thousand horses."

"The healing was terrifically violent. But you didn't wake. Korde fair feared your death, so much he ignored the rest of us, even the army marching on him. It was then Osias was able to attack."

"Why would he fear my death?"

"I think not even he would go against the Warrior-God and the Mother. Perhaps he was realizing the fight was done."

"But ours is not."

"No, my lord."

Draken spent the rest of the ride deep in thought until they broached the broken wall. Ashen guards stood bravely at the gates but Aarinnaie had them cut down without quarter. Galbrait protested and Draken silenced him with a glare.

He had never seen so much as a painting of Algir and nothing prepared him for the cold, sprawling filth that was the second busiest port in Akrasia. It was all hard lines and dim greys, streets teeming with hardened indifference, even to the hundreds in Draken's new army. People simply gave them wide berth and carried on.

The custom of tattooing the eyes was less prevalent here, or maybe it was a more sundry population. The usually pale, smooth Akrasian skin was reddened and rough, lips cracked and eyes lined with deep wrinkles rather than the black tattoos.

Monoea had to split the difference between Brîn and Algir on its approach to Akrasia, and ships usually chose Brîn with its closer access to the more populated parts of the country and longer port season. After days of plodding along on Bumpus, Draken could see why. Not only was the overland distance a hardship, but the Grassland was rife with wind, rain, and mud to plod through. He couldn't imagine travelling all that distance in a caravan of goods.

"Unlikely we'd see ships in the Rineguard Straits as of yet," Tyrolean assured him, snugging his cloak round himself closer. "I expect we will find yet an iced-in port."

Draken rubbed his hand over his face, bristly with fresh beard and chilled without the mask. The iridescence in his eyes shielded him from the light of day. He picked out the sun glaring through a thin spot in the clouds, gazed up at it for a long moment, and returned his attention to the scene around him with no halo on his vision, no spots. Just clarity.

While organizing the troops after Osias left them, Aarinnaie must have warned them about his eyes because the servii and others carefully didn't stare.

She kept quiet command of them and he left her to it. He drew up as they rode, not by her, but by Galbrait.

The Monoean Prince had grown a scraggly, thin beard while in captivity. Draken wondered that he hadn't noticed. He only knew the Prince had been shaven before, a young man's face kept smooth for courting, in Monoea where he'd welcomed Draken as emissary. The pale ruff softened his features and its sparseness made him look even younger.

"Where are they meeting? Where are they taking my daughter? It is time to tell all, Galbrait."

"And if I do not?"

Draken was tired, so weary of talking. He drew Seaborn. "Speak now or scream for a sevennight."

"She isn't what they say. She isn't important like they say—" A flick of the sword cut off his words, sliced his bottom lip. Blood welled. Bruche was that good, and despite his name, Bumpus's plodding stride was smooth.

"She is my daughter. Right now that makes her extremely important to you."

"At the flame tower."

For a brief, soul-freezing breath, Draken thought he meant the tower at Sea-keep. But he realized he had not studied Algir much beyond the broken wall, its harried, chill-bitten people, or the keep rising on the hill, an indulgence of long-ago wealth on the flat coastline. The tower rose as high as the keep from this vantage, yet it was further away through the city. Blackened stones climbed into the sky, its flame lonely and thin against the grey skies. The sight struck him as odd. Important, somehow. He was surprised he hadn't noticed it before.

"There is no way to take all these soldiers inside," Galbrait said. "It's walled . . . a small courtyard. A flame tower. Nothing else."

Draken narrowed his eyes. Anything Galbrait said could be a lie at this point. Or means to entrap him. "How do you know?"

"The priest Rinwar told me. It's not meant to hold more than a dozen people at once. They might not even be there anymore." Galbrait was already trying to talk him out of it.

"Or they might not have arrived there yet. We shall see."

A rearguard trotted alongside Draken, turning his head, maybe looking for Aarinnaie. Before he could press ahead, Draken asked him, "What is it?"

The rider frowned at him, his brows drawn in. Bruche held Draken's impatient tongue for him. He must have recalled Draken had recently been his commander. "Troops behind, my lord. I need to find Princess Aarinnaie."

"Troops . . . Ours? The Queen's?"

"Led by Lord Ilumat, my lord."

"Go back and watch them for us. Report when they breach the city." He spurred his horse ahead to his sister. "Your husband rides behind us."

She twisted back to look then frowned. "Won't be much help, that one."

"Worse than that. I fear he'll try to stop us. Will you stall him? I'll ride ahead."

"With who? You need me."

"I have Tyrolean and Galbrait."

"Three against—"

"No more than a dozen. Galbrait said the firetower is small."

"And you believe him?"

He held a moment before speaking. "I've nothing left but to trust him, Aarin."

"You need me."

Draken had a bad feeling things would coalesce here in Algir, in this strange grey city of icy cobbles and apathetic faces. "These men need you. Algir needs you. We don't know where things stand with the Ashen, how many ships will come. They could raze this city in a day if they have three ships worth of men. Right now we only have these servii and the others you brought to defend her."

"And you need time."

"Aye, to fetch Sikyra. I'll get her and ride hard for the Queen. Meet me at her encampment. We can turn the troops back over to her command there."

"You mean to return Kyra . . . Draken. No."

Bruche hushed him with a deep rumble. He couldn't answer, couldn't start that argument, or take Aarinnaie's side or lie his way through. He could only pretend she hadn't spoken. "After, we'll sort what to do about Ilumat. I won't let you languish with him."

She scowled. "I can take care of my own problems."

He gave her a grim smile. "I know you can. I'm proud of you. If I haven't said it before."

She cleared her throat. "Don't start now."

"To the Queen, then, as soon as you are able."

A long breath passed. Another. She turned her head forward and gave a crisp nod.

Draken didn't have to gesture to Tyrolean or Galbrait as he rode ahead. They both emerged from the lines of servii to join him. The firetower was close enough he imagined he could smell the wood burning, the smoke rising off great flames alerting ships to shore.

And it struck him.

The fire burned.

Why would it bloody burn if there were no ships coming?

He kicked his horse into a gallop.

◆ ◆ ◆

City planners must have been at work here early in the creation of Algir. The streets ran blessedly straight. Too straight, with few cross roads for block after block. The one he took led them askew from the tower. At this rate he'd have to ride straight for the harbor and take his chances with hordes of landing Ashen.

"Here." Tyrolean gestured to an alleyway that ended up something more like two roads over, but it looked closer to a direct shot at the tower. They trotted on, the ponies surefooted over the road cobbles. When this was done, if he survived, he'd retire Bumpus, bad attitude and all.

"You'll live the life of a king, mate." He patted the pony, who flattened his ears.

Galbrait snorted softly.

He considered checking further on at the port first, to see if thaw had actually allowed ships in. "You're certain the meet happens here?" he said to Galbrait.

"Dead certain."

Oh, he'd be dead all right, if he weren't. Still, the tower seemed too quiet. No guards at the gate. Draken frowned and dismounted. Bumpus had his strengths but carrying him into battle wasn't one of them. Tyrolean moved ahead of him and creaked one open. All three of them froze. Draken's back itched with alarm. But all remained quiet within.

I don't like it.

The lack of guards? Bruche gave an inward shrug. *Maybe not so odd. It is just a firetower and the port is quiet this season.*

There should be people here. Moonlings. Monoeans. If they are exchanging the princess shouldn't there be guards around her?

Maybe it's a small operation. Less attention drawn can mean less risk.

Draken grimaced. He didn't like it. He didn't like any of it. His daughter should be surrounded. Ashen should have materialized the moment they approached the gate. Moonlings should linger at least. They had much to gain from the exchange. Land and autonomy.

Unless they had already been there, and used the Abeyance to escape.

They would have killed or captured you were it so.

Galbrait had spoken truth. The courtyard was really only big enough for a few horses and men, with two open stalls to his offhand. The tower rose stark and steep on his swordhand. The wooden door hung open. Odd with Newseason just coming on, though the wall cut most of the bitter sea winds. Draken pushed his cloak hood back down and peered upward for movement or light. Nothing. No arrows in the slits, no candlelight glimmering between shutters. Certainly no child's lonely cry. Hooves beat the ground outside the tower gates. He turned, listening. Several riders ran by. His darksight caught flashes of green against the night. He cursed low. "Horsemarshals."

"We knew they were coming." There were very few times Tyrolean, a First Captain in said army, referred to his own army as "they." The words dropped a block of ice into Draken's gut. They were so few against two armies who wanted them dead. Even if Aarinnaie managed to keep command of the Kheinian troops, they might flee back to the Queen at their first chance. He could hardly blame them.

"Bar those gates, Galbrait." Draken strode ahead, Seaborn gleaming in his hand. He didn't recall drawing it. Bruche then, working in smooth tandem with him, wordless.

You're welcome, mate.

Draken shoved the door open to find exactly what he expected: nothing. He swore in all three of his languages. Tyrolean strode about and returned to his side, pale face carved into hard planes of frustration. Galbrait was already backing away from Draken.

"You lied. She isn't here. She was never bloody here."

"They told me. Korde himself told me . . ." Galbrait stopped. Realized his mistake.

"Korde lied to you," Tyrolean said.

Draken ran for Bumpus and threw himself on his back, gathering up his reins. Galbrait and Tyrolean barely swung aboard their own mounts to follow before he'd put the gate behind him. Bumpus laid his ears back at Draken's kicks, but he broke into a gallop, a real gallop. Draken recalled little of the ride back, flashes of building and road, the great broken wall rising ahead, the rolling gait of the pony.

Movement around him stopped. All sound faded, leaving a silent pressured void. Everything lost its sharp edges. He kicked Bumpus on, not questioning why the pony still ran. And then he was through the gates and the chaotic world swept back over him, voices and his pony's hooves and his own heartbeat.

His Kheinian troops were there, gathered around the jagged break as if to protect it. And he realized they were protecting it; they'd known but couldn't reach him in time. Aarinnaie bolted toward him on foot and looked up, her hand on Bumpus's neck. The pony didn't so much as flinch.

"I kept Ilumat out. But Moonlings." She was gasping with breath. He couldn't stop to think why. "Taking Kyra . . . We stopped. The world stopped."

"The Abeyance. The Moonlings used it against us." Draken picked out every detail in that moment. Every useless facet of his surroundings that could never lead him to his daughter. Someone among his troops coughed. Colors: green of the Akrasians, a red scrape on Aarin's brow, the faint glow of Seaborn still in his hand, an endless field separating him from his daughter. Bumpus snorted and tossed his mane, shaking off Aarinnaie's touch.

They ran.

Moonlings filled the small downturn in the land, not really a valley, but enough to diminish their stature. They were backed by thousands of grey forms, spreading out across the edges of the Grassland. All was eerily quiet until a baby cried.

Heart twisting, Draken kept on Bumpus to walk through the Ashen and then the Moonlings. They parted before him as crowds had before. *Why* chilled him. Sikyra was lost. There was no reason to fight a defeated man. All that was left was his walk to death.

Akrasians in green made a demarcation line beyond, bared swords holding back the Moonlings and Ashen, centered on Elena. Ilumat stood amid the Moonlings, holding something. . . someone . . . in his arms. A small, sturdy figure shadowed him. Curls laced with silver. Setia, alive. Draken should have taken some ease from the sight. Instead his shoulders tightened.

Bumpus carried Draken closer, his stride unfaltering and quick, for him. "Elena, don't trust him."

He heard her intake of breath. It wasn't from his words. Elena stared at her her . . . their . . . daughter. So many moonturns since Elena had put their infant into his arms, long enough Sikyra had learned to walk, could utter words. Her crying died and she tried to twist, to see him. She'd heard her father's voice.

Draken dismounted, drew Seaborn, and strode toward Ilumat. There was no other way this could end but in Ilumat's death. Escorts moved in his way, lined eyes narrowed, blades drawn. "Elena! You can't trust him! Take her."

Her eyes flicked to him.

"Don't be ridiculous. I'm taking the child to her." But Ilumat wasn't moving.

It wasn't entirely his fault. Ashen surrounded them on all sides, pressing against them, shifting Draken back. He cursed and Seaborn flared, but it was so tight the mob couldn't move. In that moment of distraction, more cries rose up from behind him, from the city. *"Il Vanni masacr." "Il Vanni masacr." "Il Vanni masacr."* The godless die.

Sikyra's round face popped up over Ilumat's armored shoulder. A pudgy arm and little hand reached out for him. She squealed for him, a desperate sound.

All these moonturns. Sevennight after sevennight of emptiness, of stinging sun and jagged shadows, of empty words and pleas, of blood, and that one sound made his heart fill. It slowed his blade.

"I'll take her to safety!" Ilumat cried to Elena, moving away from Draken, deeper into the crowd of Escorts protecting them from the Ashen. "Go with your guards!"

"No!" Draken struggled against the wall of Escorts. They slashed but he broke through. The ground rumbled only slightly; their cuts hadn't amounted to much. He snarled and spun, his sword out to warn them back. But he had no time. Ilumat was moving faster, away, not toward Elena but through the Escorts to the Ashen. Draken's darksight picked out the priest Rinwar—a bent figure in robes. Draken wondered in a flash if he realized his god was dead. Korde was dead. Long live Osias. The bloody war was won, but not this final battle. Draken used his bulk to shove through, holding his sword up. Escorts backed away as it lit, distracting Rinwar. He was almost close enough to Ilumat to kill him, to take his daughter back.

Someone shouted Ilumat's name from behind Draken. He didn't look, but used the opportunity to strike. Ilumat spun, his own blade in his free hand. The motion jolted Sikyra and she gave a sharp, frightened cry, big eyes following Draken's blade as it came down. Elena screamed. Seaborn stopped a handspan from his daughter's face, trembling. Khellian's light flickered along its flat. His arm was so cold he was numb all the way through his chest.

Bruche. Draken gasped in relief.

Sikyra squirmed, shoving with her little hands against her captor's shoulder. Ilumat's arm tightened around her. She squalled and kicked. "Fa!"

"Release her," Draken came forward a step but stopped as Ilumat's sword edge neared his daughter.

"Ilumat!" Elena, panicked.

"I'm trying to bring her to you," Ilumat said. "This sundry is trying to steal your daughter."

Draken growled. "I can't steal what's already mine."

Elena came closer, pushing through her guards, her arms out. "Give her to me, Ilumat."

Ilumat snarled, backing a step, the Moonlings clearing for him. His blade neared Sikyra's little wriggling body. She shrieked for Draken. The war cries faltered, silence spreading outward from those who could see what was happening in the tight little clearing of Escorts and Ashen, though tussling and fighting was breaking out further out in the crowd. Rinwar shouted Ilumat's name, but now desperation tinged his voice.

Elena's face hardened. Grief and the confusion of war and her fury with Draken had surely blinded her to Ilumat's lies and betrayal, but whatever fading trust she might have clung to vanished. Her hand closed around the sword at her hip. She was in no better position than Draken was, couldn't get to Ilumat before he could disappear into the Ashen, and he could use Sikyra as a shield. But she didn't move. Instead she cried out: "Tyrolean!"

It was then Draken realized Tyrolean hadn't stopped moving, shoving through Escorts and Ashen alike, coming from behind Ilumat. He whipped his twin blades from their scabbards on his back, ducked through the crowd and struck, slipping one of his thin blades between Ilumat's plate and kilt, stabbing straight through to the kidney, and then deeper, twisting the blade with a grunt. Then he shoved back and swung low with the other blade, sharp Gadye steel slashing the fine leather boots, hamstringing Ilumat.

The world seemed to halt, broken by a guttural, astonished grunt. Ilumat twisted his pale face toward Draken as he stumbled to his knees. Sikyra cried out, leaning for Draken. He lunged forward to catch her with his free arm, grabbing her up from Ilumat's failing grip. She cried out again and her tiny fists clutched at his shirt. He pulled her up to his chest with one arm, warning away the others surrounding them with Seaborn. Ilumat toppled to his side, screaming until he had no breath.

Sikyra's face pressed against the join between Draken's shoulder and throat. No one was coming at him and all he could think of was the tiny body in his arms. He dropped Seaborn and his arms tightened around her, his fingers cupped the back of her head. He pressed his face to her hair. "I have you, Kyra. I have you."

Ilumat moaned at his feet. Aarinnaie shoved forward, brandishing a knife.

"He's already dead, Aarinnaie." Tyrolean caught her and pulled her back. He bent his head to hers and whispered something. She struggled only a moment before relaxing against him.

Draken backed away, still holding Sikyra. At last he kissed her hair and lifted his head. There were noises of fighting, scuffles breaking the line between Akrasians and Monoeans, but it all soon faded again.

The Moonlings made no sound as they watched, but the world faltered into Abeyance. Sikyra froze in his arms, feeling featherlight, insubstantial. Draken grimaced. The Moonling's power of the Abeyance. He tried to shake his daughter, but knew it was for naught. He stared around desperately. The Moonlings could kill or take anyone in the Abeyance. It was when he heard Setia's voice he realized: the Moonlings weren't moving either.

"It's all right." Setia ran at the Moonlings as fast as her legs could carry her.

Everything wavered again, making Draken's stomach flip. She bore no weapon in her outstretched hands but power flowed, a light emanating from her. Weaker than Osias but the same sort of silvery light. In concentric circles the world took a breath and came back to life. The circle of Abeyance spiraled on Setia, now standing among the Moonlings. None of the tribe moved, held prisoner between place and time. The rest of the crowd shifted back into movement and life. Amazement at the frozen Moonlings spread through the soldiers and servii.

Draken raised his voice. If he spoke now he'd put off the inevitable. He purposefully didn't look at Elena. "Aarinnaie, chain the Moonlings and take care to do it well."

She was still staring at Ilumat sprawled on the ground. The white chain with Elena's pendant had twisted around his neck as he had writhed in the mud. Blood had poured from him, but he lay still. She pulled free of Tyrolean. Her voice shook but she nodded. "Aye, Khel Szi."

"Tyrolean, see to these Ashen, will you?"

"Aye, Your Highness."

Tyrolean called out a command. All around them, Escorts and servii moved. More space was made. Draken knew he should fear some trick, but he trusted the Akrasians were as sick of the foreign invaders as he was. At last he turned toward Elena.

Elena stared at him, face inscrutable. She held out her sword, pointed at the ground. A servii took it. Escorts closed around her and Draken, stepping over Ilumat, where his lifeless body lay limp nearby, his mouth open, eyes staring. "Don't speak of Ilumat. He is dead. Don't let his life and mistakes make more trouble for you. Leave that bit to me."

"You're commanding me?"

"Advising you. Offering help." Draken swallowed hard, remembering her as she wielded a sword against Monoeans when she was pregnant with Sikyra. How had he ever doubted her? "This was very well done, my Queen."

She stared at him, right in his eyes, as she hadn't done since they'd first seen one another again. A marginal nod. Then her gaze dropped to Sikyra and there was no more putting it off.

Draken reached down in the pouch at his belt and pulled out Sikyra's horse. A couple of Escorts raised their swords. Draken showed them and then gave it to his daughter. She chortled, smiling into his eyes. One of her hands clutched the horse, the other tangled in his sleeve. A leather band tightened around his chest as Elena stepped closer. He had to force himself to hold his ground, though every instinct told him to take his daughter and run.

His scarred hand closed over her tiny perfect one, pried it from his arm. "Easy, love."

Elena was close now, close enough to take her.

He kissed her curls. "That's it. Your mumma is here." He pulled Sikyra's grip free and gave her to Elena. Sikyra turned to look at him, panicked, eyes wild.

"Sh." He rubbed her arm, the one clutching the horse. His fingertips brushed hers. The band tightened. "Sh. I've much to do. Go on now."

Sikyra looked up at her mother, studying her face the quiet way Elena studied most things new to her. Her face crumpled and she tried to push away from Elena. "Fa!"

Draken stepped back because if he didn't he would snatch Sikyra back and die for it. As badly as he craved the release of death, he craved his daughter's well-being more. He couldn't let her watch him die.

"Take her away." His voice was rough. He cleared his throat. "She doesn't belong here; nor do you. I'll mop up this mess, if you'll allow it, Your Majesty."

Wasn't that what he'd been doing all along? Mopping up? Ever since he was a child slave scrubbing steps dirtied by royal boots.

Elena patted Sikyra's back ineffectually. "And then?"

He bent to pick up his sword. "And then I'll take back Brîn."

It was the best he could hope for. He strode away, Sikyra's cries puncturing great holes in his heart no magic could heal.

CHAPTER THIRTY-ONE

All around them servii and the few Brînians were taking the Ashen captive. Draken heard them invoking his name to do it. He didn't care. Whatever worked.

Draken ignored them and walked through to his sister. The horsemarshal she was speaking to snapped to attention. She turned, brows raised. "Sikyra?"

"With her mother."

"Draken, no."

"You have my condolences on the death of your husband."

Her lips parted, then shut.

"If you're finished grieving, will you fetch Galbrait?"

Her brows climbed. "Aye, my lord. Or are you Your Highness again?"

"Khel Szi. Bring the Prince to me."

A smile quirked the corner of her mouth and she ran off to do his bidding, body slight but fleet through the hardened soldiers. Many of the Ashen looked mystified, or they craned their necks to see him even as the servii and horsemarshals herded them into tight groups at sword- and bow-point. Others spat in his direction, betrayed by the image created by his betters, hating him for taking command of them. Draken shook his head, wondering what they had been told of him and wondering if he should be glad he didn't know too many details. Too many people lost this day. Half his blood-comrades, gone. Alive, after a fashion, but lost. Bruche rumbled his agreement, feeling Sikyra's absence keenly alongside Draken.

Aarinnaie came back, dragging Galbrait by the elbow. Draken studied him. The Prince faltered, leaned back a little. He still had the instinct to run. It hung on him like a thick mantle.

"You are the rightful King of Monoea."

Galbrait's wry humor faltered. "So I am told."

"These men need their King."

His face darkened. "They're traitors."

"Aye. As their King, and from your actions, you are a hostile invader in Akrasia. I should put you to the sword. But because of our familial blood, I am willing to make terms."

Galbrait blinked at him. He rubbed his hands on his thighs. "What terms?"

"All may leave freely from Algir to Monoea by your will and mine, except for nobles and commanders who you will execute as traitors and our prisoners of war. I trust these terms are acceptable."

Galbrait's brows twisted. "They are . . ."

"Fair generous," Draken supplied.

"Yes. Why?"

"Because it's much more valuable for Akrasia to have a strong King on the Monoean throne than a dead one at my feet." Gods, he hoped he was doing the right thing. The lad was green as Newseason buds.

The nobles and commanders were culled by Galbrait and brought to Draken personally. All in all he made Galbrait execute forty men in front of the other Monoeans. There were more in Akrasia, but Elena had troops to deal with them. Rinwar was last, staring up at him with a hard face marred with ash and bruises.

"You are the savior of magic and chosen of the gods," he said.

"And you are a ruddy fool." He soon was a dead one. Draken had the bodies carted to the sea.

The next exhausting day was spent sorting the injured from the able-bodied, and the enlisted servii from the previously baneridden and sending them back to their stationings and homes, if their homes even existed anymore. Geffen took command of her troops back from Aarinnaie.

Tyrolean offered to take the Moonlings to Auwaer. Draken exchanged grips with him and let him go, not knowing whether he would ever see him again. "You deserve better than serving a rough prince of a decrepit, defeated coastal city full of pirates."

"Aye, Your Highness." A smile quirked Tyrolean's lips. He bid Aarinnaie goodbye with a stiff bow.

She put her fists on her hips. "Ilumat was my kill."

Tyrolean lifted his chin. "And yet he was mine, as well, Princess."

She scowled but, wonder of wonders, she didn't snap back at him.

Tyrolean glanced at Draken, who suppressed a smile and gave him a nod. Aarinnaie stood for a long time, watching him disappear downland into the greening Grassland with his prisoners.

I expect we'll see him again soon enough.

Draken ordered a horse the next morning, and went to the paddock to collect her, a fine mare. Bumpus munched new grass with the others. "Make sure he comes along and is treated well."

The servii nodded, his confusion plain. He moved a little closer to the ugly pony, who snapped at him. "I'll, er, see to it, Your Highness."

"I am called Khel Szi."

Aarinnaie was waiting for him at the tent they'd taken over. He finished throwing things in his pack and checked that his blade was loose in its sheath, not really paying attention to her.

"I came here by Reschan." She lowered her head, then lifted it, back straight.

That got his attention. "A fair distance out of your way from Khein. Why?"

"To pave the way for you when you came home to Brîn, like I said. It took some doing, but—"

"Doing? Doing what?"

"Fighting. Killing enemy. We gave them a chase . . . or thought we did."

"Instead you just followed them here. Aarinnaie, I spent two sevennight wondering where you were. I thought you were killed or worse."

"Worse than killed?"

He gave her a look. "You do seem to attract banes."

"There are no more banes."

Exasperated: "But there were then!"

She shrugged. "Right. Well. Now you know. And now you can ride hard for Brîn, aye?"

"Why are you only telling me now?"

"I knew you'd be annoyed so I put it off."

He groaned and looked at Setia. She smiled at him.

With the weather fair clear and shed of the Kheinian servii, they were able to make good time. The few breaths Draken had held Sikyra in his arms should have faded into almost a dream. Instead the memory became sharp as a dagger that stabbed deep whenever his mind wasn't filled with logistics, fighting, feeding and leading his meager group of Brînians home. He had no idea what he'd do if he had to rout the Monoeans from Brîn and passed most of the trip worrying about that. At night though, the memories of his daughter's voice and soft hands plagued him. He told himself she would be safe and happy with Elena. Raised up a proper Princess. All to no avail.

◆ ◆ ◆

The gates of Brîn were open the morning they arrived and they were taken into quiet custody with no questions asked or answered. He found himself looking for Comhanar Vannis, though he knew the man was long dead from the Akrasian coup. He sat on a bench where directed, quieted Aarinnaie's protests, and leaned on his knees, bent in fresh, surprising grief. A small hand found his: Setia's.

They were given soldiers who took them straight to the Citadel.

The city displayed the same dichotomy. Same worn edges and rusted gilt, but battle scars from artillery marked buildings and military traffic had dug unrepaired ruts into the cobbled roadways. In the first market square they passed, several gallows at the far end hung with the dead. He stopped his horse to study the scene.

"Ashen and Akrasians and traitors," the guard said.

"Aye, I see."

When Draken turned his iridescent eyes on him, the Comhanar swallowed audibly but held his ground. It must have been more than just well-honed courtesy. Rumors of the Khel Szi's odd eyes had made it to Brîn.

The Citadel walls were clean of heads and blood. It was quiet, the same as before, as if hundreds of people hadn't died here.

"Lord Khisson will see you now," the guard said when he recovered from his shock.

At least Khisson wasn't calling himself Khel Szi. But then, the guard didn't call Draken by that name either.

He hesitated on the steps, and Aarinnaie stiffened next to him. The dead were hard on his mind. But well-trained servants bowed their way into the domed great hall. No one was present. Draken released a breath and gazed up at the familiar designs, the colorful tiled floor, the dais with the throne and the table of honor draped and ready to receive Akhen Khel, its resting place when not in use. The only aberration was a smaller chair placed beside the throne. It looked well-made, ornate, and newly painted. The colors were bright and rich next to the faded, rubbed opulence of the throne.

"I'm strangely glad to see it all still standing," Aarinnaie said.

"Strangely?"

"I used to hate this place." She twisted her marriage bracelet. They hadn't found the key on Ilumat's person, nor among his things or with his servants. They hoped to find it here. Otherwise Draken wasn't sure how they'd get it off her. Blacksmith, he supposed, but there hadn't been time.

The far doors opened and a rustling announced an entrance. Draken turned, holding Bruche from shifting his hand to his sword. Khisson entered first, followed by his wife, two sons and a young daughter, and advisors. He stopped several paces before Draken and studied him, unabashed.

The invasion and ruling Brîn hadn't treated Khisson well. His scars and wrinkles had deepened, and he'd let his hair go grey. He walked with a staff in one hand. It thumped the ground at an odd rhythm next to his bare feet, supporting a distinct limp.

"My lord," Draken said at last.

Khisson used his staff to lower himself to the floor. One knee only. But the gesture was clear. The others behind him followed. "Khel Szi."

"You've apparently done well in my absence." He offered the man his hand. Khisson gripped his forearm and Draken helped him up.

"A matter of perspective, Khel Szi." Khisson studied him closely, especially his eyes. "You're alive. I'd heard, but it's another thing to see you."

"I trust you've noticed a new moon in the skies of late."

"Aye. Bright as shined moonwrought, that one."

Draken nodded. "Brîn still stands and the invasion is over. How did you take her back?"

"Brînians are a resolute and faithful people."

"I never doubted it."

"As they never doubted you. I invoked your name and they routed the bastards."

"Well done, my lord. You've served Brîn and now I am in your debt."

"We had a deal. It's all I want."

"Aye. We did. And I'll pay it out. But I am still in your debt."

Khisson searched his eyes again as if not knowing quite where to look and then bowed his head. None of the others present seemed to know where to look. Certainly not at the Khel Szi.

Draken's heart clenched. Khisson was an ally but he would never be a friend. Draken had a god for one friend, and his only other would probably take his sister to wife and make a new life with her. He had lost all his slaves, his szi nêre, Thom and Va Khlar. Elena.

Sikyra.

Hurt ran so cold and deep through him he knew he would never be without its scars.

Two servants set out drinks on a table. Pitchers of wine and herbs to garnish it nearby. A damp, warming wind blew in through the opened doors. The familiar scent of incense drifted toward him.

He strode to the dais, laid his sword on the table, and eased down into his throne. Another servant started to whisk the extra chair away but Draken stopped her.

"Khisson, sit with me and tell me how Brîn fares."

CHAPTER THIRTY-TWO

With Newseason in full swing, leaves thickened about Draken's balconies. Each night Draken and Setia peered through them to watch Osias cross the sky. His moon was close and nearly as large as Ma'Vanni. He often followed her closely as if clinging to the Mother's skirts, and he bore a black line, curved like his bow. It was a bittersweet sight.

"Osias said he'll see us again."

"And so he does." Setia gave him a small smile. "Every night."

She disappeared into her chamber, the one that had been his daughter's, just off his. She'd taken on the role of body servant, and a sort of chamberlain. He liked keeping her close.

In eight sevennight, he'd had no word, no sign that Osias would ever return to ground. Fortunately there were no word of banes either. The mists cleared from Eidola and while no one attempted the climb, there were no signs of the dead about either. Osias must have collected them all during the attack on Algir. Removing his fetter so long ago had unleashed tremendous power.

Tyrolean returned to Brîn and asked to officially court Aarinnaie. Draken resisted punching his shoulder hard and solemnly agreed. Aarinnaie pretended ambivalence but her frequent laughter was good to hear.

Draken passed his days helping locals sort their various issues, sometimes leaning his own back to the work. He kept his mind and body busy from early in the morning when he resumed training with Tyrolean to working on whatever problems came to hand—to the annoyance of aides he should have been delegating to.

The busiest days came right after he freed the slaves in Brîn. He had to gradually release word lest there be riots in the streets, but despite many pleas against it, he remained unmoved. Had Moonlings never been enslaved, perhaps Akrasia wouldn't have been so ripe for invasion. He paid his own servants living wages despite the fussing of his coinmasters, and promised to house and feed them for as long as they would like positions with him. Many left the Citadel. The rest seemed to work hard. He had a hard time remembering all their names. None seemed to mind.

He did much and recalled little, dressed in clothes Setia chose for him, ate when food was laid, spoke when necessary, helped when he could. Inside, he felt stiff and quiet, as if he waded through deep water. Despite his darksight the world had lost its allure. Still, he pushed on.

◆ ◆ ◆

He dragged himself out hunting. With a shortage of servants, the Citadel had no abundance of meat. It was a fair day, warm enough, and it felt good to be outside the city. But upon his return, the szi nêre opened the Citadel gates to reveal a flurry of activity in the courtyard within. He paused to stare before dismounting. Royal Escorts flanked the great doors alongside his own guards. Servii saw to horses by the stables. He groaned inwardly.

Perhaps it's Elena.

Perhaps she sent someone here to take my throne away like last time.

He wished he weren't wearing clothes stained with blood from butchering during the hunt. He made a quick decision. "I'm going in the back way to change. Tell them I'll see them when I'm ready." He strode off before any could reply. He might be arrested or deposed, but he wouldn't submit to them filthy from a hunt.

He scrubbed quickly and let Setia help dress him. It was all Brînian attire: black loose trousers wrapped about his waist, armbands, a thin chain vest over his shoulders, bare feet with anklets clinking at his heels. So be it.

Someone knocked. He told Setia to get rid of whoever it was. Whoever it was protested, but Setia had developed some backbone. Or he was just noticing it.

"I should make you comhanar of my szi nêre, Setia."

Setia shook her head. "I can barely lift a sword, Khel Szi."

"And yet you protect me from my aides well enough. It's like magic." He rubbed her shoulder and went, his stomach twisting.

Cutwork lanterns lit the Great Hall, glinting on the bright tiles and shedding fresh glittering diamonds and circles across the space and over a group clustered in the middle. He walked toward the dais. All proper, this would be. They could damn well look up at him, if this last time.

Until a soft squeal and laugh tripped him up as surely as if someone had tossed a rope about his ankles. He turned. A small figure broke from the group and ran to him on chubby legs under a blue silken gown. She clutched the horse in one hand. "Fa!"

He was on his knees and Sikyra was in his arms before he took another breath. She clung to his neck. He turned his face to her hair, now in well-tended curls, and breathed her in. She smelled different: not the filth of the road, nor the spiced scents of Brîn.

She smelled sweetly floral, fresh.

Like Elena.

He bowed his head, eyes stinging.

"Fa," she whispered. She grasped the chains of his vest and shook them, giggling.

"Aye." His voice was too choked to go on. He knew he was making an undignified spectacle of himself in front of these Escorts, but he couldn't help himself.

"Leave us," Elena said.

He kept his eyes closed and listened to the boots dispersing. At last he set Sikyra back and stroked her soft cheek. "You're running now. Well done."

"Fa-fa. Run." She reached out for his eyes. He ducked away. She squealed a laugh and reached again.

He caught her hand and kissed it. "Aye, they're fair strange. I know." He stayed kneeling, looked up at Elena at last.

She stood, hands clasped before her, watching. Her face had some color from the sun, her curved, dark eyes fixed on him.

He bowed his head to her. "My Queen."

"She asks for you every day. She misses you." Her gaze shifted to Sikyra, and her expression with it. Not a smile, but softer. His shoulders relaxed a little.

"And I her. She looks quite well."

And motherhood suits you, Bruche intoned.

Draken didn't dare add that.

It's a ruddy compliment. She can hardly take offence at it.

Draken cleared his throat and pushed to his feet, his knee slowing him down. Sikyra hugged his thigh before breaking away toward the dais with a cry of delight.

"She climbs. Everything. All the time," Elena wouldn't look at him again; only had eyes for their daughter.

Fair enough. His voice was rough. "Thank you for bringing her to see me."

"It's not the only reason I came."

Draken started forward as Sikyra started to climb but felt a cool hand on his arm. He looked down. It was pale against his bicep. She didn't remove it. "My old nursemaid assures me she must fall to learn."

And crack her head open on the tile? But he held under her touch.

Elena drew a breath. Her hand slid from his skin, leaving a burning tingle, and she rubbed it on her thigh. "I need your help. Auwaer is . . . in disarray."

"Whatever you wish of me, I will serve."

"And she would like to see you more often, I think."

His heart opened a little with hope that nearly made him sway. Damn. "Sikyra . . . she is still Sikyra?"

"Kyra for short."

His lips tugged in an involuntary smile. "It's what Aarinnaie calls her." Another hesitation. So much had happened in a short time, and so much more before. Much between them; much unsaid. He took the easy road. "You've just missed her. She and Tyrolean married two days ago. They're off on their wedding trip. Wouldn't tell me where."

"She never would tell you where she went off to."

"And now she's corrupted the Captain."

"We can only hope." She studied his eyes, as everyone did. But there was no evasion in her.

He opened his mouth. Shut it. Cleared his throat. "I'll help with Auwaer. I'll help any way you wish."

"Is that the case? You will help me any way I ask?"

He bristled. "I swore that when you gave me the sword and pendant and I mean it now. I failed you. It doesn't mean I won't keep trying if you ask it of me."

Now she flinched. "I am asking. Not just because you're able to fight. Nor only for Sikyra. But because . . . I don't know who else to trust."

He studied her; really let himself examine her. Hers was a tormented mind, alone, frightened, desperate, embarrassed. He realized now how he'd avoided it, and avoided what he had to do to fix it.

"Your cousin lied to you as mine lied to me. At least yours is dead and out of your life." A mild joke; Galbrait was doing his best as King.

The stain of a faint blush stained Elena's cheeks. It might have been one of the most beautiful things he'd ever seen.

"It's all right—" His voice broke. "It's all right to ask something for yourself, Elena."

She tipped her face up to his. "I am."

"I know."

A thud tore their attention to the dais. Sikyra looked at them from where she'd tumbled to the floor, and the world stopped in that breathless gasp before a child releases a cry. They both rushed for her. She reached for Elena, muffled her tears in her mother's neck.

Elena blinked, eyes shining, and shushed her. It wasn't so bad. Sikyra settled in a few breaths. "I hate when she's hurt."

"Truth, cries are far better than silence." Draken drew them both close, their scents, their tears, their soft warmth, and at last his heart released the dagger that had buried itself there so long ago.

ACKNOWLEDGMENTS

Jeremy Lassen, Jason Katzman, Cory Allyn, and the rest of Night Shade Books, I sure am glad I went to that Night Shade party at World Fantasy so many years ago. How fortunate I've been to have grown this series inside this young Skyhorse imprint. John Stanko, you outdid yourself on this cover, and William McAusland, your maps bring Akrasia and Sevenfel to life.

Sara Megibow, agent extraordinaire and all around wonderful person, I'm so lucky to have you in my corner.

Writer friends: you know who you are. Let's have drinks soon.

Convention goers, readers, and SFF fans: you make working in our genre and industry a privilege.

Broncos crew and Stepford friends, I really do love you all despite my teasing.

All my extended family, especially Mom, love you!

Hannah and Delilah, you're the best company for this lonely writer. Good dogs.

Grace, little did I know twelve years ago what an amazing person you'd be turning into when I finished writing Draken's story.

Alex, when I started this series you had just started school and now you're facing graduation and ready to launch what I just know will be an astounding life. This one's for you.

Carlin, there isn't anything I can say here that you don't already know. Love you.

And to those enduring depression: you are the true inspiration for Draken. He perseveres like so many of you do every day. Please keep on. The world needs you.